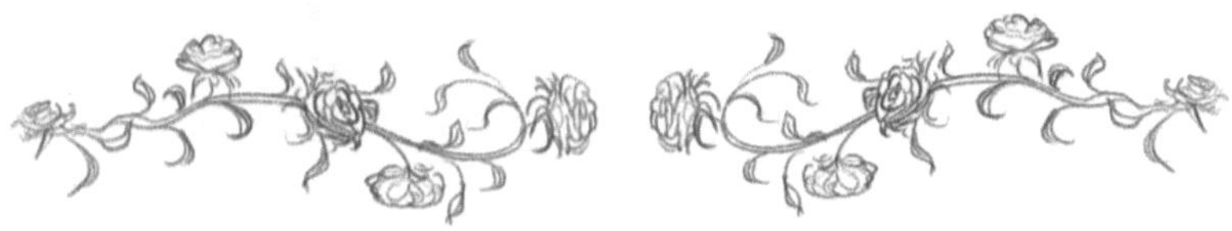

Edited by Kayla Vokolek
Cover and Illustrations by River Kai

ISBN (eBook): 979-8-9900293-5-4
ISBN (Paperback): 979-8-9900293-9-2
ISBN (Hardback): 979-8-9926605-0-0

Library of Congress Control Number: 2025910161

Our books may be purchased in bulk for promotional, educational, or business use. Please contact your local bookseller, or send a request to River Kai Art at riverkaiart.com/wholesale or PO Box 1414, Wilsonville, OR 97070.

First edition, June 2025

10 9 8 7 6 5 4 3 2 1

Riverwolf Fantasy Press
The Fantasy Romance Imprint of River Kai Art

King Luna

Book 3 of *My Shy Alpha*

RIVER KAI

RIVER KAI
King
Luna
Book 3 of My Shy Alpha
THE STEAMY SHIFTER ROMANCE SERIES

To all those
told you were one thing,
and were shamed or harmed
for your differences.

You are beautiful.
You did nothing wrong
by being you.

You matter,
you are loved,
and you belong here.

❦ 1 ❦

Closing my eyes, I tip my head back, inhaling fresh forest air. My Lycan side has taken over my senses lately, with scent taking charge—even in my human form. Between my nose and ears, I can almost pinpoint the exact location of each Greenfield Pack member around me, doing their best to scope out a safe place to build a new community structure: the Greenfield Daycare.

This morning's raindrops trickle from the trees. Tuning into their soothing song, I can picture it: a flurry of pups dashing around the forest floor in their raincoats, filling the precious first decade of their lives with connection and laughter. I can envision them nourishing their wolves' inner curiosity with hands-on examples of the world around them, tucked away in the safest area of our forest. Not only would the daycare sit a half mile from Noah's den, allowing our top Alpha to swoop in to protect them in a heartbeat, but this spot is also within walking distance to the Greenfield Pack's main neighborhood, giving parents the convenience and care we're hoping to provide.

And our pack's current pups aren't the only ones who will benefit from this future daycare building. Allowing the voices surrounding me to fade in the background, I draw my focus to the life budding in my womb.

I still can't believe I'm pregnant. Our pup is already so dear to me—scarily so. Since my first trimester began, I've had endless, OCD-stricken nightmares that everything I care about is a lie. What if my mind conjured up our desire for this child, or Noah's love for me, or even Noah's existence? Or maybe our mate connection was never mine to experience, even if the idea of him being fated to another guts me. But my mind especially loves to doubt that we're actually having this baby together. I keep waking up panting, gripping my belly to make sure they're still here.

I've never been so terrified to lose something before. Even now, my heart pounds at the mere possibility.

I love you so much, that's all, I mindlink to where I envision our baby is inside me, broadcasting my thoughts in the hopes they can feel it. Lilian, our Elder Luna and Noah's mother, thinks it's possible, claiming she formed blood bonds with each of her children before they were even born, similar to the emotional, spiritual tie Noah and I hold as mates. I want to believe her.

And I also want to believe I'm strong enough to care for this little one. Instead, I can't stop thinking about how I might be allowing a poisonous level of anxiety to seep into our baby through their umbilical cord. My stomach somersaults, souring my throat with nausea.

You okay? My best friend interrupts my thoughts, her mindlink grounding me back into Greenfield Forest.

I blink a few times at the rustling evergreens before turning to Amy beside me, her eyebrows pinched in concern.

Meeting Amy's big brown eyes, I give her a soft smile. She's framed by a sea of towering trees, their stormy greens a stark contrast to her soft auburn hair. She's snuggling her little one, Lexi—my dearest "niece." Lexi is passed out, asleep, and drooling against Amy's shoulder.

Biting my lips to stifle my adoration, I tuck Amy's silky hair behind her ear, allowing her to stop tilting her head away from Lexi's squishy cheek. Huddling in beside them with a gentle hug, I let out a slow exhale. *I'm okay. This is just surreal.*

Amy leans against me, providing cozy counterpressure until our waterproof jackets crinkle. *The fact that we're both becoming moms this year, or that we might be standing where the Greenfield Pack's daycare will begin being built by the time you come back from your trip?*

I shake my head in disbelief. *Both. All of it.*

Amy gives me a gentle smile, likely smelling my reeking nerves. I can't help myself lately; uncertainty surrounds me. I keep waiting for the bad news. Or I catch myself looking over my shoulder, expecting another hulking, angry Alpha to appear behind us with how on edge Noah has become beneath never-ending tension at our pack's borders.

On instinct, I press closer to Amy, inhaling lungfuls of Lexi's sweet scent to calm my racing heart. Amy frowns. But before my best friend can pull more secrets from me, a cheery voice calls out from the brush.

"What do you think, Luna?"

Just as my focus zips to the bushes in the direction of Rainn's voice, her head pops out of them with an explosion of flora. Leaves remain sprinkled throughout her dark brown, wavy hair as she smiles, awaiting my approval of our future Greenfield Daycare.

My mate's sweetheart of a sister breaks me out of my anxiety in an instant, leaving Amy and me in a fit of giggles.

"What do I think? Other than that you're the cutest, Rainn?" I turn over my shoulder, taking in the breezy, beautiful sight around us. Rainn's laughter widens my smile, easing the tension from my body. "To be honest, I think it'd be a shame to cut down these trees, even though I'm interested in building here. It's so peaceful."

The brusque, bulked-out Alpha woman we hired as our contractor pops out from behind Rainn, wringing her hands. "We just finished sniffing out the trees in the whole area. They were the product of improper re-seeding by humans, so a majority of them are dead, and they're way too close to each other. If they fall on their own, they might take down the healthy ones. Basically, we've gotta take a ton of them down anyway. That's why we wanted to show you this patch."

Tugging her shirt back into place, Rainn joins my side. "Can you picture it?"

Gazing out at the forest floor, I smile. "More than picture it. I can feel it. You all did an incredible job. I can't wait to show Noah."

The contractor's chest puffs in pride, tempting me to laugh at the precious, clear vision I'm given of how giddy her wolf side must look. I don't want to steal her moment by making her think her pack Luna is laughing *at* her instead of *in adoration* of her, so I turn my back, running a hand over my tiny, swollen belly.

Unfortunately, it's the first time in many minutes I've taken a single step. And one step is all it takes for me to wince, another stab of ligament pain shooting up my abdomen.

Before I can take a breath, every wolf around me dashes to my side.

"What's wrong?" Rainn asks.

"Did something hurt?" Amy asks.

"I'm fine, I'm fine," I laugh, but it's too late.

The poor contractor's excitement has fallen from her blanched face. "Did we walk too much?"

I grip my stinging heart. "Oh, gosh, no, no, please don't worry. I'm just—"

Lexi pops up, likely from the sudden influx of distressed pheromones. As she hitches into a cry, Amy strokes Lexi's bountiful curls with gentle whispers of comfort, parting from my side to leave me with a crowd of hovering wolves.

I sigh. It's been like this since the day Noah declared me the Pack's maternal protector: the Luna. Or rather, the day we announced we were also pregnant, and all 20,000 Greenfield Pack wolves decided it was their job to do anything and everything for their pregnant Luna. It's sweeter than any community support I could imagine in my lifetime, especially before discovering my hidden Lycan side, which is exactly why it's so difficult for me to accept their kindness. I'd like to think our baby deserves it, but a quiet, dark voice in the back of my head whispers, *Am I really worth all this effort?*

I know exactly where it comes from—*who* it comes from. The thought of my ex, Steven, deepens my frown.

Rainn grips me by the elbow, guiding me to sit on the nearest mossy boulder. "Are you okay, Luna? What's going on?"

Worried puppy-dog eyes surround me. I have to laugh. "Okay, let's all pause for a second before we get so stressed out."

The wolves quite literally pause, freezing in place; Rainn even halts her lungs mid-breath, her mouth hanging open.

I sputter out a laugh. "I didn't mean to literally pause yourselves! Keep breathing, at least." After a quick glance at one another, the women slump in relief. But of course, my laughter tenses my abdomen just enough to make me wince again. "Ow."

Rainn huddles against my side. "Sorry, I know I'm our pack's teacher, but despite it all, I don't know how to sit still and listen very well—especially when someone I love is hurting. Do you mind if I call Noah to come get you checked out?"

I gasp. "Don't! You'll terrify him. It's just round ligament pain. I freaked out about it last week too since it's happening early, but Natalia says it's all okay."

Rainn tilts her head, sniffing me close. "Well, you do *smell* fine. But if you're not fine, and my big brother finds out I've allowed our pregnant Luna to be not-fine, he won't be happy. And I wouldn't blame him."

Frowning, all I can do is exhale. This conversation only heightens my anxiety. I'm tempted to smile and laugh it all off, but as Amy makes her way back to my side, I shoot her a quick glance—a silent "help."

Hoisting a settled Lexi higher on her hip, Amy breaks into a mischievous grin. "I'll blame it on Aliya for you, Rainn."

Rainn gasps, but I burst into laughter. "Thanks a lot, Amy."

She winks. "You're welcome, babe."

Thankfully, my rockstar best friend swept the tension from the forest air, and these wolves live up to their short attention spans. The contractor spots our Elder Luna in the distance, her eyes widening as she sucks in an elated breath at the sight of Lilian's graceful form. And I get it; Noah overwhelms me into flustered delight each time I lay eyes on him, and Lilian is just as stoic and regal as her son.

Waving her hand over her head with a beaming smile, the contractor shouts, "Over here, Luna!"

"And… She's off." Amy laughs.

But I catch Rainn's arm before she has a chance to scamper off too. "Wait, I have a baby question for you both."

Rainn's eyes light up even brighter than the contractor's, my sister-in-law letting out a shrill squeal. I giggle, beckoning Rainn and Amy closer.

They follow my eyes as I glance behind myself, ensuring we're alone. As Lilian dives into the details with the contractor, I turn back around to find Rainn and Amy leaning in close, their eyes alert as I lower my voice.

"I have my next important ultrasound with Natalia at the Pack Doctor's Office before we leave for Sweden, but I'm really startled by how big I am. I mean, seriously, I'm only twelve weeks pregnant. Do you think this might be normal for hybrids too, or do you think we could be having… twins?" I swallow harder than I mean to, my breath cutting short. "What if she missed one on the first scan, or something?"

Amy grins, barely containing her amusement at my expense. But since she hasn't been pregnant before either, we both turn to Rainn.

Noah's younger sister is wide-eyed, but not in concern. She's smiling even brighter than Amy, gripping my arm. "Twins? Maybe."

My voice deepens in horror. "Oh, Goddess…"

Amy turns away to laugh at me over her shoulder.

"But!" Rainn whispers, tugging me closer by the arm to sniff my neck.

I blink a few times, clinging to Rainn's arm back as I allow her to sniff me. "But what?"

She nods, releasing me. "Yep, I thought so. You just smell super ridiculously pregnant."

"Well, I certainly feel it," I mutter.

Rainn laughs. "You remember the first pup I birthed, right?"

"Yes, Goddess, he's so precious." I groan, picturing the energetic little tree-climber we met on the first day Rainn allowed me to observe her Forest School class. "He looks so much like Noah."

Rainn beams, her eyes seeming to sparkle for the Lycan pup she carried as a surrogate. "Right? Well, do I have news for you."

I freeze, hanging on her words. Even Amy grows serious, her stare locked onto Rainn's animated hands as Rainn wildly gestures to her abdomen.

"*Huge,*" she hisses. "He was *huge!* He grew like a little beast!"

"Oh, my God…" I groan. "Don't tell me. Your mom already terrified me with her eight-month, full-term Lycan pregnancy for a twelve-pound Noah, and I already know Noah carries the biggest-of-big-boys gene, so—"

Unfortunately, Rainn's eyes bulge wider, her voice barely

containing her laughter as she whisper-yells. "I gave birth within seven and a half months, Luna. And he was also full-term."

My jaw drops. All I can do is grip my best friend for dear life. But Amy's mouth gapes just the same. "*Seven?*"

"And a half, she said," I rasp. "But not premature?"

Rainn shakes her head, using her hands to give us a vivid picture of her pulling that massive baby out of herself, my eyes bulging at the gap between her hands as she widens her legs, reaches between them, and pulls the imaginary pup from her vagina. "*Huge!* I screamed my freaking ass off. The second he came out, Natalia took one look at him and told me he was camping out at least a week longer than he needed to. He was just a big, beefy Alpha pup." As Rainn's focus drops to my stomach, I glance at Amy in desperation. But she's staring at my baby bump in stunned silence just the same. "Which could mean..."

I'm so shocked I can't even speak, holding my belly that's already as big as I expected it to be at four months or more, not three.

"But I— I'm part human, so we thought— I mean, my mom had a regular, human-like pregnancy, right? Didn't your mom say that she heard that from my dad, Rainn?" Glancing at Lilian in the distance, I debate on calling her over to double-check I understood the true story of my mom's pregnancy. "Isn't this just some extra bloating?"

But there's no point in rationalizing this away; the second I look at my best friend, Amy's voice lowers to the this-shit's-serious zone. "Girl, he straight up put a massive Lycan child in you."

Fanning myself, I blink a few times. "I need to sit back down."

"Oh, jeez—" Amy catches my elbow, guiding my wobbling legs to the nearest boulder.

"Hey, it's a good thing!" Rainn's voice heightens as she chases after us, waving frantically like she's wafting my worries away. "If your pregnancy is more Lycan than human after all, that means you're probably closer to the second trimester now, and in the clear like you were worried about, right?"

It fully hits me just as Amy says it aloud.

"Oh, *Goddess*. That baby could be coming out in like..." As

Amy counts quietly on a single hand, I slap my palm over my mouth, only a pained whimper escaping my lips.

Noah! I mindlink.

My mate freezes in our bond's inner world, the image of his wolf form sharpening in my mind's eye. Noah's black, puffy ears stand at full attention like I just caught him digging holes in our new rose garden again.

You got me pregnant with a huge wolf baby! And they really might pop out of me sooner, like we were worried about!

His wolf's ears slink back, his dark, fluffy tail wagging furiously. *I'm so sorry, I know. I was going to ask Natalia what she thought about how rapidly you're growing, I just didn't know for certain if it'd happen as quickly for you since there are still human genetics at work too. Especially since I still believe you when you feel like you're mainly just bloated.*

Well, I'm starting to think I might be wrong. All I can do is let out another whimper, unable to blink as Amy fans my flaming cheeks.

"Is she okay?" Rainn whispers to Amy.

"Yeah. She's probably just grilling Noah."

"Oh yeah, she does have her blank mindlinking face on again."

I glare at them before responding to Noah. *What are we going to do if we have a full-grown kid coming out of me in four, teeny tiny months?*

Noah's tail wags even harder. *I guess we'll just have to see the truth on the next ultrasound and figure things out in those four months. Plus, it could end up being five. Maybe we still have some time?*

Dropping my forehead into my hands, I have to blubber through a delirious laugh. "Oh, Goddess. I guess this is what I get for mating with the biggest Alpha any of us have ever seen."

Amy lets out a sharp bark of a laugh, capturing Lexi's full attention.

Rainn giggles, her eyebrows raising. "I mean…"

I groan, gripping my twinging back and abdomen muscles as I stand. "Maybe I should've known, especially after doing our research. Speaking of which, I need to get home. Noah brought home as many books on Lycan pregnancy as he could check out from the Greenfield Pack library, and I have to sort through which ones to pack for Sweden."

Rainn chases after me as I stand from the boulder, helping me massage my cramping back. "Oh, wow, the Alpha Summit is already in two weeks, isn't it? Have you been shifting every day yet?"

Amy bites her lips, catching my eyes.

Don't look at me like that, I mindlink Amy, then turn to Rainn with my most convincingly sweet smile. "Almost every day."

Rainn's eyebrows furrow, and I struggle to retain my composure. "You *haven't?* Oh, Luna… You didn't believe me that it's safe?"

Pretending to fix my ever-tightening waistband, I duck my head with a wince. Every damn time someone mentions shapeshifting into my wolf, unfairly realistic intrusive thoughts permeate my mind, vivid imagery appearing of our baby suffering a variety of catastrophic effects.

"Why don't you shift right now? We'll be right here, cheering you on!" Rainn says.

I meet Amy's eyes again. She flicks her focus away from me, turning to Lexi. "Hey, did you hear that? Mommy's on her way!"

Lexi blinks the sleep from her eyes, a gap-toothed smile forming. "Mommy!"

Amy laughs. "Yes! Here she comes—"

Spotting Kira's antsy wolf sprinting for us in the distance, I let out a slow exhale in relief, rubbing Rainn's shoulder. "You make a convincing point, Teacher Rainn. But I'm not feeling up to it, right this second."

Rainn frowns. "Then when? What if you need to shift to protect yourself at the Alpha Summit?"

My stomach drops. Yet another person is telling me this Alpha Summit is not only an important global tradition for Lycans—allowing every pack's top leaders to convene—but also a severely dangerous one. This barbaric gladiator competition determines this year's strongest Lycan leader of all pack leaders in the world: the King Alpha. With ever-loyal Lycans, whoever ends up on top could tip the balance between relative peace and full-on Alpha domination.

While Noah will compete to represent Greenfield Pack, Yasmine and I trained hard for the Summit all month in case we need to defend ourselves amongst unpleasant company, so maybe

I should expect everyone's warnings by now. But since I've never been to a Summit before, anticipatory anxiety curdles my insides with every mention of it.

"Actually, I was planning on shifting in rapid succession later today to get myself accustomed to it. I just want to make some last-minute changes to our den before our trip, and Amy's helping me."

"Oh, perfect!" Rainn smiles, opening her arms for a hug, and I droop in relief. "I remember those intense nesting days. Good luck, Luna!"

With a satisfying, gentle squeeze at the end of our embrace, I separate from Rainn with a smile. "Thank you, sweet Rainn. Will I see you again before we leave?"

"Oh! I almost forgot—" Rainn pats herself all over until her fingertips land on her jeans' left pocket. Digging in, Rainn whips out a thin, perfume-like spray bottle.

I recognize it instantly: Rainn's favorite pregnancy-safe, topical scent blocker, allowing me to disguise my enticing scent at the Alpha Summit without risking any hormonal alterations that could impact my pregnancy.

Apparently, dominance-craving Lycans have a murder instinct around pregnant wolves. And unfortunately for me, that especially applies to the pregnant Luna of any pack; if I die, Noah will likely die of heartbreak, eliminating the worst of anyone's competition for the top title.

So, yes, I have to travel to Sweden, knowing I'm a walking death trap for not only our baby and me, but also the love of my life.

Tipping my head back with a sigh, I cup the precious vial in Rainn's hand. "Goddess, *thank* you! I feel like you're literally saving my baby's life."

"Oh, poor Luna. I felt like a beacon of pregnancy scent too, both times I carried. But hey, you've got my big brother by your side, okay? And so many other incredible, strong allies from other packs."

I sigh. "I am thankful for that. It's just... scary. Knowing I'll be an extra target."

Swallowing hard, Rainn simply nods.

Dread strikes my core. If even Rainn is rendered speechless by the dangers of the Alpha Summit, will this vial truly help?

Am I doing the right thing?

That sounds like a classic OCD obsession, but it has a point this time.

Before I can ruminate further, Rainn leans in, her smile returning. "That's not even mentioning that this pup has *you* for a mom. I know we can't predict the future, but I'm willing to bet no one will dare mess with our Greenfield Luna."

I laugh. "Oh, stop."

"I'm serious! Yasmine told me she felt like absolute crap after sparring with your wolf yesterday, and she's not even the pregnant one."

My breath halts. "Wait, what? Who said that? *Yasmine?*"

She couldn't have said Yasmine. While Noah and I will be in Sweden, Yasmine is taking over as Greenfield Pack's leader—our top Beta that Noah keeps by his side as his right-hand protector, rather than the ever-traditional Alpha other packs employ. Yasmine's role is just like the protector my father was for Alpha Ritchie, Noah's dad.

I blink a few times, still unable to grasp Rainn's words. Since we confirmed I was pregnant, I've doubled my efforts to collect stories about Mom and Dad, attempting to fill in the gaps of this hidden side of their lives.

Which means I had to have misheard Rainn; I'm good at running away, but Dad was a menacing beast of a wolf, according to our pack Elders. I doubt my lean, sneaky wolf compares in the slightest. Plus, I thought Yasmine went easy on me yesterday. I am her pack's pregnant Luna, after all.

But Rainn tilts her head like a curious puppy, seemingly perplexed by how startled I am by this news. "Luna, do you not think—"

"Lexi's going home with Kira! Ready for nest cleaning time?" Amy calls out in the distance, tilting our focus to her.

"Yes!" I turn back to Rainn with a sigh. "I guess our den is in Amy's direction, isn't it? Anyway, Rainn, thank you so much for this blocker. I just have to massage it into my scent gland, right?"

Rainn perks up. "Exactly. I've used it both during and outside of pregnancy to make sure Alphas from other packs leave me alone, and it absolutely works; even my overprotective big brother still allowed me on my perimeter run duties if I wore it while pregnant, and he has the most annoying nose, I swear." Rainn rolls her eyes, and I sputter out a laugh. "Hey, there's an idea: have my brother apply it for you, if you want. Spice things up."

"Oh— Oh, wow. I'll, um—" I flush at the thought of Noah's stimulating touch on my scent gland, unable to hold back an erupting giggle. "I'll let you know how the blocker works. Love you, Rainn."

"I love you too, Luna! We'll see each other before you go, okay? Maybe for lunch?"

Giving Rainn's hand a soft squeeze, I slip from her grasp with a smile. "I'd love to. See you then!"

"Wait." Softly tugging me back by the hand, Rainn turns me toward her. Her smile is gone, but her eyes remain lit with excitement, staring deep into mine. "You're still early enough in your pregnancy, so even though there's a huge wolf baby in there, you don't owe anyone news. Between the blocker and discreet clothing, no one has to know."

I slump, my voice softening. "Thank you, Rainn."

"And that pup will be *healthier* if you shift often, not hurt."

Dropping my head, I laugh. "I know, I know. I believe you."

She smiles. "You're a fellow teacher, so I'm sure you know what I do right now."

Rainn's right: I can seek out a lying student with my eyes closed. Her soothing, sweet scent fills the gentle wind between us, the forest rain returning as a delicate drizzle. I soften my tense torso, allowing myself to smile.

I run my free hand over my belly. "I know what it looks like, but I really do plan to shift more. I just can't bear doing a single thing wrong to hurt your brother's precious baby."

Rainn beams, squeezing my hand. "They're your baby too. Which means they're tough as hell—not to mention they're tucked away deep in there, safely. Don't discredit either of you as fragile."

I blink a few times. I'm tempted to feel offended; is she

implying I'm the one simply *considering* myself fragile? That Alphas targeting us is my fault?

But as I gaze at Rainn's sweet smile, it's clear what she actually means. And she's right: I *am* underestimating myself. I can't help it. It's the only way I survived Steven. Otherwise, the truth of how deeply he hurt me—no matter how strong I was—would've been too gruesome to bear.

Pulling Rainn in for another hug, I shut my eyes, emitting the adoration I feel for her through my scent. "Thank you."

She inhales, her lungs expanding beneath my palms before she releases a happy sigh. "Anytime, Luna. I'll be just a mindlink away, even in Sweden, okay?"

As I return to Amy's side, waving goodbye to my sweetheart of a sister-in-law, I'm stuck in a conflicting mix of comfort and terror. While I'm so deeply loved by the Greenfield Pack, how can I not also be afraid of the outside world, constantly being stalked by predators that want me dead? Good thing Jenny and I worked on stalking triggers for my PTSD in therapy. Otherwise, I don't know how I'd survive this. I'm still unsure how I'll manage if our situation worsens, like everyone seems to be warning me of.

But I'm ready to face it anyway. I'd do it over and over again if I had to, for the sake of Noah, Rainn, and my best friend—who already protected me with her life for years. Linking elbows with Amy, I take Rainn's advice and allow myself to smile, trusting that I'll figure this out, somehow. After all, I'm not alone.

❧ 2 ❧

As soon as we're far enough from Rainn's earshot, Amy leans into my side with a smile. "You're not hiding it well."

I blink a few times. "Excuse me?"

Amy sighs, straightening her back and softening her voice. "*Oh, no thanks, not today. I'm not pretending like I've avoided shifting as much as I could since I got pregnant, or anything.*"

My jaw drops. "Is that supposed to be *me?!*"

Amy's devious giggling dissolves into loud cackling. I sputter out a laugh, tugging on her arm.

"Stop it, Amy! I know I made you come with me so that I can try to force myself to finally do it a few times in a row today without stressing Noah out, but I really can't stand the thought of my bones and muscles warping around my baby. What if the placenta detaches, especially since it's still newly attached? What if—"

Amy laughs. "No, no, no. What'll actually happen is that you'll be teaching your massive wolf baby how their body feels to shift so they have an easier time growing up!"

"Yeah. But I still don't like it," I mutter.

Wrapping her arm around my shoulders, Amy gives me a tight squeeze. "Fine, fine. I'll just wait another hour to nag you about it again."

All I can do is groan, leaning my head against hers as our laughter echoes through the trees.

Sensing an oncoming downpour, Amy and I transition from a leisurely walk to speed walking. Despite our waterproof jackets, I've been extra cold and shivery lately—which isn't boding well for how I'll handle the weather at a Swedish mountainside cabin in mere *weeks*.

Amy has a point; before we fly across the world, I want to allow my wolf to not only feel free to shift, but also organize her den. She's already in full-blown nesting mode, but to a level I never anticipated—my waking thoughts filled with the ways every nook needs to be adjusted before our pup comes. We've already gathered extra blankets to immerse in Noah's scent for our den's physical nest, and I've found my feet guiding us to our den anytime I have a spare moment—another reminder this really is more of a Lycan pregnancy over a human one.

I never thought I'd be so set on giving birth in a freaking cave, but I don't think anyone in the world could convince me otherwise. Thankfully, Noah and I have wolves jumping at the opportunity to support us through the birth and postpartum process, even beyond our friends and family.

But when Amy and I approach the edge of the den today, a putrid scent crosses my nose—the unmistakable scent of death.

Slapping my hand over my mouth and nose, I swallow hard. All I can do to keep from puking is to grip Amy. *Oh, my God, A., what the hell is that?!*

Her torso rigid in full alert, Amy presses me to the outside of the cave wall, shielding me from potential danger as we silence our breaths. Peering around the entrance of the den, Amy gasps.

She turns to me, and my stomach plummets; I haven't seen Amy's eyes this focused and wild in a long time. Not since she found me on the floor after Steven broke in.

With a firm squeeze of my hand, Amy leaves my side. *I've got you, babe. Stay right here.*

The second Amy disappears from my view, sneaking around the side of the den, my heart lurches into my throat. *What did you see? Was someone here?*

Amy sighs. "No one else is here. But I'm not gonna lie, this is creeping me out."

I swallow hard, releasing my mouth to pinch my nose shut tight. Taking a wary step, I lean over the side of our den, searching for Amy's bright auburn hair.

She's stationed right in front of the den. So is a long-dead animal carcass, hardly a single piece of it remaining beyond the bones.

"Holy shit," I hiss, joining Amy's side. I can hardly bear to look, my chest aching for both the animal and for what this could mean. "Was this a threat towards Noah?"

Amy shakes her head. "I have no clue. Whatever it is, it's ominous."

My breath heightens. "What do I do? Is it still safe to have our pup here, or should we—"

Amy and I freeze, gripping each other tight on instinct; loud, thunderous paws race through the forest.

No, not just *through* the forest. They're coming closer. Toward us.

This must be who left this here. Someone waiting in the brush, ready to attack once we stumbled across their silent warning.

Before I have time to think about it, it happens; the sprinting wolf arrives, and my wolf releases herself from my core, white fur exploding from every inch of my skin.

Claws extended, I throw myself onto the black mass whirring by, latching onto their back. The hulking wolf snatches up the carcass, dipping their spine with a sharp bark as I tear at their fur with my teeth.

How dare they try to intimidate me into submission. I bite harder, faster, sending a clear message: *don't you dare fuck with us.*

Aliya! Noah mindlinks.

Relief floods my chest as I unhook my claws from the ambusher, sprawling onto the dirt to evade, evade, evade—just like Noah and Yasmine taught me. *Noah, some asshole is trying to command me to stand down from our own den.*

But as the massive black wolf turns his head, facing me with wide, familiar eyes, my stomach drops.

Holy shit, how the hell are you stronger *than before you were pregnant and exhausted?* Noah mindlinks.

I shift back in a heartbeat, dashing for Noah's wincing black wolf. "Oh, my God, I'm *so* sorry, Noah! Are you hurt?!"

His wolf slumps, attempting to lower himself in apology as he backs out of my reach. *No, I'm fine, I'm mainly just so sorry this happened. I meant to—*

Anger floods my chest as fear still courses through my system. "Wait a second, you're right. You terrified us! Why didn't you warn me you were coming right for us like that? You sounded like an assailant."

I hadn't noticed Amy shifted into her iron-red wolf, not until she shifts back, joining my side just as butt-ass naked as I am. "For real, Noah. We were already freaked out by that dead thing."

As if he forgot about the carcass entirely, Noah sneaks one fleeting glance at it before he snatches it back up in a flash, leaping with it into the brush behind us.

"Noah!?" I call out. "Stop it, that's disgusting!"

Two seconds later, he slinks out of the brush again, his head lowered. *I'm so fucking sorry. I forgot to put that away.*

"Oh, my God. You knew about the dead thing."

Noah whines, his ears drooping so low that my heart stings. *I mean, yeah, of course…*

My jaw drops. "*You* did this? You've been eating dead things outside our den? Since when?"

No, that's not it, exactly. Well, okay, maybe I had a few bites. But I couldn't help myself when I saw it running by. It looked so nutritious, and I knew you needed iron. But yeah, clearly, it would've been a bad idea to show up on our porch with a dead thing, so I'm glad I had some common sense left and talked my wolf out of it. I also didn't want it to go to waste, so I asked a few wolves to help me bring it back to the Community Center to use for everyone's dinner, but they were like, 'Well, why don't we just allow a couple families to have some wolf-like fun for once and come eat it here?' So I told them, 'Sure, as long as no one goes into the den, or your Luna will growl at me for ruining the scent in here before I have a chance to chase you out.' And then I told them I'd come pick it up when they were done. Well, I've been too busy for that. That was two days ago. So when I smelled you in the area, I wanted to get here first. Needed to get here first. So you didn't have to… Um… See it. Like you did anyway.

It's no wonder Noah hasn't shifted back yet; throughout his story, my eyes have grown wider and wider, just like how Noah has pressed himself lower and lower to the dirt. Judging by the embarrassment blazing through our bond, I can't imagine how mortified he'd appear if he had to look me in the eyes in his human form, his wolf morphing into an inky puddle as he presses to the forest floor.

But yeah, let's hope my wolf has learned his lesson: you don't want to see anything like this 'disgusting dead thing.' Not at all.

That's when it finally hits me: this wasn't just an accidental kill, or a random animal Noah's wolf came across and wanted as a snack. This was a *gift*. For *me*.

And I just absolutely slammed its whole existence, leaving my poor mate to slink like a scolded puppy who accidentally peed on the carpet.

Amy realizes it at the same time: she slaps a palm over her mouth, but she can't help herself, bursting into such heavy laughter that she's immediately bright red.

I can't help but laugh with her. "Oh, *shit*. Oh, God, I'm so sorry, Noah! That was absolutely cruel of me, I—" I swallow hard, queasy at the thought of the carcass. I fan the nausea hot flash from my cheeks, attempting to sound excited. Instead, my voice wavers through a near-gag. "I really appreciate the sentiment, um—"

Noah grumbles, burrowing his snout under both paws. *Stop. Just stop. I know it's gross, I just cannot stop my wolf for the fucking life of me. He's dying to feed his pregnant Luna, and—*

I groan, dashing for him. He refuses to lift his head, forcing me to glomp onto it as his wolf grunts. Thankfully, he still gives me a sneaky little tail wag.

"My poor, big boy. Look at you, working so hard to hunt for me and our baby." I sputter out a laugh as his tail thumps the ground hard enough to vibrate my feet. "And here I am, not even appreciating your sweet gift."

Aliya, please. Please, *don't encourage this.* Noah's wolf grumbles beneath me, his tail only wagging faster. *Seriously, stop. I don't know how to play with you while you're pregnant without tackling you from how much I love you.*

Stooping over with a hand on our baby, I kiss his snout before releasing him from his suffering—backing up as quickly as I can. "I can't help it. You're such a sweet, adorable Alpha that I have to love on you. And I'm so horribly sorry for making you feel bad."

Noah rises to his paws with another growling grumble, turning his back to us to reenter the brush. *Let's stop talking about it before I actually die of embarrassment. I've gotta go bury this thing.*

"Okay, okay. Just know I love you and I— Well, I want to say I liked it, but I can't pretend I wasn't a little freaked out." I laugh as Noah's wolf whines again, shoving his head into the brush. "But I really do appreciate the sentiment! If I lied to you, you'd just feel it in our bond, anyway."

Noah's tail wags just before it disappears into the brush, and that's the only response I get.

I laugh, cupping my hands around my mouth to shout. "I love you!"

I love you too. I'll be back… After brushing my teeth.

With one look at Amy, we cling to each other, Amy letting out a desperate squeak as she suppresses her laughter. Biting my lips, all I can do to keep from torturing poor Noah another minute is to turn my best friend around with frantic waves, rushing her deep into the den where we can settle ourselves in peace.

Amy flips around with a sly grin. "Did you notice yet?"

I freeze. "Notice what?"

"You shifted."

Amy's rising smile evolves into giggling, but I cringe, gripping my bare stomach. "Holy shit, I didn't even think about it! Are you sure the baby's okay?! I just went crazy on poor Noah's back!"

Amy laughs, bringing me in for a hug. "Hi, Aliya's OCD: I'm not answering that. Didn't the Pack Doctor basically prescribe you to shift as many times as possible in your first trimester?"

I grimace. "Maybe…"

Amy laughs, releasing me to head to the back of the den. I follow her, fetching two sets of spare shirts and sweatpants for us before we get to work, gathering stray rocks for our newly forming rock wall. We're building a small enclosure in the den's furthest depths, creating a sturdy surrounding for the nesting blankets I'll continue piling up until my wolf is satisfied.

But ten minutes into our rock collecting, I can't focus; even with Amy's back turned, her scent calls out to me, a sadness crawling across my bones as if she's aching for help. I don't wait for her to turn around, slipping my arms around her from behind and huddling into her back.

Amy sighs, hugging my arms around her waist. "I'm sorry."

My gut sinks. I hadn't realized she was this upset, but with how low her tone has dropped, I'm afraid of what she's thinking. "What's wrong? Is something going on with you and Kira? Or my sweet niece?"

Amy turns, releasing herself from my grasp with a weary chuckle. But she can't even pretend to hold her smile as we meet eyes. Her eyebrows lift, contorting in sadness before she withdraws her gaze from mine. "No, sorry, it's just—"

"Oh, *A*. What's wrong? I'm here." I let out a helpless sound, rubbing her back as her scent erupts with a heavy, stinging sadness.

But Amy tilts away from my touch, grasping my hand instead. "No, it's really fine. I didn't want to make this about me."

"What? What's making you so upset? I haven't seen you like this since— Well…"

My breath catches as Amy's expression warps. Her silky hair swoops across her features as she ducks her head, obscuring her distress from me. "I don't feel like I have the right to be upset about this."

I swallow hard. "About Steven?"

Amy shakes her head, but in my heart, I know this "no" is in denial of the horrors Steven caused, rather than in answer to my question. This is absolutely about Steven, and it guts me.

"I'm so sorry," Amy chokes out. "I'm sorry I didn't protect you more, especially if he was one of these Alpha-domination Lycans."

My stomach sinks to the floor. "Oh, *babe*."

"I know we had everyone to help at the dress shop, but seeing you back in that state with Mason stalking you, and knowing there are more of these guys out there… I'm really scared of you going to the Alpha Summit. I wish I could go with you, but maybe that's thinking too highly of my capabilities. I didn't even protect you just now."

I groan through the ache in my chest, gathering Amy in my arms. "That's probably because you're not pregnant and overprotective, so your rational brain saw that it was Noah. Plus, you did protect me, keeping me from approaching the den the second you felt something was off, and investigating it yourself despite the possible dangers. Then you also had the courage and kindness of a best friend to still let me see that someone left a 'disgusting dead thing' here, even if you knew it would freak me out."

Amy sputters out a laugh. "Well, still."

Swiping her tears off with her head hung low, Amy dissolves back into overwhelm. Her quivering lip claws at my heartstrings.

"You mean to say that still, you couldn't be there the day Steven showed up," I whisper.

Amy simply nods.

A piece of my broken heart rips back open, memories flooding my mind. All I can do is stroke Amy's hair as she fights back tears, just like she held me as I sobbed on her couch all night long for a week after Steven broke in. Nothing felt safe except this woman aching in front of me, misunderstanding herself as "too late to be the hero" when really, Amy was the only person in the world who could save my life that night. And she did.

"He wouldn't have let you stop him," I whisper. "Especially if he was a wolf, and knew you were a wolf. What if he went all the way and killed us both?"

Amy's voice wobbles, tearing my heart in half. "I guess, but—"

"No, there's no 'I guess.' You were still the one I chose to call in my worst moment."

Slumping into me, Amy drops her head against my shoulder, letting out a true sob.

I shut my eyes hard, struggling not to stoke my bitterness against Steven. But there's truly no end to the pain he caused that night. I'm sure my parents rolled in their graves, having to witness what he did to me in their home, ruining the safe space they left behind for me. We knew the system to prosecute Steven was broken, but Amy and I had to witness the gory depths of its failings, the cops refusing to charge him no matter the evidence upon evidence we provided. It was my fault in their eyes too for not bending to Steven's desires, and therefore, Amy had to be reminded she was never safe either.

If someone did this to her, how helpless would I feel if all I could do was hold her through the pain, depression, and suicidal ideation that followed? Knowing this trauma was now embedded into her for the rest of her life, but not knowing if she'd survive another night through her suffering?

Guiding Amy to the back of the den, I urge her to sit by my side. Luckily, she obliges, dragging her feet until she slinks to the ground against me. I have to smile.

Holding her head to my shoulder, I drop my temple against it. "I told you I don't want you to feel imposter syndrome from having trauma from this too, right?"

She fiddles with my fingers. "Yeah, but it's nothing compared to the pain I found you in—"

"Yes, it is something. Because you witnessed a traumatic event through me, just the same. Don't discount this for yourself."

She huffs. "Okay, fine. But that doesn't change wishing I could've been there with my wolf. To tear his fucking head off."

"Maybe not. But you said it yourself: if he really was a Lycan, he probably smelled I was part-Lycan and used intense scent blockers ever since, ensuring he never let on what he was, right? If that really is true, he succeeded in disguising himself, and that's *not* your fault. That means he was hiding from the start, from *all* of us."

Amy shakes her head, her eyes vacant as she stares at the rocky ground.

And I can't stop it: bitterness crawls up my throat, anger shortening my breath. "I can't say I trusted a single other person in the world to come find me in the heap on the floor, and to have the internal strength to lift my soul out of the depths—" My voice catches with emotion.

Amy dives in for a hug. "Fuck—"

I hold her close, shaking my head. "You held me, you helped me clean my damaged body, you fed me when I had no strength to even open the fridge, you took me to the doctor to rid him from me, you took me to therapy—"

Amy's pained cry puffs hot air against my chest, striking my heart.

My voice shakes as I stroke her head. "Steven did what he wanted, no matter who would be there to protect me. So when I had no other family left, you stepped in and did everything in your power to mend my shattered soul. That's more than I could ever, ever ask for, Amy. I literally owe my life to you."

Amy's shoulders finally loosen. She nuzzles in, cuddling me as close as she can.

I silently vow to hold Amy for as long as she needs me to, just like she did for me that day. By the time she slumps against me in pure exhaustion, her breath slowing into near-sleep, I break into a smile; I really have been best friends with a sweet little guard dog puppy, ever since we were little. I can't believe she doesn't think she did her job well; for all we know, what if she was the only reason I didn't have a shitty boyfriend growing up like all my friends did? Not until one literally prevented himself from meeting Amy and everyone I knew, refusing to meet them—and isolating me in the process. Neither of us stood a chance against his manipulation.

I hope she can let this go. I know I've struggled to, but I can't stand the thought of her suffering too deeply over him. In that way, I understand how she feels, to my core.

Combing through her shiny, soft hair, I lower my voice to just above a breath, just in case she's asleep. "Thank you. I love you."

She sighs against me, readjusting herself to curl into sleep with her head on my lap. Gazing out to the entrance of the den, I sit in silence, observing the world around me. Birds peck for worms in the grass, the rain crashes against the flora as it ebbs and flows in its downpour, and Amy's lungs rise and fall beneath my hand on her back. As I exist in the stillness, my heart settles into pure peace. I hope Amy's does too.

When Noah finds Amy and me still huddled up in the den half an hour later, his adoring smile brightens my heart the rest of the way. He settles in on my other side, holding the healing quiet with us.

❧ 3 ❧

"Are you sure you'll be okay with staying a few hours? I know you've been feeling extra sick this week." Amy bites at her nails in her apartment doorway, Kira's arm draped over her shoulder.

Shifting Lexi to my hip, I smile. "Are you kidding? We're so excited to be with this sweet one—and to get some parenting practice in before we have our huge wolf baby."

"Girl, that kid really did look massive," Kira mutters.

"*Kira…*" With my groan, we all break into laughter. We're not having twins, after all, our latest ultrasound showing one big baby growing just as rapidly as any other Lycan pup at fourteen weeks. This also means we'll likely have a baby in our arms in a mere four and a half months… or less.

Noah reaches around me to give Amy's shoulder a soft squeeze. "Seriously, though, you're both doing us a huge favor next week by helping us keep Greenfield safe while we're in Sweden. Giving you a break for a date night is the least we can do to thank you."

"Oh, come on. You all spoil us too much here already, Alpha. We wouldn't raise Lex anywhere else." Kira scrubs Lexi's head, giving her one last cheek kiss before Kira urges her anxious wife down their apartment steps.

"Let's say, 'See you later, Mom and Mommy!'" I hoist a sniffling Lexi higher on my hip, waving to Kira and Amy as they grimace on their doorstep. *Amy and Kira, leave, right now. You're torturing yourself, and we want you to go have fun.*

"See you later, Mom and Mommy," Noah echoes, helping me model for Lexi what to say with a small wave. Except, coming from him, these words widen Kira's and Amy's eyes in unison.

Dropping his head in a flustered giggle, Noah pushes the four of us adults over the edge, laughing as Amy and Kira dash down their apartment steps.

"I'm not forgetting that for a long time." With a wide grin, Kira drags Amy along faster. "We'll be back in a few hours!"

Amy waves to Lexi. "Have fun with your Auntie and Uncle, Lexi! We love you!"

Lexi waves back with a sad, quiet whisper. "Love you."

As we close and lock the front door, I try my best to remain calm. But I can't help myself; I brace for the inevitable, my heart already wrenching into my throat at Lexi's potent, pained scent.

Fetching Mr. Wolfy—Lexi's favorite stuffed toy, a fuzzy gray wolf with massive eyes and long, floppy legs—Noah opens his mouth to speak. But before Noah can say a single word, Lexi's little face scrunches into an agonized grimace. The first gut-wrenching cry she lets out hits my soul so deep that my eyes burn hot; the grief in her scent is unlike anything I've felt in my preschoolers when they're homesick.

"Oh, my love… I know, you're so sad." I rub Lexi's back, rocking us gently.

"They'll be back soon. We're right here with you, okay?" Noah pats Lexi's tears with his sleeve, his voice so soft that my chest fills with grief alongside Lexi—Noah's serenity allowing my body to express deeper emotions.

Poor Lexi's tears shift into screams.

But this isn't something we can just take away. Lexi's not only crying over missing Amy and Kira, she's crying because her first parental bond with her biological parents was ruptured when they were killed. Whenever Kira or Amy leave, it reminds her of this deep, never-ending wound in her young heart.

My heart gallops, a sweet, comforting scent rushing from me in an attempt to soothe her.

But with my scent comes a trace of my anxiety and pain permeating the air. What if I'm amplifying Lexi's fear, no matter how much I shush and cradle her?

"Hey, hey, you're okay. While we wait, let's play together. Or maybe we can watch a movie? You love that rabbit movie still, right? With Bun Bun?" Noah's deep, rumbling voice extends past

Lexi's desperate cries, but not even the mention of Lexi's beloved Bun Bun grabs her attention.

"Oh, Noah, she's *so* heartbroken," I whisper.

"I know. Poor sweetheart." Noah joins me in stroking Lexi's back. She cries to the absolute depths of her ability, her sobs so vicious that fear strikes my core, the grating tone to her voice begging my primal instincts to ease her suffering.

Noah isn't just comforting Lexi now; one of his wide hands smooths warmth over my back too.

Dammit. He must be noticing my internal freak-out. We were prepared for Lexi to potentially react like this the first time her new moms left the house together, so why can't I keep it together?

A flood of Noah's protective scent fills the air, softening Lexi's cries. But it's only momentary; her next scream is sharp enough to send her into a coughing fit.

"Oh, Lex, I'm *so* sorry." I sit us down at Amy's kitchen table, shifting Lexi in my arms to hold her chest to chest. Noah smooths Lexi's curls back into a ponytail, blowing cold air on the back of her neck—attempting to calm her flaming red skin. But as Noah speed-walks across the kitchen, preparing a damp towel for Lexi's forehead, her little body quivers hard in my arms, wrenching at my soul as she grips me tight. When Noah turns around, his eyebrows warp in shared pain.

Glancing up at Noah with wide eyes, I feel lost. My breath shortens as I cradle Lexi's head to my shoulder, my insides somersaulting with Lexi's loud, heaving cries. I'm supposed to be the experienced caregiver here, but the harder Lexi cries, the more panic I feel; I understand her better than ever. Now that Noah and I are preparing the rest of our lives to include our baby, I miss my parents more than I can withstand.

Amy and Kira don't know what exactly Lexi experienced on the day her parents died, but as Noah smooths slow, sweeping touches down her back, keeping his voice soft for her, my eyes water alongside hers. The sharp sting of trauma emits from her scent; Lexi witnessed something horrible as she lost them, even if she can't remember the details. Amy and Kira have mentioned how hard it was to console Lexi in the first couple of months she came home with them, but I underestimated how deeply it'd hurt my heart tonight, no matter my professional experience.

Like Lexi, I know my loved ones might never come back home.

"I don't know how to help," I whisper.

Noah nods. "Keep holding her. She needs time to process this abrupt change in her safe space."

As Noah stands over us, wrapping us in his big arms, I grip him tight. What if he dies from one of these violent Alpha attacks too, and we leave our future pups behind like Lexi? I never want our kids to feel like this.

But just before I slip into deeper fear, a cozy, sweet scent washes over my skin, drawing a pleased sigh from my lips.

Noah tenses above us, a flash of surprise crashing through our bond.

Oh, my God. This scent is *Noah's*.

He's emitting that rare, Omega-like scent I've smelled from him before. It's beyond comforting, wrapping me in a nourishing warmth that seeps all the way into my aching heart—like he's cradling it until all the pain in me washes away. I slump in relief, but Noah takes an uneasy step back, his chest tight.

"S-sorry," he whispers. "I d-don't know why— Uh—"

My heart stings when I meet Noah's wide stare; he's mortified by his own scent.

I grasp his hand, drawing him closer before he can second-guess my initial reaction a second longer. "No, no, my love, this scent is *beautiful*. Look at how deeply you're comforting her."

Immersed in Noah's scent, Lexi's cries shift from screams to whimpering tears, her body loosening until her arms fall limp at her sides.

"There you go, Lexi. We're right here with you until your mommies come home." I attempt to steady my voice, taking a deep breath as I look back to Noah with a wobbly smile. "Keep going, Noah. She loves it, see? And I do too."

Noah swallows hard, his eyes wide and jaw taut. It's clear he's uncomfortable, but it's almost like his scent is beyond his control today; both of our eyes widen as a far sweeter scent fills the kitchen.

My mate ducks his head, but as he steps closer, returning us to his embrace, Lexi lets out a soft, purring whimper. Then her little arms pop up—outstretched for Noah.

I stare in awe. Not because she's aching for Noah—that comes as no surprise to me with how loving my mate is—but because I've never seen a simple gesture hit Noah's heart like this. As his eyebrows flinch, his big hands hoist her into his arms, tucking her under his chin in a desperate snuggle. Noah squeezes his eyes shut tight, cradling her. As a far more potent scent spills from him, my heart flips.

I stand, rubbing Noah's back as he nuzzles Lexi's hair. His cheeks flame red.

"Oh, my love. This is so good. You're a natural nurturer, see? And your scent is just what we all needed," I whisper.

Noah is far too flustered to speak, keeping his head lowered.

I press my knuckles to my lips, my shoulders raising at the gorgeous picture Noah and Lexi paint before me. She nuzzles closer into him, peace washing over her as he holds her little, tired body in his massive arms. Noah softens his warped forehead, his hand sweeping down Lexi's back through her leftover shuddering. When a different, sweet scent fills the air, my breath catches; Lexi is returning Noah's loving scent with her own pleased emotions.

Noah lifts only his eyes to meet mine, his eyebrows contorting like he's near tears. From how touched he feels in our bond, I know this moment strikes a deep nerve for him. I stroke his hair from his eyes, biting back tears with him. Our bond unearths a deep pain hidden on Noah's side of our bond, but Lexi's adoration of Noah's uncontrollable, nurturing scent appears to be healing something in both of them.

"Okay, my loves. Let's sit down and watch a movie with some snacks and cuddles." Guiding Noah to Amy and Kira's royal blue tufted couch, I adjust the pillows for Noah before he sits. But instead of sitting right away, he holds Lexi close, stooping over me to plant a shaky kiss on top of my head.

My shoulders soften. Looking up, I steady Noah's arms, gazing at my mate with a quick look of recognition at how powerful this moment was for him.

Thank you, Noah mindlinks, his eyes racing across my face to absorb my expression—as if he might've been wrong, and that I'd still end up judging him for his scent.

Stroking his cheek, I smile. *I love you, Noah. No matter what.*

Noah's eyelids blink slower, his taut torso slackening before my eyes. I didn't realize how worried he still was about his unexpected scent, but between Lexi and me showing him how beautiful it was, I hope he can take it easier on himself tonight.

Lexi has no plans of moving, content to be bundled in Noah's arms, even as he repositions her to settle on the couch. Fetching a blanket from across the room, I turn around to find Lexi staring up at Noah in deep trust, her hand fidgeting with his shirt collar. When Noah breaks into a soft smile, gazing back down at Lexi, my heart flips into my throat.

Noah, you're going to keep me gushing over you all night at how gorgeous you are with each other. How am I going to survive when you're holding our pup like this?

Widening his grin, Noah peeks at me as I drape a fuzzy, royal blue blanket over them both. Lexi purrs, nuzzling her stuffy, red nose into Noah's chest. With it, she urges out another surge of Noah's nurturing scent, stirring my heart into overwhelm. Noah's breath speeds, but this time, he doesn't look to me for reassurance. He stares down at Lexi, unblinking—as if he's in awe at how contented she seems, thanks to him.

"You're her lifeline right now," I whisper, running my fingers through his dark hair.

Noah doesn't respond, but our bond certainly does; the most precious hope stirs his wolf's tail into a happy wag, the sweet sight of it in my mind deepening my breath.

Goddess, help me. I didn't realize how deeply Noah not only wanted kids, but also needed to nurture. Has he been hiding this part of his scent intentionally?

Noah feels far too shy and nervous about this for me to point it out later tonight—and the last thing I want is for him to feel like this type of scent is a bad thing, especially since shame was his default response. I don't know what convinced him that this nurturing scent was shameful, other than what's clear from my experience in Greenfield thus far; this is not a scent I've *ever* smelled from an Alpha.

I don't want to label it for Noah, but I recognized it right away. Comforting Lexi in Amy and Kira's kitchen, he smelled purely of Omega.

But what does this mean? My scent wavers between pheromones like this too, but it doesn't seem like either of us are exhibiting "normal" Lycan scent behavior.

Staving off my overwhelm, I kiss Lexi's cheek, then Noah's. "So, do you both want some blueberries?"

"Bluebears." Lexi's eyes widen.

Noah grins. "Doesn't she only know like 50 words at her age? She recognized that immediately."

I break into giggles. "Ah, yes, you are your mother's child, Lex. Mom *loves* blueberries."

"Bluebears," Lexi says, sucking back snot. Noah smiles, wiping it off for her with his sleeve.

I straighten Lexi's rumpled shirt. "Yes, blueberries! Your mommies also said it's okay if we have some chocolate too while we watch our movie. What do you think of that?"

Lexi's head lifts, her curls poking out in every direction. She beams up at me with puffy eyes, finally giving me a smile.

Noah's deep chuckle widens Lexi's grin. She turns to him, gripping his chin with her little hand and letting out a bright squeal of excitement.

"Chocolate and blueberries, coming right up!" Handing Noah the remote, I giggle as Lexi peeks over Noah's wide shoulder, keeping her eyes on me while I fetch her favorite snacks.

Noah flips to the kids' selection of movies for us to watch. "Good thing you're a Lycan, Lex. Chocolate would be a sad favorite food to have as a wolf-wolf."

"Choc-it! Woof woof!" Lexi's volume raises, drawing a deeper laugh out of Noah.

"'Woof woof' works too."

"Woof woof!"

Noah's bright giggles fill the living room, followed by Lexi's huffing, excited breath as she squishes his cheeks, marveling at his scruffy jaw.

With one hand gripping the sink handle, the other holding a colander of blueberries, I'm frozen, entranced by them. Lexi plops herself back against Noah's chest, giving an excited shout at her favorite movie's opening title appearing on the TV.

As I fetch Lexi's baby-proof bowls for us to use, my heart won't stop flipping in delight. I keep checking over my shoulder, afraid I'm dreaming a good dream for once—that I'll be sad to wake up instead of relieved. But no, this is real.

I have to pause. Staring at the picture of the two of them, my eager hands press over Noah's growing child in my womb. An excitement bursts through our bond that I haven't let myself feel in a while, gratitude filling me for a chance at a future like this.

Sweeping my hand down my belly, I resort to filling our bowls with one hand, unable to convince myself to let go of our baby. The deepest love I've ever felt lifts my soul higher and higher, and they're not even here yet.

Noah turns over his shoulder, meeting my eyes. *I love you.*

I love you so much. I can't wait to give you this pup.

Noah's mouth is covered by the couch cushions, but as his eyes squint in the most delighted smile, I beam at him, unable to stay away from his side a second longer.

Carrying an armful of snacks to two of my favorite Lycans, I snuggle into Noah's side. Like clockwork, Lexi scrambles off Noah's lap, wedging herself between us.

Noah laughs, freeing me from one of Lexi's straying legs as it flings over my lap. "Be careful with Auntie Aliya's belly."

"Belly. Annie 'Liya." Lexi snags a fistful of blueberries from my bowl, ready to cram them into her mouth.

I catch Lexi's hand just in time, sputtering into laughter as I pry most of them from her shockingly powerful grip. "One blueberry at a time, please."

Mumbling into her palm as she munches on her surviving berry, Lexi stares at the TV, no longer caring about anything I could say if it's not about blueberries or chocolate.

Noah chuckles, draping his arm around my shoulders. I lean into his warmth, drooping into the couch in a sudden exhaustion. Just as my neck softens beneath his touch on my shoulder, a mindlink interrupts my thoughts.

I'm so sorry, I know I said I wouldn't mindlink you, but I can't help it, Amy says.

I shake my head as I smile. *I love you, A. I knew you'd do this.*

Just you wait until I'm watching Baby Greenfield for you. You'll nag me all night too.

I bite my lips, holding my breath to stave off a laugh. Noah glances at me, and I grin, mindlinking him. *Amy's already asking about sweet Lexi.*

I don't blame her. I was about ready to die inside, watching her so upset, Noah says.

My heart flips at his sincerity. He braved so much stress and fear for us tonight. But I blink a few times, refocusing on Amy's worries as she floods my mind.

How did she handle it when we left? Is she okay now? Is she still crying, or not as much, at least?

Hang on, I'm sending you a text, I say.

Snapping a secret picture of Lexi and Noah snuggled up on the couch beside me, I smile wide, sending it to Amy and Kira.

We had a small rough patch, but we're all good now! I mindlink Amy.

Thank the Goddess. I'm so glad she loves you both so much. Also, Kira and I are dying; Lex looks like a tiny doll against our Alpha's massive pecs. Anyway, don't work too hard, A. I'll see you soon!

No, you won't! Take a break, and have fun with Kira! Get frisky if you want to—we can stay as late as you need us to after we put her to bed. Noah and I like to curl up on the couch to chat until late at night anyway. We're all good here, A.

But as soon as I say that, Noah and I are mindlinked by someone else.

Where are you both? Lilian asks.

I freeze, whipping my head to Noah. He remains perfectly still, his eyebrows knitted. Only Noah's eyes drift to meet mine, not wanting to disturb Lexi despite the shared concern rising in our bond.

Noah is likely thinking the same thing I am: his mom never reaches out like this. Especially not to Noah.

We're babysitting Lexi at Amy and Kira's place. Would you like to come over? I ask Lilian.

Lilian doesn't answer at first. I straighten, alarm tightening my chest until she replies. *Oh, it's okay. I stopped by your cabin, but I'll figure it out.*

Okay, this really isn't right. Lilian might be implying something is wrong, but her brushing it off makes me think her situation must be even worse than if she openly admitted she needs our help. And whatever it is, she came all the way to our cabin to confide in us—even though her relationship with Noah still holds an uneven pace.

Noah's uneasy feeling heightens in our bond, raising my shoulders as he mindlinks me privately. *I don't know what's best. Should I leave you here with Lexi and go meet her, or have her come here? Would it even be okay to invite her over?*

When he looks at me, I nod. *I'm ready to help her however we need to. She's been invited over here a bunch of times while we were planning for the daycare, so as long as Lexi is safe, I think Amy and Kira will understand.*

As if he's unable to wait a second longer, Noah's focus zips off mine as he mindlinks Lilian. *Mom, please come over—no questions asked. Are you with someone who can drive you, or can I come pick you up?*

No response.

Noah tenses, closing his eyes. When he reopens them, they're half shifted, a stark green staring back in alarm. *Wait, Mom, are you shifted?*

Yes, she says. My stomach lurches into my throat. Did she need to defend herself from someone, and that's what's wrong? *I'll be there soon.*

Noah doesn't need to speak to tell me he's alarmed; his shell-shocked stare, alone, drops my heart to my feet.

"Would you like to sit on my lap for a bit, Lex?" I open my arms up for Lexi. Thankfully, she crawls into my lap right away, settling her back against my chest as she continues to watch her movie.

Noah shuffles off the couch, keeping his movements slow and steady despite the rippling concern in our bond. *Thank you. Sorry that I'm so worried. I don't mean to scare you.*

No, I'm worried too. Are you going to meet her outside?

Yes. Readjusting our blanket over Lexi and me, Noah's voice softens for Lexi. "I'll be right back in a minute, okay? I'm just grabbing Grandma Lilian."

My heart flips hearing him call Lilian "Grandma," giving me another glimpse into the future. I wish I felt settled enough to enjoy it.

You don't think her being shifted means she's being followed and needs backup, do you? I ask.

Oh, no. If she shifted, they probably already learned the hard way that they fucked with the wrong wolf. They're lucky if they're getting away alive. Something else must be wrong.

I blink a few times, startled. I knew Noah came from an intensely powerful father in Alpha Ritchie, but I haven't witnessed any situation in which Lilian had to fight. With how fierce she can be, I shouldn't be so surprised Noah thinks this highly of her strength.

Noah strides to the plushy chair in the living room's opposite corner, grasping a fresh blanket. He's already ten steps ahead of my train of thought—from what it sounds like, his mom likely had to shift in an emergency, leaving her with no clothes to change into once she arrives.

But by the time Noah opens Amy's door, Lilian is already here.

I jump off the couch, my jaw tightening as I clutch Lexi closer, holding her on my hip. Lilian is, indeed, fully naked on Amy's doorstep, hurrying into the blanket Noah provides.

But as Noah urges Lilian inside with a taut arm around her, slamming the door shut, my heart drops; Lilian isn't just naked, she's coated in blood.

I thought it was a trick of the moonlight on her skin, but as I set Lexi down on the couch, my head spins at the sight of blood, forcing me to clutch the coffee table. Lilian drips blood onto the floor, each heartbeat pumping out another dribble from beneath the blanket. Her tan skin pales in the kitchen light as I flick it on, gripping her shoulder.

I gasp. "*Lilian*, oh, my *God*—"

Lilian ducks her head. "I knew I shouldn't have come here to stress you both out. It's fine. I'm—"

"No, it's not fine. How bad is it?" Noah tugs Lilian's blanket open in an attempt to see where she's bleeding from, but Lilian yanks herself back.

"I said, I'm fine."

I don't expect Noah to growl so deeply. "Mom, let me help you."

"You're not helping, acting like that," Lilian hisses.

Glancing at Lexi, I'm relieved to see her still absorbed in the movie—I guess she's used to Amy and Kira laughing and chattering at top volume, so this must seem like nothing unordinary.

Lilian huffs. "Maybe I should go."

But as Lilian turns to the front door, she must've lost more blood than I thought, stumbling with flickering eyelids. I catch her with a yelp, Noah grasping her other side. We support her exhausted body to the kitchen, easing her into a chair.

When Lilian tears herself from Noah's hands again, he grips his hair. "Are you *serious?* If you don't want me to help you, why didn't you go straight to Doctor Natalia? Do you still think so low of me that you believe I'd be fine with you bleeding out?"

"Noah," I say. Meeting his wild, golden eyes—his wolf showering us in terrified, angry Alpha musk—I shake my head. *It's not fair, I agree, but she's acting out in embarrassment, not hatred. Take a deep breath.*

Huffing out a harsh exhale, Noah turns his back to us, leaning both palms against the kitchen countertop and dropping his head. "Sorry. I just can't believe one of them felt justified enough to do this to you. I don't even need to ask what attacker profile we're looking at: Alpha, large, solid or near-solid coat, male."

Lilian simply hums in agreement, not meeting my eyes.

My heart drums into my ears, knowing these attacks are what we're dealing with for the foreseeable future. Many Lycans hold a bias against Rogues, claiming Rogues are the violent ones, but these are no stray Lycans; they're bloodthirsty, angry Alphas from neighboring packs. Similar cases are stopped at the edge of Greenfield Forest by our toughest pack members, every single day, now that we've identified ourselves as a sanctuary state for anyone escaping a growing Alpha-domination dogma.

But like Noah said, Lilian is a high-profile wolf. To go after her speaks of a terrifying boldness that only an egotistical Alpha could commit to.

We all know the most dangerous encounters are violent Alpha men; they're willing to break social conventions to prove they're owed power. And who can safely stop them? The truth can't budge their unmovable beliefs, and stopping them physically is too great of a risk for most wolves when Alphas receive the most physical training of us all.

But attacking a globally recognized Elder Luna to this degree changes the game; their private organizing has emboldened Alpha-domination attackers beyond what we previously thought.

As our bond steeps in distress, Noah sighs. "At least this one won't have the guts to do it again. I'm positive they're shitting themselves and counting this as a second chance at life, knowing your wolf."

"You're right about that," Lilian mutters.

Stooping over, I tuck a stray piece of Lilian's gray hair behind her ear, her bun lopsided and dotted with leaves. Keeping my tone kind but firm, I use my serious teacher stare on her. "Luna Lilian, show me where you're hurt, please, and I'll get to work stopping the bleeding."

Gritting her teeth, Lilian unfurls her blanket. The second I see the gashes across her forearms and side, my vision reels. I let out a slow, shaky breath, assessing the claw patterns; thankfully, Lilian's attacker missed her vital organs, the worst cut down her side being from the second claw, just like I always see on Noah.

I roll out my shoulders, relieved. These wounds are long, but they're shallower than I expected. I can help her.

Instincts take over, my wolf urging me to lift Lilian's arm to my tongue. The faster I lick her wounds, the more I salivate.

Turning around at the sound of my purring, Noah strokes my hair out of my face for me, humming in concern. "I know you're my little vampire wolf, but you'll feel sick again if you don't spit that blood out."

I can't help myself. I growl at him, my pregnant wolf insisting this is what she's doing to nurture and protect our Elder Luna, regardless of her mate's opinion. Noah's breezy chuckle lowers my hackles in our bond.

Within minutes of my determined licking, Lilian's wounds fade into fresh scars. Lexi has returned to Noah's arms, her head drooping against his chest as he fills a cup with water for Lilian. Thankfully, Lilian accepts Noah's help this time, taking slow, steady sips of water the second the cup lands in front of her.

As Lilian closes her eyes, clutching her glass in both hands, Noah's arm lifts from his side—but it stays there, hovering. I silence my breath; is he about to hug her?

Lilian's eyes are still closed. Just as Noah moves in, Lilian straightens with a sigh. Noah yanks his arm back, a flash of his disappointment stinging me to the core.

She doesn't even look at him, instead turning to me. "Thank you for your support. I don't want to intrude on Amy and Kira much longer, and I don't happen to have a spare change of clothes with me."

Noah's brows furrow. "Mom, I can let you borrow some spare clothes we have in the car. You don't have to—"

"Truly, I hate having to do this to you."

Gritting his teeth, Noah drops his chin to his chest—giving up before they move into argument territory once again.

I get it. *Really* get it. With Steven I'd give up, over and over again, anticipating greater hurt if I dared stand up for myself—until I no longer stood up for myself at all.

But as I cup our baby in my womb, I can't bear to look at Noah like this. With how connected I already feel to his pup, how could his mom not see she's pushing her precious son away? Doesn't she know they could only have mere years left in life together, if that?

It kills me to watch him reach for her when she won't reach back.

Doesn't she take one look at him and feel what he's thinking in the depths of her bones? She might hate inconveniencing him, but he wants to be inconvenienced. He needs her.

And she's not there for him.

My eyes overflow before I can stop them, forcing my lungs to hitch. Lilian and Noah whip their focus to me, brightening my flushing cheeks. "Sorry, ignore me."

Lilian stands, her eyes wide. "Oh, no. Did I say something hurtful again?"

I don't know what to say. All I can do is look at Noah.

He stares back, his eyebrows lifting as he registers the reflected pain in our bond; I'm mirroring his overflowing emotions, expressing his pain for him whether I want to or not.

Providing me with a steady hand to grasp, Noah guides me to his side. Wrapping his free arm around me, he holds me close to his chest, cuddling a sleeping Lexi between us. His heartbeat throbs beneath my palm as he kisses my forehead, the silence stretching between us as Lilian simply watches.

"Clearly, I have. Maybe I should go," Lilian whispers.

Noah's low voice buzzes through me, sweet and soft. "You can stay, Mom. This is just an overwhelming time. A lot to process for all of us with the Summit coming up, and I think seeing you so hurt was a daunting reminder."

He's attempting to cover this up. Not for his sake, but in spite of it—sacrificing his feelings for Lilian's and my comfort.

But I swallow hard, hating how his pacifying words seem to sharpen his pain. Lifting my chin to find his loving eyes staring back, I bite my lips to keep from crying more. *Do I have to pretend that's really all it is?*

Noah softly smiles down at me. *Of course not, my sweet Luna. But it has to be, with her. It's okay. I'm okay.*

I shake my head, unable to accept this conclusion. *I would never want to distance our baby like this. I can't stomach watching you get hurt like this, Noah.*

Shutting his eyes, Noah shakes his head. *That's because you're not her. This is just how it is.*

"No," I whisper.

Blinking through a sudden rush of my frustrated scent, Noah's focus flits between my eyes.

Turning to Lilian, I hold out my arm. "Tonight was a lot, like Noah said, but I think we also need you here right now. Will you join our hug, Luna?"

Noah's chest stiffens against me. But as Lilian turns her head to hide her eyes from us, to my surprise, she steps closer—straight into her son's side.

He sucks in a shaky breath before holding it tight. When Lilian remains pressed against us, even as our arms settle around her, Noah finally exhales, the weight in our bond loosening just enough for me to breathe slower alongside him.

Maybe this is a step in the right direction, or maybe they will never come around to each other. I don't know. I just have to hope this is progress. Otherwise, I'm at a loss: as I stare at Lexi snuggled against Noah's chest beside me, her eyes still swollen with grief, the last thing I'd want to do is cut ties with our baby's last surviving grandparent.

We settle ourselves back on the couch, cuddling Lexi for a while before putting her to bed. I can only hope that Lilian's lingering glances at Noah's turned back might mean something— that soon enough, she'll finally reach for him first.

❧ 4 ☙

Tomorrow, we leave for the Alpha Summit. I grumble in bed, not wanting to let Noah go. We still have way too much to do today besides packing, and carrying this little bean of our pup has exhausted me beyond belief, despite their size.

Noah suddenly buries his nose into my neck, giving it a quick nip.

It startles a screeching giggle out of me, sending a tingling shockwave to my toes. "Noah!? What's going through that wolf brain of yours?"

He growls against my throat, prowling over me to cuddle me closer. "I don't want to let you go for the day."

I laugh. "Me neither. I wish we had enough time for you to knot me at least twice like I want you to. We're almost out of cuddle ball time, sadly."

Groaning, Noah rubs his forming erection against my thigh. He sucks in a breath to speak, but halts. Then he blows out a slow exhale. "I know."

Holding the silence by biting my lip, I wait to see if he has something more to say. Sometimes all my shy Alpha needs is a few extra seconds to gather his thoughts—and the more important they are, the more time he needs.

But Noah growls deeper, nipping my neck faster.

I sputter out a laugh, digging my nails into Noah's back as my toes curl. "Stop it, you wild wolf!"

He sighs, propping himself up on one elbow to look me in the eyes. Swiping my sprouting baby hairs off my forehead, Noah turns a deep shade of red.

I have to laugh. "Okay, you *really* have something spicy on the mind."

Breaking into the most gorgeous smile, Noah lets out a soft laugh that squeezes my heart. "Maybe I do, maybe I don't."

I roll my eyes. "Oh, no. You definitely do."

Erupting into giggles, Noah nuzzles our noses. Planting a soft kiss on my lips, Noah pulls back to laugh again. "Okay, yeah. I do. But I'm a little—"

He hums in thought, blinking faster as his eager scent hits my nose. I inhale a lungful of it, a heartbeat forming between my legs as his delicious scent swirls into my core. Except instead of Noah's sharp, lusty Alpha musk, his scent contains a flowery sweetness—one he almost never allows out.

I stroke his back in an effort to keep us both from overthinking this sudden change. "You're a little, what?"

He drops his forehead against mine, taking a shaky breath. "Nervous."

"Oh? It's that good of a fantasy, huh?" I can't help but grin as Noah breaks into hearty giggles.

"I mean— W-well, yes."

Turning on my side, I shimmy up to him until we're melded together again, pushing more gorgeous laughter out of him. "Tell me more, my shy Alpha. We only have ten more minutes before we have to get out of this bed, and I won't be able to focus during therapy if my imagination is running wild."

Noah chuckles, shaking his head.

But he still doesn't speak. As Noah traces my eyes with his gaze, his big hand covering my whole hip, I stroke his hair, parsing through our conversation thus far. After all we've done in bed— and the wild sex we've had in the forest, in front of the whole damn pack—what sort of sex-related thing could still embarrass my mate? My heart leaps in excitement. Maybe Noah's thinking of confessing a kink he's never tried before, and he needs a little encouragement—needs to know I won't make fun of him for it.

I soften my smile. "Would it help to mindlink it?"

Noah twists his lips. But to my surprise, he doesn't mindlink me; he leans closer, pressing our foreheads together until our eyes are only an inch apart. When he speaks, his breath tickles my lips. "I'm just working up the courage."

My heart softens for my sweet mate, his determination exciting my wolf into wagging her tail in our bond. Noah breaks into a smile, blinking faster, and I do my best to stifle my wolf.

"Sorry, I don't mean to pressure you. I'm just a little excited because I can feel it; this is something coming from your heart, isn't it?"

Noah sucks in a sharp breath, blinking a few more times as nerves rattle our bond. Then he gives me a quick nod. "Yeah."

"Okay. I'm here to listen, but we can always wait to talk about it if you need to—"

"Your Alpha musk makes me feel safe," Noah blurts out.

My breath escapes my lungs. I'm afraid to move, to even blink; Noah's breath speeds into an anxious jog, his eyes racing between mine to read any minor rejection he can find in my reaction.

But Noah's words strike deep into my heart, igniting a joy I've rarely experienced. I've never considered my occasional, strange, Alpha-like scent bursts to smell like a *true* Alpha musk. Does Noah? I didn't expect to feel so enticed by the possibility—so desperate to know the truth.

I hold Noah tighter, searching his eyes just the same. Waiting to see if there's more.

"I-it heals a part of me I'm afraid to show," Noah whispers.

Letting out an aching sigh, I slide my hands up his wide back. "Oh, my *love*."

I understand his hidden meaning: just like my scent is Alpha-like, Noah's scent has a hidden, Omega-like edge. One he's felt tremendous shame about, even in the short glimpses of it he's allowed me to witness.

If "allowing" me to witness it is even the right word. His Omega-like scent has seemed to slip out without his permission, surprising us both.

Just like it did today.

Noah clings to me, hanging on my every word as his breath quivers with nerves.

Cupping his cheeks, I stare him in the eyes. "Goddess, Noah, thank you for even telling me this. I know how hard this is, so I want you to know two things: one, I *love* that side of you. And two, you don't have to show every side of yourself unless you feel ready. Not even with me."

"I want to be ready—with you," Noah mutters.

A thrill shoots through my core. I'm unable to keep my proud wolf from smiling through me. "Okay, then let me hold him, whenever you can. I'd be honored."

Noah blinks hard and fast, likely processing my words. I figure our conversation is over, but his eyes shift from their oceanic teal to a vivid green, his wolf pushing forward. "No, I want to, as soon as possible. My wolf won't stop thinking about it, and I feel a little—" Clearing his throat, Noah lowers to a shaky whisper. "I feel a little bad for him."

I'm stunned. Since we've met, I've only heard Noah disparage his wolf. I'm usually the one looking out for the goofy Lycan, aching for him whenever I think about how hard he works for all of us, no matter if he receives gratitude or hatred in return.

But it's written in Noah's pained, half-shifted eyes; his wolf needs freeing, and he would love my help loosening the reins.

"I feel bad for him too," I whisper.

Noah's eyebrows flinch, and my heart drops. What if he's hurting deeper than he ever lets on?

I skate my hands down his chest, softening my voice. "You said my Alpha musk helps you feel safe? Do you mean that it helps in bed, while we're already feeling more open and intimate with each other?"

Noah's heart jumps beneath my palm, kicking into a pounding pace. Goosebumps rise over his bare skin as I circle my nails through his chest hair.

But Noah nods. "Can you practice letting that side of yourself roam free with me?"

Excitement strikes my core. I prop myself up, snaking my arm around his waist. "Oh, so you enjoyed me being on top again at the Luna ceremony, huh?"

Noah breaks into giggles, his warm palm sweeping down my lower back until he presses us belly to belly, hugging our baby between us. Dragging his gaze down my bare skin, Noah coats me in tingling pleasure. "It's a bit deeper than that."

It's my heart's turn to race. I know what he means; I don't allow my Alpha-like side out to play very often either. Not even with Noah—at least, not as often as my wolf begs me to.

The second I think of her thinly veiled disappointment every time I reject her, a gnawing sadness reveals itself in my chest. Judging by the pain in our bond, I'm willing to bet Noah's stifling of his Omega-like scent hurts him too. My heart aches for us both.

As I push Noah's hair back with slow, gentle sweeps over his scalp, his eyes flutter shut, and the twisting in my stomach subsides. He trusts me. And thankfully, he just gave me an opening to help him sort through his pain. *Our* pain.

"Okay," I whisper. Noah's eyes jut open, but he doesn't move a muscle—his hand frozen on my hip as he holds me in tense silence. "It'll be a little scary since I'm still confused about myself, but that doesn't mean it won't be tremendously fun."

As I break into a giddy smile, Noah's sweet scent erupts. Despite his side of our bond wavering in anxiety, my wolf stirs, urged to the surface.

"Let me treat you." I cup the base of his head, not wanting him to slip deeper into fear. "Let me soak you with as much Alpha musk as I can allow myself to release, and however you show up beneath me, I'll hold this sacred space for you. I'll love you through it, no matter how scary it might be for both of us."

Noah huffs out a fragile, broken breath—before crashing against my lips. I moan into his kiss, my heart thrumming through the rising gratitude in our bond.

"Thank you." Noah's aching voice strikes me to my core.

I sink my lips back into his, throwing my leg over his hip. Noah kisses me deeper, dragging his tongue over mine until I squirm against him, heat pooling between my legs.

As I pull back, I'm relieved to find Noah in a flustered yet giddy silence, his human cheeks flaming red as his wolf nips at mine in our bond.

Until my phone alarm rings, pushing a surprised squeak from my lips.

Noah breaks into a delighted giggle as he fetches my phone for me. "Precious."

I groan. "So much for being your tough Alpha."

"Maybe you're my Alpha mouse."

"Noah!"

He lets out a deep belly laugh, spurring me into hearty cackling. I shut my alarm off before rolling over Noah, pinning him beneath me as I straddle his hips. "Alright, wild wolf. Let's get ready for the day before your pregnant Alpha mouse pees herself."

Noah's bright laugh fills my heart and lungs with hope as he follows me to the bathroom like an excited pup.

As if Noah didn't spoil me enough with the Moon Goddess's blessing necklace—the most gorgeous, glimmering moonstone crystal hanging around my neck in the shape of a crescent moon—Noah insisted we follow at least one human tradition with an intimate courthouse wedding last month. That, and I insisted we do so for legal purposes, ensuring there are no human-world custody issues for our future kids.

Eloping in front of our closest family and friends, we gifted each other engraved wedding rings; an endless moon cycle circling our left ring fingers as our initials rest against our skin.

Spinning the ring as he holds my left hand in his lap, Noah settles into our forest drive out of Greenfield. I love to steal quick peeks at his profile as he drives, waiting for his stoic expression to soften as he spins the ring. We've never discussed it aloud, but a wordless sense of security within our bond tells me the rings remind us both of our forever connection, a quiet, soothing hum falling over us as we coast through the cozy autumn gloom.

Unfortunately, I can tell our peaceful silence is about to be broken; Noah's emotions wobble in our bond. Despite his stoic expression, darkness creeps into our shared connection, allowing me to spot the slightest hint of tension between his brows.

When he catches me staring, I bite back a smile, and Noah's forehead softens.

"Damn. I tried to keep it to myself, but I should know better by now," he mutters through a smile as it spreads to his cheeks.

I laugh. "Let's talk about it, love. We have a few minutes before we reach Jenny's office anyway."

Noah sighs, tipping his head back against his headrest with a *thud*. "I don't think you're going to like it."

My smile widens. "Too bad for me, I guess."

With a chuckle, Noah comes to a stop at a red light. Meeting my eyes, he lowers his shoulders. It's just enough to take the edge off my forming anxiety—no matter how lighthearted our conversation feels, my wolf will always be on edge when her mate is tense. Maybe he's simply being considerate of the emotional heavy lifting I'll have to do today in therapy between pregnancy anxiety and our upcoming overseas travel. But I can't forget the truth: my mate never deliberately hides things unless it's *bad*.

Noah's smile fades, sadness overwriting his features. As he shuffles in his seat, returning his focus to the road when the light turns green, I can hardly stand the silence. But I know my mate by now, and I'm well aware he needs me to hold space for him to formulate his thoughts.

As soon as I release Noah from my stare, he slumps in my peripherals. If I didn't know his voice better than anyone's, I might not be able to pick out his pained, soft-spoken words. "I feel so bad that you haven't been able to talk about Mason with Jenny."

My focus zips back to him. Between all we've had to accomplish before the Alpha Summit, I had no idea Noah's mind was still steeping in this deep of guilt beneath the surface over that jerk. My heart aches with Noah's, pushing a soft groan from my lips.

I grip his hand. "Do you not believe me that I don't blame you for what he did? Because I don't think you could've stopped him, Noah. I know we can't go back in time to know for certain, but it's not your fault some power-hungry Alpha decided to use me to get to you. It's Mason's fault." Noah lets out a tremendous, frustrated sigh. Nothing more. "And like we talked about, you wanted to give me freedom without being followed around all the time by security. I really appreciated that, especially with my history."

Noah's expression darkens. "It's because of your history that I feel even worse. I'm sure you need to talk this out with her in greater detail, don't you?"

I frown. "What makes you say that? Am I doing more

compulsions without noticing or something?" Instead of answering, Noah bites his lips. My stomach sinks. "I have, haven't I?"

Noah does a double-take, giving my hand a squeeze. "Not quite. Keep breathing."

Drooping into the passenger seat, I sigh. Noah's right; the second I suspected OCD had taken a stronger hold over me again, my whole body tightened up, preparing for the worst. As Noah slips his hand from mine, smoothing it over our budding pup, my chest swirls with excitement, loosening any remaining fears.

We're about to turn into the parking lot outside Jenny's office, a silent reminder we're out of time to get too much deeper into our conversation. Noah rubs his thumb over my baby belly, stirring my heart muscles into action. "You've been so jumpy, my love. Ever since then."

As the ache in Noah's tone deepens, I bite my lip. "Dammit, I guess you're right. I didn't put two and two together until now, but Amy was still really upset about that stalking incident too— when she helped me nest a couple weeks ago."

"Ah, I see. I was wondering why she seemed so distressed."

"I know. She's a sweetheart, like you." I sigh. "Is that all you've noticed?"

Shifting the SUV into park, Noah meets my gaze once more. We share a sad smile, shuffling against the center console to drop our foreheads together.

"Not exactly," Noah whispers against my lips. Placing a soft kiss there, he flutters my eyelids. "You've been restless in your sleep. I don't know if it's mainly pregnancy stress dreams like you've mentioned, but my wolf is on high alert now that you're carrying our pup, and…"

"He thinks it's more on the side of PTSD nightmares," I mutter the quiet part out loud. With Noah's wince in confirmation, I nod, even though my heart drops. "I trust his judgment. Thank you for letting me know."

Noah's hands cup my cheeks. "I know you've got your own treatment covered, so I'm not meaning to tell you what to work on, or what not to."

"I know, my sweet Alpha. You don't have to worry about that." I close my eyes, nuzzling into his palm's comforting scent.

"Maybe I do, though. Because I know you haven't said anything directly to me about it, but I'm pretty sure not being able to tell Jenny about Lycans existing makes getting proper treatment really fucking hard. Especially if you'll have to use Prolonged Exposure. I hate to put you in that place."

My eyelids snap open, but no words form in response.

Noah has stumped me. I don't know how to solve this problem either, and it's a huge one—especially when Mason antagonized me not only as a stalker, but also as a hulking beast, intensifying the major trigger he provided.

But with humans involved, the truth often comes with a fatal price. My stomach sinks at the thought of our fathers' deaths. If disclosing the existence of Lycans risks losing Noah, or any of our pack members, it's not worth it. I know firsthand nothing can replace a life.

So as Noah's guilt threatens to bend our pack's rules for my sake, I shake my head. "I can continue to work around it. I'll bring up the incident to her today, just explaining he's been watching us lately and freaked me out."

Noah frowns. I kiss him, but his lips aren't as urgent to kiss me back; my mate is too deep in thought.

"I mean it. I can't risk your safety either. All of our safety, rather. Our pack is too precious," I say.

Noah finally softens. "Yeah, that's how I feel about all of you too. But it's not black and white; you don't necessarily have to expose everything in order to talk about it... And I finally thought of an excuse that might work." My eyes widen as Noah breaks into a mischievous smile, his wolf coming out to play with a flash of his fangs. "We *are* in the Pacific Northwest, you know. If you told her you witnessed some supernatural, crazy shit, even as specific as shapeshifters, she might actually agree with you that there's more out there."

I sputter out a laugh, pulling back with flushing cheeks as he gives my tiny belly a soft pat. "You can't be serious. What if she thinks I'm hallucinating or something?"

He shrugs, his incisors enticing my wolf into nuzzling him in our bond. "Maybe she will. Or maybe you could lean into that white lie, and it'll be fine, as far as I'm concerned—as long as you can get the support you need. I trust you to be safe about it."

I suck in a breath to speak, but all I can do is stare in awe. Knowing how deeply Ritchie's death torments Noah, I'm stunned to receive his trust on such a tender issue. Maybe he wants me to take care of myself, but I don't want to bend our rules for my sake. His permission to do so has the opposite effect, tempting me to keep our Lycan secret even closer to my heart instead, protecting sweet Noah for life.

Hugging Noah's palm to my belly, I beam at my mate. "You're so smart. But still, I'll see what I can say without disclosing much of anything."

Noah nods, glancing at the dashboard's clock once more. "Shit, sorry. You only have a minute to take the elevator up."

As his smile fades, I can tell he's also eager to leave—someone must be mindlinking him for backup. Stressful mindlinks seem to be endless for Noah these days, and I hate it. My stomach twists beneath his hand, hating to lift his warm palm off our baby. Kissing his knuckles to make up for it, I smile the best I can, not wanting to make him feel even worse.

"Stay safe, my shy Alpha. I'll see you after my appointment."

I open the passenger door, but I'm caught by my elbow. The second I turn my head back to Noah, he smushes a heavy kiss against my cheek, sending me into giggles. My wolf's fur stands on end, delighted by her mate's sneak attack. When I meet Noah's eyes, I'm relieved to find them more relaxed than they've been all morning.

He grins. "See you soon, gorgeous Luna."

No matter how many days we've lived together now, my wolf still slumps in disappointment to part ways with Noah. I laugh, hurrying to the office doors for all of our sakes. Well, at least, I *try* to make it easier on us. I can't resist one last glance over my shoulder to wave goodbye.

But I freeze in the open doorway, surprised to see Noah has thrown his SUV into park. He hops out, ripping off his jacket— eyeing the treeline like he's desperate to shift into his wolf. Did I keep him too long?

Noah's forehead creases—a millisecond before he whips his half-shifted eyes in my direction. I let out a squeak, scurrying into the building.

Spying on me, huh? Noah's wolf wags his tail, softening his urgency I feel in our bond to dash into the forest. *It's all okay, Luna. Let me be the one to deal with the usual bullshit today. You can just focus on holding the baby for me.*

Biting my lip, I overflow with fuzzy warmth as I step into the elevator. *I love you.*

I love you too. I'll see you before you know it.

I want to relax, to ease Noah's concerns rather than feed into them, but in the end, I can't control my pacing wolf. She's restless lately, hesitant to part ways with the goofy Alpha giving her a chance to carry her first pup. But I know that's not the only reason why. Ever since Mason gathered 250 Alphas to leave Greenfield behind, I've been unable to shake the paranoia that it's not truly over. What if his mindset poisoned pack members beyond the Alphas who left alongside him, and the rest are waiting their turn to hunt us down at our next vulnerability? What if they're spying on us to tell Mason everything he's missing? What if it's not just Mason's pack, but something far more sinister—a global super pack, like our international allies suggested?

Noah has too much to focus on. We both do. Especially when we're leaving our pack behind for two weeks at the Alpha Summit—the perfect opening to strike.

My pregnant wolf is all instinct—nearly impossible to ignore, as if someone dialed up the volume to her thoughts in my mind. Rushing my feet down the hall, she changes her mind about chasing after our mate, instead demanding I huddle up safely indoors and stop distracting him.

But once I step into Jenny's waiting room, I'm surprised to find her staring out the window. Normally the muted, forest green walls calm my wolf, allowing me to sink into my favorite gray, textured armchair in the corner, worn in by dozens of other patients like me whose lives have changed thanks to Jenny.

I was expecting to find an empty room; to have to wait for Jenny to open her office door, her warm smile welcoming me into her sanctuary. But today, Jenny's back remains to me. With my nimble wolf at the forefront of my being, I must not have made a single sound entering the office.

But Jenny's tense shoulders set me on edge. I soften my voice, not wanting to scare her. "Jenny?"

No response.

Fear slithers up my sternum. Have they come for us now?

I stand frozen on Jenny's welcome mat, unease tightening my throat. This has never happened before. Jenny has always greeted me with a cheery hello and a hug. Lately, she takes our greeting a step further, playfully challenging my OCD fears around losing our baby with a bright "How's my pregnant client doing today?"

Today, it's like I'm not here at all.

My jaw opens and closes, my fingertips busying themselves with picking at my thumb. Is Jenny in danger? Are we *both* in danger? Whatever she sees out the window, she's locked on. If I say something else to break the silence, I know I'll scare her shitless.

But Jenny gasps, gripping the windowsill.

My focus zips outside, following Jenny's gaze. I have to take a few steps closer to get the right angle, exposing a dark treeline—overcast skies deepening every murky shadow below the evergreens.

But that doesn't stop me from spotting a familiar shape: the tail end of a big, black shadow, accompanied by Noah's wolf heightening his primal instincts in our bond, ready to protect our pack.

It takes every ounce of control in me not to gasp. Did Jenny see Noah's wolf? Or even worse, did she see him *shift?*

Our car conversation replays in rapid speed in my mind. Noah was afraid of keeping me from sharing enough, but now I'm afraid Jenny has seen too much.

I can't control my anxiety, exposing itself in my quivering voice. "What? What is it?"

Jenny is silent for a long moment, leaning deeper into the window. Her fingertips grip the windowsill even harder, bending until they squeak against the glossy paint. I ease closer, my jaw clamped tight in fear.

Shit, Noah, are you safe? I mindlink.

I'm fine, I'm just pissed at this straggler ignoring our borders again after Yas chased them out. Fuck, did I distract you in our bond?

Locked onto Jenny's frozen profile, I can hardly breathe. *I'm scared Jenny saw you. Out her window.*

Fuck, no way. I thought I was deep enough into the brush. Did she say anything?

She's just… staring. My gut churns as an intrusive image flashes across my mind: Noah coming back home to me with fresh gashes across his chest. Again.

He can't afford me distracting him like this.

Straightening my shoulders, I suck in a shaky breath. *It's fine, I'll play it off. Act like I didn't see anything if I have to. Or maybe she missed the shift and just thought she saw an unbelievably big bear. Focus, and I'll update you later.*

Great. Poor Noah must feel even more terrible than before my appointment, thinking the same thing I am: now I *definitely* can't bring up anything close to shapeshifters in therapy. At least not today.

I'll have to talk this through with Noah when we get home.

For now, it's time for damage control.

Except Jenny is still so absorbed in her shock that she still hasn't realized I'm here. I hate scaring people. Should I say something again, or does she need a soft tap on her shoulder to come to her senses? My hand hesitates in the space between us, but that seems like a terrible idea. If I were her and that's how a client got my attention, I'd probably piss myself. Maybe that's because I have to pee constantly right now anyway, but still.

Bracing myself with no choice but to terrify the poor woman, I wince preemptively. "Jenny?"

With a jolt and a screech, Jenny grips her chest. I scream too, causing Jenny to scream yet again.

The second we meet wide eyes, she lets out a breathy laugh, gripping my outstretched hand. "Oh, goodness. Aliya!"

I grasp her tight with a groan. "I'm so sorry! I didn't mean to startle you, but you seemed so concerned when I walked in that I wanted to make sure everything was okay. Are you safe?"

Stooping over in relief, Jenny laughs—her usual, bright smile on full display with bouncy, ringlet curls framing her face. "Oh, you are such a sweetheart. It's nothing, just a huge animal of some sort."

"What, where?" I laugh along warily, but my guts flip. She *absolutely* saw something. Something so unusual that she doesn't give me a single detail more before waving me into her office.

"It's gone now. Sorry to lose track of time!"

And now I'm ten times more nervous to talk about Mason, hobbling on shaky legs to Jenny's cushy couch.

"Are you okay? Did that trigger you?" Jenny asks.

Settling into the cushions, I huff out a heavy breath. I'm a bit relieved she just gave me an easy out; maybe I can talk about Mason retriggering me after all.

But all I can do is nod. Post-adrenaline weighs me into the couch cushions, upsetting my already-rocky stomach.

"You're doing a great job at regulating using your breath, so let's keep doing that together." Jenny softens her voice, taking a few slow breaths with me, in and out. After three rounds, she gives me a gentle smile. "You're right here with me. You're safe."

I nod, but I'm sure my smile looks as weary as I feel. I'm tempted to shift with Noah, stealing him back to bed to sleep off the stress.

But Jenny's grin grows. "Plus, there's this big, burly, outgoing accountant next door that I could scream for help from, God forbid anything happens."

I laugh, my shoulders softening. "True, I've seen him." I've also smelled him; pregnancy made scents strong enough to bulldoze my brain with one wisp of a scent. Just walking by the accountant's door a couple weeks ago, I realized he was another Greenfield Pack wolf.

"Are you noticing any extra anxiety or hypervigilance since your pregnancy began?" Jenny asks.

Anxiety stings my veins. "Yes."

"Like what?"

Dammit. I don't think I can avoid this any longer. My whole body tenses, warning of old PTSD symptoms resurfacing. Pregnancy exhaustion tugs on my limbs like I'm wearing a coat of bricks, yet I shuffle in my seat, unable to hold still. "Sorry, I know I'm a bit quiet, but something happened recently, and I've been a bit nervous to talk about it."

Jenny keeps her eyebrows in check, but I see it: that near-imperceptible twitch of concern in her forehead. "Are you nervous to talk about it with me?"

I bite my lip. "Not exactly. It was just so weird; this one guy from our town was following me and being gross, except this time, I had a whole group of my best friends around, and I felt completely fine afterwards. Poor Amy was triggered by it too, though."

Jenny's eyebrows arch in reflected sorrow. "I'm glad you both have each other."

"Me too," I whisper.

After updating Jenny about my heart-to-heart with Amy, she hums in thought, tilting her head. "So what part about this latest stalking incident still makes *you* distressed?"

"Well, it's over, and I'm talking about it with Noah and Amy, so it's helping to avoid a PTSD-like reaction. But I still feel a little creeped out. Like he's going to return. Just like—"

I hesitate, my insides churning; it's been a while since I've been afraid to say Steven's name. I don't want to lose progress.

But Jenny nods. "Correct me if I'm wrong, but since we know each other kind of well by now—" I giggle, and Jenny smiles. "I have a *pretty* good guess about where this is going."

I groan, shutting my eyes. "I can imagine."

Jenny's infectious cackle fills the room, leaving me laughing with her. But she's right; we know each other well, and the second I open my eyes, I know she's seen right through me.

"Are you worried that he'll return, or are you worried about being worried that *he'll* return?"

I frown, wanting to be annoyed. But I can't help but let out a giggle. "Maybe you do know me."

Jenny joins in on my laughter until our smiles lighten my heart.

I sigh, cupping my belly. "I don't want to go back to how I

used to be. I'm really scared that I'll not only hurt Noah with my trauma now, but also our sweet baby."

Jenny nods, and I flush; I didn't expect my voice to come out so shaky when I finally admitted this aloud. Tears sting my eyes, and I swallow hard.

"Guess what?"

I laugh. "I know. Maybe I will, maybe I won't."

Jenny grins. "More like you most likely will. We can't avoid making any mistakes ever, can we?"

My heart flips. "Unfortunately." Jenny laughs, and I'm grateful to have a reason to smile again.

"Now, I don't want to give you reassurance here, but could it be possible that you've developed the tools by now, to where even if your child does end up with similar mental health conditions, or inevitably experiences trauma in this crazy journey of life, that you might be able to support them far better now? Not because you suffered, but because you now hold the knowledge of how to heal?"

My lip wobbles, forcing my voice to come out as a strained whisper. "It's definitely possible. I hope it's possible."

Jenny nods, her eyebrows contorting in reflection of mine. "I think it is. And I think this could be hitting you so hard because you care so deeply."

"Which is also why my harm fears are resurfacing," I mutter.

Jenny smiles bright. I know what she's thinking even before she says it; I *do* have the tools. I just have to give myself a chance to use them before jumping to the worst conclusions possible.

But I huff. "It's just hard to grasp still sometimes when I've had so much proof the world is unsafe."

Jenny hums. "It is unsafe. *And…*"

"And then there's Noah. And Amy. Kira, Yasmine, Rainn…"

As my body softens, I run my hand over our budding child, imagining how many loving hands will hold them alongside mine and Noah's.

I can hear Jenny's proud smile in her gentle words. "*Exactly.* Just like there are unsafe pockets in this world, there are pockets of safety that you've created for yourself too. There can be both."

My eyebrows furrow. Logically, I know she's right. I'm just having trouble believing it.

❧ 6 ❧

Anticipatory jitters charge my exhausted limbs the night before our flight. I shuffle through our luggage, hiding a sexy surprise for Noah during our trip to Sweden. I think he'll need it; whether it's the Alpha Summit or the additional Alpha-domination Lycans he had to chase away from our borders thirty minutes ago, Noah's stress has increased to a level that seeps through his scent glands, soaking the air in a persistent sense of unease.

As I approach him, Noah's tight shoulders droop. "Sorry, I know I reek, it's just—"

"I know. I'm not upset, just concerned for you."

Noah shakes his head. He says nothing more.

Wrapping my hand around Noah's limp arm at his side, I guide him to our cushy mattress. But when he plops down on it beside me, he bounces me in the air, pushing a yelp from me.

Despite his upset, Noah cracks a smile, grabbing me by the hips to stabilize me. "Oops. Sorry, Luna."

I laugh, sorting his hair out of his eyes. "I know what I signed up for when I mated you."

Giving me a soft smile, Noah kisses my forehead. But then he drops his head into his palm, scrubbing his face with a growl. "I had to add *twenty* fucking people to the blacklist today. Just that I know of."

Dread creeps up my throat. But I know the only reason I haven't panicked over our rising outbreak of domineering, violence-focused Alphas is because Noah is there to protect not just me, but everyone. He's shouldering that fear for us. I'm afraid it's wearing him down by the day, digging into the corners of his eyes.

"You're under *so* much pressure, my love," I say.

Noah slumps.

And I can't take it anymore. "Forget the bed chat: you've probably had enough of talking about this all day, every day. For tonight, let me wash your body."

That came out before I could stop it. I freeze, realizing I didn't phrase my offer as an option, but a demand. That, plus my Alpha musk is showing. What if I didn't leave enough room for Noah to consent to what he wants?

But Noah seems to loosen in relief, his arms slackening as he gazes up at me. "Are you sure? You're pregnant."

I laugh. "So? I can still thank my mate's gorgeous body for being here. I'd love to do you a favor."

Dropping my stare, Noah smiles, giving me a soft, "Thank you."

My wolf spins in circles in our bond as I take Noah by the hand, guiding him to rest on the toilet seat while I prepare our shower.

Dragging my fingers beneath the water to gauge its temperature, I check on Noah over my shoulder. I'm relieved to see his eyes closed, my mate doing his best to regulate his wavering stress in our bond.

Which also gives me an opening. As quietly as I can, I tug my hoodie over my head, slipping my fingertips beneath my sports bra to relieve my achy breasts. Noah draws a heavy breath, letting out a growling sigh. But he doesn't open his eyes. I bite back a smile. Despite Noah's wolf hearing, I manage to be quiet enough to yank off my leggings too, setting them on the cool tile below my feet with one hand as I tug my socks off with the other. All I'm left with is my underwear.

I speak as softly as I can. "Hey, gorgeous."

Noah's eyes flutter open. He sucks in a harsh breath through his nose, his focus zipping straight to my swollen breasts. "Oh, fuck."

I smile, turning around but holding eye contact with him. Pulling my long hair over my shoulder, I ensure Noah has a clear view of my entire back.

Tugging at my waistband, I ease my panties over the curve of my ass. My wolf puffs her chest out in our bond as Noah soaks me in, his focus dragging up the length of my body. When we meet eyes, his irises flash green—and a burst of Alpha musk wafts from my scent glands.

My breath shakes. I've let my wolf's Alpha side out to play with Noah before, but this feels new. Intentional, and, therefore, far more potent.

As Noah's eyelids flutter, his lungs flex his rib cage, dragging in an extended whiff of my scent. When he opens his eyes again, his heavy-lidded stare rattles me; he's *pleased* by my Alpha scent. My heart squeezes tight in my chest, pushing a flood of oxytocin through my torso.

Before I can finish turning back around, Noah catches me by the hips. Purring over my skin, he plants soft kisses up my spine. Goosebumps crawl up my body, hardening my nipples as I suck in a sharp breath.

Pulling me closer, Noah sweeps his palms down my thighs before dragging them back up my hips, circling them around my waist to rub my bloated abdomen. My lips part, relaxation washing over me as tingles cascade my torso; I *love* when Noah caresses our baby, and he knows it.

Before Noah can convince me he's treating me instead, I spin around in his arms, my shins bumping the toilet seat beneath him. "Your turn."

A thrill pierces my chest; I'm met with ravenous, golden eyes, staring deep into my gaze.

His wolf isn't challenging mine for dominance, but he seems tempted to, his Alpha side still hesitating at the forefront.

But a slow smile creeps up Noah's cheeks, breaking the intensity of our staredown. Glomping onto me, Noah sighs against my chest, soft kisses on my sternum sparking waves of pleasure down my belly.

When I stoop over, gripping the hem of his T-shirt, Noah slackens, allowing me to ease the grass- and dirt-stained fabric over his head. He reattaches his palms to my waist the second they're free, spurring giggles from me.

Gathering his wide, sturdy hands, I help Noah to his feet. His jeans sink to the tile with a *plop* of heavy denim, but I make sure to ease his boxers' waistband with care over his forming erection, his shaft bobbing at my brief touch.

Drawing my eyes up Noah's bare body, I suck in a tight breath; he's still staring straight at me, spiking excitement through my chest. Heat pools low in my belly, swirling between my legs.

By the time I guide Noah by the hand into the shower behind me, my lips remain parted with the thought of his rising pleasure—I'm dying to lather him up, making him feel good all over. Pumping body wash into my palm, I scrub my hands together, desperate to massage my soapy fingers over his dense chest.

But just as I place my hands over Noah's pecs, he cups my cheeks, holding me in place. I freeze, blinking up at the gorgeous man above me. Water spills down his neck, cascading over his clavicles in a tantalizing waterfall. Full lips part above me as Noah's pointed stare roams to my mouth, but he doesn't pounce yet, his thumbs stroking my cheeks. Steam mixes with a blast of my scent, carrying a quick burst of Omega-like submission to anything and everything his hands wish to do to me. But my wolf shakes herself off, determined to keep flaunting her Alpha side.

As I meet Noah's eyes once more, his sharp gaze greets me with a delighted, sugary, Omega-like scent to match my own. I can hardly keep my knees from dipping with desire, inhaling his enthralling scent as a burst of Alpha musk erupts from me once more.

Deep down, I'm terrified by how new this scent swap feels. Is this too much? I analyze Noah for his reaction to our scents, afraid to make another move. But now that I've let myself go just a little bit, my wolf fights back, refusing to stifle her Alpha side and pushing more and more of her truth out instead—especially as her mate welcomes her Alpha side with open arms, our bodies communicating with each other through desirous pheromones. Within seconds, I douse poor Noah with more Alpha musk than I've ever allowed myself to express.

The second Noah lets out a soft, helpless sound, I'm done for. Responding with my own moan, I slide my soapy hands down Noah's thick arms, working out their tension. He doesn't allow me to lather him for long; Noah locks one hand around my waist as the other sinks into my soaked hair. Pressing me against the

icy shower door, Noah coats my front half in his blazing warmth, sinking his lips into mine with a growl. My breath hitches through my nose as I tilt my head, gripping Noah's shoulders to deepen our kiss. My tongue slips over his, tasting our sweet, aching scent for each other in the steam. I moan through the pulsing ache in my pussy, my inner muscles clenching in preparation for him.

As Noah's erection prods my belly, it takes all of my strength not to squat down and blow him, right here. Pulling back from his lips with a shiver-inducing *click* of our heavy kiss, I hold burning eye contact with Noah. When I dig my fingers into his hair, his eyes roll back in bliss. I smile as I give his scalp a slow, tender massage, bubbles crinkling beneath my fingers.

"There you go. Good boy," I whisper.

Noah sucks in a deep breath before letting out a heavy shudder—his desire evident on his slackened lips alone, even without his cock poking me for attention. I place soft kisses across his chest, humming through the rising pleasure in our bond as Noah runs his big palms down my back and ass, washing me in return.

We don't have to plan ahead aloud: the urgency rising in our speeding hands tells me Noah wants to get out of this shower and into bed as badly as I do.

After scrubbing any remaining bits of myself, I grip Noah's arm—stopping him just before his hands run over his swelling shaft. Sliding my soapy palm beneath his heavy balls with one hand, I sweep down his plump cock with the other, giving him a gentle rub. Noah's breath hitches as my fingertips skate down his shaft's sensitive underside, just before they circle his tip. His erection boosts to full mast, and I can't help but smile at the heavy flushing I've created on his tan cheeks. Cupping my palms, I collect warm water, rinsing every last bubble from his sensitive, swollen shaft. Noah shudders, pressing my wet forehead to his lips and holding me there.

Reaching behind Noah, I shut the shower off. "Let's get you dry."

Noah hobbles after me out of the shower, not allowing me out of his range of motion a single inch—his hands dragging over my hips and lower back until my pussy flexes faster.

I laugh, scooting my hips out of his reach to throw one of our fluffy, white bath towels over his broad shoulders. As I quickly scrub him off, Noah growls, pressing our hips back together.

"I have a feeling you're about to kill me," he mutters.

Sputtering out a laugh, I scrub my legs dry, gripping Noah's arm for balance. "*Kill* you? That wasn't exactly the plan."

After a sleepy chuckle, Noah groans. Letting his towel flop to the tile without a single care, he ushers me out of the bathroom with a steady press of his palm on my back.

I have to laugh with him. "We're still soaked!"

"Yeah, and we're gonna get soaked again in bed, at this rate. By both of us."

Letting out a giddy cackle, I chase him to the bedroom, leaving little puddles on the hardwood floor with every step.

Noah drops himself onto the bed first, helping me up after him with eager hands. "How do you want me?"

Biting my lip does nothing to stop my bursting smile—it erupts from me as heavily as my Alpha musk. My heart hammers as I witness the intense reaction my scent spurs in Noah: inhaling hard, Noah's irises flicker back to their brightest gold, his cock flexing with urgency.

By now, I'm bathing Noah in my scent. It feels miraculous to free this unexplored side of myself, but that doesn't mean it's perfectly comfortable; nerves spiral through both of us in our bond, likely the only thing keeping us from caving early and fucking in the shower.

I don't want to overwhelm Noah. In my heart, I know I don't.

But a core, unavoidable part of me is taking over my body. My Alpha-like tendencies likely don't compare to Noah's full-fledged Alpha side, but I'm filled with empathy for how Noah must feel when he falls into a rut: I'm shocked by how overpowering the urge feels to surround Noah with my Alpha-like scent until he writhes beneath me with pleasure. It takes tremendous effort to focus on anything else.

My voice shakes. "On your back for me, please."

Noah swallows hard, his eyes sweeping down my bare body. But despite our clear nerves, Noah lays back; he still wants this.

And I want to top him.

Straddling his waist, I kneel above him. My soaked hair has glued itself to my breasts and back, so I fetch the hair claw I left on my nightstand, tossing my hair up behind my head.

With a clear view of all of me, Noah's palms land on my damp thighs, warming them as his thumb catches a stray water droplet trickling down my inner leg. I suck in a sharp breath at how sensitive it feels, catching his hands before his electric touch jolts me into the air.

Noah's eyes zip to mine. My heart lurches; it's the first time his Alpha side has made a true effort to challenge me back all night. I hold his stare, my wolf shivering with excitement in our bond. But as I settle myself down over Noah's lap, pinning his seeping cock against his abdomen, Noah sucks in a tight breath. With gentle circles of my hips, Noah's eyes roll back as they shut. Another gush of his Omega-like scent hits my nose, and I purr.

Yes, this is what I want.

But I should make sure Noah's faring okay; a flash of nerves crash through him with this last release of his scent.

It takes everything within me to steady my voice. "You okay?"

With lips parted, Noah simply nods. But when his eyes flutter back open, I freeze.

This is him; Noah's wolf stares back with those vivid, golden irises. While I intended to draw out his Omega side over time, I didn't expect him to show up now. Not right away. His scent might still be subdued, afraid to fully present itself, but no matter how many times I draw in another breath, all I smell is a blissed-out *Omega*. Which means Noah trusts me to witness him at his most vulnerable.

And the emotions laced into Noah's scent scream as clearly as his heaving chest; he's craving me.

Yep, this is the last time I'm seeing in full color for the night. Before I can stop her, my wolf takes charge, lacing her fingers with Noah's. Pressing his hands to the mattress beside his shoulders, I purr over him, dragging the tip of my nose down the mark I left on his jugular's scent gland. Noah's breath hitches, his jaw tilting in a near-fawn. I can't get enough of it, inhaling lungfuls of his delicious, flowery scent.

Prowling over him, I drag my tongue down his sternum,

lapping up every water droplet I find. Noah hisses, his cock twitching beneath me and bumping my clit. A growl pushes from my chest, my grip tightening against Noah's hard squeeze of my hands. My tongue trails the edges of his pecs, cherishing their swell as of late—every day, my poor mate chases Alphas who don't understand they have no damn chance, bulking Noah out even further by giving him an extra boost of training. But when I slather his left nipple in my attention, giving it a soft suckle, Noah jerks beneath me, letting out the smallest gasp.

It takes everything within me to force myself to sit up, checking in on Noah's expression. But he eases back into the pillows, his lips parted and cheeks darker than ever as another desperate, saccharine blast of Omega-like scent hits my nose.

Fuck. He's a blissed-out puddle of lust, and it's all my fault.

I can't get enough of it.

Is this how Noah feels when he melts me into the bed sheets, burying me in his Alpha musk? Just like the day I let Noah mark me, it's not dominance I'm craving over him; it's Noah's buttery, whimpering reaction. *I'm* doing this to him. He's squirming beneath me, and I want more of it.

But Noah knows my weaknesses too: his big palms drag up my rib cage, forcing me to jerk upright with a cry. Gripping his hands around my over-sensitive breasts, I prevent Noah from roaming further.

Noah's sly grin sinks deep into my core, pulsing wet heat through me until I'm certain I'm more soaked between my legs than on the back of my neck, my hair dripping down my spine.

Chuckling, Noah blinks up at me. "Sorry, little Alpha. I had to tease you back before you made me come in, like, sixty seconds—and with you barely even touching me."

I huff out a breathy laugh, rolling my hips over his cock. "Don't tempt me."

"Does it still feel okay if I touch you here, though? After you acclimate for a second?" Noah brushes my darkened nipples with wide thumbs, pushing hard, heated breaths from my lips. "You seem extra sensitive. More than the other night."

I grip his hands tight to my chest again, shuddering. "Every part of me is extra sensitive now, but you're so gentle with me that it's nice."

"And you don't feel sick? Or too tired?"

My shoulders soften. "I'm okay, my love. I'll tell you if we need to stop."

With this, Noah seems to finally, fully sink into the pillows. I rest my weight over him too, my thighs squishing over his hips. As I drag my fingernails up and down his stomach, back and forth over his chest hair, Noah purrs. Deepening my touch into a kneading massage, I can't stop more and more of my Alpha musk from leaking out. How can I, with the sight of my gorgeous mate in front of me, his eyes heavy-lidded and his jaw softened in bliss?

Shimmying my pelvis, I spread my labia over Noah's hardening shaft. With a groan, Noah grips my thighs, raising both of our hips as he grinds up against me.

I slow my massage, sweeping down his torso. "Relax, my love. Keep letting me treat you."

Noah smiles, his eyes flickering back open. "You want me to be a pillow prince?"

Giggling, I slip my wet pussy over him faster, delighted by his slow, heavy blinking in reaction. "Yep, you got it."

Noah chuckles, but he peers at me through his eyelashes—his puppy-dog stare presenting itself.

That's when the true depths of his scent hits: beneath his usual cinnamon, spicy-yet-sweet scent, a blast of enticing sugar hits my nose. I've never smelled Noah like this before. Never so raw, so vulnerable, or so afraid—yet so absolutely daring, as if to say, *Fuck it all, I'm showing you this part of me, anyway.*

He's mesmerizing.

My fangs extend beyond my control, a growl escaping my lips as I roll my hips in rapid circles, struggling to stave off the pulsing ache in my jaws—my wolf begging me to mark him again. Noah sucks in a startled breath below me, but it's a heated one, squirming against my rocking movements. Tilting my weight forward, I slip back and forth over his tip, using my clenching pussy to suckle the sensitive gland. He's already leaked against his abdomen, so I drag our fluids between us, circling my widening core over his flexing shaft.

Noah's chest labors beneath my hands, another eruption of his scent escaping him with a hard squeeze of his eyes. But before I can ask if he's okay, he whispers, "*Thank* you. Keep going. *Please.*"

My heart flips as I realize I just soaked him with another deluge of musk, pushing more of his sweet scent out; he's not thanking me for using my pussy to give him a sloppy, wet handjob, he's thanking me for showing this hidden Alpha side of myself, allowing him to do the same with his Omega side.

I can't believe this is happening to us. A deep part of me questions if it's okay. If it's allowed.

But there's no mistaking that my wolf loves it, courting Noah's wolf with hard, heavy licks of his neck in our bond. Noah's eyelids flutter as his breath escapes him in harsh gasps. With that, I can't hold back anymore, my scent pouring from me.

As I slip my pussy faster over him, his tip dips into my core; I'm aching so badly for him, my body has opened up wide on its own. But I want more. Tilting my hips, I work my gaping core further over his tip before pushing my ass back, immersing him inside me.

When Noah gives out a faint, pleased moan, every inch of my body shivers, delighted by how soft his skin feels inside me. I work him deeper, arching my spine until I can drop my ass back on his lap, massaging my G-spot with his spongy tip. As I let out a purring moan, Noah's back arches beneath me, his moans amplifying. I pound myself over his cock again and again, craving more of his reaction. His touch sweeps up my body, his breath rapid.

Wild, ravenous eyes meet mine. Gripping the back of my neck, Noah pulls me to his lips. I drape myself over him, moaning into his mouth as I inhale a deep lungful of his hungry scent. His scent's sweet, desperate cry of arousal flexes my pussy around his shaft. Noah tightens his grip on my ass until his claws poke my skin.

I growl. "You smell *so* good, my love. I can't get enough."

With this confession, I'm hit with another wave of Noah's sweet, flowery scent. It jerks my hips over him, my body shuddering with delight. Noah urges me into a heated kiss, his hips writhing beneath my thighs. As we hum through a thorough, tonguing makeout, I smush my ass down in his lap, gripping his cock with soft squeezes of my core to slow my pace. Noah's fingers tremble over my hips as I roll them in circles, massaging every angle of his shaft inside me.

"A-*Aliya*—" He breathes.

"Does that feel good, gorgeous?" I whisper, tracing his heaving chest with my fingernails.

But Noah can't seem to speak, soft gasps of pleasure escaping his lips as I rub him from base to tip with each squeeze of my inner muscles. I glide my massaging fingers up his chest to his scent gland. Instead of tracing my scarred mark there, I give his neck a swirling massage, urging more scent out. I don't have to hope it feels just as delightful as when he's done this to me; he jerks up into me with a soft cry, gripping my wrist hard as if I'm fingering his prostate. With this stimulation comes the most potent burst of Omega-like scent I've ever smelled from Noah, dropping my jaw as I salivate over its delicious sweetness.

With how heavily Noah's hips press up into mine, his expanded cock filling every inch within me, I can't control my body's reaction; fluid gushes from my pussy, spurred on by Noah's lusty scent. Sweetening the air, his sugary scent envelops my nose with spicy, cardamom undertones. I let out a whimpering moan in delight, but Noah moans louder, gripping my hips hard to meet my every bounce with an eager thrust.

He's an absolute puddle of pleasure beneath me, my poor mate arching in desperation for release.

As he lets out a far more pleading moan, I tighten my inner muscles around his shaft, my heart flipping at how delicious his plushy counterpressure feels. "I've got you, Noah."

Planting my palms beside his shoulders, I bounce over him. Noah pants like he never has in front of me before, his eyes flashing an even brighter yellow to join my wolf where she's at— lost in the throes of our connection.

As Noah's burning palms caress every inch of my bare skin in gratitude, I pound myself over his swollen cock—until he breathes hard and fast, warning me he's on the edge of a heavy orgasm.

My thighs burn, but I don't care. Spreading my knees, I bury him to the hilt within me, chasing my own release as my clit bumps his abdomen with every bounce.

But Noah's massive hands suddenly grip my hips down over his lap. I pant through harsh gasps, Noah's pelvis jerking as he floods my core with wave after wave of heat. I squirt with him, riding him on the edge of my own impending orgasm as I chase his knot.

But as Noah slackens beneath me, his breath shaking through every moan, I try not to let my surprise show: his knot didn't form.

Instead, he slumps onto the pillows, his cheeks flushed and eyelids drooping as he continues to shudder.

"Sorry," Noah whispers, blinking through the haze. "You made my muscles so weak that—"

A moan escapes my lips as Noah helps me rock my hips back and forth over him, keeping my pelvis pinned tight to his lap. Between his heavy rubbing against my clit and his softening cock giving itself room to massage my G-spot even deeper, I can hardly mumble through the pleasure creeping up my chest. "No, no sorries. You're so gorgeous that I'm—"

I whimper in delight, Noah tracing tingling touches up my sides. A sparkling pleasure climbs my spine, my nerves lit up in awe of him.

"*Good* girl," he breathes.

"*Noah*—"

As I rock my hips, Noah writhes beneath me in leftover bliss. Between his breathy moans and his thick thumb rolling my clit, I cry out in pleasure, my thighs quivering around his waist. Tingles caress my body, buzzing comfort covering every inch of my belly, breasts, and neck until the nerves trickle to my face. I keep my ass pressed tight to his hips, Noah's big hands pressing down hard on the junction of my thighs as he rubs my clit faster. As his fingers wrap to my ass, squishing me into him with a tender press of his tip against my G-spot, I come hard enough to steal the breath from my lungs, my pussy clamping down rapidly over his cock. He gives me soft bounces of his hips, rubbing out every last drop of pleasure from me. My skin washes in goosebumps, satisfaction spilling from my lips as Noah massages me from the inside out.

As I slow to a trembling stop over Noah, he smiles beneath me, hardly able to keep his eyes open.

I pant in absolute delight, unable to stop softly moaning. "Oh, my God. I can't believe how lucky I am. I've never seen anyone more beautiful."

Noah covers his eyes with the back of his hand, but he doesn't hide his deliriously happy smile.

I can only stare at him, my heart dancing in circles. Is this how good it feels for Noah to top me, turning me into a mushy mess on the mattress?

"I might need to do this again tomorrow," I whisper.

Noah sputters out a sleepy laugh, daring to look at me again. "I can't believe my pregnant mate did this to me. I was right: you might actually kill me next time from how hard you just made me come."

I laugh, gripping my chest as I catch my breath. "Oh, good. At least we'd both go out with a bang."

Noah groans through a laugh. "I saw the Moon Goddess, that's for sure."

Draping myself over him as I giggle, I kiss his sweaty chest. "We're going to need another shower, but it looks like it'll have to be in the morning."

"Ugh, I know. I think you sucked the life out of my limbs. I don't even know how I'm speaking."

I can't help myself, letting out a loud, hard laugh and accidentally squeezing him inside me. Noah's breath hitches before he lets out a hiss.

I freeze, struggling to stifle more laughter. "Sorry, sorry—"

Lifting my hips, I free myself of his softening, oversensitive shaft, not thinking of anything else but easing him to sleep. Noah snags tissues beside us, but he's too late, cupping around his sides as his cum spills from me, dripping across his abdomen.

I gasp. "Oh, my gosh, I'm so sorry! I totally forgot. My legs are so weak that I can't even think."

Noah just laughs, flopping back into his pillow as I pat his stomach dry with tissues. "It's fine. I don't even care if I'm soaked in us all night. Just hurry back to me, please. I'm about to fall asleep, mid-sentence."

All I can do is giggle; he's not joking. I'm loving the absolute bliss and relaxation on his slackening face as his head droops to the side, especially since he's been so stressed lately.

As I rush to the bathroom to pee, my wolf spins in giddy circles, dying to top her mate again. Not only that—to show off her newfound musk that made him whimper and writhe against the sheets. She chases her tail, unable to contain her excitement. My human side flexes at the delicious memory of him coming hard inside me, my knees pressing together as I settle onto the toilet seat. My wolf only inflates in deeper pride of herself, clinging onto this new, enticing challenge we've created.

From the other room, Noah lets out sleepy chuckles.

Giggling, I open the bathroom door, calling down the hall as I reach for the toilet paper. "Sorry! I can't calm her down."

"Want to hold her. Now," Noah grumbles in the distance.

I sputter out a laugh at how precious and soft his demand sounded, nowhere convincing, whatsoever. After hurriedly washing my hands, I wring out a wet washcloth, dashing back to his side.

Warmth fills my heart when I find Noah spread out on the bed, his chest slowly rising and falling—as if his body was so heavy with pleasure that he couldn't move a millimeter from where I last left him.

Tip-toeing to his side of the bed, I soften my whisper. "Here I am. Let me clean you up, gorgeous."

As I run the warm washcloth over his bare torso, Noah sighs. That sweet, gentle sound fills my heart to the brim with the purest love for him.

My eyes sting hot; with Noah's guard fully down, I'm hit with how deeply held he feels—knowing I accepted his Omega side this intimately. How long has he been begging to show every side of himself, too afraid of how everyone would treat him?

I thought I'd panic about what this all means about us once the lust wore off, but all I'm left with is a deep need to cuddle up to my mate. Especially this hidden, raw side of him. I don't care if I never find out what it means. All I know is that I love him.

And we both needed this breakthrough—more than I ever realized.

Tossing the used washcloth on the nightstand's glass table top, I snuggle into bed with Noah, burrowing into his warmth. Not only his warmth, but a potent cloud of our lingering scents in our bedroom.

As I breathe us in, it really hits me: the depth of what we just did. There's a reason why I've never seen Noah like this before. Why I've never let myself top him this freely before.

Noah was terrified of this part of himself. I could feel it, even when he worked up the courage to tell me I helped him feel safe. Lately, he's been wound up, tense, and more hypervigilant than I've ever seen him—afraid to show a single second of vulnerability around anyone, thanks to these asshole Alphas.

But he braved it all tonight. I thought it'd take him months, maybe *years* to open up, but the freedom in his breezy, purring breath tells a different story.

What if this is only scratching the surface of Noah's inner depths? How incredible will it feel to only see *more* of this hidden, tender side of him? To chase our inner freedoms together in only the way we can, and to heal suppressed parts of ourselves in the process?

I knew I loved Noah to death, but at the sight of him showing this hidden piece of himself to me? I'm beyond smitten for life. I want to embed myself in his joy, again and again, as long as it takes for him to free every side of him. I want to show him he's still loved, no matter what, until he roams free, his wolf prancing through the fields in our inner world without fear of who sees him.

A part of me is still tempted to analyze this: what his Omega-like smell really means, and my Alpha-like musk.

But I don't think it changes anything between us, regardless of what I discover there. Whatever that side of him really is, it was *beautiful.* And my wolf wants to not only protect this side of him, but to cherish this part of her mate too, forever. As if he can feel it, Noah nuzzles in closer, breathing in my hair as I hold him tight.

❦ 7 ❦

In the morning, I can't stop smiling; Noah keeps stealing glances at me as we scurry around the cabin, gathering our remaining toiletries and chargers before our flight. Every time I catch him staring, his focus zips away, but he smiles wide.

We giggle as we pass each other, Noah leaving me with a soft pat on my ass.

"Wild wolf," he mutters. "What did I get myself into?"

I laugh, zipping up my suitcase. He's saying that now, but he has no idea what devious items I have in here. I double-check that my surprise won't be visible if Noah opens my bag for me when we land; he's been sweet enough to gather a change of clothes for me in the mornings when I feel too nauseated to move, and I definitely don't want to spoil this treat I'm packing for him.

Shoving a fuzzy, faux tail into the depths of my clothes, I call out down the hall from our bedroom. "Don't speak too soon."

"Oh, Goddess." Noah chuckles in the kitchen. But as his car keys jangle, I can hear his sharp inhale from here. "Oh, *Goddess.*"

My eyes widen; whatever he's reacting to, it doesn't sound good. Heaving myself to my feet with a grunt, I attempt to dash for Noah. Instead, I'm forced to stoop over the wooden dresser beside our bedroom door, struggling to retain my vision as a flurry of lights waves across it.

"What's wrong?" I try to call out, but my voice comes out a flimsy whisper. Closing my eyes as darkness creeps across my vision, I ease myself to the floor, propping my back safely against the wall as the *thump thump thump* of Noah's feet speeds down the hall to our bedroom.

Big hands shuffle my legs into a better position, my knees bent and feet planted on the floor as Noah holds my shoulders in place—just in case I fully pass out.

"How did you know?" I mumble.

"I know you well enough by now." Noah strokes my hair back, planting soft kisses on my forehead as my vision returns in patches. "Do you need a bag to throw up in?"

I groan, my stomach swirling. "Not this time. Did you pack enough of them, though?"

"Oh, yeah. We're all prepared, even if you puke twenty times on the plane."

Raising my head slowly, I laze my eyes open with a weary chuckle. Noah softly smiles back, sorting my long hair into place.

I sigh. "Sorry."

As Noah's smile fades, my heart hammers. I can't tell if my raging heartbeat is the after-effects of my blood pressure dropping from pregnancy, yet again, or if it's a trauma response, afraid of what a partner's serious, unhappy face might mean for my safety. Even though I trust Noah, a part of me still tightens in defense, especially while my conscious mind is hazy from feeling god-awful.

Softening his features, Noah lowers from his crouch beside me, joining me on the floor. He's facing me, scooting as close as he can until his bent knee bumps my thigh. With Noah's wide palms stroking my shoulders and arms, I swallow hard, staring deep into his serious, concerned gaze.

"Did I say something bad?" I whisper.

Noah blinks a few times, tilting his head in thought. "Actually, yeah. Towards yourself."

I straighten. "What? What did I say? Just 'sorry?' How's that bad when we're about to be late for—"

"How's that *not* bad when you're carrying this baby for both of us, and fighting like hell through every second of it?"

I laugh. "Not *every* second—"

Noah's jaw hardens, and I freeze. My heart thunders in my ears. But after the trust we shared in each other last night, I face Noah's upset head-on, my focus switching between his eyes.

Settling his hand over my belly, Noah lowers his voice. "I know

I need to work on this too when it comes to my wolf, but I don't like it when you talk about yourself like this, either. You're not a burden on me. I don't think you realize how much you do for me, and for the whole pack, even before you were pregnant. But now that you are pregnant, there's nothing that should require you to continually apologize for feeling sick, or to downplay your pain. It's not fair to you. I don't appreciate it."

With a rapid breath, I stare in awe of my mate's words. He's genuinely angry, but he's so gentle about it that I don't know what to do. How to process it, or what he wants me to say.

But Noah drops his stare, his thumb tracing the soft swell of my stomach. "It fucking kills me that you have to suffer through this in the first place, but I don't want you to feel like you also have to feel bad for it. You can't control when you throw up, pass out, have body aches—any of it—and I would never ask you to."

"Okay, well, we really are about to be late. I know what you're saying, but I also don't want us to miss our flight." My chest rises, defiance building in my chest.

"What if we did have to miss it from you not feeling well, though?" Noah stares straight into my eyes, challenging my rising Alpha side. As our scents build and clash, Noah's chest puffs, his wolf holding strong. "I'll tell you: I'd just get us another flight, as long as it meant you felt well enough to fly. I'd stay home, forgetting about the Summit, if you needed me to. I'd stop the whole fucking Lycan world for you, Aliya."

Dropping my stare, my face flushes hot. "That's a little extreme."

"Is it, sweet Omega? Or is it what my badass Luna deserves?"

I blink a few times, struggling to grasp his words. "I don't know, if I'm honest."

Lifting my chin, Noah catches my gaze once more. "Then I'll tell you: it is what you deserve, and more. Honestly, I feel like shit from how little I'm able to do for you compared to what you're going through. I know sometimes you feel okay, but that's also because you don't let anything stop you. And it's not just me that you support. This pack did not function nearly as well without your grounding presence, Aliya. Not just because of what you do, but who you are. Your value is far deeper than you give yourself credit for."

Biting my lip, I struggle to fight back tears. I hear what Noah is saying, so why is this hitting me so hard? Meeting Noah's eyes, I huff out my frustration, hugging my stomach. "Then what am I supposed to do now that I feel like shit, right before we leave?"

Lifting one eyebrow, Noah breaks into a smile. "You're going to stay sitting right here, even when I tell you there's a huge crowd outside our door, waiting for us to say goodbye."

My jaw drops. "What?! Noah, why didn't you tell me?"

Noah laughs, hoisting himself to his feet. His wolf's sly, teasing grin spills from him as he towers over me. "Because I meant it when I said I'd stop the whole world for you. And that I want you to take care of yourself, please."

Dropping my head back onto the wall behind me, I hide my face in my palms. "Bossy Alpha."

All I can do is laugh alongside Noah's chuckling as he strides down the hall, knowing what he's doing to me; while I'm annoyed, butterflies also erupt in my belly, spurred on by his cocky wolf.

I don't know what's gotten into him today. It's almost like his Alpha side's confidence has skyrocketed since I topped his Omega side last night.

And I can't deny that I'm flushing down to my chest, heat pooling in my groin at Noah's demands that I *matter*.

I'm left to wait in silence as Noah fills a cup with water and fetches a snack to help stabilize my heart. It finally sinks in; pregnancy is no joke, I know, but I'm no exception. I don't think it hit me how hard I've been struggling, not until Noah pointed it out.

If it were Amy or Rainn going through this, would I blame them for making us late after almost *passing out?*

Fuck no.

Now my cheeks burn from embarrassment, rather than the flustered state Noah left me in. As his footsteps return down the hall, I swipe tears from my eyes, not wanting to worry him more.

But why shouldn't I let myself worry him? How wonderful was it when Noah braved his raw emotions with me last night, allowing me to worry so I could better support him? Wouldn't Noah want the same from me?

Halting in the doorway with water in one hand and a plate of nausea-safe snacks in the other, Noah slumps. "Oh, my *love*. Was I too harsh?"

I shake my head, unable to look at his aching stare as my heartache floods our bond. Hitching through a soft cry, I swipe off more tears. "I didn't realize how cruel I was being to myself, at all. I don't want to accidentally teach our baby to treat themself like this. But I can't help it; I still think badly of myself, sometimes."

Letting out a pained sigh, Noah settles back down beside me, handing me my water. He strokes his mark on my neck, spreading soothing warmth through my belly as he extends a sweet, comforting scent. "That's why we're both learning. I don't want you to think I'm not proud of you. I just want you to give that wild, proud wolf I saw last night more credit. I love you. So, so much."

Leaning against Noah, I cram saltines in my mouth. "Even though I still feel bad for making everyone wait outside?"

Noah chuckles, nuzzling my cheek until I smile with him. "Is that a genuine question? If so, I probably shouldn't answer your OCD, huh? But you're braving this like a fucking rockstar. I can feel how goddamn uncomfortable you are."

Sputtering out a laugh, I shrug. "You basically just gave me new Exposure and Response Prevention homework to complete, so yeah. But you're right: I want to take care of myself better. Especially if that means I'll be taking better care of our baby."

Noah's focus drops to my hand around my stomach. His wavering smile spikes emotion through my heart. As he bends, my lungs swell; cupping my tiny baby belly in his massive hand, Noah kisses our pup as delicately as he can. "I can't thank you enough for doing this."

Goddess, his voice is shaking. Burying my hands into his hair, I stroke Noah's head as he hugs my waist, a conflicting mix of his awe, gratitude, and guilt stirring in our bond. I didn't realize how guilty he felt for putting me through this, but the second I recognize that angle of his words, my heart softens.

"I want to do this, gorgeous. And I'm so, so happy we're getting to do it together. Thank you for taking such good care of me. Of us, rather."

Smiling against my belly, Noah gives our baby another kiss, fluttering my heart.

After a few silent moments, my heart rate settles enough to allow me to rise to my feet—with Noah's help, just in case. Pulling me in for a tight hug, Noah gives me a slow but tender kiss, massaging my lips with heavy, comforting pressure. Gazing into each other's eyes, we smile.

"I hope you know I'll have your back at this crazy Alpha Summit too, even when I inevitably feel sick," I whisper.

Stroking my hair, Noah smiles. "Oh, trust me, I do, my feisty Luna. They better watch their fucking backs, judging by how you attacked me outside our den."

With a laugh, Noah and I pull ourselves together, collecting our bags and doing a once-over of the cabin for anything we may have forgotten to pack. Once we're ready to leave Greenfield, we open our cabin door to a crowd of smiling faces, pack members flooding the driveway with their adoring excitement.

Amy, Kira, and Lexi push through the crowd, giving us hugs goodbye. We said goodbye to Yasmine, Dave, Rainn, and Lilian yesterday; they're spread around Greenfield Forest, too busy taking their positions to hold down the pack in our stead for the next two and a half weeks. I'm surprised how deeply my chest aches to step into the car, taking one last look at everyone's smiling faces to wave goodbye.

As we take the first turn out of Greenfield Forest, winding down the country roads, I stiffen at the sharp ache in our bond. Noah bites his lip, his concern heavy enough to bring tears to his eyes.

"Oh, my love." Rubbing his knee, I breathe through the pain in my chest as Noah takes a few slow, steady breaths. "They're going to be okay. We'll be back soon."

"I know." His stuffy nose distorts his voice. "This is important. I need us all to be safe, and I don't know how else to do it except at this stupid fucking Summit."

My stomach recoils. He's right: with how severe the Alpha-domination outbreak seems to have taken over, the Alpha Summit is our best shot at preventing global chaos amongst all

Lycan packs. I don't want to say it aloud, but I know we're all thinking the same thing.

We don't simply need to go to the Alpha Summit. Noah needs to *win*.

～∽ 8 ∽～

To my relief, Noah and I relax into his SUV for the rest of our drive to Portland International Airport, settling into a cozy hum of laid-back conversation for the next hour and a half. I've kept my hand on his knee, rubbing it as we chat, and I'm delighted by how much it softens his shoulders.

I hope this is a good omen for our trip. We're leaving three days early, allowing us today for traveling, and two additional days to bond with four of our best allies. Our hosts Viktor and Annika, the King Alpha and Queen Luna lead their pack in Sweden, where they're giving us a room to stay in their lakeside Community Center. Tāne and Waimārie will arrive shortly after us, catching an even longer flight from Aotearoa—the land I've known as "New Zealand" until learning more about its indigenous roots from these new friends.

Judging by everyone's lighthearted natures the last time we talked, I'm relieved to know we'll start our trip on a pleasant note.

But as Noah and I grip the door handles to exit the car in the parking lot, Lilian's sharp, furious mindlink freezes us in place.

You two need to wear scarves on that plane before you inevitably mate. I've never seen more pregnant wolves in my lifetime! They're so ravenous in the Community Center kitchen that I'm going to have to make more food—all because of your wild Luna mating ritual.

Noah's eyes widen so far that I burst out laughing. He beams at my heavy laughter despite his darkening cheeks.

"I guess we better listen to our Elder Luna," Noah mutters, hopping out of the car.

Laughing, I follow Noah to the SUV's trunk. He tugs one

of my three scarves out of my backpack, draping it around my neck. But when my abdomen accidentally brushes against his belt, Noah freezes.

"What's wrong?" I ask.

He holds me back by the hips, rotating me left and right. "Holy shit, Aliya, you have such a clear little bump today."

My stomach flips. "It's— It's still just extra bloating, I think. Isn't it?"

"No, no, no—"

Noah spins me until my back presses against his chest. Whipping out his phone to take a photo of us, he grasps the back of my bulky hoodie until it's wrapped tight around my belly, exposing the smooth curve of my stomach. My heart catapults into my throat as Noah skates one hand down it, his eyes locked on mine as I gaze in awe at his phone's screen. "That's not bloating like last month, sweet Omega. You've stayed this big for over a week, and you've only gotten bigger. That's our baby."

Tears cloud my vision, but when I blink them away to meet Noah's dazed eyes above me, I release a wet, giddy laugh; he already looks like a terrified yet euphoric new dad.

Gripping Noah's hand on my belly, I turn over my shoulder, planting a hard kiss into his lips. Noah breathes me in, holding me even closer. Except he's not just holding me. He's holding the faint, new soul I keep feeling between us—occasionally poking their little head into our bond to say hello. My breath restarts as elation crashes between us, amplified by the heat of our lips.

When I pull back to gaze at Noah, his electrified eyes squeeze my heart. I trust him, not only with our pack, the world, and myself, but also with this baby we're carrying together.

Tapping his recent photos on his phone, Noah grins wider, adoration flooding our bond. I stretch on my toes, tilting his hand for a better view of his screen. I thought he put his phone away after showing me how pregnant I looked, but Noah took a sneaky photo of us afterward, and it steals my breath away.

He's right: my bump looks like it's here to stay. In the photo, Noah's big hand swoops under it to emphasize how it curves past my hip bones. My heart flips at the way he's cradling our baby while also snuggling me tight against his chest, gazing down at

he hoists all of our luggage along, his coat flung over one shoulder. As he glances at me over the puffy fabric, excitement builds low in my belly, stoking heat in my groin.

Noah smiles up to his wild, eager eyes, ducking his head with a sharp turn away from me. I have to laugh, quickening my steps to rejoin his side. But Noah guides me to a lone, empty row of chairs near the first set of escalators, motioning for me to sit.

The second I do, Noah towers over me, blocking the blaring lights above us with his wide shoulders. As I blink up at him, I realize he's barely suppressing a smile, biting his lips as he plops my stuffed backpack in the empty chair beside me with a squeak of the vinyl. As he digs through my bag, I can't stop myself, stealing one of his hands away. I purr, dragging my neck over his wrist to mark him with my pleased scent.

Noah breaks into giggles, wriggling his hand from my ravenous grip. I try to catch his wrist again, but a large hand comes down over the top of my head, pinning me in place.

"No," Noah says.

I try to sputter out a laugh, but a soft gasp follows it, my thighs squeezing together as Noah's stare lands on mine.

A grin stretches across his face. Noah checks over both shoulders before allowing me to see a quick flash of green in his teal irises. "Naughty girl. You better let me get this scent blocker out, or we'll both get ourselves into trouble."

Shit. Maybe I'm more of a mess than I realized. Heat strikes my groin harder, my core clenching from his words. Like clockwork, a yearning scent seeps from my scarf, flooding the space around us.

Noah stifles any outward reaction towards my exploding scent, but he can't hide his internal response from me; as Noah's desire builds in our bond, his chest inflates, heightening my breath. Keeping his hand stationed over my head, he finally digs out the small vial with his free hand, passing it to me.

I shakily screw off the lid. "God, I'm all over the place today. What the hell is going on?"

Stroking my hair back, Noah doesn't respond. He squats, cupping the back of my neck with one hand as he brings the other to my forehead.

Meeting my eyes, Noah lifts one eyebrow. *Do you feel like you're going into a pregnancy heat? Look at your wolf.*

This shocks the horny haze out of me. I blink a few times, gripping Noah's forearms. Like Noah said, my wolf has rolled over in our bond, begging to be mated.

I grip Noah's wrists. *Wait, do you think? I know pregnancy can really do a number on Omegas and cause all sorts of hormonal waves, but I've never understood this one: normally, all I want during my heats is for you to get me pregnant. But I'm already pregnant. Why would I ever need to go into a temporary heat?*

The point isn't only to get pregnant. It's to bond with a heat partner worthy enough to take proper care of you—and your pups. Which means I need to do my job of cooling you off, as soon as possible.

Tugging my scarf off, Noah reaches for the base of my hoodie. I squirm, my chest rising on instinct to present myself to him, but Noah's sharp, focused stare lands on mine.

"*Behave.*" Noah's growling grumble pins me in place, forcing me to take sharp, quiet breaths: a rabbit freezing beneath a wolf's stare.

But as Noah's smile spreads back over his cheeks, mine quickly matches his; he's both taming me and teasing more reactions out of me, just the way I like it—and we both know it.

I try as hard as I can not to continue wiggling in my seat, loving the thrill racing through my chest as I challenge his wolf back, staring him straight in the eyes.

"Make me," I whisper.

Noah chuckles, shaking his head. "Be careful what you wish for, little Alpha."

I frown. "You're lucky I'm little, and you know it."

This rouses a rumbling, infectious laugh out of Noah, stirring my heart in absolute delight. I beam up at him, lifting my jaw to flash his mark on my neck—teasing him with a silent invitation to bite me again.

Noah swallows hard. "Not fair."

Dabbing a bit of the scent blocker onto his wrist, Noah covers up the spot I just scent-marked on his arm. I scowl, and Noah chuckles, bringing it to his nose.

"Hmm. Pretty effective… Sadly."

My shoulders soften, my wolf perking back up now that she knows her mate hasn't rejected her doting scent mark.

Noah hovers his wrist in front of my face. "But what does my pregnant Luna's nose think? You're way better at this than me."

Inhaling softly, I'm surprised; I don't smell a single thing. But gripping his wrist, I sniff a little deeper. Then I frown. *It still smells like horny Omega scent at its core.*

Noah sniffs it harder this time, and my eyes catch on a passerby behind us. They're polite enough not to stare, but I bite my lips, staving off laughter as Noah pretends he's bringing that hand up merely to fix his hair. *It's a bit more natural that way. I think it mainly removes your delicious, sweet pregnancy scent, rather than erasing your scent, as a whole.*

As Noah grips the vial, I gather my hair off my neck, holding it up behind my head. Dotting a few drops onto his fingertips, Noah stoops over me, slipping the cool liquid over my burning neck. I suck in a sharp breath, my knees squeezing tight as he gives my scent gland a soft, circling massage, sending a tingling buzz down my torso until pleasure pools between my legs. My pussy flutters with every circle, and Noah's eyes locked on my reaction only heightens my nerves.

"Breathe through it," he whispers.

I let out a slow, shaky breath as his hand retracts, hovering over my neck's opposite side. But as he strokes over the second gland, his swooping, tender pressure drops my jaw. I lean into it, purring at the echoed sensation it stirs between my legs.

"Fuck." Noah slips both hands over both sides of my neck to block out another wave of my scent creeping through. "You might need more of this stuff, at this rate."

I blow out a shaky exhale. "It'll just make it worse if you keep rubbing me with it. It feels so nice."

Adjusting his pants, Noah groans. "Then let's quit while we're ahead, and try to calm ourselves while we walk. We at least have to get through security before I can—um—do something about this, worst case scenario."

The thought of flying sobers me to the bone. With a tightened jaw, I stand. "No, you're right. Let's get going."

Walking hand in hand with Noah, I steady my breath until

my temperature settles. Thankfully, we have plenty of time before our flight, pausing on every walking escalator as it rolls us closer to security. But without a near-heat to distract me, I'm buried in nausea and exhaustion once more, dragging at Noah's side like a wilted plant.

While Noah checks our bags in, I droop into another floppy vinyl chair. Portland's airport is far less crowded than any others I visited with my parents as a kid, but I haven't been around this many strangers lately—at least, not anyone I've viewed as a "stranger." Even if I've never met most of our pack members, they still feel like home. And home is far more comforting than the unfamiliar faces whizzing by, their clashing scents stinging my nose.

By the time Noah returns to my side with only our carry-on luggage, nausea thickens my throat. Noah's eyebrows cinch in concern, but he stands at my side without a word. Extending a soothing scent, Noah combs his fingers through my hair until my abdomen uncoils.

"There you go." Noah's deep voice cuts over the crowd, allowing me to inhale deeper. "I'm so sorry, my love. I didn't think about how much longer that walk would be for you while pregnant. I should've dropped you off at the front instead."

My heart flips; he saw right through me. "I didn't think of it either. It's okay."

"No, it's not. I'm going to get better at thinking your needs through. We both can, yeah?"

Flushing at Noah's earnest, concerned eyes, all I can do is nod.

Noah kisses my forehead. "Take your time. We still have a little under an hour."

I give Noah's hand a soft squeeze. "I'm actually alright to keep going. You're more effective than my ginger candies."

Chuckling, Noah drops his head. The sight of my shy Alpha lifts my cheeks into a smile, no matter how terrible I feel.

But we can't seem to catch a break today; despite arranging for both of us to skip most of the security line with a pre-check, poor Noah is far too bulky and intimidating for TSA to allow him to pass, selecting him for a "random" pat-down.

Dread crawls over my skin, leaving me shaky. As I collect

my bags, awaiting Noah at the security exit, I feel sicker by the second. I know Noah isn't meaning to allow me to feel his distress through our bond, but he can't seem to help it. I'm terrified of what it means: that my theory could be correct, and his trauma stems from sexual violence too.

I find a spot where I can keep an eye on him, but he's caged in by curtains. *Are you okay?*

Fine enough for the circumstances.

Oh, God. That means "no."

Noah meets my eyes briefly before turning to the TSA officer pointing at his waist. My jaw drops when they instruct him to remove his pants for a far more invasive, second round of pat-downs. It's humiliating for too many reasons to list, the base of the wall barely doing enough to cover him with how tall he is compared to everyone around him.

I clutch my stinging heart. *Oh, my love. I'm so sorry they're being so difficult. I'll be right here, waiting for you the second you're done.*

Noah doesn't respond. His stoic, collected form emanates relaxation on the outside, even when all I can see is his back, but the discomfort in our bond only heightens, forcing me to pick furiously at my thumbnail.

When Noah fetches his pants to leave, he shoots me a glance. I do my best to smile back, nodding in reassurance that I'm here for him, but my stomach grumbles in complaint, sympathetic nausea rolling through me. He's trying to appear brave, but the sinking disturbance in his heart weakens my knees.

Shaky thighs drop me onto the nearest bench. But I don't have long to rest before Noah retrieves his carry-on suitcase and backpack, striding back to me. I gather my luggage around myself, rising to my feet so I don't give him something else to worry about.

Reaching for him as he approaches me, I slide my hand into the nook of his elbow. "Are you okay? What did they say?"

"Nothing important. It's always something different—something wrong with my pants button this time, my left boot last time. I'm wearing the same ones too, actually."

I rub his arm, gazing at his eyes. But he doesn't seem to want to look at me, glancing around the nearby shops and restaurants.

"Anyway, I'm fine. Do you want anything before we go to our gate? Are you hungry?"

I know it's a deflection and he's not *that* okay, but I oblige his silent request to move on. "Actually, let's find some good, iron-rich meat for you to enjoy with me. It'll keep us both stronger for the long travel day ahead."

With a smile, Noah rests his hand on my lower back, soothing the tension there. "Sounds good to me. You've got the better nose for delicious food these days, so lead the way, sweet Luna."

Grabbing his hand behind my back, I loop it around my waist, burying it into my hoodie pouch and sewing us together in the process. The second our palms cup our baby—our little secret with how hidden our hands are inside the pouch's black fabric— our bond finally settles into equilibrium.

Noah's eyes soften into a genuine smile, and I adore every second of it. Even as his distress lingers while we select a restaurant, I'm content with letting go of what just happened for the sake of his trust. He'll tell me if there's something deeper here, when or if he needs to, but I never want to force him to disclose his trauma. TSA's pat-down reemphasizes how force is a major trigger for Noah, so I'm glad I've learned better by now.

Settling into a barstool as we wait for our food, I stroke Noah's hand. "Have you ever played the game 20 Questions?"

Noah tilts his head. "No, what is it?"

Ah, okay, I wondered if it was just a human game, so it must be. It's one we all played growing up. I smile wide as Noah's wolf perks up in our bond, rotating one curious ear. "Let's play it on the plane. It's simple: we'll just take turns asking anything we want to know about each other. That's pretty much it."

Noah's brows furrow. "Oh. So no one wins, you just ask questions? Twenty times?"

I laugh. "Actually, I don't think the number of questions really matters—it's more about holding a mindset of having plenty to ask. I realized I used to love playing this game with my crushes growing up, but you and I got to know each other so quickly that we skipped some of the silly, simple stuff at the start of dating."

Noah lifts one eyebrow, a genuine smile returning to his face. "Oh? Now I want to know what you want to ask."

I laugh. "Good. I'll let some suspense build, then I'll ask you something really pointless, like, what's your favorite color?"

Chuckling, Noah shakes his head. "You already know my favorite color."

"Dammit, you caught me. I was planning on sneak-attacking you with something juicy."

"You were, huh? I'm in trouble." Beaming, Noah traces my stare with ocean-teal irises, the storm behind them finally having settled. My heart lifts, dancing in my chest. I draw Noah closer for a quick peck on the lips. His warm hand only adds to the fuzzy bliss in my belly as he rubs my arm.

"Here you both are!" The restaurant's waiter drops our food bag on the bar counter in front of us. Noah jerks back, eyes alert like a startled puppy. I have to bite back a laugh, stroking his back to quiet his wolf. But the waiter doesn't seem to notice, their smile widening as they look between us. "Aren't you two just the cutest! Newlyweds?"

Noah's stare drops to the counter, his cheeks blazing, and I giggle. "Actually, yes. I'm the luckiest woman on the planet."

"No, m-me," Noah mutters. Then his eyes bulge. "W-wait, no—Man. I'm the luckiest man. S-sorry. Um—thanks. Excuse us."

As Noah stiffly pops up from his barstool, the waiter laughs. "Enjoy your meal!"

"You too—" I gasp. "Wait, I mean, thanks!"

Sputtering out laughter, I chase after Noah as he scurries from the restaurant. When I spot the back of his ears reddening, I laugh even harder.

Rejoining his side, I grasp his arm, peeking around his wide chest to find him covering his face with his palm wrapped around his forehead. Noah whimpers, barely stifling his laughter at my epic fail, despite still being beet red because of his initial slip-up. We both break into giggles, carrying our hot food to our gate.

Floor-to-ceiling glass provides a clear view of the tarmac on either side of us, framing each gate with a display of soft rain. When we finally reach our gate, Noah places his arm around my shoulders, his voice a low, humming rumble as he whispers into my ear.

"I really am the luckiest."

Grinning wide, I give his shoulder a quick nuzzle. "No, I am."

But the second our butts touch the rubbery vinyl chairs outside our gate, Dave's mindlink cuts through my thoughts.

Alpha and Luna, this is just a heads-up, and this is nowhere near Yas's fault—

Fuck, they broke through, didn't they? Noah jumps to his feet, his thigh bumping my carry-on suitcase and forcing us both to lurch for it before it topples over. *How bad is it?*

Noah's urgency both frightens and saddens me. After already having to work hard to make the best out of this trip, it seems determined to create chaos, only three hours in.

I grip Noah's tense forearm, hardly able to process this news. "Wait, what? They really did wait until after we left? But don't we have people lined up, in case—"

My breath halts. Noah's teal eyes have already half-shifted, a stark green staring back. "I'm so sorry, Luna. If it's bad enough for them to tell us, I don't know if we can make this flight." Flinging both our backpacks over his shoulder, Noah mindlinks, *Yas, it'll take me at least an hour and a half to sprint back through the forest, so—*

Don't underestimate me, you jerk, Yasmine's sharp mindlink widens our eyes. *Before you interrupted him, Dave was trying to tell you that I downed five of these Alpha-dom assholes myself, and the rest scampered home.* As Noah's shoulders droop, I let out a slow breath. *We wanted to tell you some better news too: they seem to be lowering in numbers, like you and I thought. I don't think they'll be trying so hard here after the hell we've given them lately. Go relax on your trip—and win the title you're owed.*

Noah rolls his eyes, slapping his forehead. After huffing out his stress for a good ten seconds, Noah drops his palm, facing me with a strained stare. But the second we make eye contact again, we both smile in pure relief.

"You okay?" I ask.

Plopping back into his seat, Noah sighs, gathering my hand in his. "Sorry, Luna. The last thing you need right now is me freaking the fuck out over nothing."

I giggle, leaning across the armrest to kiss his cheek. "You just care, my love. I'm glad it turned out to be nothing."

He shakes his head, closing his eyes. "Same."

Another plane races down the runway, engines roaring loud enough to shake the floor beneath our feet. I'm surprised how calm I feel about our upcoming journey today, dare I say excited. Part of it's from how powerful Noah's wolf seems today—refreshed and renewed as he struts around in our bond. He might've been stressed a moment ago, but his ever-present wolf has settled—and so has his human form, melting into his flimsy vinyl seat no matter how uncomfortable it is.

I sweep my gaze down Noah's slackened chest, picturing how hard he panted in desperation beneath me, a mere twelve hours ago. If this loosening effect is the result, maybe I should treat him in bed like that more often.

Noah's eyes zip to mine. I straighten, whipping my focus back to the massive glass windows in front of us. But Noah giggles, drawing my hand into his lap to spin my ring. *Don't entice my wolf, little Alpha. We have to get through this flight first, at least.*

I laugh, snuggling into his arm. *You said that about security, earlier.*

True. He sighs. "This has already been a long day. But I'm glad it's been with you."

A strand of hair slips past his brow. I ease it out of his eyes for him, my smile rising as I stare at the most loving person I've ever met. "I feel the absolute same, my love."

Handing me my food, Noah doesn't say another word. He doesn't need to: his emotions flood our bond with a giddy shyness, all while his wolf zooms around mine before playfully nipping at my neck. I giggle, stretching to kiss his cheek, but he steals the kiss from me, pressing hard into my lips. I blink back at him with a pleased hum before we close our eyes, smiling through our kiss.

With Noah's palm settling over my thigh, we dig into our meals, preparing for the long journey ahead.

❦ 9 ❦

With our stomachs refilled, we shuffle onto the plane, today's tiredness already taking hold of my dragging limbs. Our plane is wider than any flight I've been on—as I expected with a longer, international trip. But instead of the roomy seats I've usually walked past in first class, this plane has expansive rows of reclined chairs. They look much more like individual, spacious beds.

When Noah stops us here, plopping our backpacks into the wide cubbies beneath the seats, my jaw drops. "Wait, really? This is us?"

Noah grins over his shoulder with a soft giggle. "Mhm."

I double-check that the numbers above our heads match our boarding passes, my eyes widening by the second. Two aisles stretch down the plane, giving enough room for multiple passengers in each row of economy seating. In this luxury section, however, there's so much space dedicated to each of us that only three passengers fit in each row. Tall screen dividers line the aisles, allowing for total privacy.

But the seats Greenfield Pack purchased for us are special: our row has two seats smushed together in the middle, clearly designed for a pair of travelers who intend to fly together without the big dividers between us. As I lean closer, relief wells in my chest; there's an armrest between us in case we need it, but the squishy seats stretch all the way across our section without dividing, creating a proper bed with our own personal screen.

I bounce on my heels. "Noah, this is *unreal!*"

Helping me into my seat, Noah laughs. "That's right, you've never been on a flight like this, huh?"

"Are you kidding? No way. We're absolutely being spoiled."

"Yeah. Greenfield likes to spoil the hell out of me with overseas flight tickets every year for the Summit, no matter how much I argue with them that I don't need it." Noah rolls his eyes. "But now that you're here, I'm glad they did. My mom said they wanted you to be comfortable, in particular, so I didn't have any complaints this time. It was nice of them to find us a pair of joined seats too. Normally, I'm sectioned off by myself."

My heart clenches. "Noah, that's so sweet of them. I can't tell you how grateful I am to be able to fully lay down and relax. This will be way easier on my body."

To my delight, Noah's entire torso loosens. "Good. I'm happy to see you happy."

I beam at him, taking his hand in mine. "You're sweet. Even if we didn't have these seats, I've already been thinking about how grateful I am that I'm getting to go on this trip with you."

Noah's cheeks flush hot, and I giggle. He's gushing with affection as he lifts the armrest between us, pulling me to his edge of my wide seat. With full access to me, my mate promptly nuzzles into my cheek with more soft kisses than I can count, but I don't feel smothered. Gentle caresses over my arms, abdomen, and sides lull me into a meditative state.

Breathing in Noah's scent, I allow myself to doze against him as the rest of the passengers board. But by the time the plane roars to life and the safety instructions begin, I'm left with no choice but to inhale jet fumes. My nausea returns full-force, aggravated by my anxiety around flying.

As the muffled safety protocol drones over the plane's speakers, I try to lay perfectly still, not wanting to aggravate my stomach further.

Noah rubs my hand with a gentle whisper. "Are you feeling sick?"

"Yes, but it's fine. It's the jet fuel smell that's—" I swallow thickly, and Noah winces.

"Can I see your scarf?"

Using the last drop of my limited energy to shakily bend over, I fetch my scarf from my backpack in my personal cubby. When

I hand the plaid red fleece to Noah, he eyes the passengers across the aisle, ensuring our tall dividers cover us.

Clutching my scarf, Noah releases a saccharine, soothing scent, sending tingles down my spine. I'm already feeling better just from inhaling his loving pheromones, but when he scrubs my scarf against his scent glands, I curl my toes in anticipation.

As I hoped, Noah wraps the scarf around my neck, swooping the fabric over my nose—immersing me in lungfuls of his comfort. I can't help but purr, burrowing in deeper.

"How's that?" Noah asks, but he's already grinning wide; my eyelids droop in absolute bliss, my stomach swirling with delight despite still recovering.

But as the plane jerks back, driving onto the runway, every sensation in me is replaced by fear.

I grip Noah's hand hard enough to turn my fingers white. A furious, commanding urgency in my gut tells me to lean past the dividers at our sides and check out the window, ensuring we're safe. Then check it again.

That's OCD talking. I know it. That doesn't stop OCD from holding an absolute chokehold over my brain, shuffling me in my seat in discomfort. Noah's protective scent rushes past the fabric covering my nose, but it's not enough to settle my racing, shallow breath.

"What's going on, Luna?"

I groan. "Dammit, I thought I worked on this enough with Jenny."

"Are you scared?"

"Yes. But I don't want to miss out on your first game of 20 Questions."

Noah's eyes widen as I visibly quiver. If I wasn't so freaked out, I'd laugh, rubbing his arm to reassure him that I'm not dying, but I'm not so convinced myself.

"O-okay, uh— You're sure it's not an avoidance compulsion to play that game instead of facing your fears, head-on?"

"Good point..." I frown, thinking through the details. "I normally wouldn't be sure, except my brain is demanding that I consistently check outside the window to make sure we're okay, which usually means it's time to live my life as I would without the obsession nagging at me."

"Got it. Then how about I ask the first question to get us going?"

"Okay." I clutch his hand.

Noah grips my hand back, allowing me to squeeze harder. It's cathartic enough for me to take a deeper breath.

But Noah focuses hard—conjuring his first question with a deep stare into the blank screen in front of us. When his eyebrows raise, I lean in, curious what's stirring a sudden shyness in our bond.

Lowering his voice, Noah turns to me with serious, furrowed brows over his puppy-dog stare. "Who was your first crush?"

Tension washes from my limbs as I erupt into giggles. "Are you trying to make yourself jealous?"

Noah grins, softening his expression. "No. Everyone who made the mistake of leaving you should be insanely jealous of *me*."

I bite back a smile. "Well, actually… My first crush was Amy."

Noah's eyebrows lift—a much milder reaction than I anticipated. But within seconds, his true surprise explodes in our bond.

"It's not what it sounds like. It's more like—" I laugh. "I was six, and I thought she was the most powerful girl I'd ever seen. I wanted to be just like her. Then, when everyone thought I was a weirdo, she was so kind to me, which is my weakness."

Noah breaks into a massive smile. "It is, huh?"

"Yes." I laugh, gazing straight into my mate's adoring eyes. "But I quickly realized I loved her as a forever-friend, and it was more of a deep admiration thing."

Noah softens into a gentle smile, his thumb tracing my palm. "Cute. So fucking cute."

Clearing my throat, I fidget with Noah's thumb. "Well, until college when we kissed for fun and I realized I was attracted to girls too. But then she met Kira about a week later, so nothing else happened, of course."

Noah tilts his head. "Was that hurtful?"

I'm so relieved that he's not upset that a fizzy excitement spreads throughout my chest. I break into a smile. "Not too hurtful, thankfully. I felt more connected to her as a best friend, so it was actually a bit of a relief to not have any dating expectations."

Noah hums in understanding, dropping his stare to our hands.

I nudge him with my shoulder. "Your turn. I want to know the answer to the same question: your first crush."

"My turn? Uh, shit—" Noah flushes bright red. "I didn't think it'd be turned around at me."

I laugh. "It doesn't have to be. Actually, I should've deflected your second question with a question of my own, but bending the rules for this game is more fun. And I'm really curious. We haven't talked about our exes much—well, beyond Steven."

As Noah's expression morphs into a disgusted glare at the thought of my ex, I can barely contain a laugh, even as the plane lifts its nose. Noah captures my full attention with a tighter squeeze of my hand, keeping our eyes locked as we lurch into the air.

"My first crush—" Noah clears his throat. "Was a-another boy too. But not as a friend."

My heart hammers, but I break into a smile. I don't know if Noah identifies as "bisexual," or if he considers himself pansexual, omnisexual, or something else on the bisexual spectrum, but I've always been curious to know how fluid his sexuality has been for him. How long did it take for him to accept this piece of himself, living in a different social structure than mine? Lycans seem decades ahead in supporting queerness, but that doesn't mean it's been easy.

I can't stop my curiosity from pouring out. "A Lycan boy? Did you tell him you liked him? Wait, sorry. That's two more questions."

Noah frowns. "Our version should allow more questions, I think. Like, 20 Subjects instead. Or 20 Questions Per Subject, knowing us."

Grinning, I snuggle in closer. "I love that. Then, did you tell him?"

Noah softly smiles, but he fidgets with his seatbelt, his wolf just as antsy in our bond. "N-no, I didn't tell him."

"What was he like?"

"H-he was, um—" His eyes dart away from mine. "He was all Alpha."

My heart flips. At first, I thought Noah was shy about telling me about liking a *boy* for the first time. But now that I'm face to face with my sweet mate, I think he's shier about liking another *Alpha* than anything else.

"How did you realize you liked him?" I ask.

"I-I— Well, it's embarrassing." He runs his fingers through his wild hair, messying the dark strands further. "I couldn't stop watching him chase this rabbit around. I thought it was the coolest thing."

My mouth opens, but my breath catches. "Wait— Watching him? Like, from the bushes?"

"Yep… Like an absolute weirdo." Noah rubs his forehead, wavering between laughing and sighing through the mortification in our bond. "But he could never catch the fucking rabbit."

I bite my lips to keep from laughing, but it's not doing much to help. I'm forced to hold my breath, trying to think of anything else. With one look at me squirming in my seat, Noah breaks into hearty giggles. I can't help but laugh with him, gripping his wrist as I lean in.

"So then what?"

"I wanted to catch it for him one day, but some other Alpha beat me to it, and my crush was so angry." Noah's eyes widen. "B-but then they started kissing? But with too much tongue?" I burst out laughing with Noah, and his grin widens. "Which is when I realized I wasn't ready for this courting thing yet and ran away."

Noah and I dissolve into giggles, leaning into each other for support.

"Oh, my God. I wish I could've met little Noah! How old were you?"

"Only a-about eight."

"Ugh, you cutie. I'm going to explode with affection when I see your little one."

Noah's smile gushes at the thought of our pup. He huddles closer to kiss my mark. "Me too, sweet Luna."

Shivers race down my spine as Noah's fingers trace my small bump, filling my belly with warmth beneath his gentle touch. I stroke our future pup with him, our bond igniting in the brightest, adoring hum.

I still have no idea if it works, but I've been mindlinking our pup anyway. *I can't wait to see your dad holding you.*

"My turn," Noah says.

I blink, almost forgetting what we're doing. But Noah's hyper grin alerts my wolf's ears, perking them up to the sky in our bond.

Rubbing slow, wide circles over my stomach, Noah flutters my heart into my throat. "Speaking of this one, how does it feel to carry them this week? I know you're beyond tired and have a lot of uncomfortable physical symptoms, but other than the round ligament pain, does it feel like a lot of pressure in here?"

My heart flips; he's been so curious about my feelings and sensations during pregnancy. It makes me feel seen.

I smile, stroking my belly with him. "Actually, yeah. The bigger they're getting, the more pressure I feel on my bladder, especially." We laugh, knowing how obvious that is by how many times I keep interrupting our lives to pee. "And you know how it's making all my organs travel?"

Noah winces, but he's still smiling. "Oh, yes. I will never forget that vivid imagery."

I laugh. "Well, I still feel that strange sensation sometimes, and that's probably the most off-putting type of pressure, just because of the thought of it. Otherwise, I actually kind of like the thought that they're still growing bigger in here, and that's why I'm having to stretch and adjust so much."

"Goddess, that's—" Noah's eyes brighten, widening my smile. "You're precious. It's not too unbearable, though?"

"I definitely notice it, but it's not too bad this week. I'm imagining the pressure part will feel way more intense later on, but I don't know how much either. I'll have to tell you what it's like."

Wild, excited eyes flit between my stare. Instead of asking another question, I grin, waiting.

Sure enough, Noah blurts out his thoughts. "Would you like to give our baby a nickname, for now? One we can use between us, at least until we think of more names?"

Joy floods my heart. I sit straighter than I have all day, clinging to Noah's hoodie. "Really?"

He chuckles, slowing his hand until he cups my belly. "Is that a yes? It's okay if it feels like too much. I just feel like constantly calling them 'the baby' is too vague for how attached I already feel."

Dropping my forehead against his shoulder, I groan. "That's so cute, it hurts. It makes me want to bite you."

Noah laughs, softly gripping my open jaw. "You're probably serious about that, mother wolf, so I'm going to put you back in your own seat before I get mauled."

Breaking into giggles, I allow him to lift my head off him. Meeting my eyes, Noah's irises seem to sparkle, even beneath the dim cabin lights. I'm delighted by every inch of his existence. How in the world will I be able to handle how much I'll love his child?

Softening my voice, I beam back at him. "I've been calling them 'little one,' sometimes. But I think with how sweet and adorable you are, we'll have to call them something even cuter."

Noah's eyebrows raise. "Wait, you mean you've been calling them that in your head?"

My cheeks flush hot. "Um, yes… And I know it's a little silly, but I've been trying to send them my thoughts too."

Through mindlink? Noah's eyes widen, and my heart thumps faster.

When I nod, Noah groans. Planting a soft kiss on my lips, Noah smiles against my mouth before pulling back to stare me in the eyes.

"What the hell? That's *way* too cute. You really must be trying to kill me this week."

I laugh, shaking Noah's arm. "Stop saying that! I love you to death."

Raising one eyebrow, Noah breaks into a sly grin. "You're not helping your case."

He startles another laugh out of me, but a flight attendant eyes us from down the row, so we duck closer, giggling beneath our breaths like teenagers in the back of class.

"Do you really think they can hear me, though?" I whisper. "I know your mom and sister think so from the feelings they got while pregnant, but what do you think?"

Noah hums, sweeping his wide palm over my belly once more. I'm melting into a gooey mess with every stroke, huddling closer to him as he beams down at me. "We'll have to look through the books we packed, but I believe it, especially since you're carrying a blood bond with them. We just don't know for certain how soon they can hear it, which I've been really curious about too. Pups don't know how to respond to us through mindlink until they learn how to talk, and they can't remember anything from the womb once they're older, of course, so maybe we'll have to see what we think. See if it feels like they're replying to us in their own way."

My heart flutters. *So, in the meantime, your sweet baby might be able to at least feel this love you and I are sharing in our bond, don't you think? And I might be able to feel them reacting in some way?*

Blinking rapidly, Noah presses his forehead to mine. Our bond swells with elation, speeding my breath into short bursts. *I'm pretty sure, yes. Just like they can feel your other emotions, or you can feel mine. Theirs might just be more vague to us for a while.*

I can hardly contain my excitement. It's reflected in Noah's rising smile as he spills into giggles with me.

Using one finger to trace gentle circles over my swelling uterus, Noah whispers as softly as he can. "This little wolf in here is going to be so lucky."

My heart muscles squeeze tight. "That's how I feel whenever I think of you holding them as sweetly as you hold me."

As Noah's chest rises, my stomach flips at the loving intensity in our bond. Grasping Noah's hand, I hold our baby with him, my heart throbbing with joy.

But my eyes widen. "That sounded so cute just now, actually—what you just said. What if we call them that, for now? Little Wolf."

Noah blinks. Then he breaks into the biggest smile, his eyes crinkling as he brushes my nose with his. "Little Wolf. That's way too sweet. I love it."

We're a mess of giggles, whispers, and soft touches. If we weren't so tucked away, I'd feel terrible for expressing this much mushy PDA, but I can't help myself; each touch seems to erase every last ounce of stress we've both carried for weeks.

But after sharing a few more laughs with Noah, my shoulders slump. "Dammit, I wanted to revisit our plans for the Summit, but I can't think."

Noah strokes my cheek, softening his voice. "Let's save that for later—on our shorter flight from London. You don't look like you feel very well."

My jaw tightens through a wave of nausea the second I focus on it. "You're not wrong."

"Take a nap, gorgeous. You need it."

"You'll be okay?"

"Yes, my love. I've got all three of us covered—Little Wolf, included."

I freeze, not expecting the sharp spike of emotion Noah created with our pup's nickname. Noah's wild eyes meet mine, his cheeks blazing, and I laugh.

"You're waking me back up with excitement."

Noah's deep, purring chuckle widens my smile. "Oh, yeah? I think I can fix that."

He's right; I hum in delight, unable to keep my eyes open against Noah's warm hand as he strokes my belly with bigger, slower caresses. He soothes me from every angle, running soft touches down my face until my head droops, ready to doze off against his shoulder.

There you go, precious wolf. I love seeing you at peace, Noah mindlinks.

As I lose my conscious thoughts to sleep, I can feel Noah's telling me the truth; with his full focus locked on me, I'm amazed by how happy his heart feels. I hadn't realized it until now, but prioritizing my needs during this pregnancy supports Noah's wellbeing too.

The tranquility flowing between us sinks me deeper into my chair. Curling up on my side with one hand on Noah's chest, I cherish every heartbeat beneath my palm, counting them until I lose track.

But the next time I open my eyes, I'm shaken awake by

turbulence. My throat scrapes dry, my heart races, and my whole body pulses with an achy vengeance.

It's too much stimulation at once. My mind struggles to find its bearings, leaving me wide-eyed and breathless.

Noah perks up, alert eyes tracking my every breath. "Are you having a panic attack?"

After gulping down a few mouthfuls of water, I close my eyes. "Maybe, actually. I'll try to ground myself."

"Okay, I'm right here."

I do my best to meditate despite my racing heart, feeling the weight of Noah's palm on my thigh. I want to relax, but I grimace, unable to shake off the aches consuming me. Doubling over, I let out a slow, quivering exhale.

"Oh, Luna… What do you feel like?" Noah whispers.

I sigh. "Sorry, I think I just have really bad body aches from being in one position for too long. Everything hurts."

Worry creases Noah's brows. "Stand up for me and turn around, gorgeous. I'll give you a massage."

"Goddess, you're sweet—" I struggle to swallow. Glancing around us, I rise on shaky legs. "Actually, are we allowed to get up right now? The seatbelt sign is on. I'm also a little worried I'll throw up unexpectedly and won't be able to turn around to get a bag in time."

"I've got you." Fetching a bag for me with one hand, Noah keeps another sturdy palm on my lower back.

His touch soothes me, tethering us together like a lifeline. When he hands me the bag, I huff out a touched breath, my eyes stinging; not only did he stuff the bags with paper towels, keeping anything from splashing back and dirtying my clothes, but he knows I get embarrassed by the see-through bags, concealing it for me inside another waterproof, machine-washable bag.

Noah doesn't seem to understand my sudden, gushing affection for him, stroking the back of my head as he swipes away my tears. "Don't worry about the seatbelt sign. We'll just let them have to instruct us to sit down. But if you want me to block anyone from seeing you while you get sick, I can."

"It's okay, I—" Clenching my teeth, I decide it's safer to keep my mouth shut for now, trembling through too many aches to keep track of.

"Keep breathing," Noah whispers. His palms sweep down my arms, back, and hips, warming my sore joints. I shut my eyes, leaning into his touch with a soft groan when he reaches the dimples behind my hips. "There you go. You're doing so well."

My heart flutters at his words. Thankfully, I don't feel like I'm at the level of nausea where I have to fully throw up, but I'm still producing so much excess saliva in preparation that I'm forced to continually spit into the bag. It's gross.

But Noah's breath skates over the back of my neck, sending tingles down my spine. As he continues to rub, knead, and caress me, my muscles loosen, lessening my nausea.

"That's helping so much. Thank you, love," I whisper.

Noah sighs. "Fuck, I'm just so sorry you had to fly this far while pregnant. It seems absolutely *miserable*."

"It's okay—" I pause, clearing my throat; my trembling voice is nowhere near convincing. Taking a deep breath, I steady myself. "Like I said, I want to be here with you. And I'd do anything for this baby."

"I know, me too. So keep leaning on me and allowing me to carry this struggle with you, okay? You're doing great."

I nod, but I can't bear to waste my energy on speaking a single word more. I'm forced to breathe deeply with my eyes closed, gripping my sickness bag tight.

"Are you both okay? Do you need anything?" A new voice chimes in.

Dammit, that must be a flight attendant. I pry one eye open, but Noah's hands slow into gentle sweeps on my back, a silent reassurance he'll take care of things. As he applies climbing pressure up my spine, I drop my chin to my chest, allowing my neck muscles to loosen between gentle, swirling presses of Noah's thumbs.

He keeps his voice soft. "She's just feeling a little stiff and motion sick. We'll try to sit back down in a minute."

"Would you like some ginger candies or sparkling water?"

"Sure. Thank you."

As the flight attendant's heels *clack* away from us down the aisle, I expand my rib cage further with each breath, allowing Noah's pressure to deepen beneath my shoulder blades.

But a different voice in front of me snaps my eyes open.

"I'm so sorry to accidentally eavesdrop, but I have something else that could help, if you'd like."

A fifty-something woman pokes her head around the privacy divider across the aisle. She's wearing a tailored gray business suit, her silky black hair wrapped in a perfect bun.

My heart drops. For a second, she looks just like my mom— her kind, dark eyes radiating with care.

When I regain my bearings, my eyebrows pinch in worry. "Oh, gosh. I'm so sorry to disturb your luxury flight like this."

Her eyes widen. "Oh, no, not at all! You've both been incredibly quiet, actually. I just noticed your discomfort as I was trading another book to read from my bag, and even before your sweet husband commented about your pregnancy, I knew I could relate to your struggles."

Shit, sorry. Maybe I was louder than I thought, Noah mindlinks.

Don't be sorry for how incredible you've been, Noah. I think it's more like you said in the parking garage; I'm starting to look pregnant now too. Maybe it was too wishful of us to think we could hide it at the Summit.

Noah's uncertainty rises with mine in our bond, but his hand wrapping around my belly reminds me he's here, figuring out this trip alongside me.

This stranger scoots to the edge of her chair, facing me in the aisle. Placing two gray, wide elastic bands into her palm, she extends her hand. "Ever since my first pregnancy, I've had terrible motion sickness. I have an extra pair of sea bands, if you'd like them."

A sharp spike of surprise hits my chest. My emotions waver, uncertain how to react to such thoughtfulness. I'm tempted to apologize or dissuade my way out of this, preventing myself from being a burden on this kind stranger. But Noah's hand still cupped around Little Wolf reminds me why I agreed with him this morning; I don't want our baby to learn this false belief that they can't accept help.

And if they were in my position, feeling sick on a plane, I'd want our future pup to use a stranger's sea bands. *Especially* if they happen to be missing their mom.

So I take the bands with a smile, even as my ribs tighten in discomfort. "Oh, my gosh, how kind. Thank you!" I lift one band to analyze it. A small, round bead is sewn into the elastic. "I've seen these before, but I've never used them."

Noah's fingers loosen around my sides as he peeks over my shoulder. "What do they do?"

"They're for an acupressure point on your wrist. Here, let me show you how to use them." The woman holds out her hand with a smile.

The world must be testing me today. I give her a shaky smile, cautiously extending my wrist. After adjusting the band into the correct position with thin, nimble fingers, she rubs its small, sewn ball attachment into my wrist. Noah copies her on my other hand, and I relax my back against Noah's chest at their gentle massaging.

After a minute of silence, my nausea reduces enough to stop swallowing as hard. "Wow. That actually helped a lot. Thank you so much, seriously."

The woman breaks into a bright smile. "Of course! Keep them."

"What? Are you sure—"

She laughs. "Really, I mean it. From one mom to another."

Blinking a few times, I'm hit with a wave of excitement. God, I'm a mom.

The flight attendant returns with more than just ginger candies and sparkling water: she also offers me her pregnancy sickness suggestions once she hears us talking about it. As Noah's eyes light up beside me, enthusiasm lacing every shy, quiet question he asks about how to better care for me during pregnancy, my heart pounds, touched to my core that so many people offered to help. The world might be testing me, but the universe decided Noah was right this morning, and it gave me plenty of practice accepting support—and feeling like a burden.

With how much these strangers seem to delight in sharing their advice, another aspect of my thinking is tempted to change; after months of watching our backs, wherever we go, maybe there are safe strangers in the world too.

I can't stop smiling. "How are you all so nice? Can I send you both a card, or something?"

We all laugh, but surprisingly, both women share their emails and PO Boxes with me. As we each settle back into our seats, I scribble down my thoughts on the comfort they've provided me, vowing to write to them on a postcard from Sweden.

Noah chuckles beside me, kissing my temple. "Goddess, you're so damn cute. I know you have your concerns, but personally, I'm not worried about you getting along with other Lunas."

I sputter out a laugh, loving the tenderness I find in his eyes. "I need to write you a card too, after all this. You're my hero, Noah."

Noah drops his chin to his chest, easing back into his seat with a smile. I giggle, snuggling in at his side.

Maybe today is a good omen, after all; despite how rough we've had it, we've continually ended up smiling together, surrounded by kind strangers.

❧ 10 ❧

Fourteen hours later, after two layovers and scattered sleep, we touch down in Kiruna, Sweden. While waiting for our luggage to be loaded off the plane, a luxurious vanilla scent entices my nose. I close my eyes, taking a deep breath. Before I can stop myself, I groan in bliss.

Noah chuckles. "What do you smell, Luna?"

"Something delicious."

"Yeah? Follow your nose, and go treat yourself. I'll wait here for our luggage."

My heart clenches in delight. "Thank you, my love."

I don't wait for his reply, chasing the vanilla scent to the airport's nearest cafe, and Noah laughs in the distance.

But when I spot the delicious scent's source, my heart sinks; it all looks so good. Cinnamon rolls do, in fact, line the bakery, but so do decadent Swedish pastries I've never tried before—glaze, sugar crystals, and vibrant berries glittering beneath the cafe lights. How do I choose just one?

Fuck, I'm about to cry. I clear my throat, half-weeping, half-laughing at myself. But as my stomach rolls, threatening to sour my appetite, it's no longer funny anymore. Suddenly, I'd kill to eat one of these cinnamon rolls. And if I embarrass myself by crying in this cafe over food, I'm going to be pissed.

I try my best to remain centered and rational, but my wolf begs me to scramble over the counter to snag a pastry.

Okay, enough. I'm paying for one and leaving before my pregnant wolf loses the last of her self-control.

As the cashier hands me my prize, thanking me in Swedish,

I have to swallow a few times so I don't drool. I cup a chunky cinnamon roll in both palms, the protective paper barely containing its dripping, hot glaze. I shove a bite into my mouth, my tongue smothered in sugar and cinnamon.

"Ugh, *yes*—" I breathe.

But as the cashier's eyes widen, my heart spikes into my throat.

Oops. I moaned out loud, and I'm still at the register. I flush, wiping a drop of glaze off the corner of my mouth. Checking behind myself, I'm relieved to see no one in line behind me. "Sorry, I— I think I'd actually like to order one of each, please."

On my way back to baggage claim, I devour the cinnamon roll first in three more bites—even after eating my two meals and half of Noah's on the plane. I check my reflection in my phone screen, making sure I don't still have sugar on my lips.

But when Noah finds me with my massive haul and one of my pastries already missing, the wrapper crumpled in my fist, he grows serious. "Oh, fuck, wait—maybe we still aren't feeding you enough of something else, now that they're growing so quickly. That could make you extra nauseous, right?"

My tight shoulders soften. For a split second, I thought he was about to scold me—another reminder of Steven's old scars on my brain.

I sigh. "Yeah, but too much food at once could make me nauseous too." My stomach sinks. "Maybe I'm doing something wrong by eating too big of portions in a short time."

"No, my love, please don't think that way. You need to eat as much as your body asks. Pregnant wolves need even more food than pregnant humans to grow such a complex baby. That, I know for sure." He clears his throat, no longer meeting my eyes. "E-especially because they're usually big. Which I'm still sorry about. Maybe we should've decided to call them Big Wolf."

I break into giggles—until Noah rubs my belly in tender circles, and my heart nearly explodes. But my wolf leans in for more, gripping his hand.

"That's so soothing, Alpha. Please keep going," I whisper.

"Okay, sweet Omega. I've got you. You're safe."

I indulge in every second of his hands on me—until a stranger glares at us for loving on each other in public.

Oh, my God, Noah, I forgot what it's like to be in human spaces. This is weird of us.

We separate quickly, sorting out our clothes to busy ourselves.

But when I look back at Noah, his rosy, flustered cheeks make me smile. "Cute Alpha."

"You mean King Alpha," a voice speaks behind our backs.

I stiffen at the sound, sending Noah back into stoic Alpha mode.

But Noah's shoulders loosen when he meets the stranger's eyes. He breaks into a genuine grin, his incisors on display. "Shit, Vik, you didn't have to meet us all the way out here."

Flipping around, I'm eye-level with a massive man's chest, his full height towering at least a foot and a half above mine. This isn't just any man: standing beside me is Viktor Abrammson, Scandinavia's top Alpha, and the current King Alpha of the entire *world*.

And holy shit, he's even more striking in person. Viktor's bright smile threatens to break hearts, the deep brownish black of his irises complemented by his slender suit jacket and the tight, midnight black curls atop his short fade. Just the sight of him looks expensive, and his chuckle comes out like premium velvet. "Oh, but I did. I had to be the first to meet the Greenfield Luna in person, of course."

Noah rolls his eyes, but I know it's lighthearted; his sweet smile makes me laugh.

Which draws Alpha Viktor's attention straight to me.

The second Viktor's eyes land on me, I can hardly breathe. He radiates power, and I haven't even caught a whiff of his scent yet. My wolf tucks her tail, petrified of this unfamiliar Alpha.

But Noah's hand on my back sets my racing heart at ease. I'm grateful for it—as Viktor opens his arms for a hug, my heart only pounds faster. "Luna Aliya, it's a pleasure to meet you in person."

"Oh, it's a pleasure for me to be invited, and to finally meet you both!" I'm enveloped in Viktor's potent musk as he gives me a tight squeeze. I blink rapidly, fighting through its sting. "Where's Luna Annika?"

Viktor chuckles. He releases me, only to lean an elbow on Noah's shoulder. "Anni's coming. Probably waiting for Alpha

Noah and me to be a nuisance before having to deal with us. Your mate drives me insane."

Noah sputters out a laugh, giving Viktor's shoulder a playful shove. "*I* drive *you* insane? Fuck off."

Viktor's rich laugh attracts eyes across the baggage claim. "Excuse me?! *You* fuck off." Vik leans into Noah, a sly grin overtaking his smile. "…King."

"Don't start with that." Noah isn't smiling anymore. "I'm not the King."

"This year." Viktor grins wider. "At least not officially. Asshole."

I blink a few times, struggling to follow. What is Viktor talking about? I thought he was this year's King Alpha?

Noah breaks into a dark grin, coating my skin in goosebumps. "You still haven't gotten over it… King?"

Viktor shoves Noah, who grins even wider.

Before shoving back.

"Um— We're in a human airport!" I whisper-hiss.

Maybe I don't have much Alpha in me, after all. Their playful shoving is so aggressive yet full of laughter that I gape in pure culture shock, shrinking by the second.

Until I spot the most gorgeous woman I've ever witnessed in my life—and she's headed straight for us.

Annika Abrammson, the Queen Luna. With bountiful curls tinted a light strawberry, Annika floats to us like an angel, her white dress flowing around her petite frame with the speed of her wide strides. I have no idea how she's not freezing; her pale, bare ankles shine beneath the airport lights, her puffy, champagne-pink coat left open to flap at her sides in Sweden's biting wind. Meanwhile, I'm having to plaster my arms to my sides just to stay warm, and I have at least two extra layers on.

But Annika shakes her head with a frown, calling out from the other end of the baggage claim. "Boys!? What did I tell you about sparring in public?"

Viktor and Noah freeze—Viktor with his hand gripping Noah's jacket, and Noah's fist wrapped in Viktor's buttons. As Annika approaches faster, they slump in embarrassment like scolded pups with drooping ears.

"Sorry, my love." Viktor releases Noah, straightening his jacket. Annika just sighs.

My heart flips. Am I imagining the startlingly sweet smell in the air, or did their pheromones just combine to create a saccharine explosion of a perfume?

During our London layover, Noah warned me about this: the way Viktor and Annika tag-team, using their scents to lull other Lycans into security, including their enemies.

Noah might've prepared me mentally, but witnessing this phenomenon in person is a whole different beast. I'm unable to control the butterflies in my belly from a single whiff of their scent, my mouth watering for more.

Annika perks up when she meets my eyes, breaking into a smile. "Luna!"

My heart flutters when she calls my name. Every feature of her body emanates gorgeous regality, so it feels like a miracle she knows me at all.

"Luna, hello!" My voice is squeaky, but Annika's smile is warmer by the second.

Oh, God. Speaking of girl crushes. Noah raises a knowing eyebrow, and my cheeks burn. Guilt spikes through our bond, but before I can say anything, Noah chuckles, kissing my head. *This is exactly what I was talking about.*

I want to respond, but I'm too overwhelmed; Noah's arm around me doesn't stop Annika from throwing herself at me in a near-tackle. "Oh my goodness, look at you! Hello, beautiful!" She squeezes me tight, but her arms are so soft that I feel like I'm being embraced by a cloud.

"Are you kidding? Look at you!" My laugh comes out awkward and wary.

Why the hell am I so flustered? Never in my life did I think I'd look at anyone other than Noah, let alone have any desire to. I glance at Noah, terrified I'll find a blazing hurt in our bond, any second now.

But Noah chuckles, stroking my back as the four of us separate into our prospective pairings. *Don't worry. These two look innocent, but this is why I warned you; they win every sexual attraction contest we hold. On purpose.*

My heart still hammers. *N-Noah, I swear I only have eyes for you.*

He beams down at me. *I know. It's not you—there's something about their scent that allures other wolves. They use it to their advantage. Thankfully, they use it for good. At least, in my opinion. This is light, compared to what I've seen them do. They've mastered their scent, alluring dangerous wolves into submission. It might be a manipulative tactic, but it's a far more peaceful one than other packs who choose to kill their enemies. It's the main reason Vik and I get along.*

I want to agree with Noah, but my stomach churns. *Doesn't that mean they're manipulating me on purpose right now?*

Noah hugs me closer. *No. I almost don't smell it, so it must just seem extra strong to my poor pregnant Luna.*

As if Annika could hear Noah's mindlink, she closes her eyes, breathing me in. Gasping, she turns to her mate. "Oh, my love, did you smell her? She's *delightful.*"

The second Viktor's eyes land on me, Noah settles his arm back around my shoulders.

So it wasn't just me overanalyzing their behavior: Noah is guarding me from Viktor. It's borderline possessive, which is so unlike my mate. Is this another effect of their scent tactics? I lift an eyebrow at Noah, but he pretends not to notice.

At least one person can control himself: Viktor sniffs the air from afar to catch my scent, not daring to come anywhere near my neck.

He pulls back, his eyes wide as he meets Annika's eager stare. "So sweet!"

"Beautifully so, yes?" Annika beams. "And it reminds me of a particular hormonal phase, Luna."

"Dammit. So much for that," Noah mutters.

Viktor grins. "Ah, I see. Scent blockers not working?"

"That's okay. When you're this far along, you have to apply it every few hours." Annika gives me a knowing smile, and even though Noah frowns even deeper, all I can do is giggle.

"I— Um—" I tuck my hair behind my ear, glancing at Noah. "It's still a bit early, and things are a bit rocky in our area, so Noah and I haven't decided if we'd like to advertise the news of our pup to other Alphas and Lunas yet."

Annika gasps. "Oh, I'm so sorry! I didn't mean to put you on the spot! I won't speak of it without your permission again."

"Oh, no, I'm excited to be pregnant. But maybe it can stay between us, Tāne, and Waimārie? At least for a day or two?"

"Oh, goodness, yes! It will stay between us until you give the word." Annika squeezes my hand before nuzzling into her mate. "Although, Vik, I do have baby fever again now."

Viktor's smooth chuckle softens my shoulders. "Oh, Goddess. I don't have enough limbs for another pup, my love." He plucks a stray hair off Annika's cheek, sweetening his voice. "But maybe we can discuss this over dinner?"

Noah's jaw drops, but Annika and Viktor are too busy making out to notice. *Fuck, we're gawking at their pheromones, but maybe our scent really does do something to other Lycans. Is everyone at the Alpha Summit going to get pregnant because of us? My mom's really going to kill me.*

I can barely bite back a laugh, and when Annika meets my smiling eyes, she grins.

"Please know you're safe with us, and so is your pup. Come to me whenever you need support from another mom, okay?" Annika hugs me again, enveloping me in a far more relaxed, nurturing scent.

I sigh. "Thank you, Annika. You're so sweet."

"I just know what it's like to be pregnant around all these reckless Alphas."

Viktor laughs. "Hey! I'm not reckless!"

Annika ignores her mate, looping her arm into my elbow with a giggle. "Let's go get you warm in the car, mama. I just adore you already."

11

Wolves are affectionate, sure. But as Annika nuzzles me towards the car in a near-courting gesture, I have no idea what to do in response except glance back at Noah for his reaction.

Viktor and Noah are buddied up just the same, chatting about the Summit with Viktor nuzzling in closer than any man I've seen dare snuggle up to my mate. But Noah is staring straight at me.

I trust you, sweet Omega. Don't worry about me.

I break into a smile at the warmth buzzing through my chest, turning my attention back to Annika. *I trust you too, Alpha. Is she flirting with me?*

Not exactly. She just really likes your scent, enough to want it on her. It's a compliment. Noah pauses in his mindlink, his soft giggles filling the air as Viktor breaks into rambunctious laughter.

I'm grateful you have a buddy here too, I mindlink.

Viktor is a wild card. But Annika is a good ally for us and has an even kinder heart. I figured you'd get along well. I hope you can enjoy having her as not just an ally, but a friend. I've been so excited for you to be around so many other Lunas.

Thank you, sweet Alpha. My heart flips as I peek back over my shoulder, met by his loving, gentle smile.

Viktor is still chattering away, his voice low and hands gesturing wildly. Now that I can see the two Alphas from afar, I'm shocked by their similar height and build. Noah still holds a little more bulk in his dense muscles than Viktor's lean athleticism, but not many Alphas can come this close to matching my massive mate's stature. It's no wonder they're so competitive. I can hardly resist rolling my eyes as I turn back around, leaning a little closer to Annika's supportive hold on my waist.

After a short walk, I'm cuddled into Noah in the nicest limo I've ever seen. Outside, hillsides roll in and out of view, Kiruna's country roads stretching over the land in a gentle dance as we pass sweeping lakes. Thankfully, I'm used to winding, uneven roads in Greenfield Forest, otherwise I'd feel even more nauseated by yet another car ride.

I have other things to worry about; something weird is going on between Viktor and Noah. I feel it in our bond, but they're hiding it with playful smiles and laughter. What is it, frustration? Annoyance? It's so muddied with our overwhelming surroundings that I can't pick it apart for long before powerful eyes snap me back to the present in a continuous cycle.

All I know is Viktor is the current King Alpha after winning last year's Alpha Summit competition, yet he won't stop calling Noah "King." Noah seems to hate it.

And I'm feeling really out of the loop.

Annika senses my wariness—probably in my obnoxiously loud scent. She slinks from her Alpha's arms, scooting to my side on the wide, black leather bench.

"How are you feeling?" Annika's breezy tone softens my shoulders.

"A little spoiled. I haven't been in a limo since prom," I say.

Annika laughs, huddling in closer. "Prom? I know it's a human thing, but I thought the excitement around it was mainly just in American movies!"

I laugh with her. "Nope, it's sort of like a milestone everyone talks about, growing up. But it turned out to be kind of disappointing, to be honest. My boyfriend and I broke up a few weeks beforehand, so I had to tag along after my best friend and try to have a good time while her girlfriend kept stealing her away to make out with her."

Annika laughs, grasping my arm. "Oh, no! How old were you?"

"Seventeen. Did you and Viktor know each other by then?"

Biting her lip, Annika gives Viktor her best puppy-dog eyes. "Oh, we knew each other. That was the age he marked me."

Viktor's eyes glaze over in pleasure, his left knee bouncing as he taps his heel faster. I blink through the sudden haze of hormones in the car, my body flushing. Noah shakes his head, silently laughing to himself.

I'm tempted to ask more, but I wouldn't dare give them the opportunity: I can only imagine how horny these two can get, and my cheeks are hot as it is.

Thankfully, Annika fills in the silence. "How are you feeling in terms of health, though? You said it's still early in your pregnancy?"

"Well, for me. I'm about fifteen weeks pregnant, which I know is farther along for Lycans, but I'm part human. We have no idea how long my pregnancy will be, so all I know is that I'm still having to adjust to these hormones, more than the average wolf."

Annika's smile brightens. "So you feel terrible, huh?"

I laugh. "Kind of."

"We were planning to show you around our Community Center before the Alpha Summit begins, but let me know if you need to rest, okay? We can always give you a tour tomorrow."

I sink into myself, knowing I'm running on fumes. I don't want to miss out on everything, though. Maybe I can get through it.

Noah looks at me from the corner of his eye, sensing my distress.

But Annika leans in, cupping one hand over my ear. The other laces into mine, spiking nerves through my chest.

"Hey, I'm serious. Don't let these Alphas push you around. I'm on your side, and I'm sure I'll need you on my side too. Not every top Alpha and Luna are friendly."

A fire ignites in my lungs, my stare clinging to Viktor and Noah's tense, hushed conversation. My wolf is all riled up. She must instinctually sense the truth beneath everyone's words clearer than I can. There's danger ahead, but just how bad will it get?

I squeeze Annika's hand, trading positions so I can cup my hand over her ear. "I agree. When it comes to protecting people I care about, I'm a different wolf. If you ever feel unsafe, come to me."

Without warning, my Alpha musk trickles from me. I stiffen, hoping my scarf blocks most of it.

But Annika bites her lip with a blushing giggle. "You have a… *rebellious* side to you, Luna. I like it."

When Annika flashes her neck, revealing Viktor's scarred and re-scarred mark, I suck in a shocked breath. She's fawning for me?

Is this normal? Other than Noah, I've never had a single other wolf flash their vulnerable scent gland to me like this before, let alone witnessed anyone doing this to other wolves. Isn't this a gesture reserved for mates?

The sight makes me fear for Annika's safety, a protectiveness welling up in my chest. Before I can help it, even more Alpha musk leaks out, softening Annika's lips.

Viktor growls in warning.

It's gentle, but he's also one of the most powerful wolves I've ever met. Before I can control myself, I jolt back, ripping my hand from Annika's and plastering my back to the limo seats in submission.

In a flash, Noah jumps on Viktor, pinning him to the leather cushions.

Viktor raises two empty palms. "What the fuck?!"

Annika grasps fistfuls of my jacket, shrinking behind my back. "I-I'm sorry, Alpha Noah, it was my fault! I took it too far!"

Noah doesn't seem to hear her as he snarls over Viktor, his eyes flashing yellow. I'm shocked to see how much Viktor has to strain against him despite being physically equal.

"Shit, bro! Calm the fuck down!" Viktor says.

But Annika snaps back. "Vik, she's pregnant! You can't growl at her and expect him to be fine! Apologize already, and he'll lay off."

She continues to argue with him in Swedish, but Viktor fights against Noah's grip, his deep brown eyes flashing to green. Noah's fangs have extended, and I cower into Annika, all traces of my Alpha vacant.

"N-Noah? P-please," I sputter.

He releases Viktor the second he hears my shaking voice, dropping back into his seat with his head in his palms.

"Fuck. Sorry, Omega... Goddess, I'm so sorry. That was fucking immature."

A heavy silence hangs in the air as Annika rubs my back. Everyone's eyes are on Noah. Waiting for him to shift the collective energy...

Like a king.

But like Noah keeps insisting, he's not the King Alpha. There's definitely more going on here. I have a feeling this Summit will be rocky, even between our allies.

Viktor scrubs Noah's head until his hair pokes out in every direction. "No, man, that was my bad. I know how it is, especially with your first pup."

Nudging Noah's shoulder, Viktor laughs nervously. But Noah keeps his head buried in his hands.

"Seriously, it was my bad. Anni and I flirt with everyone—you know how it is. It's ridiculous of me, actually. For a second, I forgot your sweet little Luna wasn't another Alpha I had to be worried about. Maybe her mother wolf energy is extra strong, or something. They are rightfully fearsome, after all."

My stomach drops to my heels, spiking through our bond so heavily that Noah sucks in a sharp breath.

Noah, I did accidentally release my Alpha scent while talking about who we're up against at the Summit. I'm sorry.

It's okay, Luna. I've got you covered.

His wolf gathers himself into a brooding calm I recognize from our Pack Safety meetings, sitting on his haunches with collected, solid stoicism in our bond. Human Noah shakes his hair out. When he relaxes back into his limo seat, Viktor's shoulders soften almost imperceptibly.

Noah's low chuckle sends a shiver down my spine, his arm draping over my shoulders. "No, I lost my cool too. I should know my Luna knows her way around angry Alphas. You should've seen her: only a week before this one guy left, the dude took one look at her snarl and bolted with his tail tucked. He probably couldn't bear to stay after that, so he made a show of threatening her, orchestrating the biggest Alpha split from my pack."

Viktor's expression hardens, leaning in with tense fingers gripping his spread knees. "Yeah? Which guy was this?"

Noah's jaw ticks, losing a bit of his calm. My stomach groans in complaint.

"Mason Hart." Noah's soft murmur escapes more like a growl.

Viktor's eyebrows lift, but they settle just as quickly. "You mentioned him over the summer, but I didn't get to ask at the time…"

Noah grumbles. "Go ahead."

"You meant Hart, like… Jack Hart? The same family?"

When Noah doesn't answer, my instincts urge me to rub his chest. He barely softens.

Viktor nods. "Alright, I'll keep an eye out. For both of them."

I swallow hard, fighting off nausea. That's right. Jack Hart is still out there too, and every wolf I've met so far seems terrified of him.

Noah kisses my temple, breathing me in. *You're safe, Luna. No one working with Vik would let the Harts anywhere near here.*

When Noah's musk becomes stronger still, I'm tempted to comfort Annika; she leaves my side, plastering herself into her mate with tense shoulders.

But Viktor's scowl scares me too much to approach his mate again. His musk sharpens alongside Noah's until I have to breathe through my mouth to lessen the smell.

Viktor scoffs. "Alright, are you still pissed at me, or what? Spit it out. You're freaking out my Luna."

Noah sighs. "S-sorry, Annika. I'm not pissed at either of you. A-and I really am sorry I overreacted. I already have someone else on my mind today to warn other Alphas about, and it has me on edge."

"Shit, well, then let's talk about it. A little scuffle doesn't change things between us. Right, King?" Viktor's smirk churns my insides.

Noah isn't smiling. "It shouldn't. Right, Vik?"

Annika shoots Viktor a glare, and Noah huffs out his frustration, shaking his head.

So Viktor *is* pissed about last year's Alpha Summit competition. What really happened?

Viktor rolls his eyes. "Fine. Sorry. I'll drop it already. I really mean it, though. I want to know who's making you—" He waves his hand over Noah's tense form, one eyebrow raised. "Like this. I've never seen you so on edge."

Noah chews on his lip, glancing at me. *Are you okay if I ask about—?*

My heart drops, but I'm no longer confused. *Yes, you can ask them about my ex. But do you really think Steven's worth mentioning? These two are important wolves.*

And so are you. Whether he turns out to be a wolf or a human, he needs to be blacklisted.

Just because he's my ex? Isn't that a misuse of our power?

No, it's because what he did should never happen again. It should never have happened in the first place.

My throat thickens with nausea. *You're right. I don't want that to happen to anyone else, ever.*

The dread in Noah's emotions mixes with my residual anger. He closes his eyes with a heavy sigh.

But Viktor's tone softens a little. "Alpha, seriously. Who is it? Are you both okay?"

"Someone I knew," I say.

Noah stiffens at my admission, but I nod, urging him to continue.

His voice deepens as he leans in. "Do either of you happen to know a—" Noah winces like he swallowed spoiled meat. "A Steven Barrett?"

My stomach churns at Steven's name in Noah's mouth, his tightened voice reflecting his repulsion in our bond. But when Annika and Viktor look at each other in thought, anticipation burns my chest. I can't decide if I want to hear their answer. I need Steven far away from us and our allies, so I don't want to hear he's close by, but not knowing where he is scares me just as badly.

"A Lycan?" Viktor asks.

"Or a human. It's… complicated," Noah says. "I'm wondering if he used scent blockers. He isolated Aliya from friends and family, in part to control her, but it's also very possible he was distancing himself so no other Lycans could scent him out, even with a blocker."

Annika and Viktor frown, glancing at each other.

Oh, God. I hope they still believe me. I had no idea Lycans existed back then, so I didn't know how to differentiate Steven's scent. And if Noah's theory about scent blockers is true, Steven could've easily been hiding it. He's right: Steven never met a single member of my family, and stayed far, far away from Amy, forever calling her "your clingy friend."

Noah pulls me closer, giving my hip a soft squeeze.

But Viktor shrugs. "We don't know a Steven Barrett. Not here, and not that any of our allies have warned us about. But we can ask them directly, in private conversation. If he's violent and also this calculated, they need to know about it. He's North American? Pacific Northwest origin?"

"Yep. I'll give you a full profile. He's somewhere near our territory, as far as we know. Which pisses me the fuck off. I can't find him anywhere, and—" Noah's wolf bristles in our bond, too angry to continue speaking.

Viktor dares to lean even closer, staring Noah straight in the eyes. His deep voice quiets to a low hum. "What'd he do? You look like you want to kill him."

"No, I—" Noah's jaw clenches. "Aliya and I discussed this, at length. And I agree with her; if he's a human, we're pursuing legal action, and if he's a wolf, we're capturing him—not killing him. No matter how much I fucking hate his existence, we're not playing God, like he did."

"Hurting him won't magically erase what he did to me, it'll only make me feel even worse," I say.

Viktor frowns. "Well, sure, we'd do the same here in Sweden, opting for rehabilitation by social workers instead of inhumane punishment like most human societies choose. But like Anni has always told me, there are limits to which men like this will ever change."

Meeting Annika's somber eyes, a fire ignites in me. "I've struggled with that exact fear; I have my doubts he could be rehabilitated at all, no matter the amount of love, support, and training we could provide him. It's his decision in the end, not ours. I can't see the Steven I knew choosing to pursue compassion over power, maybe not even in his lifetime… But I won't prevent us from giving him the opportunity. We're planning to sentence him to some form of service that benefits survivors like me— without compromising anyone's safety, of course. The rest will be none of my business." I straighten, fueling my confidence with the heat in my gut. "But don't underestimate his capabilities.

Steven is a dangerous man to any woman he meets, Lycan or not. He— Um—"

My voice cracks, and I have to swallow my fear as it surges up my throat.

So much for confidence. I've never spoken about Steven so directly to strangers. This is already beyond my limits.

But Noah gazes at me with such pain, yet such intense admiration that my heart flutters.

My Alpha has my back. I'm going to tell them the full truth.

"We dated for a while, but he was verbally and emotionally abusive, and he couldn't handle my rejection." I fist my scarf, its fabric still doused with Noah's comforting scent, hoping it calms my heart; the poor organ hammers every beat into my ears. "When my dad died, I finally saw Steven for how he was using me—manipulating me into 'serving' him, no matter how horrible I felt while grieving—and I broke up with him. But he stalked me, waiting for the right time to approach. So, shortly after my mom also died of heartbreak—" I struggle to catch my breath, but Noah stares with such pride and awe that I continue without thinking. "Steven broke in and raped me."

My heart isn't the only one smacked with a barbed pain at my words: Annika's eyes widen in horror, gazing deep into my soul. Just her stare alone tells me she understands. It hurts me just as much to think she's been hurt like this too, my throat tightening as I gaze into her aching expression.

Viktor hums, a darkness surfacing in his eyes. But he's not looking at me: he's locked onto Noah's furious frame. "Alright, King. If I see him, I'll deal with him."

"And we'll make sure our allies will too. They don't need to know the details, but they'll listen to us." Annika reaches across the seats, grabbing my hand. "We believe you."

Without warning, my lip wobbles.

Annika's eyebrows warp. "Oh, Luna, I…"

Noah's walls break down, my mate slumping even though anger flares in his heart. He nuzzles into my hair. "I'm sorry, sweet Omega. I-I shouldn't have brought it up without warning, and—"

"No, it's not that." I force the best watery smile I can manage. "It's just really nice to—" I take a moment to stifle my tears with a held breath, touched by the display of comfort I'm receiving; the three wolves hold my hands, stroke my arms, and rub my back. "It's just nice to be believed."

Annika's eyes water, nodding along with me. "I know, mama. Trust me, I know."

My heart plummets. "I thought I could see it in your eyes."

"I could recognize it the second you started speaking about your ex too. Which is why we'll do anything to protect you, Luna." Annika's tense stare flits to Noah. "Especially after what your Alpha has done to trap my own monster with Vik."

Noah can't bear to look at any of us, rubbing his forehead to keep from crying, but my heart can't stop pounding.

Is Annika saying Noah helped defend her from an abuser too, tracking them down?

I always knew my mate was a protector, but I hadn't thought about how vastly influential he might be beyond Greenfield. Which means that not finding any trace of Steven, no matter who Noah orders to investigate after coming up empty-handed himself, must make Noah feel powerless.

As I huddle into my mate, my hand stretching across the limo seats to hold Annika's, a peaceful quiet falls over the car. No one speaks for at least two minutes.

When Noah breaks the silence, his voice is softer than I expect. "My Luna could kick most wolves' asses. But after a certain point, a victim's physical, mental, or emotional power can't protect them. Not when their abuser doesn't allow anything or anyone to keep them safe." He takes a sharp, furious breath. "That's how dangerous he is."

Annika nods. "Yes, I understand that too. And the manipulative ones often sneak under everyone's radar."

"Which is why we're taking this seriously. Sweden will be a safe space for you, we swear it," Viktor says.

The four of us huddle up in the limo with softened voices and a new perspective on one another, bonding over adversity. I can see the purpose of our allies more than ever now. Noah isn't just a strong Alpha for our pack, he's also smart in his strategizing.

Even if he's behaving so weirdly today.

As our limo approaches the Alpha Summit Community

Center, the mountainside parts, revealing a rich brown lodge. Stretching along a vast lake, the Community Center holds a modern elegance to its warm wood, rather than the rustic edge I envisioned. Bushy trees coat the rolling land, cradling the Community Center in a central clearing. The sheer size of the lodge screams of how expensive it must've been to craft, alongside its wide porches carrying a view down the lakeside.

The sunlight glimmers in hot white across the lake's crystal blue water, rippling through the forest's reflection. When it finally sinks in that this is where we're staying, I gasp loudly enough to perk up all three wolves beside me.

I turn to find their wide, alert eyes, like a crowd of curious pups, and let out a giddy laugh. "Sorry! It's just so beautiful!"

Annika smiles. "Isn't it, mama? We're so lucky to be here."

"It's wonderful. I'm so excited to look around with the three of you," I say.

But it's clear looking around isn't an option, my knees buckling when I step out of the car.

Noah scoops me against his side, carrying a majority of my weight with a panicked gasp. "Oh, Goddess, Luna. Are you okay?"

With Annika's and Viktor's wide, worried eyes, I do my best to laugh it off. "I'm fine. Just a little tired."

But Noah's concern seeps into my chest. *I'm so sorry, Aliya. I know you're looking forward to this, but you look like you need to rest.*

My shoulders droop, knowing he's right.

With my defeated nod, Noah turns to our King and Queen. "Vik and Anni, we're both looking forward to seeing the Community Center and how hard you've worked. But we've been traveling for almost a full day, and we need to sleep off some jet lag. Can we do this again tomorrow morning?"

Annika rushes to my side, stroking my arm. "Oh, poor mama. Let's show you to your room and send you some food and water. Like I said, we can absolutely wait until tomorrow, okay?" She whips her head to frown at her Alpha. "Vik, come help. You put her under a lot of stress."

Viktor's eyes bulge. "I'm sorry—"

"It's fine!" I step back, anxious from how much they're crowding me.

But Annika's dejected expression makes me wince.

"Sorry, Annika. I just don't want to pressure you to take care of me. I'm not usually like this, but everyone's fighting over me, and I'm just a nauseous mess, and—"

Annika puts on a half-hearted smile. "No, it's okay, I understand. I just feel bad it turned out this way. I was so looking forward to meeting you. I hope we didn't give off too bad of a first impression."

Oh, God. It's true I'm not enjoying how everyone's clashing, but I don't want anyone to feel bad if I admit it. At the same time, that sounds a lot like OCD talking.

I straighten my shoulders the best I can. "Hey, there's still tomorrow to try again."

Annika's frame softens as she breaks into the biggest smile, and my heart warms.

"But still, I really appreciate how you both listened to us and believed us today. I'd love to get to know you better... Maybe without any sparring in the background?" Viktor and Noah slump in unison, and my stomach drops even lower. "Ugh, I'm sorry. I need to stop talking before I say anything else I don't mean."

Annika gives my shoulder a playful squeeze. "Hey, I'm with you. Someone needs to speak up against these Alphas when they go too far, or they'll never stop. Let's start over again tomorrow after we've all rested and had time to cool off."

My shoulders loosen. "That sounds wonderful. Thank you."

After giving Annika the biggest hug I can manage, I follow her to our room with a heavy heart. I wish I felt ready to sleep after that exhausting meeting, but I'm upset Noah didn't tell me about the tension between him and Viktor. I have to confront him, which sends my anxiety through the roof.

Noah can sense it, glancing at me every few seconds as he helps me hobble my way to our room. Today isn't turning out how I expected at all.

12

Annika and Viktor drop us off in what I'm certain is the most beautiful guest suite they own; tall, wood-lined ceilings frame broad windows, giving us a panoramic view of the lakeside below the lodge. Geometric black-and-white furniture brings out the natural beauty of the warm wood surrounding us, a ginormous bed sitting in the middle of the suite with enough space for me to spread my sore limbs—and still leave room for my massive mate. My muscles ache at the thought, dying to be immersed in soft white sheets.

Once I'm seated on the bed's edge, slipping off my shoes, I gasp at the clock. "It's 8 p.m.?"

"Y-yeah. It s-stays lighter out in the evenings here until October." Noah crosses the room to shut the blackout curtains, but his back remains to me.

When he still hasn't moved after I change into one of his big, gray t-shirts, my heart hammers into my throat.

Oh, God. I hate fighting with him. I love him so much.

But I'm hurt by what he hasn't told me about him and Viktor. Of course he can have his own personal secrets, but this is different; with unstable Alphas on the loose across the world, any important information we don't share with each other could cost our lives. Are there other vital secrets he's keeping? And why?

Noah turns around, wringing his hands. His puppy-dog stare is in full swing.

No matter how upset I am, I have to smile. "You're too cute, my love. I'm struggling to remember why I'm upset."

Noah gives me a soft smile. "W-well… I wish I could ask you

to not be mad at me." He drops my stare, deflating. "But I don't blame you. I'm really fucking embarrassed by how I acted."

My heart tears at the seams, pushing a sigh from my chest. "It wasn't that. I know you were trying to protect me and our baby, and I love you for it."

Noah slumps, his expression warping as he meets my sad eyes. "Oh, my sweet Luna…"

He speed-walks across the room, sitting beside me on the bed to stroke my back. But with the gap he leaves between us, my stomach rolls.

"Please, tell me what's wrong," he says.

"I will, but I want you to know I didn't mean to shame you or make you feel embarrassed, just now."

Noah stiffens. "No, that's not why I just told you that. Don't stifle your upset for me. I want you to be honest with me about what you're feeling, no matter how I feel."

His rising frustration makes my cheeks burn hot. "Why aren't *you* being fully honest with me then?"

Noah's eyes widen. "W-what? Are you saying I'm lying about something?"

"No—well, actually, I don't know. How can I know if you're lying or not when you're avoiding telling me important information?"

"Okay, let's slow down for a second—"

"No, I'm really hurt." I huff, barely suppressing tears. "We're really deep into this Alpha Summit thing already, Noah. I wish you told me more about the dangerous things you're dealing with here, especially before we already got here today."

Noah shuffles in his seat. "Which dangerous things?"

"Like with Viktor. I don't want you to be overprotective of me by lulling me into a false sense of peace."

"Overprotective? You mean when I snapped at Viktor?"

"You didn't tell me about this 'King' thing with Viktor, which turns out to be a pretty big deal. It scared me to see one of our main allies butting heads with you so badly and not having a clue why, or what to do if he stopped being lighthearted about it. How can I support you properly if I'm left in the dark?"

Noah gapes in genuine surprise, leaving us in silence. After a painfully extended five seconds, Noah's knee bounces. "O-oh. I'm sorry. I guess I didn't realize there was something to tell."

My chest stings. "How could that be true? You remember to tell me a lot of things. I thought you trusted me as your partner in our pack. That was confusing and frightening to have thrown at me. Not to mention I—" I grip the hem of Noah's shirt I'm wearing. "I felt really left out."

"Luna…" Noah's breath shakes as he stares at me in my peripheral vision. When I don't say anything more, he drops his head into his hands. "Goddess, I never thought about how I'd feel it in our bond when I hurt my mate. This is *horrible*." Noah shrinks into himself, scrubbing his face as he sits on the bed's edge. "I-I know it's not an excuse, but I'm really not used to having anyone by my side with pack things yet. And when things are tense with other Alphas, I feel like it's my job to deal with, and my job only." He grips his knee hard enough to turn his knuckles white. "They're all aggressive as fuck, so I don't like putting it on anyone else. Especially not on you." He takes a few short, hot breaths until he freezes. When he speaks again, his voice cracks. "You've been around enough aggressive men."

My heart drops. "Noah, I didn't realize that's what you were thinking…"

"Fuck, I know, and I'm sorry. I just fucking *hate* how so many Alphas are like this. It makes me so irrationally mad, and—"

As he growls beneath his breath, my shoulders soften.

I sweep my nails down his spine. "Okay. I can see that. I think I took this way too personally."

"No, you were right; I fucked up by not talking about it with the wolf I trust the most. I just don't know what else to do in these types of situations." He looks up at me for the first time in minutes. His vivid, teal eyes ignite a flame in my belly. "Which is also why I should turn to you. Because it's true. You're my partner in leading this pack."

My tight stomach muscles finally relax.

But Noah isn't finished. "I see you as my equal."

My heart jolts into my throat. "Your *equal?*"

He furrows his brows. "Of course. Do you not feel like you are?"

My head spins, but Noah doesn't seem to realize the depth of what he just said.

I wouldn't call us "equals." He's the top Alpha, guiding the whole pack, including me. And with every hour we've spent away from home, the more I'm convinced he's not just a top Alpha in the Pacific Northwest, and not even just the United States, but also a *global* Lycan leader. Isn't he?

Before I can keep thinking it through, Noah launches into another mood entirely.

"What's really causing problems is that my wolf clashes with what I want. He gets so fucking agitated around aggressive Alphas. But I don't like that. I don't want to be like them." He shakes his head, but our bond stumbles into panic. "But you're also pregnant, so he has a point. What if I can't protect you from dozens of powerful Alphas at once, and—"

Noah huffs hard and fast, gripping the bed's edge hard enough for it to creak. My eyes widen as Noah's emotions shift faster than I can keep up with, each one spiraling darker.

"Hey, hey, Noah—"

"I don't want to see another Omega hurt by another fucking twisted Alpha again! I— I can't—" He sputters. "I can't handle that, Luna—"

The second Noah's breath rises to an unsteady sprint, I close the gap between us, my wolf on high alert as I grasp for his tense hand on his bouncing knee. I recognize that familiar, sickening feeling in our bond; his PTSD is going haywire.

God, this makes so much sense. Noah's wolf might be over-reactive now that I'm pregnant, but the more time we've spent around agitated Alphas lately, the worse he has seemed to feel. Maybe his agitation today wasn't just situational, but also a PTSD symptom.

Pheromones gush from me, coating the room with my nurturing scent. I pulse squeezes down Noah's shoulders, arms, and hands, pressing firmly enough for him to feel it if he's dissociating. "Look at us and where we're sitting right now, okay? I'm safe in this room with you, Alpha. You're safe too, right here with me. We're safe, and we have each other covered. Nothing's happening to you, me, or our baby."

Noah chokes out a frantic breath. "God, you're too sweet. And I'm just— I'm a fucking coward, I—"

"No, gorgeous, don't listen to that dark chatter. Just breathe. Please, breathe for me."

Noah shakily inhales into his hands, a tense silence stretching between us as he labors through it. And as this moment catches up to me, the dots connect.

Does this mean another Alpha did this to him? Another Alpha *here?*

My jaw clenches until it aches. I want to bite them to fucking shreds.

I hold Noah as tight as I can, enveloping him with my whole body. After two agonizing minutes of his poor body shaking the trauma out in my arms, he can finally take a deep, steady breath.

I exhale with him. "Oh, good job! You did it, my love."

Noah's expression remains flat. When he speaks, it's barely above a whisper. "Fuck. I'm so sorry."

I comb my fingers through his hair, but he still won't look at me. "Noah, please listen for a second, okay?"

He nods, flattening his loose shirt over my belly so he can see its small curve. As he gives our baby a gentle rub, my heart flips. I'm dying to be nestled together again.

"If something impacts you this much, I love you so deeply that I don't care if it doesn't involve me. I don't even care if it disturbs me. I still want to know how you feel—good or bad. I want to protect you, just like you want to protect me. And just like you'd tell me: don't let yourself be alone in this anymore."

After a heavy swallow, Noah nods. "O-okay. I'm sorry. I love you so much. I would never want to leave you out on purpose."

"I know. I see that now, and I'm sorry I assumed otherwise." I run my fingertips down his neck until he buries his face into my shoulder, pulling me into his lap. I giggle. "Don't hide, my shy Alpha. Kiss me."

When Noah peeks at me, his sad eyes slowly glint into a gentle smile. "You still want to kiss?"

I sputter out a laugh. "What?! Of course I do! I still love you, even when I'm mad."

Noah sighs, tucking me closer. "Luna…"

I nuzzle his cheek, relieved to see him smiling again. "Does that mean I should kiss you first instead?" I dare to nibble his earlobe, testing the waters.

Noah's wolf smashes his nose into my wolf's ear in our bond, washing me in excited chills. But his human form breaks into a sly grin. "Not until you're horizontal, my exhausted, pregnant Luna."

"Wha—"

I giggle-shriek as Noah wraps an arm across my chest, pressing my back tight to his rib cage, and flops back on the bed with me in his arms. Noah chuckles, cradling me as he flings open the covers.

But his rippling torso captures my full attention as he tears his clothes off, desperate to hold me skin to skin. As my eyes sweep over his body, Noah raises an eyebrow.

I bite my lip. "Alpha…"

He gives me a low growl, prowling over me to kiss me. "Don't give me that look. You're too tired for sex."

I laugh. "You're not wrong."

As Noah dissolves into the mattress beside me, he presses kiss after kiss into my lips, each one growing more passionate. I worm my way in closer, aching to be bundled up with him. Unfortunately, our baby is big enough to block our true cuddle ball formation.

Before I can frown, Noah grins. "Don't worry. Flip over, my angry Luna."

I laugh, turning my back to him. "I'm officially your *angry* Luna now?"

"Sorry—angry *pregnant* Luna. That I forced to carry my 'huge wolf baby.'"

As I groan-laugh, Noah growls against my neck, enveloping my entire back half in his body heat. Once we shuffle ourselves into our modified cuddle ball, he purrs over me in a smooth prowl, kissing me everywhere except my mouth.

I groan. "Noah! Why are you teasing me so much?"

"Because your fiery Alpha side came out to play with me a little, and now my wolf's all excited."

I burst into giggles as Noah nips at my neck, his wolf doing the exact same in our bond.

But as my toes curl in delight and my eyelids grow heavy, Noah nestles me into the curve of his body.

"I really am sorry, Aliya," he whispers.

"I'm sorry too. I don't like fighting with you."

Noah doesn't respond right away. After a few breaths, he mutters, "Weirdly enough, I do."

I let out a loud, scoffing laugh, whipping my head over my shoulder to meet his eyes. "Noah!?"

"S-sorry, sorry, that came out wrong." Noah ed into my neck, his ears flushing bright red. "I just mean, when we fight, we still treat each other like we're on the same side. I'm not used to that." His voice softens just above a whisper. "But I love it."

My heart flutters into my throat as we nuzzle each other. Now that I think about it, that's the key difference between my soft-spoken "fights" with Noah and my blowouts with Steven. I don't feel like I have to defend myself from Noah, let alone "win" against him to survive. We're usually "fighting" to understand each other better, as a team.

If this is how Noah actually sees us, maybe I need to rethink the next time I'm reading his intentions.

He tucks my hair behind my ear, furrowed eyebrows creasing his forehead. "Oh, no. You feel sad again."

"I'm sorry for acting like you were lying to me."

"Oh. Is that what you're worrying about? I was starting to think I just said something horrible again."

I laugh through a whine, my heart aching with love for him. "No, it wasn't horrible at all, and you're way too cute! I actually loved what you just said. It made me think."

He traces my eyes as I sink into the mattress with him, our cuddle ball requiring us to share a pillow. "Let's talk over it more tomorrow. Give that beautiful brain a rest." He kisses my temple before settling back down, digging his fingers into the roots of my hair.

There's no chance of keeping my eyes open with his big hands massaging heavy purrs from me. Slipping my loose t-shirt collar down my shoulder, Noah kisses my bare skin, washing my body in a satiating warmth.

As my limbs loosen, Noah hums in delight. "There you go.

Relax, gorgeous wolf. All you need to know right now is that I love you, and I feel so close to you."

"Good. I feel close to you too. Closer than ever, now that we talked this out."

My body blends into Noah's, huddling into him like a calming anchor. Each slow draw of his lungs against my back eases me closer to sleep, sweeping away my worries.

But there's one thought I can't let go of.

I whisper as softly as I can in case he's asleep. "Noah?"

"Hmm?" His voice still sounds awake, but it's sweeter and gentler for me.

"I wasn't scared of you when you attacked Vik. You're not a scary Alpha to me, and you never have been. I trust you more than ever."

Noah's heartbeat gallops against my back, doubling the pace of his breath.

But Noah massages me slower, liquifying my limbs. After a few hesitant breaths, his deep voice comes out cracking with emotion. "I-I trust you with my whole heart, sweet Luna."

With a soft hum, I'm too tired to respond with my voice. I tug his arm tighter around myself, nestling our joined hands at the base of my swollen belly. *I love you so much.*

❧ 13 ❧

The next time I stir, my wolf growls at Noah for trying to exit the bed. He doesn't listen, attempting to slip away from me, just slower—as if I wouldn't notice. I growl deeper, not entirely conscious as my lips lift in warning to flash my incisors.

When I crack open one eye, I find Noah barely containing a laugh. "O-oh, Goddess. You're totally turning into a mother wolf."

My jaw tightens. "Don't laugh at me. I want to hold you."

Noah bites back an even heavier threat of a laugh. "I know, and I-I love you. But I also need to pee."

I gasp, retracting my claws. "Oh. Sorry."

"Shh. Go back to sleep." Noah struggles to contain himself with a shaking voice as he pries his body from my limp arms.

The next time I open my eyes, my wolf growls through me again, pawing Noah's gentle touch away from my face.

"God, you're the cutest wolf I've ever fucking seen. You don't have to get up, and I won't disturb you for much longer. Just open those scowling lips to drink some water for me, my love."

I fumble for the cup with my eyes closed, downing the whole glass with how thirsty I am. As I catch my breath, I groan. "This bed isn't right."

Noah's breath hitches. When I pry open one eye, almost all color has left beyond blues and yellows, my furiously attractive mate biting his lips in grayscale. He stares back, wide-eyed. I shut my eyes again, grumbling at the glimpse I caught of the disastrous state of my bed.

"Mate, help me. I need more blankets." I huff, shoveling armfuls of the comforter around me to plump up the mattress.

"Oh, shit. Are you…?" Noah whispers.

His hand brushes my forehead, and it takes everything within me not to snap my jaws at him, barely opening one eye again to glare and growl.

"Sorry, sorry— Blankets, you said?" Noah backs up quickly, flinging open the cabinet behind him and grasping for anything soft he can find. I close my eyes, satisfied with his efforts.

"I'm so tired," I groan, unable to stop my arms from digging, digging, digging, not willing to stop until everything around me feels plushy enough.

"I know, Luna. Listen to your maternal instincts. Are you almost done?" The laughter in Noah's voice deepens my frown.

"Don't make fun of me, Alpha. I really am tired. It hurts."

"Oh, sweet Omega. I'm so sorry. I'm not laughing at you, my love. I just find you so endearing. You're going to be such a good mom."

Purring, I nuzzle my face into the blankets, unable to lift my arms a single time more—not even to drop my body back into bed, my ass left high in the air.

Noah purrs back, easing me onto my side until my body droops into the mattress in submission. "There you go. Crawl back in and go to sleep, okay? I won't disturb the bedding again."

Growling at the thought of my blankets being disrupted, I burrow deep into the fresh blankets Noah supplied me with, cocooned by squishy fabric.

"Good girl," Noah purrs, sending a tingling warmth between my legs. I wiggle my hips, too tired to fully invite him into bed to mate, but Noah shushes me gently. "No, no, sweet Omega. I'm not meaning to get you riled up. Get your sleep."

"But don't I need to get up soon?" I mumble.

"No, my love. I'd make the whole world wait for you if I had to, yeah? But there's no pressure at all today. Just rest."

I'm so exhausted that the only thing I can sense is Noah's giddy adoration. His gentle touch on my cheek lulls me back to sleep with a weak smile.

The next time I wake up, my bladder is about to explode—as if our baby is sitting right on top of it. I scramble to the toilet just in time, sighing in relief.

That's weird. Noah isn't in our room or the bathroom. Maybe he had something to do?

It's silly, but I miss him already. I have a feeling we'll be mushy around each other the entire Summit—like proper newlyweds.

Hey, cutie. Where'd my big, scary Alpha go? I mindlink.

Noah's wolf perks up in our bond with a floppy tail wag. My laugh echoes throughout the marble bathroom.

I didn't think you'd wake up just yet. I just bought a few things, and I'm on my way back, Noah says.

You bought a few things? Is there something we forgot to pack?

N-no, it wasn't that. I know you were feeling like we researched human pregnancy too much when this one's turning out to be pretty Lycan, so I was cross-checking the differences between Lycan and human pregnancy at the beginning of the second trimester and grilling my mom about it while you slept. She had some more ideas for your dizziness, other than forcing my poor Luna to eat a shit ton of red meat.

I'm tempted to cry. *Noah, that's so sweet.*

It's the least I can do while you carry that huge wolf baby for us. Wait for me, Luna. I'll be right there.

After a quick brush-through of my hair, I exit the bathroom to find Noah entering our suite.

I can't help it; I break into the widest smile my cheeks can manage. "There he is."

Noah drops his stare to his feet with a grin. He accepts my glomping hug with just as heavy of a kiss, wrapping his arms around my waist to snuggle me in close. I didn't realize how tense I felt to be alone in a different country until my entire body slackens, content to be immersed in Noah's scent once more.

Hi, Luna. When Noah releases me with a happy purr, greeting our baby with a soft stroke on my belly, my heart skips a beat. "And hi, Little Wolf."

My face flushes until I'm certain I'm beet red. Noah laughs, drawing me in for another kiss—or five.

But when Noah pulls back, my eyes widen at the bag in his hands; it's stuffed to the brim. "What's all this?"

"Just a few things." The bag hits the table with a solid *thunk* despite Noah carrying it with one finger.

I laugh. "A few, huh?"

"Mhm." Rummaging through the bag with a tucked-away smile, Noah pulls out the usual morning sickness snacks for humans: crackers, ginger candies, and peppermint tea.

But my eyes widen when Noah hoists a hefty variety pack of Swedish baby food onto the table—a clear answer to why the bag sounded so heavy.

"Um… Wow, those are—" Biting my lip, a wave of nerves crawls over me, eating up my adoration at how sweet Noah is for trying. But how the hell am I going to explain this to him without crushing his pride? It'll be over a year before our baby can eat any of those, and my wolf already tenses into a protective stance at the thought of not doing the proper research on each brand's ingredients first to find the right fit.

Noah chuckles, kissing my cheek. "Cute. So fucking cute. I know it's weird, but my mom, Rainn, and Annika swore by baby food for Lycan pregnancies, and so did the Pack Doctor. They think you need way more nutrients and salt, beyond more iron—especially on days you feel like you can't stomach solids. I can try all the flavors with you if it feels too ridiculous."

"Oh, that's— That's for me?" My heart hammers, tears pricking my eyes. "Y-you did *all* this for me?"

"Oh, sweet Omega. Of course I did." He cuddles me into his warm chest, settling my eager wolf with luscious strokes of my mark. I hum, and Noah sighs with me, our bond swirling with love for each other. "So, are you feeling up for dinner with our friends in an hour, or should we sit this one out?"

I gape at Noah, struggling to grasp his words. "That's supposed to happen on Tuesday evening!"

"Ah, um— It *is* Tuesday afternoon, my love. 4:30, to be exact."

"I slept that far into the next day?! What was that, twenty hours?" I cup my mouth, muffling a panicked groan before gripping Noah's forearm. He simply shrugs. "Oh, God, this is terrible. After Annika and I planned to make things better today, I just blew her off? What'd I miss?"

Noah's sweet laugh softens my pounding heart. "Nothing, Luna. No one's flying in until tomorrow, except for Tāne and Waimārie who arrived this morning, and they needed a nap before meeting us after flying across the entire world. Annika and I agreed you also needed your rest. She told me a lot more about Lycan pregnancies too, actually."

I groan, wrapping my arms around my mate to cuddle into his warm chest. "Did she say anything about why I could eat the equivalent of three wolves' meals, five times a day?"

"Actually, yes." Noah digs into his bag, his wide back obscuring my view. I try to wedge my head beneath his arm to peek, but he turns his hip, blocking me with a giggle.

As a thrill crashes through our bond, I smile. "Hey, what else do you have in there? Something to hide?"

"Maybe. You'll see later, when you're feeling better."

I quirk one eyebrow at Noah when he briefly glances at me over his shoulder, and he chuckles. When he turns around, he's holding an aromatic, rustic loaf of bread, packed with colorful crunchy bits. I gasp, grabbing it before I even know what's in it; my nose knows, and that's all that matters.

Fuck, yes, this smells heavenly. I have no thoughts, only a deep, snarling urge welling up in my belly as my mouth gushes with drool.

I smash my face into the loaf, crumbs cascading down my cheeks as I cram it into my mouth.

"U-um…" Noah's voice fizzles out. I give up on raising the loaf to my mouth, opting to bury my face into it where it sits in my palms. "I-it's pumpkin bread," Noah mutters. "Pumpkin soothes wolves' stomachs, but Annika has this recipe with extra nutrients… And… It's gone."

I moan with my mouth stuffed, sucking off the crumbs from my fingertips. *Thank you, Alpha.*

When I finally have a spare second to look at him, Noah's eyes are almost as wide as his gaping mouth. He presses his closed fist to his lips, losing the battle not to laugh at me. I hum in recognition of how wild I must look, hiding my reddening cheeks as I continue to chew.

But a muffled grunt of surprise escapes me when I take a closer look at our room. The bed sheets are wrapped into a beehive-like tower, my pillow has deep claw marks, and empty plates litter the floor.

I gulp down the last of my bread, gripping Noah's arm for stability as I struggle to catch my breath. "What the hell happened in here?"

Noah bites his lip, collecting the crumbled food wrappers at the bedside. "Y-you were nesting. Making a new den."

"What? No, I'm pretty sure I would remember that."

"You—" Noah can't contain his giggles now, his shoulders shaking hard enough to vibrate his voice. "You had your eyes closed."

With one bewildered look at each other, we burst out laughing.

"Noah, what am I putting you through?!"

He scoops my cheeks into both huge palms, his beaming smile stirring warmth through my heart. "Everything I've always wanted. And I'm loving every second of it."

My full belly flutters as Noah's smile grazes my lips, my sweetheart of a mate kissing me softly enough to stoke an aching heat in my groin. I'd need all the time in the world to thank him how I'd like to—dragging him back to bed until he's the one groaning in delight.

But I grip Noah's shirt with a gasp. "Shit, the dinner!"

Noah springs into action with me, turning on the shower as I strip my pajamas.

When he approaches my suitcase to fetch my dinner dress for me, I yelp. "Wait, don't!"

Noah freezes, his eyes wide. Then he melts into a mischievous smile. "So I'm not the only one hiding things in my bags."

I flush down to my chest, gripping the icy glass shower door. "I told you: I have a surprise for you in there."

Noah's smile curls into a sultry, teasing grin, flashing his incisors. "Then I better behave myself so you'll still want to give it to me."

He flusters me speechless. All I can do is laugh, scrubbing myself down beneath the warm water as fast as I can.

By the time I'm braiding my wet hair, my stomach churns itself into a rocky sea. I'm about to meet Tāne and his Luna, Waimārie, in person for the first time, before I'm honored by Viktor and Annika tomorrow as Noah's new Luna. I've never met other pack leaders before this Summit, so I'm grateful we at least had our video call with Viktor and Tāne over the summer, and the limo ride from the airport yesterday—otherwise, I'd be even more of an anxious mess.

Thankfully, my moonstone necklace elevates anything I wear—and distracts from the dark circles stuck beneath my eyes throughout this pregnancy. Zipping my navy blue dress behind me, Noah eyes me in the mirror as I decide to ditch the bra, sighing in relief as I slip it from the bodice. A wave of Noah's loving pheromones wash goosebumps down my skin, enticing me to inhale deeply.

But as his eyes drift lower, his scent changes.

He's enjoying how I look lately, and I know it, but his eyes aren't focused on my body tonight; I didn't realize it, but I've been rubbing the base of my belly, unable to keep my hands off Noah's baby.

As our stares meet in the mirror, my heart flips. Our bond whirls with an emotion so deep and complex that I'm struggling to place it. Is it awe, gratitude, admiration, or all three? Whatever it is, it ignites my cheeks bright red, the effect of Noah's gaze spilling down my chest with how flustered he's made me.

"Goddess, the way you hold them so lovingly is—" Noah ducks his head, his voice coming out soft. "I fucking love you."

Flipping around, my breath is stolen at the sight of my mate; he's wearing a lean black suit jacket that sculpts to his muscles, and beneath it, his dress shirt matches mine in a dark navy blue. The color draws out the blue in his irises, turning them an oceanic teal. I step closer, snaking my hands around his waist—embracing him beneath his jacket. Wrapping me in his warmth, Noah purrs, his nose ruffling my hair with his affectionate nuzzling.

All my nerves wash away. Pulling back with a smile, I smooth Noah's suit collar, relaxing my bump against him. "Dammit. I really can't believe my wolf took over me like that for so long. I wanted more time to talk to you before we went."

Noah stiffens. "R-right. Are you still upset about last night?"

"No, my love. But I wanted to give us a chance to talk about anything that might come up at the dinner. And any last-minute ideas you might have about our team plan, especially when we move into talking Alpha-dom politics."

"A-about that…" Noah plops onto the bed's edge, tugging his tie off his throat. "I-I don't know if you have this, but PTSD gives me some serious issues with memory recall, and—" He drops his head, digging his fingers into his hair. "Sometimes, when I'm already nervous or stressed, I can't remember fucking anything about these people in words, only my wolf's impressions of them. I'm really afraid to tell most people that because they might think I'm not fit to be their leader, but— I don't know. It's brief when I do forget, but I can't deny it happens. Especially around certain… triggers."

The ache in my stomach is replaced with fire. According to last night, "certain triggers" means asshole Alphas.

So it *was* another Alpha who hurt him. It better not be anyone here.

Noah notices the uptick in my emotions, shrinking into himself. "I-I'm sorry—"

I gasp. "Oh, God, not you, Noah! I completely understand. I'm just mad someone hurt you, just like you were mad someone hurt me."

"Oh." Noah rubs his brow with one hand, staring at the other clamped on his knee. "W-well, anyway… Seeing everyone's faces on the blacklist tonight will help jog my memory, and even more so when they arrive tomorrow. I know it's not ideal, but—" He glances at me. "D-do you think I could tell you if there's a-anything else I remember as we go? I really do want to tell you more."

My shoulders soften. "Absolutely. I love that idea."

I *wanted* to feel relaxed, at least. Now I'm quivering with nerves, arm in arm with Noah as we exit our room.

Noah's pheromones are exploding, overwhelming me with his protective scent. *No matter what happens this week, I'll be with you through it all, okay?*

I stop Noah in the hallway, drawing him down for a sultry kiss. As I bury my nails into the back of his hair for a soothing scratch, my Alpha musk shows itself. *And I have your back before anyone else's. Goddess help anyone who threatens you.*

Noah freezes, staring deep into my eyes. Gathering my cheeks into his hands, Noah closes his eyes. An overpowering wave of safety swirls through our bond as Noah's hips fall flush with mine, pressing me against the wall with his deep purr.

But someone clears their throat. "Well, shit. We might need to postpone the dinner after all."

Noah and I hurriedly pull away from each other; we're face to face with the King and Queen Lycans. Decked from head to toe in black and white, Viktor's and Annika's forms are sleek and smiles immaculate, a perfect vision of elegant, powerful leaders.

Annika giggles. "Don't stress yourselves, please! It's so good to see you both!"

My shoulders slump. "Oh, Luna, I'm so sorry I slept for so long. I feel terrible about it!"

"No, mama, please don't be sorry. I wanted you to rest!" Annika grasps my hands, but I pull her into a hug.

"Thank you. Your pumpkin bread saved my life."

Noah's soft chuckles rumble behind me.

Pulling back to face me, Annika grins even wider. "It's good, isn't it?"

Viktor's laugh echoes throughout the tall, arched hallway. "My Luna's pregnancy pumpkin bread is to die for, that's for sure. But if I ate it while she was pregnant, she'd maul me."

Annika gasps. "Viktor! I would not!"

After a playful nuzzle, Viktor guides Annika down the hallway. "I hate to break up the love fest, but Tāne and Waimārie are probably excited and waiting for us, knowing them. Let's get going."

Like Greenfield, Viktor and Annika's Kiruna Pack has a community kitchen, but it's framed by vaulted, castle-like ceilings with old chandeliers dangling low. We have to sneak through a dim hallway reserved for staff, preventing ourselves from causing a stir in the dining hall, but I catch a glimpse through a small opening in the kitchen. Facing one another across round wooden tables, pack members chat happily in the dining hall, their pack just as expansive as ours with Lycans of all ages and ethnicities. People must travel from all over to find refuge here too. It settles my twisting stomach.

Viktor and Annika guide us out the kitchen's back door, passing through another hallway until we reach a small alcove of the lodge—an old restaurant nestled beside the dining hall. Intimate, streamlined modern tables line the walls, immersing the surrounding brick with dancing candlelight. There are only about ten tables, and it's reserved just for us tonight, the restaurant's front doors shut tight.

Seated in the back of the restaurant, there they are: Tāne and Waimārie from Tawairauriki Pack. The second Tāne spots us, he leaps from his seat, arms outstretched. "Kia ora."

We smile, echoing the Māori greeting as Tāne dashes over to us. His bulky form is at least twice the size of Waimārie, the Luna known for her warmth and generosity. As she shuffles out of the curved booth, she pulls her long, black hair over her shoulder, allowing it to cascade down her flowing, hot pink dress.

But Waimārie winces as she rises, gripping her back.

I flinch with her, extending my hand to help her to her feet. "Oh, gosh, Luna. Are you alright?"

"Sorry, I reckon I'm just stiff from all that flying, and—" She blinks a few times before she recognizes me, but the second she does, the table's candlelight shimmers in her eyes, complementing her wide, infectious smile. As if our wolves recognize each other as old, dear friends, my chest bursts with excitement.

"Luna Aliya!" Waimārie cheers, throwing her arms out for a hug—just like Tāne.

I catch her as she envelops me in the biggest, warmest embrace. When Annika piles on, we erupt into giddy laughter, the three of us snuggling in close. Waimārie douses me in her excited scent in the process, loosening any remaining tension in my limbs. But as Annika copies her, blanketing me in a nurturing comfort as they nuzzle me, belly laughter spills out of me from deep in my chest.

But their comfort also frees my honest scent—heightening it enough to break past my scent blocker.

"Wait, *Luna*, you're—" As Waimārie pulls back with a loud gasp, her gaze zipping to my belly, I already know what's coming.

Ducking my head, I cup Little Wolf with flaming cheeks. "Yes, Noah and I are about to be new parents."

As Annika looks to Waimārie, eager for her response, I almost can't believe what I'm seeing; they're not even our packmates, but Annika's beaming eyes shine just as vividly as if we were family, encouraging Waimārie into a cheer of pure joy. The two women make my eyes water in happiness.

At least until I jolt out of my skin, startled by Tāne's resulting happy-scream.

I turn around just in time to see Tāne smack the hell out of my mate's arm, Noah not bothering to dodge. Instead, Noah shoves Tāne back just as hard, unable to hide his face from us as he flushes just as red as I do.

"Bro! Your first pup!?" Tāne wraps Noah into a hug, and my heart dances along with Noah's, unable to process such a display of joy in front of me alongside our bursting bond. Before I know it, Tāne reaches for Viktor and us three Lunas, gathering everyone for a group hug. As the empty restaurant fills with our celebratory laughter, Noah meets my eyes over our wiggling bundle of happy Lycan allies. His wide smile hits me to my core, bringing me to full tears; after all he's been through, he's genuinely, truly happy. Not only that, he's so loved. We both are.

Before I can reassure everyone that my tears are a good thing, Waimārie strokes my arm, unfurling her fresh napkin from the table to dab at my eyes. "Oh, Luna, poor girl. Those pregnancy hormones really do a number on us, eh? Sorry to overwhelm you."

"Isn't she beautiful, though?" Annika whispers.

I blubber out a laugh, unable to respond. Bewilderment rattles me to my bones, forcing me to take in a shuddering breath.

But warm, wide palms sweep down my arms, embracing me in a scent rich with cinnamon-sweet comfort. As if my body knew who he was before my brain, I don't panic at Noah approaching me from behind; I lean into him, allowing his presence to root me back into the earth. Both women soothe me with gentle touches as Noah leans over my shoulder, pressing a slow, loving kiss onto my cheek.

I sigh, steadying my breath. "Sorry. I wasn't expecting anyone to be so excited for us tonight, but I could really feel it and— And it means a lot."

"We absolutely get it, Luna. Come here—let's all get settled." Taking my hand, Waimārie guides me to sit beside her, followed by Tāne. With Noah on my opposite side, Annika and Viktor snuggle into the bench across the table from us.

The couples take turns showing us baby pictures of their pups as we get to know one another. Noah seems looser than I expected, smiling far more than he was yesterday during our limo ride. He sticks close to my side, so I keep getting distracted by him; he seems to shine from within with his cheery smile, now that he's included as another dad.

Noah does a double-take, meeting my stare. I don't avert my eyes, instead leaning in with an affectionate nuzzle. No one else seems to mind, sharing their own affections across the table as we chat. I'm still not used to it, marveling at the way Viktor and Tāne touch each other's hands and arms as they chatter away, Annika and Waimārie pressing into Noah's and my sides as they have a heated discussion about this new Lycan baby formula that I'm absolutely never buying based on the disgusting, clumpy sound of it.

But I freeze when Viktor turns to me; the King Alpha stares with unwavering, focused eyes.

"Aliya, I heard you had some thoughts about our current plans on how to handle the Alpha-dom cultists. Would you like to share while we're waiting for our food to arrive?"

My stomach flips; the whole table falls silent. The ever-present wolves gaze at me, waiting.

Noah gives my thigh a gentle squeeze, but my throat locks tight.

I told Noah I had my reservations about our pack's safety plans, but I didn't expect all five top-of-the-top Lycans to place their full focus on me to start us off. It's probably only been mere seconds, but it feels like I'm taking an eternity to gather my bearings, grappling with the truth; Noah wasn't lying last night. Not only does he see me as his equal, but he's also presenting me as one to our allies.

And I have to try not to allow OCD to overtake my mind. No matter what I say, its ruthless reminders chime in: if I make a mistake here, the whole world of Lycans is at stake.

But I want to do this anyway. Need to, for the sake of everything I value.

I clear my throat. "Thanks for asking. I did have a theory that might change our strategy, but I wanted to get everyone's opinions on it first. You're far more accustomed to Lycan traditions than

I am, but that's what got me thinking; after living through and understanding an abuser's mindset intimately, I'm concerned we may have overlooked something huge."

Viktor's brows furrow, and I tense, preparing to be dismissed. But he's not shutting me down yet, tilting his head like a curious puppy.

His low voice hums over the soft music playing throughout the restaurant. "Alright, let's walk through it together."

The remaining wolves follow his lead, leaning closer. I lean in with them, pausing as our waiter rushes by to grab something from his staffing stall. My stomach gurgles, thinking of how horrified he'd be if he happened to overhear this conversation. Guilt stings my chest, knowing our allies are about to be disturbed by my thoughts, just like I was—and I have no choice but to allow them to also experience this pitting disgust in my guts.

The second our waiter dashes back into the kitchen, I drop my focus to our table's flickering candle, nerves striking my chest with every heartbeat.

"So, the plan has been to keep our second strongest wolves at home, protecting our packs while we're gone—as in, when the pack's most vulnerable, right?"

"Right," Tāne says. "That's the usual protocol for the Alpha Summit, as well, but we amplified it ten times this year, stationing a few of our skilled members across the world in smaller, less experienced packs that have remained peaceful with us."

"Which I think makes absolute sense." I open my mouth to continue, then close it—my nerves wash over me far more intensely than before, shifting into nausea.

Hooking his hand in mine, Noah gives me a gentle squeeze. *You okay? Do you need backup?*

They won't like this, backup or not. I know it.

Probably. But this is what they all signed up for, yeah? And I'm not letting anyone ignore my genius Luna. I trust you, and so do they. Look at them.

That's what's making me sick. They look so sincere—so dedicated to their beloved packs.

And I don't want this to be true either. But the more I think about it, the more I can feel it. We're reading these cultists wrong.

Viktor's shoulders ripple beneath his suit, his expression darkening. "Wait, you think the plan makes sense? Then what's wrong? Why do you look so terrified?"

"*Because* it makes sense," I mutter, unable to keep my voice from shaking. "I understand there's a natural order to things. That customarily, you fight for dominance, wolf to wolf—just like at the Alpha Summit."

"And? What's wrong with that?" Viktor stiffens, and I freeze. He stares me down, and this time, I'm certain I shouldn't hold eye contact.

"Vik," Annika hisses beneath her breath.

"What? I'm genuinely asking."

Noah clears his throat. That's all it takes for everyone at the table to soften their glares, loosening in their seats. Still, it's dead silent.

"What's wrong with that is that this is what *you all* would do as pack leaders. But these Alphas aren't the same as us," I say.

Viktor sighs. "Okay, that, I absolutely agree with."

"Right. They don't act like us, which also means they don't think like us."

This time, when it falls silent, no one dares to speak up in response to my thoughts. The collective scent reverts into a bitter unease, unsteady eyes latching onto me in the hopes I hold the answers for them.

A heavy pit forms in my stomach. "They have the perfect advantage to attack. We're grouping global leaders all in one place, and they have multiple leaders on their side to infiltrate from within the Summit. I think we're right about a possible global super pack forming, an alliance spanning across hundreds of packs for the sake of Alpha-domination extremism. And I think they'll try to kill us all here."

I expect Viktor to fight me on this, but Tāne's eyebrows shoot up his forehead. "*Here?* Where they'll get beaten senseless by the strongest Alphas in the world, all at once?"

"That's exactly what I'm saying," I mutter. "These are volatile, power-hungry Alphas, a large majority of them with records of abuse. And abusers can't be reasoned with. Their decisions often don't make sense because they don't play by society's rules.

They don't have to. Not when their manipulation, coercion, and intimidation breaks the whole game, forcing victims into a never-ending, losing battle: no limits, respect, or compassion in sight."

Tāne and Viktor exchange the subtle, fleeting glance I expected; the one I've seen many times as a woman trying to speak up for myself or my loved ones. I don't expect a flash of anger to broil through me at the sight of it, but as fury rips through me, I know it's not actually directed at anyone here. With the thought of these Alpha men barging in to not simply fight us, but likely take at least some of our lives, I quiver against Noah.

But his deep, rumbling voice stabilizes my breath.

"Think about it," Noah says. "Maybe they challenged us face to face in the beginning, but in the past few months, have any of you fought cordially with a single one of our worst offenders while they played by our traditional rules?"

Silence.

My heart throbs faster; their silence is a horrible yet necessary validation. I grip Noah's hand tighter, inhaling through the burst of pride Noah feels for me in our bond.

You've got this, Luna, Noah says.

"No one's forcing Lycans to fight for dominance by the rules—we just do, out of respect for one another. But these Alphas want to put us in our place. Specifically us pack leaders, who represent everything they want," I say.

"That'd be reckless," Tāne mutters. "Yeah, sounds like them."

"Exactly," Noah says. "That's what pissed me off too—it proves her point, right? It isn't just straggler extremists anymore. And the leaders using this dogma to abuse their own packs are just as reckless. What do these jackasses do to us every year at the Summit?"

"Fight way beyond their physical limits, nearly getting themselves killed." Viktor's voice has never been so quiet.

"And imagine them now, emboldened by how widespread their belief system has grown," Noah mutters.

Annika shrinks, her eyebrows knitted in clear fear. But I perk up, courage building in my chest at the Alphas' affirmation of my thoughts.

"What tipped me off the most is that Mason Hart decided to

intimidate, disturb, and frighten us when he left our pack—not challenge us. He was distorting us, psychologically."

I swallow hard as Noah fidgets, his Alpha musk stirring up Tāne's and Viktor's protective scents until my eyes sting.

"So, do you reckon they'll target literally everyone at the Summit, or just us?" Tāne asks.

"I don't know. They might be cocky enough to fight everyone, but I think we were on the right track with protecting the most vulnerable, smaller packs first. Maybe they know they wouldn't be able to kill the strongest of us. At the same time, who they kill might not matter to them. By killing off as many leaders as they can, and then splitting up to divide and conquer packs while they're overwhelmed and grieving, they can continue building what we're all pretty sure is a global super pack—until they're too huge for even us to stop. I mean, can you imagine what they could do if they overtook a pack from just *one* of us here? Enlisting even a quarter of the Alpha pack members from any of our huge packs would be devastating. Not to mention how they'd probably abduct a ton of Betas and Omegas as forced mates."

This time, the silence stings. All four of our allies glance at one another, their expressions unreadable. I can only imagine what they're mindlinking about this—like I said, they hate this possibility too. The sour sting of fear and anger lingers in the air, verifying it.

But the silence stretches one second too long, burrowing hurt into my gut; they don't believe me, do they?

Noah sucks in a tight breath, but I can't bear to look at him— not even as he applies slow, soothing pressure down my thigh in an attempt to comfort me.

I drop my chin, unable to watch this unfold a second longer.

But Annika's soft, shaking voice cuts through the silence. "She's right."

Viktor drops his head into his palms, rubbing his eyes hard.

Waimārie's jaw flexes. "I was about to say the same. And to add to Aliya's thoughts, I wouldn't put it past them to kill us with weapons, not just their wolves."

My heart drops to the floor. I hadn't thought about that, but

Waimārie is spot-on; what would stop them from stabbing us? No, *shooting* us?

"Oh. Like Alpha Ritchie and my dad," I whisper.

Noah's form tenses beside me. His eyes zip to mine, flashing golden.

A wave of turmoil strikes our bond. My jaw clamps shut, my whole being wracked with horrendous nausea. As I stare Noah in the eyes, I feel every flicker of dread, denial, and grief tearing through us. But beneath it all, a deep knowing roots itself in our bond.

Fuck. This really could be our answer to how they died, couldn't it? Noah mindlinks.

Dropping my eyes to my lap, I chew on the inside of my cheek, fighting off tears.

Our waiter chooses this moment to bring us our food. No one says another word for a long time, struggling to smile and thank our waiter with tight shoulders and fleeting, cautious glances.

But before I slip into full despair, Waimārie grasps my hand. "Ki te kotahi te kākaho ka whati, ki te kāpuia e kore e whati." As Tāne's eyes soften in adoration for his Luna, Waimārie beams back at him. "It means, when we stand alone, we are vulnerable, but together, we are unbreakable."

Her words strike my core, leaving me breathless. Like a true Luna, she reorients my focus to one of hope in an instant, and nurtures my heart in the process.

Waimārie straightens in her seat. "Alright, now that our Greenfield allies have shared this important revelation, let's adjust our plan. Anyone have ideas?"

Tāne and Viktor leap into action, spouting off idea after idea. Although we don't acknowledge it aloud, it's clear our allies are joining me in allowing Noah his space to contemplate quietly in the corner as he picks at his food, still reeling at the thought of our dads' murders. But as we sort our tactics together, pointing out additional ideas and possibilities, I stroke Noah's hand, loving the tight pressure he applies back—returning my soul back to this earth, no matter how unsafe this realm may feel. It's true; no matter the attacks coming our way, we're not alone in facing them.

Soon, I'm comforted enough to dig back into my food. Whether it's intentional or not, Noah softens his rigid torso beside me. He glances at me eating, gradually lifting his fork faster to his mouth. I smile; I guess I'm modeling security for him too.

As we nourish ourselves over a discussion to keep us all safe, I can feel our hearts returning to safety too. I don't know how we'll get through it if a super pack does arrive, but for now, I'm relieved Noah's here to experience this with me. That he doesn't have to experience his grief alone anymore either.

⧼ 14 ⧽

Once we've finished dinner, our allied group heads down the Community Center halls for the meeting room. Tall, arched windows line the hallway on one side, old knotted columns bracing wooden ceilings above our heads. Muddled sunlight streams in, painting the floor in a soft blue hue as it bounces off overcast skies.

Viktor stops before two wooden doors, iron bars lacing the front. He swings it open, waving us inside with a flashy smile. "After you."

As Annika, Waimārie, and Tāne filter in in front of me, Noah and Viktor trail behind us. Thankfully, there's no seat at the head of the pristine white table, or else Viktor might torture Noah about being the King again.

But when Viktor sits at the computer at the front of the room, he frowns. "Anni, I already forgot how to turn this fucking thing on."

Annika's eyes widen. "Turn it *on?*"

Viktor's frown deepens. "I'm a big meatsack designed to protect you, okay? I don't know how to do any of this shit."

Annika shakes her head as she leans over him, setting up the computer with an adoring smile.

Tāne's chuckle is hardly contained, his shoulders shaking as he runs wide fingers through his bountiful, long curls. "It's alright, bro. It'll be even more worth it for me when I successfully kick your ass *and* run my own tech."

Viktor barks out a laugh. "Shut up."

Waimārie smiles at me, but when I turn to Noah, his eyebrows are knit.

I slide my hand into his. *What's going through your mind, love?*

Noah huffs. His eyes lift to the screen, glaring as a massive list of names appears. *That. I've been dreading this list.*

Every muscle in me tightens. Noah mentioned a handful of trusted allies were joining us in collecting a list of names of violent, Alpha-domination-leaning Lycans they've encountered, and we'd review our findings at the Summit.

But our combined list can't be this long… Can it?

As Viktor scrolls, the list stretches on and on, each subsequent page stifling my breath. Just like Noah's list, it starts off in the red zone, the most dangerous names like "Mason Hart" littering the page—many of them with locations "Unknown." Then there are active participants in the yellow zone: names of traitorous pack members who were actively hateful enough to leave us for Alpha-domination packs, such as Mason's crew of followers. The gray zone is the largest, filled with wolves that *might* be involved, but none of us could prove it. I wish that could provide some hope, but I advised Noah to come up with a set of qualifying rules, including at least one report of verbal or physical violence.

Which means *everyone* listed has acted on their Omega-hating beliefs, in one way or another.

Viktor speaks low to Annika in Swedish, pointing at the end of the list. They add three additional names from this morning.

The room falls eerily silent, not even Tāne daring to speak a single word. As we stare in solemn silence at our King and Queen Lycans, Annika meets my eyes, giving me a somber, aching smile.

All I can do is shake my head in horror.

"Alright, we've already banned everyone from the Summit who's in the red zone. Which leaders will be here tomorrow from the yellow and gray zones?" Noah asks.

Annika opens a second tab, pulling up a far shorter list of names: a mere thirty-two. I want to loosen my stomach enough to exhale, but I wrap my arms tighter around our growing baby on instinct: these Alphas are all qualified as dangerous pack *leaders*. How many Lycans follow them?

The Alphas get to work, highlighting names of Alphas they

consider a serious threat in the upcoming Summit battles. Since Viktor is King Alpha this year, he gets to decide who fights who, so we split the worst offenders amongst Noah, Viktor, Tāne, and a few of each Alpha's other closest allies.

Waimārie takes Noah's seat beside me, leaning in close with the softest, kindest smile. "Luna, we're here with you."

I bite my lip, struggling not to plummet into deeper fear. "Am I catastrophizing, or is it as bad as it feels?"

Waimārie doesn't answer right away. I glance across the room at Annika for answers, but her eyebrows warp, threatening tears.

I drop my chin; I can't bear to look, knowing Annika experienced something deep and dark in connection to this as well. As Noah's emotions fluctuate between anger and horror, I close my eyes, slowing my breath. I want to be here to protect Noah from this. But as my hand covers my belly, guilt burns like acid down my limbs. Was it wrong of us to try for this baby amidst all this? Not only am I putting them in danger, but I'm also not in an optimal state to protect Noah.

At this thought, my wolf tenses in our bond, snarling fiercely. I blink a few times, startled by her intensity. I've never felt her defy me so greatly before, but her message was clear: *we're not backing down from this fight. Especially not now.*

But I want to protect her too. She went through hell with me, all while I was denying her presence inside my heart.

Viktor clears his throat, struggling to keep his volume down with how deep his voice is. But as Annika turns to him, I'm startled to find Viktor's eyes on me.

They flit away, returning to Noah. With my wolf on high alert, and the help of reading Noah's lips, my hearing heightens, allowing me to catch something I'm not sure I was meant to hear: *strongest wolf... pregnant.*

That's all I manage to catch.

A memory comes to mind that I nearly forgot; Noah mentioned his strongest Alpha once before. Outside of Celestial Couture, Mason claimed he was leaving Greenfield alongside "our strongest Alphas," and Noah mocked him for it. I still have no idea who Noah's strongest Alpha is, and I forgot to ask at the time, terror taking precedence as Mason stalked us.

Are they discussing the same "strongest wolf?" Maybe they're also discussing the dangers of this situation, considering my pregnancy? Or maybe Noah's strongest wolf, Yasmine, is different from his strongest *Alpha*, and they're just talking about Yas after all. But what if Noah has some hidden Alpha assassin we haven't talked about, and this wolf happens to be pregnant right now too?

Noah claimed Mason knows Greenfield's next strongest Alpha—Noah takes first place, of course. But what else was it that Noah said that day? It was something Mason didn't like.

My chest tightens as it all comes flooding back. That's right; Noah claimed Mason not only knows our strongest Alpha, but also would never admit it.

Was that because they're an Alpha woman, or a non-binary or transmasculine Alpha carrying a pup?

But who else is also pregnant that we know?

I can't think of a single other person. The more I rack my brain, the angrier I become: why is Noah keeping this wolf so private, anyway? In terms of his personal life and traumas, that's one thing. But we just had a discussion about this. With that threatening list looming above our heads on the projector screen, this sounds like crucial information for our survival.

What if I'm wrong? What if Noah is another man who has used manipulative tactics on me, and I didn't notice—again?

"Who are you talking about?" I ask.

Noah's eyes zip to mine. The whole room falls silent. Everyone glances from me to Noah, awaiting his response.

But Noah doesn't flinch; his gaze remains locked onto mine. "I'm sure you've heard us joking about 'mother wolves,' but it's not actually a joke. Pregnant wolves are often feared by how strong they become to protect our pups. You're a powerful figurehead, so while we've been concerned you could be a target while pregnant, it's also possible they'll be even more intimidated by you if they happen to find out you're pregnant."

I tighten in defense, my nails digging into my palms. "So you're talking about me? But you were whispering about your strongest wolf as well, so is there something that I don't know?"

"There isn't anything you don't know, we're just talking quietly to reduce everyone's stress. But—" Noah's mouth opens, then closes. "This is a big misunderstanding."

Viktor's eyes widen. His fleeting glance at Tāne ticks my anger up a notch.

My frustration rises, but I mindlink Noah, not wanting to embarrass him. *Are you sure you're not whispering because it's something secretive? Is your strongest wolf different from your strongest Alpha that you mentioned to Mason? I don't know them either.*

They're all the same person. And it's not a big secret: I've told you the truth, many times. But maybe not directly enough, Noah mindlinks.

My heartbeat gallops. *I don't get it. Please, just tell me clearly.*

I will, but I don't think it's fair of me to rub it in constantly, and this misunderstanding is making it sound even worse. I just didn't want to make you even more uncomfortable. I know how much pressure it is to be viewed like this, and it's not like you can control it. But I forgot about the Alpha thing I said to scare Mason. I didn't realize how fucked up that was for me to blurt out in the heat of the moment, and I'm really sorry. You're an Omega, even if you have an Alpha side, and I know that. I won't assume otherwise unless you tell me.

I shuffle where I stand, my cheeks flaring hot. *Wait, you're talking about* me? *No.*

Noah's shoulders stiffen. *I would be pissed in your position too. I really shouldn't have phrased it like that to Mason, especially not in front of so many others. But that doesn't change the truth about—*

No, it's not even the Alpha thing. Mason hates Omegas and could never see us as strong as any Alpha, so I'd do the same thing. I'd summarize my occasional Alpha-ness as full Alpha-ness just to shut that asshole up—if only that 'strongest' label you tacked on were anywhere near true. That's the problem. You're glorifying something that doesn't exist in me.

Noah doesn't move. He continues to challenge my staredown, not daring to back down. *I disagree.*

Oh, my God. He's serious.

I grit my teeth. *It can't be me.*

Noah's chest tightens. *Why not?*

No, this is ridiculous. You have to be mocking me.

Mocking you? I'm not the one mocking your strength right now. I'd never, not once in a million years, categorize you as 'weak,' Aliya.

My chest puffs. *Then I disagree too. This makes no sense.*

When Noah's jaw ticks, I'm tempted to let out a genuine growl, my wolf edging to the surface with my rising frustration. But as a wave of hurt pummels both sides of our bond, my chest cavity stings.

Viktor's brows furrow, glancing between Noah and me. "Uh… Should we step out?"

Fuck. I didn't realize it, but my Alpha musk has been creeping from my scent glands, forcing wary stares out of our Luna allies.

Wait, no—out of *everyone*. Viktor and Tāne eye me just as closely as they eye Noah.

What the hell is happening?

Gritting my teeth, I try my best to stay centered, quieting my scent. But I can't help it; my eyes burn hot at how frustrated I am, replacing my furious Alpha musk with a hint of terrified urgency.

But as Noah fidgets, gripping his palm at the front of the room, his puppy-dog stare pulls at my heartstrings, loosening my wound shoulders.

"Can we talk? Outside?" he mutters.

I sigh. "Sure. Sorry."

As I step away from the table, I wobble a little—my knees quivering beyond my control in response to any and all conflict. Noah freezes, eyeing me closely. When I regain my balance, straightening my back and striding for the door, Noah drops his gaze, holding the door open for me to step out.

My heart pounds into my ears. I don't know why I'm so upset, I just know I don't like how this is going. Not only how Noah didn't tell me what he's decided to be true about me, but this is only a day after I discovered he neglected to mention this "King" debate with Viktor, adding insult to injury.

But with the workload we have left to accomplish, we better sort this out as soon as we can. I stop only a few steps into the hallway, facing Noah's wide-eyed stare. "Overpromising what I can do is not safe for any of us. What if I can't protect everyone, but they're trusting me now, all because of what you're claiming about me?"

"Aliya, can we take a step back?"

"No." I fight back panic, my chest rising. "I'm not dropping my upset for others anymore."

Softening his features, Noah lowers his voice. "I know. I won't ask you to, okay? I know I fucked this conversation up, so let's just take a second to reset ourselves. I don't feel like you're sounding like yourself."

I grip my forehead, my heartbeat frantic. "Oh, God. I'm fighting with you like you're him, aren't I?"

But Noah reaches for me, and that's all the invitation I need; I cling to him, desperate to be by his side again.

"You're okay, sweet Omega. We're okay. I'm still here with you, just like you reminded me last night."

As Noah wraps his arms around me, I suck in rapid, shaky inhales as the true depth of my emotions come crashing in, stinging my heart with an icy vengeance.

"Shit, I'm so sorry, Noah. I know you're not my enemy, but I don't want to be wrong about someone I love again. The second I thought about losing the honest person I know in you, I got so scared. I overreacted, jumped to conclusions, and—"

"Hey, hey, don't explain yourself. Like we talked about, it's not right of me to keep important information from you. And I want you to feel like you have room to stand up for yourself, even around me. I'm proud of you." Noah strokes my head as I quiver in his arms. "It's going to be okay. We're going to talk through this, okay? You can be upset with me."

"I don't like being upset with you," I whisper. "Why didn't you talk about this with me directly first?"

Noah slumps. "I didn't do it on purpose. I didn't realize it wasn't clear enough to you, and I thought you were already under so much pressure to begin with."

I groan. "Avoiding it like it's a secret won't help."

Noah leans back, looking me in the eyes. "There aren't any secrets here. It would be weird of me to go around, declaring you my strongest wolf. I don't have to declare that Yasmine or Dave are strong, so why do I have to declare that about you? Just because you're an Omega? Plus, I already kind of did announce that you're my strongest wolf. Why do you think you're running this pack with me?"

My jaw drops. I gaze into Noah's eyes, waiting for the punchline.

But Noah's expression warps into sadness, a fresh, stabbing pain rippling through our bond. "Who's been telling you you're weak? Do you really believe that about yourself?"

I step back from him, gripping my arms. "I don't feel like we're talking about the same person—especially not after seeing you, Viktor, and Tāne making that huge room feel so small. Not only are you all two or three times bigger than me in size, but I'm not like you guys at all. I don't fight well, and I don't want to, whereas you're all batting at each other playfully like it's nothing. What if I'm just a sad copycat of an Omega or Alpha? I'm not even a full Lycan."

Noah's expression hardens. "You *are* a Lycan. *And* you're a human. They don't cancel each other out."

I drop my head, pain striking my gut.

Stepping closer, Noah lowers his voice. "Are you sure there isn't anyone telling you these horrible things? My mom?"

"No, no, I just—" I swallow hard, my eyes stinging hot. "I just figured, that's probably what everyone still thinks of me, right? Beneath the surface? And who am I to come in here, suddenly acting like I have power? Who am I to think I'm good enough for any of this?"

Huffing out each word, I gaze deep into Noah's eyes. He stares back, his fierce stare not giving me an inch of room to continue disparaging myself.

"So you're defending yourself from others' abuse in advance—committing it for them in the hopes they'll spare you."

His words strike deep into my core. My wolf shudders, enraptured by him. But even my wolf feels disconnected from me, unsure where she stands to exist.

"How did you put that into words so well?" I whisper.

Noah's eyes soften. "We're not too different at heart, my love."

Dropping my head, I blow out a slow, pained breath. I can't bear the thought of Noah perpetrating his own hurt in advance to protect himself, but it's true: I see it in the way he treats his wolf.

And in the way I treat myself.

"What do you think a true pack leader looks like?" Noah mutters. "It's not a quiz, I'm asking for your honest opinion."

Furrowing my brows, I study the uneven, old tile beneath our feet, tracing my thoughts. "Historically, an Alpha man has almost always been in power, right? But morally, hypothetically? I'd hope—"

My chest tightens as I dare to dream, afraid it'll only raise my hopes to fall that much harder. But as Noah stands here with me, shouldering the discomfort alongside me, I whisper my thoughts—even if they might sound cheesy.

"I'd hope they were someone who loves their pack so fiercely, they'd do anything in their power to improve their lives and safety."

Noah hums. "Everything *in their power*. Not everything in the world."

I swallow hard, lifting my gaze. Noah gives me a soft, somber smile, taking my hand.

But I can't accept this. "So you think I'm just not giving myself enough credit? But that's not what we're really talking about, here."

Noah nods. "We're talking about strength. And do you know what stood out to me about what you just said?"

I furrow my eyebrows. "Someone who loves their pack fiercely? I agree, that's important, of course. And I know you guys like to tell me I'm good at that. But when it comes to you calling someone your 'strongest wolf,' aren't we talking about physical strength?"

"Partially. And you have a lot of it. But that's not *all* of what I'm talking about. Not with Lycans."

I bite back tears, unable to stop my voice from quivering. "So this is another cultural thing I don't understand?"

"No, this is something I think applies to humans too. All species." Cupping my cheek, Noah catches my tears with his thumb as I growl, annoyed with myself. "Do you want a leader who thinks they're invincible? One who lives to prove themself as the strongest in the world?"

I swallow hard, thinking about someone I know like that. The person who comes to mind bitters my throat, forcing me to swallow hard. "No. Not at all."

Noah slides his hand down my jaw, cupping his palm over my mark. "Me neither. What if true strength came from someone willing to question herself, no matter how powerful she is? What if she's someone who loves so deeply that she's afraid she could never measure up to protect the people she vowed to protect—and yet she still shows up. What if she even shows up to one of the most terrifying meetings of her life, shaking where she stands, in order to save a world she didn't even grow up included in, all while knowing she'll probably never get recognition for it in a world made for Alphas, not Omegas?"

My breath catches in an attempt to hold myself together, but I can't help it; tears stream down my cheeks. Noah's words hit deep in my soul—from a trauma standpoint, a grief standpoint, and so much more. How deeply I've longed to be a part of a community like this, to the point where I'm willing to uninvite myself before anyone has a chance to—otherwise, it'd hurt too much to bear.

But I also couldn't see myself giving up on our pack, even if they didn't want me here. I just happened to be Noah's fated mate.

My voice comes out shattered. "Wouldn't other people do this in my position?"

"You and I both know they wouldn't." Noah gives me a sad smile. The second I see the pain behind it, I hitch through a harder sob. "We've had horrible, awful examples we'll never forget that prove it… And yet you still show up."

"You're right," I whisper.

"I don't want to speak for you, so you can absolutely tell me I'm wrong. But from what I can feel in your heart, I think you're just so in love with our fellow wolves that the thought of failing them terrifies you. Which is why I never, ever, intended to put more pressure on you than I thought necessary by drilling it in your head that you *have* to be the strongest—because honestly, Aliya, you don't need anyone to instruct you to stand up for us. You're the type of wolf to just do it. But at the same time, I absolutely *will* tell our allies where your heart is, because whether you mean to or not, your wolf stops even seasoned, powerful leaders like Tāne and Viktor in their tracks, inspiring them to look at you, hear you, whenever you speak—providing a beacon of hope for their survival, no matter how petrified you are. *That* is raw fucking strength."

I suck in a sharp breath, their earnest stares returning to my mind. I hadn't realized it, but maybe Noah is right about how warped I still have the order of things: when I envision a leader, I still picture someone slamming their subordinates into submission, claiming their dominance. But that's not what I want in a leader, at all.

What if there was another way? What if, together, Noah and I can create something new?

Swallowing hard, I grip Noah's hand on my cheek, tugging it to my pounding heart. "Goddess, you're freaking me out. I want a new reality for us, so badly. And you think we—" My voice tightens, afraid to admit my thoughts out loud. "You think we can actually make a difference? That I have some say in our future?"

Noah breaks into a genuine smile—wide enough to crease his cheeks. I huff, hugging his hand tighter to my chest.

"Seriously, Noah. You don't think I'll fail you all somehow? Let everyone down, possibly at the cost of their lives?"

He laughs. "Those are questions I ask myself every day, my love. And I'm so sorry to say it, but I don't have the answers. I think we just have to keep doing what we can to help, even if we end up failing at it. Which we probably will."

I shut my eyes, blowing out a slow breath. "You're right. And facing that possibility, even while you come home to me every night, hurt and scared, has made you the best leader for us."

"And you."

My heart flips. Tugging my forehead to his lips, Noah lets out a soft sigh, his breath ruffling my hair. I inhale his sweet, soothing scent as he soaks me in it, leaving me in a cozy warmth.

"I want to be better at it, though. More confident," I whisper. "For myself too."

Giving my forehead a last, punctuating kiss, Noah sighs. "I know. I feel the same about myself, always. And I know reassurance is an OCD nightmare for you, but I need you to know that I didn't promise anyone you can take them all down in battle in my stead or something, okay?"

Breaking into a smile, I groan. "Okay, okay. Maybe that was a bit extreme of me to assume."

"No, I get it. Like I said, I completely fucked this up. And I learned my lesson too: I won't keep my thoughts about you from you anymore, even if it's a lot of fucking pressure on you. All you have to do is to continue believing in your wolf, and giving yourself more credit. Can you try that for me? For yourself?"

Nodding, I press Noah's hand to my belly, unable to fully feel sure of myself yet, no matter how badly I crave it.

But Noah grins, barely suppressing a giggle. "You're badass enough just standing here, but I've gotta admit; they're lucky they don't have to face off with your wolf. We'd need to hire a team of extra medics."

I groan. "Alright, alright, sure. Let's just go back inside and try to figure this out."

Laughing, Noah follows after me, his hand on my shoulder reminding me he has my back too. A small, delighted piece of me perks up from Noah's words, desperate to be the one he leans on, especially with the unwavering, gorgeous strength I witness in him every day—a sturdiness in his heart that keeps me rooted in the earth. Maybe it's selfish, but I want Noah to be right about me. To be seen as strong enough to be his grounding force too, even when I feel my most vulnerable.

15

Tonight marks the Alpha Summit's official first day. Nerves course through me, souring my appetite.

Fetching a silvery, beaded cocktail dress to complement my moonstone necklace, I shimmy into the fitted fabric, having to tug it down a lot harder than I expected to with my expanding waistline. But when I turn to the mirror to finish tidying my appearance, I gasp at what's reflected back.

"Um, Noah?"

Noah pokes his head into the bathroom, straightening his tie. "What's wrong?"

I cover my breasts just in time, my eyes wide as Noah meets my gaze in the mirror.

When he steps into the bathroom, furrowing his eyebrows, I swallow hard as I get a full look at my mate. Of course, Noah's about to give me a heart attack with how classy he looks, his dark, disheveled hair accentuating his polished black suit.

But as Noah blinks a few times, taking a good, long look at me, I turn red hot. "I'm— Um— Not quite fitting in this, anymore."

Turning toward him, I lower my palms, revealing the front of my low cut dress. The deep V-neck stops at the base of my sternum. Its silvery fabric is designed to frame the outer halves of my chest without a bra, the back sloping into a low arc.

Except I'm spilling out the front of it, my nipples peeking past the fabric strapped over them.

Noah's eyebrows lower—curiosity dissolving into a serious focus. It's doing nothing to stave off the building heat in my belly from having his smoldering eyes all over me.

"Fuck, well, that's— Hmm." Noah's Adam's Apple bobs sharply before it glides back down, just like his eyes drifting down my form. As his gaze sweeps back up me, I swear I feel it tingling over my skin.

His quiet focus stirs my heart into overwhelm. Then I smell it: a sharp, hungry Alpha musk stings my eyes, forcing me to blink through its mouth-watering spices.

I fidget with my wide dress straps, tugging the fabric inward as I attempt to ignore the sudden throbbing between my legs. Noah clears his throat, his ever-alert wolf eyes catching on every minor movement.

"Well, what if—" He attempts to pull the fabric over the outer slope of my breasts, but I suck in a tight breath, squirming away from how sensitive I've become.

Noah freezes. Without lifting his chin, his gaze flickers up to mine, and my belly lurches through the sharp thrill it gives me; the second his eyes flash green, his Alpha musk returns even stronger.

His soft voice comes out deep enough to buzz through my chest. "I'll be gentler, yeah?"

Slipping a finger beneath the edge of the fabric at my cleavage, Noah tugs the straps inward until they no longer cup my chest. Repositioning them like wide panels of fabric down the middle to cover my nipples, Noah exposes my side boob as a trade off.

"There," he mutters.

I swallow hard. His hands roam low on my waist, skating over my hips before he steps back—his fingers lingering until he can't reach, like he doesn't want to let me go.

Except I can feel he really doesn't. Our bond pulses with heavier desire by the second, spiking higher each time I meet his ravenous stare. Noah and I both know we're running out of time before dinner, otherwise this pull in our bond would make me ask him if he'd like to drop everything we've planned to mate each other senseless. I fist the back of my long skirt, debating if I should turn around, hoist the fabric up and over my hips, and ask Noah to mate me anyway.

No, Aliya. You're about to meet the top Lycan leaders in the entire *world*. We can have sex later.

Forcing myself to flip around and face the mirror, I'm startled by how breathless I look—lips parted beneath rosy cheeks. Noah's hands station themselves back at my waist, closing the distance between us. But with his presence comes a heavier dose of his scent.

Heat builds in my core, my body calling out in response to his pheromones.

I can't help it; I rub my knees together, craving his affection.

"Hey." Noah's voice is sharp, no matter how quiet.

I grip the icy marble countertop, meeting his eyes in the mirror. "Yes, Alpha?"

"We only have twenty minutes, but you're squirming."

"I know," I whisper.

A flash of excitement moves through Noah's eyes. When he speaks, his voice is even gentler, but it's far rougher around the edges, morphing into a rumble. "I don't have time to do what I've wanted to do to you the second I saw you in this dress. Which, no, does not fit."

Staring into his eyes, my Alpha side surges forward, loving Noah's unspoken dare to squirm *more*.

We've teased each other back and forth like this more and more lately, mainly when our Alpha sides are both present. And as I tremble with excitement under Noah's stare, I think I was right; his Alpha side is even wilder now that I topped his Omega side, his confidence thriving.

So I stand up straighter, removing myself from his arms and making him think I'm cutting our playtime short. Like the sweetheart he is, he silently follows my lead, stepping away to respect my consent.

But I turn side to side, analyzing my swollen chest in the mirror with gentle caresses down my now-exposed side boob.

"Well, this is what I'll have to wear, then. So you think a little more skin showing on the side is better?"

Noah blinks a few times, his eyes widening as I shove myself back into the halter, propping up my breasts so they're spilling out the center again.

"And not this, right?" Straining to keep a straight face, I stare Noah dead in the eyes.

Stark, yellow irises stare back.

I break into devious giggles, my chest bubbling with excitement at the sight of his hunting stare. Noah's cheeks rise with a sly, eager grin, but he doesn't waste a second as I lift my foot to escape him; just before I dash from the bathroom to tease him further, Noah catches me in a hug.

"*Naughty* little wolf." Purring against my mark, Noah nips a laughing yelp from me. When he straightens to gaze at me in the mirror again, I snuggle back into his arms, dousing his dress shirt with my scent as delighted pheromones escape my neck from his affections.

Meeting his eyes in the mirror, I soften my voice. "Twenty minutes might be enough for what *I* wish I could do with you, my sweet Alpha. I think I could make you squirm much harder than I am."

Noah's stare loses its airy playfulness, replaced by a determination that shocks heavy giggles out of me. "Then I'll make you come twice in thirty."

I sputter out a laugh. "Noah!"

He chuckles, planting hard, punctuating kisses over my cheeks until I'm laughing even harder. "Oh, I'm not kidding. All my instincts point to pleasing my pregnant Luna, so everyone will just have to meet without us."

I freeze, startled by the eagerness in his stare. Any second now, I'm expecting him to bend me over the sink for quick, rough sex.

But the next time Noah moves, his touch is slow and calculated. Wide palms skate beneath my arms, Noah's pointer finger inching up my cleavage until I gasp.

Noah grins wider. "You're dying to know what I was picturing when you teased me like that, aren't you?"

I can't respond; Noah's fingertips glide over my nipples, sending a tingling shockwave across my torso. I try to moan, but the sound is cut off as I shudder hard, jerking back into Noah's chest. A hot, solid erection presses against my lower back, and I rub against it, unable to hold still against Noah's touch.

Noah's low, purring growl builds a fire in my belly. I reach over my head to cling to his sturdy shoulder, doing my best to hold myself up despite my knees dipping as he teases my breasts faster. Fluid trickles into my panties as my core flutters in preparation for him.

"On one hand, I could still do what I wanted to when I first saw you in this." Sliding the fabric just a touch further, Noah pops my left nipple from my dress. With easier access, his fingertips swirl faster. Sharp bursts of sensation build with each circle he makes, my nerves buzzing strongly enough for me to writhe beneath his teasing—until I can't take it anymore, gripping his hands to freeze them in place.

As I pant, trembling through each hard breath, Noah's grin softens into a yearning stare. I swallow hard, my pounding heart pumping heavier blood flow between my thighs. Noah's shaft prods me in the back, as if in response to my urgency.

Pulling my dress straps back up and over my nipples, Noah exposes the sides of my breasts again. "But now that we've tested out this quick fix, there's a lot more I could do without overstimulating you. I don't even have to undress you."

All ten of my fingertips grip the marble countertop, anticipation boiling in my core. Noah leans over me, smoothing hot palms around my swollen belly before swooping back up my hips.

On instinct, I bend over. Stretching up on my toes, I try my best to reach his throbbing shaft through his slacks, my ass rubbing up against him as my wolf begs me to present myself for mating. Losing his calm coolness, Noah huffs out a harsh breath, his hips jerking against me as one wide palm grips my lower back.

Noah hugs me around my shoulders, lifting my chest. One hand holds my hips tight to his as the other releases my shoulders, dragging down my sternum—until he scoops my breast into his palm.

Dragging his lips down my shoulder, Noah exhales his hot breath over my exposed skin. I let out a soft moan, urging his cupping hand to squeeze my breast a little tighter. When he gives in to my request, my skin plump between his thick fingers, I tremble at the heavy, massaging pleasure he pulses through my torso with each soft squeeze.

As Noah plants soft kisses over the outer curve of my breast, licking and nipping my side boob, I can't help but let out a needy whine. By this point, he's drowning me in his horny scent, and

I can hardly stand how heavily my clit has swollen—aroused until it aches.

And Noah hasn't even touched me below my waist. My mouth parts through my airy breaths as my pussy flexes urgently; I can't stop picturing how heavily we'll mate in mere minutes, loving the spontaneity of this moment.

Noah's gaze zips to mine in the mirror, his wolf shining through their focused intensity. "I've got you, sweet Omega. Back up so your cute little belly doesn't bump the countertop while we have our fun."

"Like this?" Grinning, I shimmy back until my ass falls flush against his hips.

Noah chuckles. "That's my good girl. Now lean your weight against the counter and relax, please."

Easing onto my forearms, I flinch as my exposed breasts bump the chilly marble. But my focus is quickly brought lower; my thigh muscles flex as Noah grasps handfuls of my skirt, pooling it up and over my waist. He shoves my skirt far up my back, his hands smoothing over my skin as I bend over deeper in a wolflike stretch.

"Beautiful," Noah whispers, his hands limbering up my muscles with luxurious, deep massages along my arched spine. "That's my girl. Keep feeling into your instincts for me."

My claws extend on their own, urged out by Noah's purred praise. I'm overwhelmed by how pleased my wolf is; I don't think I've felt this taken by Noah in a while—not with how sick I've felt lately—but now I can't seem to stop letting him see more of my primal, wolf-y behaviors. Especially when he reacts to them. Notices them, and encourages me to be more like me.

Nuzzling my face in my folded arms on the countertop, I flush red hot as I purr along with him. Noah drops his slacks to the floor with a clatter of his belt. My back arches at the sound, lifting my ass higher in the air.

Kissing up my spine, Noah purrs between my shoulder blades. "Gorgeous, gorgeous Omega. You smell so beautiful, my love."

"*Noah,*" I breathe beneath the cover of my arms. "You're too sweet to me."

"Good," he whispers, caressing me all over.

By now, I can hardly stand him hovering behind me without rubbing up on me. But I don't know how to reach him in this position—not unless he stoops low for me, like he does when he's rutting. If he wasn't so tall, it'd be easier to have sex like this without him having to bend so deeply, and while I'm also forced to lift myself higher on my toes.

But as I prod him with my ass, his boxers work in my favor today, pinning his cock at the perfect height to nudge my core. I suck in a tight breath, loving how warm he feels between my legs. When I push myself back a little heavier, rubbing the soaked core of my panties against his tip through his tented boxers, Noah hisses.

"Fuck— Hang on, I was about to—" Noah's hands roam up and down my sides, his hips bucking against my urgent rubbing until his shaft glides between my labia through our underwear.

Noah lets out a genuine growl this time, but to my dismay, his hips disappear from behind my raised ass.

Lifting my head, I try to control the disappointment in my expression, but I can't; I watch in the mirror as my eyebrows contort in distress, my lips parting in complaint.

But in the reflection, Noah's devious grin returns behind me. I don't have time to contemplate why; thick fingers shove the clingy, soaked core of my panties to the side. They rub wide, slick circles through my wet labia, blurring my head with the pleasure he swirls up my abdomen. I let out a louder moan than I mean to, my hips rocking in time with the wet sounds he's producing between us.

Embarrassment seeps through me before I can prevent it from flooding our bond; my volume caught my attention in the mirror. I take a better look at myself quivering over Noah's fingers, quieting myself in the process from how raw it feels to watch myself enjoy his touch.

But Noah growls through his purr. "Don't think. Keep letting yourself be all instinct."

Huffing out sharp breaths, I settle my burning forehead against the marble countertop, spreading my knees wider to allow Noah easier, deeper access to my pussy. To my delight, Noah's fingers slip in and out of me, gathering lubrication to lather every inch of the sensitive skin between my legs.

I don't care if he's making a mess of me; I let out a shuddering moan, unable to fully process how loving of a deep massage he's already giving me. With each swoop in and out of me, thick fingers splay my pussy wider, opening me up before sliding back out, treating my clit with wet, focused swirls of his fingertips. Each time he repeats this cycle, my pleasure heightens. By the time his fingers push far enough inside me to knead against my G-spot, Noah pressing slow and deep against the front wall of my pussy, I'm a sputtering, gasping mess, my calves aching with my desperation to stretch higher on my toes.

But my wolf growls through me.

Noah meets my eyes in the mirror, his lips parted in pleasure as he toys with me. "What's wrong? Are two fingers not thick enough?"

My eyelids flutter as he sticks three fingers deeper inside me, widening the space between them to gently stretch me. I groan, my thighs quivering, and Noah purrs.

"Was that what you wanted?"

As Noah works my G-spot deeper, harder, all I can do is shake my head, groaning at how tenderly he's stroking the absolute depths of me. *You're not enjoying yourself alongside me.*

Noah lifts one eyebrow, his grin returning through his heavy-lidded stare. "I'm not enjoying myself, am I?"

Stepping to the side of my hips, Noah reveals his throbbing cock in the mirror. It's grown so large that it's poking out from the stretched leg of his boxers, every flex revealing how dark pink and swollen his tip has become. My mouth waters; the vanity light above the bathroom mirror glimmers along his tip as it shines with precum, dripping down the base of his shaft.

I grit my teeth, staving back a heavy moan. "Maybe you're enjoying the view. But you want to mate me, hard. I can smell it. Why aren't you, Alpha?"

Noah huffs. "Because you're releasing such a fucking delicious scent that you've made me swell to the point where it almost hurts. I'm worried about hurting you too if I don't properly prepare you."

I'm stunned speechless.

Noah knows it. Revealing a flash of his incisors with his teasing smile, Noah grips my hip in one hand, dropping my jaw as he pulses faster against my G-spot while his thumb presses down on my clit in rhythm. I sputter through each breath, moaning with every dip of my knees.

I can't believe how sensitive he's made me. With every few pulses, he repeats the rhythmic cycle he's created—pulling his hand out of me, teasing my clit until a bundle of pressure forms between my thighs, then diving back in. Each time his fingers re-enter me, he applies faster and faster pressure to my inner walls—until I let out a hearty cry. He's stroking my deepest nerves, moving far beyond "preparing" me. My hips lurch higher, begging for more. Noah pumps hard and fast into me, stirring my breath into a startlingly rapid urgency. That familiar feeling of fluid builds in my pussy, aching to be expressed.

But I don't squirt, stuck on the edge; Noah chooses this moment to slow down, allowing me to quiver against the countertop as I catch my breath through his soft, steady strokes.

By now, he's made me soak my own thighs. Noah slips his boxers off with his free hand, stepping out of them behind me. My inner muscles clench hard over his fingertips, begging him to enter me. I widen my knees, but the elastic of my panties digs deep into my thigh, restricting me from opening myself up to him further. I'm forced to settle back down with a groan.

"Am I frustrating you, sweet Omega?" My mate smiles, knowing what he's doing to me. He inhales a lungful of my desperate scent, his irises bright golden as they challenge my staredown, but I don't let him speak another word.

Before my gorgeous mate can tease me further, my wolf growls through me. "I asked you to stop holding yourself back for me."

Noah blinks a few times, inhaling my eruption of Alpha musk before regaining his cool. Except now that he's gazing at me through serious, heavy-lidded eyes, my heart lurches into my throat.

"I see. I thought you were worried about my annoying dick nudging you to enter you too early, so I was trying to keep you enjoying yourself instead of worrying about me. But it seems like I read you wrong."

I can hardly gasp as he slips his fingers out of me, my knees dipping at the sudden emptiness in my core. As I tremble in a heap against the counter, Noah slips my panties off my hips, letting them fall over the tops of my feet.

"So, when you told me to mate you hard like *I* wanted to, was that actually a request of what *you* wanted, my feisty Alpha?"

My cheeks burn hot in the mirror. I lose the battle to bite back a smile as Noah rubs his shaft against my soaked core, stirring me back into overwhelm. My pussy flexes urgently, my teeth releasing my lips as they part in pleasure.

"Maybe," I breathe.

Noah hums, his smile widening. "Why didn't you tell me directly? I'd rather not have to guess what you want, even though I try."

My heart sinks. "You're right. I'm sorry."

Sweeping his hands over me, Noah is suddenly so soft with me that I'm tempted to turn away, embarrassed. But he draws me close, his heart aching with me. "Don't be sorry, my sweet Luna. But I think you still need to get clearer with me tonight since I'm not understanding. So, tell me what you want, and I'd be happy to do it how you'd like."

My heart pounds into my ears as I stare up at him, our lips ghosting over each other as our eyes remain locked. I grip his suit jacket, my breath heightening as warmth pools far deeper into my core—I might be uncomfortable with how I just acted, but Noah presented a true challenge for me just now, and now that I'm facing it, I absolutely *love* it.

"Be rougher with me," I whisper against his lips. "I miss it, and I don't want you to think I'm fragile now that you got me pregnant with your huge wolf baby."

Noah hums. "I have a lot of thoughts about that, my very not-fragile mate. But for now, by rough, do you mean you want me to be rough with my hips once I work you up, or to be rougher with your whole body—minus Little Wolf, of course."

My heart flips, anticipatory anxiety spiking its beat into my ears. "My whole body."

"Good girl." His deep whisper comes out more like a growl. "Is that a request from my sweet Omega? Or was it my grumpy little Alpha speaking, so it's more correct to call it an *order*? An order to mate you rough and hard—until your moans morph into yells again."

I'm not smiling anymore. Noah stares so closely that my wolf bristles, overcome by goosebumps beneath her fur. My feet shuffle as I breathe faster, my core empty and craving him.

"If it's something you want to do too, then—"

"It is." Noah's rapid declaration swells my lungs.

Staring him straight in the eyes, I whisper, "Then it's an order."

To my surprise, he still doesn't explode into action. Breaking into a fanged smile, Noah sends chills racing down my spine. He releases my hips, smoothing his hands over my back. "Alright, Alpha. I need you to relax as much as you can for me."

Excitement grips my heart. I loosen my shoulders over the countertop, lifting my ass higher in preparation for Noah's entry. But as he slips a hot palm behind my right thigh instead, I meet his eyes in the mirror again, startled.

"Tell me if this position still feels comfortable for you with that cute pup belly, gorgeous," Noah murmurs.

My heart races as I allow him to lift my knee on top of the counter, forcing my left foot to stretch higher on my toes.

"It's fine," I shakily whisper.

"*Good*," Noah hums, spreading my labia wider with his fingertips until I moan.

My breath picks up the pace as I brace my hands against the countertop. Keeping our baby far from the cabinet, I shudder as Noah trades his fingers for his cock, nudging a whimper from my lips. He swirls his leaking tip around my core, fluttering my eyelids.

But when I meet our reflection in the mirror once more, sensing him moving my hair off my back, I freeze at what I find.

Noah wraps my thick, long ponytail around his hand. I suck in a tight gasp as he glides his tip into my pussy—just before he softly tugs my head back.

Crying out, I shove my hips back, gripping my raised thigh to open up further for him. Noah seats himself deep inside me with one slow push, breaching my pelvic opening with a delicious flood of pressure in my core. He groans with me, his breath beating against my exposed back as he arches in delight.

"Relax for me more." Noah's rough purr coats my skin in goosebumps, my nipples hardening against the cool countertop. "Right here."

Massaging the outer edges of my pussy, right where he's stuffing me full, Noah urges a heavy whimper from me, tightening my inner muscles harder over his engorged length instead of relaxing me to allow him in deeper. Closing my eyes, I melt at Noah's soft rubs between my legs, smushing my cheek against the counter as he gives my hair another delicious, massaging tug.

We wait a few more seconds for my core muscles to loosen, my back relaxing into a deeper arch as Noah strokes down my spine like he's petting me from head to tail, washing my torso in fuzzy comfort. The more he caresses me, the wider my pussy blooms, giving his tip soft squeezes along the way until his breath deepens with pleasure. As soon as I loosen my grip on him enough, Noah grabs my ass to spread me wider, allowing himself to push further—until his thick shaft ignites pleasure up my spine, rubbing against the G-spot he worked earlier.

I groan when my ass finally presses against his hips—Noah fully immersed in me. "*Oh,* my God—"

Bending over me to kiss my cheek, Noah gives me soft, slow thrusts as he quiets his voice. "There you go. Good job, gorgeous Omega. I know I'm not mating you heavily yet, but keep breathing. Enjoy yourself on the way there."

I sputter out each breath, unable to speak as Noah glides in and out of me. *Goddess, no, you were right. You're so big tonight, filling me up so deeply that I can't—*

My pussy attempts to clamp down hard over his shaft, but with how heavily he's dragging against every surface of my inner muscles, I can hardly squeeze him, meeting plushy counterpressure that tingles every nerve in my core. As my breaths heighten into moans, I reach behind my head, gripping his hand on my ponytail.

"Pull—" I gasp. Noah's eyes flash in surprise, meeting my drooping eyelids in the mirror. "Pull harder."

"Fuck me," Noah whispers to himself, his jaw taut. His hips

jerk, pushing a heavy cry from my lips as he hits just the right spot. The second he tugs my hair a little harder, my jaw drops, my arching back tightening my pussy over his cock until he massages every inch within me—like he's stuffing me with blissful pleasure. Each avenue of Noah's stimulation builds on the other, the massaging pull Noah creates over my scalp colliding with his thrusts in my core. I moan hard, his tip pumping faster against my G-spot until my hips twist.

With my knees pulsing wider, Noah's prediction comes true: I moan loud enough to echo across the whole bathroom. "There! Right there—"

Noah groans, his eyelids fluttering as I squeeze him tighter. "Oh, fuck. Fuck—"

Pressing my shoulders down flat with a shudder, Noah shoves himself deep in me, freezing his hips in place.

"Don't move," he rasps.

I groan, my thighs shaking as I drop both feet on the ground, too weak to hold myself up with how good he feels inside me. "Oh, Noah. Don't edge me right here. *Please.*"

Giving my hair another gentle tug, Noah hisses again when I squish my ass against his hips, my pussy flexing faster. "Oh, *Goddess.* No, I'm serious. I can't knot you—it's already huge, and it's not even fully formed. We'll be stuck here until we're twenty minutes late, not ten."

At the mere thought, my breath rises until I pant. "Okay, yeah, I can feel it growing. It feels stupidly good."

Noah huffs. "I said I'd make you come twice too, but I haven't yet."

I groan. "It's just for fun. It doesn't matter—"

Noah's words come out pleading and breathy. "Aliya, I can't help it. I'm going to knot you, hard."

"Please," I gasp. "Please do, Alpha—"

As if he can't help himself, Noah lets out a strangled groan, his hips restarting. I choke out a gasp as his budding knot stretches me wider at the base of his cock, applying tingling pressure on my clit—all while his tip rubs the deepest part of me. Noah's hand drops my ponytail in a frenzy, grasping my thighs. He drops his weight over me, rocking into me with my ass pressed tight to his hips.

I feel so full with his pleasure in our bond that my moans escalate beyond my control, rising until a flood of fluid gushes from me. Noah's resulting heavy, sated moans send me over the edge, my pussy fluttering hard over his forming knot as I come. My knees jerk inwards, every limb squirming at the delightful, full-body buzzing Noah creates within me. He pumps faster and faster, his hard breath beating against my shoulder. He draws out every second of my orgasm, massaging it out of me until I'm liquified on the countertop.

But as Noah cinches us together tight, releasing a flood of warmth in my lower belly as he comes, I'm startled by how good it feels—the pleasure flowing throughout my abdomen strong enough to build another orgasm. What's even more shocking is that I don't seem to be alone. I gape in the mirror as Noah's incisors stretch, his hands roaming over my breasts. He clings to me tighter, his hips rocking us as we remain tied.

Noah moans hard and loud against my neck, sending a thrill racing down my spine. "Fuck, Aliya, I don't know what it is about your scent, but I— I'm—"

My eyes widen. He wanted to make me come twice, but I'm about to make *him* come twice.

As Noah's fangs whisper over my neck, I cry out, pushing myself from the counter to smash my ass hard into Noah's pelvis. He responds with a throaty growl, nudging inside me the best he can with his thick, heavy knot wedging us in place. So I bounce my ass up and down, rubbing him back and forth inside me. As Noah's pleasure triples in our bond, my eyelids flutter at the beautiful, desperate sounds he makes against my neck, his drool slipping down my collarbone until I shiver.

"Do it—" I moan, bouncing faster. I fawn for him, tilting my head to reveal his old mark on my scent gland. "Follow your instincts too."

Cuddling me tight to him, Noah presses his tongue into my scent gland, slathering me in its heat. The pressure of his tongue echoes down my torso until my pussy pulses hard over his knot. Noah's eyelids flutter as he groans against my neck, his breath frantic. I slow my bouncing, opting to circle my ass over his pelvis until Noah's breath deepens into moans, the blissful sounds keeping time with each circular motion. I gasp for air with him, pleasure rising in my chest just before he clamps down—his fangs piercing my skin as he floods my core with his cum. I cry out, the pain replaced by an earth-shattering bliss as I flex over his knot, coming hard alongside him.

Our bond warps as a new flood of emotions crosses through our reformed connection, Noah's fresh mark stunning me speechless with how much gratitude and pride he carries for me—as well as the raw, tender Omega side of him. I've never witnessed Noah's wolf feeling this nurtured. Through his eyes, I can finally see the strength I hold; Noah views me as his beacon of hope for survival.

Our inner world blooms before my awareness. Flowers are replaced by turning leaves, a soothing rainfall pittering across their reds and browns. In the center of the field, our wolves snuggle up in the warmth of each other. At the mere sight of Noah's silky, midnight fur, I love him deeper than I ever have.

As I come back into awareness with Noah's slow, soothing touches down my breasts, sides, and belly, my heart aches with how much joy I contain. Noah seems to feel the same, his eyelids blinking ever-so-slowly as he unlatches from my neck, giving me thorough, tender licks to stop the bleeding.

Urging Noah closer over my shoulder, I nuzzle deep into his hair. *You were telling me the truth of how you see me.*

Tears cloud Noah's eyes as he smiles, still washing me with pleasure as he strokes my fresh mark. *So were you.*

But when I glance at us in the mirror, I'm met with a horror scene: sweat and streaky makeup cake my face, and that's not the worst of it. Blood coats my breasts, splashed down the right half of my dress.

I sputter into laughter, gripping Noah's arms as he groans.

"Oh, Goddess—" Noah lifts his head, prying open heavy eyelids. "What's so funny—"

Noah genuinely gasps. I laugh even harder at his gaping jaw, groaning along with Noah as my inner muscles squeeze his knot.

"I don't think this dress is going to work out," I whisper.

"Fuck." Low, rumbling laughter buzzes over my back, Noah

burying his forehead against my stinging shoulder. "No, no it won't—pretty much ever again. I'm so sorry."

Giggling, I comb his hair. "I'm not. I'll never forget this."

Meeting my eyes, Noah's puppy-dog eyes overpower his expression, a touched shyness flickering through our bond. Judging by how Noah first described marking to me, I'm certain the true depths of my comment lands; not only did I choose Noah as my mate, but each time I allow him to mark me, I'm choosing him again, vowing to bear his mark to the world as evidence of our bond. I kiss his reddening cheek, my heart fluttering as he huddles closer.

As we snuggle in the bathroom, allowing Noah's body to settle, he lets out a rumbling sigh against my cheek. "I wish we could skip this dinner, but I might also be more prepared for it than ever now. I feel like nothing can stop us."

A smile creases my cheeks as I look at us in the mirror, my heart full to the brim. "Me too. Let's do this."

⚬∽ **16** ∽⚬

After cleaning ourselves up, we rearrange my ponytail in a bun behind my head, pinning back any stray hairs. I'm forced to use a dress I had set aside for later this week, but it matches Noah's outfit well enough, a halter dress with a ruched skirt draping over my bump in a classic Luna white. With a touch of mascara and lipstick, I decide I look fine enough, considering the fresh, hot red bite mark on my neck; it'll draw far more attention than anything else about me. Noah eyes his bite pattern with pride when he thinks I'm not looking, his wolf's chest puffing in our bond. I stifle my amusement, grabbing my scent blocker vial on the way out the door.

Thankfully, Annika and Viktor stumble out of their room upstairs a few minutes after us. Their outfits are even more rumpled than ours, Viktor yanking his suit jacket back into place as Annika's thumb scrubs off her red lipstick from his bottom lip in an emergency spit bath.

We take one whiff of one another, the hallway's air suddenly reeking of deodorized sweat and relieved lust, and we all laugh.

"You both ready?" Viktor grins.

"Absolutely," Noah says.

He tucks me to his side as we follow Viktor and Annika to the event space, their harmonizing pheromones stinging my eyes; now that Noah mated every last drop of lust from my bones for the night, I find their combined scent way too overpowering to be alluring.

Noah spots me wrinkling my nose from the corner of his eye, breaking into a smile. *When I said they seduce anyone and everyone,*

I meant it. They're into group sex and host an orgy every year. We might've dodged a bullet by all four of us getting sex out of the way.

I hug Noah tighter, my cheeks flushing as Annika eyes my mark, giving me one quick wink behind Viktor's back.

I try my best to smile until Annika turns back around. *Do you think it's to manipulate their friends too, or just for enjoyment's sake?*

I think it's both. It's easier to keep someone on your side when they're whipped for you.

I bite back a laugh. *So… Does that mean you've tried it with them?*

Noah drops his head, stifling a smile. *They only create groups with even numbers. A-and I usually come here with my mom, so I've never been invited. Or, well, I have, but I would've been paired with some random, unmated Alpha, so I don't even consider that an invite.*

I see. That doesn't tell me what you'd think about joining now, though.

Noah can't bear to meet my smile, his bright teal eyes dropping to our feet. I giggle, stroking my shy Alpha's back. Is he flustered because he wants to join, or because he absolutely does *not* want to?

Before he can reply, Annika returns to my side at the dinner party's entrance, lowering to a whisper. "We'll head in first, then you and Alpha Noah. Stay strong, Luna. Remember what I said in the car ride over, okay?"

I swallow hard, forcing a smile. "Thank you. I'm by your side too."

Annika props herself at Viktor's side, kissing his hand before entering the hallway across from the event space.

As my heart pounds faster and faster, I cuddle deeper into Noah. He wraps his arm around me, stroking my side. *I've got you, Luna. Just be yourself.*

They're going to want to smell me, right?

Noah leans in, taking a deep sniff of my neck. *You're golden. I hardly want to eat you alive anymore.*

I roll my eyes. *But what if I get all Alpha-y and weird again?*

Noah stoops over me, lifting my chin for a deep, toe-curling kiss. *Then everyone will be lucky enough to see another side of the badass Luna who stole my heart.*

Stuffed with happiness, I beam at my loving mate as we

enter the Alpha Summit's introductory event, hand in hand. No matter how many eyes are on us, I step forward with my chest held high, my wolf standing proud in our bond thanks to Noah's encouragement.

It's easy to trust the world under his lead. He remains serious but relaxed, his warmth flowing through our clasped hands.

Viktor's top Beta, Johannes, stands at the edge of the room, his lean, toned figure streamlined by a jet-black, pristine suit. While Johannes is nowhere near as physically powerful as Viktor must be, there's no question why his wide shoulders were chosen to aid Viktor in protecting their pack.

As we meet eyes for the first time, Johannes's warm smile greets me, settling my shoulders.

Gesturing to us with an open palm, Johannes directs the crowd's focus in our direction. "Introducing our next guests of honor, the Luna and Alpha of Greenfield."

Wolves gawk at us, skyrocketing my nerves as they display a range from clapping to glaring.

But Noah isn't looking at anyone else but me, his adoration flourishing in our bond. *You're sexier every day I know you.*

I flush, squeezing his arm. *Noah, don't wake up my horny wolf again.*

He chuckles, kissing the top of my head. *I won't... Yet.*

The crowd stills as Noah leans into my side, his soft voice rumbling beneath his breath. "I love you, sweet Luna."

"I love you too, my shy Alpha."

He stops me in front of everyone, tilting my chin to reveal my fresh mark.

My claws prick his arm with my nerves—I feel more vulnerable than ever to fawn for him in front of so many powerful figures. But when Noah presses a featherlight kiss on my neck, my eyelashes flutter.

I mean it. I really love you. I'm not the King, but you've always had the grace and kindness in you of a Queen Luna. Let them see it. Let them see it, right now. Noah's proud, heavy-lidded gaze stirs my heart to new heights. It bolsters my confidence tenfold, rolling my shoulders back and unclenching my jaw.

Once we've officially entered the event space, we're swarmed.

Wolves nuzzle and sniff me, new names blurring until I can't remember a single one.

You're doing great. Keep breathing, Noah mindlinks without needing to turn his head; our bond fluctuates faster than I can keep up with as we're overloaded with sensory stimulation.

Most wolves give Noah a much wider radius than they give me, but if anyone inches too close to me, all Noah has to do is look at them.

A thrill runs through me each time an Alpha scampers away from him—submitting to Noah, even though we're in the company of the world's top Alphas. It's clearer by the second that, like me, Noah is far more powerful than he gives himself credit. He might not be the King Alpha, but my mate carries himself like one.

I stare up at his sharp profile, my heart fluttering at his rapid tracking of any and all movement he sees.

Anyone here I should watch out for, gorgeous? I attempt to follow his gaze.

I'm scanning for them. But mainly, I'm looking for my one true ally. I want you to know who to go to if you're in trouble.

I swallow hard. Noah has mentioned him before: the top Alpha in Idaho, Reid Nordskov.

But Reid is even more aloof than Noah. No pictures exist of Alpha Reid online—not officially, at least. All Noah has on his phone is an old picture of the bottom half of Reid's face, only a wide smile peeking through. The rest of the photo is blocked by Reid's wide palm covering the lens.

Reid is special to Noah. I've heard Noah calling him on the phone sometimes to get his opinion on pack issues, but Reid never seems to want to be involved in the top global rankings, preferring to aid the state of the world from the shadows. I don't blame him. The weight on Noah's shoulders pains my heart too, and Reid might even be able to accomplish more out of the spotlight. While it's different from our strategy, it's an ingenious one.

Needing support at the Summit is a recurring concern between every pack leader I've spoken to thus far. Things must get tense here.

And I'm gravely disappointed; there are hardly any women or

non-binary wolves leading as top Alphas here, let alone fellow queer couples—unless the men and women I see are bisexual, like us. Not to mention almost none of the top leaders are Omegas or Betas in the first place, top Alphas touting their Lunas like accessories.

Greenfield Pack seems to be more of an anomaly than I realized. I'm positive powerful Lycans exist in these packs beyond the Alpha men attending the Summit in the vast majority, but this must be what Noah has been worried about. How can packs thrive with domineering Alphas shoving their own pack members down? It only creates a culture of hurt.

Worry consumes my rocky stomach. While Noah defies the Elders in our pack, does this mean he defies a large majority of the Lycan world's traditions too? How are we going to be able to make things safer if Alpha-domination culture is this widespread?

The second that thought crosses my mind, my focus latches onto the murmuring behind our heads.

"That's him, Luna. The shy 'King.' I bet he's too much of a little bitch to fight anyone. Real Alphas don't exist anymore, thanks to cowards like him."

Before I think it through, I turn around with a snarl. "*I'm* not shy. Don't come anywhere near my mate."

The Alpha raises his hands in defense, flashing a sly grin. "No harm intended, little Luna."

His smirk wavers as Noah's chest puffs beside me. Noah slowly turns to the Alpha with his expression completely flat—until his lips curl into a vicious smile.

A smooth darkness seeps from Noah's rumbling tone. "You're the top Alpha in Illinois, aren't you?"

Everyone around us shrinks, anticipating Noah's next move—except one Alpha in particular. A tall, stoic leader paces a few steps behind the Illinois Alpha, his stare sharpening until a chill runs down my back.

My feet shuffle in anticipation. I don't recognize this pacing Alpha, but he looks like he's waiting to strike. Is he on our side?

When Noah places his hand on the Illinois Alpha's shoulder, multiple wolves jump. "Well?"

The Illinois Alpha hardly breathes. "Y-yep, Illinois. Logan Brightville of Brightville Pastures Pack. No harm intended to you either, King."

Noah frowns—at first. His smile creeps back up one cheek, exposing his incisors. "I'm not the King."

Logan's jaw ticks, his torso twitching through shaky breaths in a failed attempt to remain stoic.

Noah lifts one eyebrow. "But I do know what your Alpha-domination buddies are up to. And I think you know how I feel about that."

Despite puffing his chest, Logan releases a strong whiff of fear. The pacing stranger stops, his eyes locked on Noah.

A deep, insidious chuckle reverberates through Noah's chest, stealing my breath. Not a single eye blinks, the entire mass of us locked on his form.

Noah doesn't raise his voice. He pats Logan's shoulder, releasing him with a gentle shove. "I'll see you on the field Friday… Illinois."

Logan mumbles an excuse to drag his Luna and allies away.

That's when my mate finally allows himself to scowl, mirroring the anger boiling in the depths of our bond. I don't attempt to settle him; Noah's annoyed scent diminishes the crowd for us, wolves eager to turn to smaller, safer groups of conversation.

But the lone, pacing Alpha remains, unafraid of Noah's anger. He locks eyes with Noah.

Noah freezes.

My heart flips as a timid affection blooms in Noah's heart. Their eyes linger a second longer than I'd expect, only broken by Noah's duck of his head.

My jaw drops. But I have to laugh, nudging my mate with my elbow. "Who's *this?*"

His eyes widen. "T-that's…" Noah resorts to scrubbing his face as it flushes bright red. "That's y-your ally to turn to if you need protection. The Idaho Alpha. Reid Nordskov."

Reid and I meet eyes, grinning at Noah's shyness just the same. I laugh. "Hi. Thank you, Alpha Reid—our dear friend."

With a bashful nod, Reid leaves us.

And I put my hands on my hips, turning to my now-sheepish

mate. In stark opposition to his brutish form that protected us mere seconds ago, Noah's shoulders strain, rising to his ears as his wolf paces frantically in our bond.

Noah takes my hand, tugging me closer. "L-Luna, um…"

I break into giggles, rubbing his arm with my free hand. "*Noah Greenfield.* You naughty Alpha. I know you've crushed on other Alphas, but you didn't tell me you had a hot Alpha *ex*."

Noah covers his eyes before diving for me, burying his expression with a heavy hug. "I don't love him like that. Not like you."

I laugh, allowing him to hide in my shoulder. He groans as I scratch his head, but I can't stop giggling at how precious he is.

"Really, Aliya. We already weren't working since we both wanted to lead our own packs in separate states, but the second I started dreaming of you and realized you could be real, we broke up. Before that, I thought I didn't have a fated mate at all—just like him."

My heart flips. This is new information too, but it's one that burrows a giddy warmth in my belly. I still marvel over how we dreamed of each other, but my stomach flip-flops, touched by how seriously Noah took my existence, even when I was a mere *possibility*.

When I kiss his mark, Noah's shoulders drop, relief flushing his anxiety from our bond. "I'm just teasing you, sweet Alpha. I know you might've sensed a little jealousy at first, but I don't mind if you have a history, my love. I have a history too. And I'm happy you seem to still be in good spirits around each other. I've never felt any emotional romantic tug in our bond when you've called him on the phone, or just now when you met. It feels like you have true friends in each other."

Noah pulls back, biting his lip. "W-we do. H-he's still my best Alpha friend. He's—" Noah's voice softens. "If I'm not by your side at any point this weekend and you need help, I'd recommend going to him. He's safe."

The hidden meaning beneath Noah's words halt me in place: Noah hasn't called a single other wolf outside our pack "safe." Everyone else he's introduced me to has been our "allies."

I stroke Noah's cheek, my eyes catching on the secretive Idaho Alpha disappearing into the crowd.

So that's the only wolf Noah *actually* trusts at this Summit, besides me. I hope we won't need Reid's help.

❧ 17 ☙

On the second day of the Alpha Summit, we gather outside, the sun whited out by smatterings of overcast clouds. Everyone else must be already acclimated to mountain temperatures or something. I'm plastered between Waimārie and Annika at the lakeside, shivering if they separate from me even a centimeter, but other wolves jump in and out of the water, some shifting to play and relax on the shore in their wolf forms.

Most of the other Lunas are inside, enjoying the sauna, but I can't join them since I'm pregnant. Waimārie and Annika were sweet; they decided to stay with the Alphas and me outside so I wouldn't be alone.

When Annika bends away from me to fetch another slice of pumpkin bread from our picnic basket, I tighten my jaw, attempting to keep my teeth from chattering. She does a double-take at me over her shoulder before erupting into laughter. "Oh, Goddess, Waimārie, snuggle her closer!"

Waimārie laughs, rubbing my arms. "I am! I think we'll have to resort to desperate measures."

I smile, unable to keep my voice steady. "I-it's o-okay. I'm wa-arming up."

"Oh, shush." Waimārie chuckles, turning to the shores and waving her arm over her head. "Alpha Noah, your mate is a shivering little bunny over here!"

In unison, Noah, Tāne, and Viktor freeze in their wolven romp. I almost can't tell them apart, each of their black wolves towering over the other Alphas playing further down the lake and in the forest. But as my eye catches on a particularly fluffy Alpha on the left, I'm right about who it is; Noah shifts back into his human form in a blink, hopping on one foot along the shore as he slips into his pants. Viktor's wolf shakes out his luscious black coat, nipping at Tāne's equally dark fur to instigate another chase. They dart down the shore, shrinking into black specks in mere seconds.

But as Noah jogs over, Waimārie sputters out a laugh. "Steamy Alpha!"

Noah quite literally steams before our eyes, his overheated chest smoking against the frigid air with wisps of evaporating water. As he tugs on his jacket, I laugh with our ally Lunas, reaching for him. Dropping his stare with a smile, Noah joins us on the blanket, helping me climb into his lap.

"Goddess, thank you—" I hum, loving his delicious warmth.

Noah bundles me inside his jacket with him, soaking me in his body heat. Slinking his arms around my belly, Noah chuckles beneath his breath as I break into satiated purrs. "My poor girl. You really are a shivering little bunny."

"Aww, look at you both! I want in." Annika nuzzles up to my side.

Within seconds, we've created a new wolf pile, Annika and Waimārie curling against us as Noah kisses the top of my head.

But as I lean back, I gasp, gazing up at the tall trees stretching into the sky and framing my mate's face. "Oh, wow. It's absolutely beautiful out here… But maybe we should go inside before your fingers freeze off, Noah."

He laughs, kissing my forehead. "I just sprinted four miles and back, so I'm fine. I think we should actually go inside for *you*."

Waimārie laughs. "Aliya, aren't you used to the cold in Oregon?"

"It's only just starting to cool off at home for autumn, so I'm not used to it yet after a ridiculously hot summer. Otherwise, I'm just pregnant and anemic." I sigh. "Hey, wait—how are *you* not freezing? Isn't it even hotter where you are?"

Waimārie rubs her cheek against my arm, grinning. "Oh, I'm used to being a little cold. Tāne and I may or may not have regular outdoor *excursions* at night, out in the wop wops."

Annika and I exchange a puzzled glance, breaking into giggles. "The *what?*" Annika asks.

Waimārie bursts into laughter with us. "The wop wops! You

know, somewhere out in the forest or mountains? Where no one lives—as in, no one's going to interrupt us."

"Like ass-crack nowhere," Noah mutters.

"*Excuse* me?" Waimārie laughs so hard she snorts, spurring us all into laughter. "There sure are ass cracks involved, but I don't think that's a requirement for the wop wops."

Tears form in my eyes as the four of us melt into silent laughter, Noah's belly shaking my whole body in his lap.

Annika hugs both Noah's arm and mine before releasing us with a sigh. "Speaking of which—Waimārie, do you and Tāne want to join us for a couple's massage tonight? And then head upstairs for some other fun?"

My jaw drops. That was perhaps the wildest conversational transition I've ever heard, but I can't fully laugh along with everyone else; Viktor and Annika really *do* invite everyone to join orgies.

After Noah brought it up, we didn't get to talk about this possibility, at all, and I'd never consent to something like this without him. I don't even know if I'd want to join. What in the world am I going to say if we're invited next? What if I offend her, no matter what I say?

"Don't laugh, Waimārie, I'm serious!" Annika reaches over me, shaking Waimārie's arm.

She takes Annika's hand, giving it a quick squeeze. "We'll ask Tāne in a minute, eh?"

I'm flustered to my core, unable to keep myself from stiffening in Noah's arms. He chuckles, and as I lift my eyes to check his expression, I find him shaking his head over me, his smile growing at my wide-eyed stare.

"Stop laughing at me!" Annika chuckles. "Luna, your mate makes fun of Vik and my sexual hobbies, every Summit. But you're going to turn down my offer too, aren't you?"

"O-oh, um—" I erupt into heavier giggles, my face flooded with heat.

"Don't torture her, Anni," Noah says. "And I don't make fun of your sex life. I make fun of your not-so-well-disguised code words. You and Vik have sex in front of everyone at least once every Summit, so at this point, you might as well straight-up ask to have sex with people." Noah's sudden sass, spoken with such a flustered shyness, spurs us back into laughter.

But Annika straightens. "Wait, are you jealous? Does this mean you're finally interested, now that you've found your Luna?"

My eyes widen, heat crowding my face. But as Noah's frown deepens, his arms curl tighter around me, jealousy creeping into our bond.

Annika was on the right track, but I'm almost certain she misplaced his upset; he wasn't jealous when he wasn't invited, his heart is protesting now that he's picturing the possibility.

I'm smiling again, gazing up at him from his lap; I know exactly what he's about to say.

"Not interested," Noah grumbles.

I chuckle. "Thought so."

Annika groans, dropping her head against my arm. "Boring."

Waimārie sputters out a laugh. "Nah, he's simply consistent. Care to share why, though, Noah? I always look forward to your creative rejections."

Noah's glare deepens. "Hmm…"

Waimārie rubs his arm. "Ah! If you're not open to sharing, no worries, eh? But you do smell even more jealous now, so… Did Anni hit the mark?"

"No. I—" Noah huffs, turning to scowl at the rocks beside our picnic blanket. "I'm not usually l-like this, but yeah, I'm jealous. But not because we'd be left o-out if we don't join. I don't know what Aliya thinks about group sex, so I'm not speaking for her, and, to be clear, I'm fine with us watching others or being watched during mating rituals. But with this, for me— It's different when other people get directly involved because I—"

Noah clears his throat, shuffling beneath me. When he speaks, his deep voice is soft enough that if we weren't all bundled up together, I might not hear him.

"I want her to myself."

Butterflies fill my chest. I gaze up at him, his burning jealousy in our bond mixing with a burst of passion.

As emotions flicker between our connection, I realize he's not telling the full story. He doesn't simply want me to himself, and it's not as if he claims ownership over me. Just like he said, I've never felt a spark of jealousy during our public mating rituals.

On one hand, it could be due to trauma; we've both had to trust each other to our cores in order to fully let go during sex.

But I know my mate. Judging by everything he's shown me thus far, Noah craves the emotional intimacy of our privacy. Our physical union is sacred to a vulnerable piece of him, and he must want to keep that between us. To resolidify our bond each time our bodies connect, in a way only we know.

Heat races down my core. The second my pheromones gush from me in response, Noah's body reacts, mirroring me with an equally eager scent.

And Annika breaks into a sly grin. "Oh? What's going on here? Do I spy a jealous, possessive Alpha, Mr. I-hate-Alpha-domination?"

Burying his face from our view, Noah grumbles into my shoulder, hugging me closer as his ears burn against my cheek. As I pat his head with my puffy gloves, I can't help but giggle.

"At least I'm all warmed up inside now," I whisper.

Waimārie lets out a sharp laugh. I chuckle with her, covering my icy cheeks beneath my fuzzy gloves. Soon, all three of us Lunas are laughing, and Noah joins in, shaking his head.

"Well, Anni, I know Tāne will be happy for another massage, at least—and a bit of group fun tonight won't hurt," Waimārie says. "Let's see what happens if I ask."

The four of us return our gaze to the shore. In the distance, Viktor and Tāne scamper in circles, their massive wolves taking occasional dives at each other to rile themselves up again.

But as Waimārie breaks into a grin, one wolf halts. Tāne remains frozen—even as Viktor nips at him all over, dancing around his chest.

Then Tāne bolts.

Waimārie erupts into heavy belly laughter, collapsing into my lap. I can't help but cackle with her, loving Tāne's speedy run as he races toward us; his tongue flops out the side of his mouth as he bounds down the bank, black fur slicking back in the wind until his alert eyes look absolutely unhinged.

Annika and Noah laugh just as hard, our amusement only

rising as Tāne can't stop, accidentally flinging himself through the forest brush behind us. A moment later, he bursts out in his human form, butt-naked and grinning.

"I'm ready!"

Waimārie hops to her feet, glomping onto her mate with a beaming grin. "I guess you really are, e te tau. You don't even have to get undressed for the massage."

Once Viktor catches up, laughing along with us, we head into the lodge's main lobby. More wolves linger inside than I expected, a few Alphas pulling Noah and Viktor into a conversation just beyond the lobby in the nearest event hall.

"The massage?" Annika calls after them.

"I have one question for our Alphas first," Viktor says.

Annika sighs, but Waimārie simply smiles. "More time for us to chat!"

I smile with her, but my gut wavers; the distance between Noah and me increases, filling with unfamiliar wolves.

Keeping his eyes on me, Noah nods. *I'm right here, if you need me.*

Thank you, my shy Alpha. Actually, I'm a little worried, going into an enclosed space with so many wolves. Hasn't it been a while since I applied the scent blocker?

Noah's eyes widen. He smiles politely at the Alphas around him before slipping from their conversation, ignoring everyone else as he weaves back to my side.

Placing his hand in mine, Noah passes off the vial discreetly, leaning over me to kiss my cheek. *Would you like help putting it on?*

I kiss his cheek too. "I'm okay, thank you. Go have fun, if you'd like to stick with the Alphas a bit longer."

"Yes, he'd like to!" Grabbing Noah's arm, Viktor tugs Noah back down the hall, prompting an unhappy grumble from my mate.

I smile, shaking my head as I buddy up to Annika and Waimārie. "Before you go to your massage, can you hide me for a moment? I need to reapply this."

"We've got you," Waimārie whispers before raising her volume. "Luna, can I help you fix your hair? It got all windblown."

Annika giggles, joining Waimārie in smoothing a stray hair

behind my ear. "Can I just say I adore how sweet Noah has been around you? He's so excited for your pup. I told him I'd answer pregnancy questions, so he asked me a million while you were asleep."

My heart twirls. "He told me, and that was so sweet of you too, Anni."

"Oh, I loved seeing him so invested. He even took notes! I had so much fun, but Viktor was sick of him talking to me by the end."

I laugh, imagining Noah's serious-yet-excited focusing face. "I can't wait to see him with our pup."

Annika beams, and that's when I notice something missing: the conspiratorial glaze to her eyes has finally softened. This is an honest Annika, staring right back.

"I'm so glad you have him." She hugs me close, rubbing my back.

I release a burst of grateful scent, Annika's warmth easing my worries. "Thank you. I desperately needed a mom hug."

Annika juts back from our hug to look me in the eyes, her forehead warping. "Oh, Luna… You don't have your mom?"

I can't bear to respond, my mouth gaping as it struggles to form words.

I can't believe I just told her that. I don't usually tell new friends these things, and I wasn't planning to.

But she *is* the Queen Luna, and she certainly feels like it. The second her maternal, reassuring emotions hit my nose, I swipe at my gushing eyes, the pang in my heart only deepening.

"Oh, *sweetheart*." Waimārie strokes my arm, her sugary, comforting scent pushing more tears from me.

"Sorry—" I mutter.

"Don't be, please. Oh, I can't imagine going through this without my mom." Annika digs out a fresh tissue from her bag for my tears. "Hey, you can ask me pregnancy questions too, you know? Let's stay in touch after you go home, mama."

Waimārie grins. "Oh, me too! Please, let's chat!"

I sigh, turning my back to the open door in response to Noah's obvious fretting in our bond. "God, you have no idea how much I'd love that. You really are the sweetest Lunas we could have."

My shoulders loosen beneath Annika's and Waimārie's gentle touches, allowing me to shut my eyes and relax my aching stomach.

"Let's get that applied, eh?" Waimārie whispers, tapping my fingers clasped over the vial.

"Ah, right—thank you." Turning to the room's corner, I swing my long hair over one shoulder, pretending I'm finishing combing out my hair. As I rub the blocker into my scent glands, my torso slackens in relief. But the second I turn around, an unfamiliar Luna locks eyes with me.

When this Luna strides straight for us, Waimārie's torso tenses. She steps in front of me, blocking me from the stranger Luna's view. "Hey, Luna, how are—"

"Hello! Sorry, I have a question for Luna Aliya." She nuzzles into Waimārie in greeting, and my wolf's defensive walls go up. The unfamiliar Luna is all smiles as she leans over Waimārie's shoulder, locking eyes with me to whisper-shout. "You're pregnant too, aren't you?"

Oh God. Without Noah's musk masking my scent, and with how stressed I am, did my pregnancy scent leak through the blockers again? Did I reapply it too late? Or is my bump just that obvious now, even beneath my thick jacket?

I'd be fine with everyone knowing I'm pregnant—if I didn't remember what Noah said about Mason's Alpha pack possibly wanting to kill us before we produce an heir. Some of his top allies are present. How do I know this Luna isn't fishing for details too?

I shrink, crossing my arms over my belly. "Why are you asking me this?"

The Luna waves her hands, her eyebrows arching. "No, no, wait, I'm sorry! I wanted to relate with you, if so—see?" Smoothing her high-waisted skirt down to show me her barely-there bump, the Luna beams. "I've got a little one on the way too!"

The fear in my chest evaporates, replaced by relief; this Luna is the embodiment of an excited puppy, not the conspiratorial enemy I feared. Waimārie and Annika relax alongside me, sighing in unison.

I take the stranger Luna's hand, drawing her closer in the hopes she'll mimic my hushed tone. "Oh, my goodness, sweet Luna, how exciting! How far along—"

Another Luna whispers from about ten feet away. "Did Talia just confirm the Greenfield Luna is pregnant?"

My blood runs cold. It wasn't just her; *everyone* heard this unfamiliar Luna, Talia, declare our pregnancies.

Waimārie's voice remains gentle but serious as it lowers. "Dear Luna, you don't just ask people sensitive questions like these."

Talia gasps, following my glare over her shoulder. "S-sorry! I wasn't thinking, I'm so sorry—"

Far more wolves have turned their focus our way. No, they're coming straight for us, racing faster the second they see others attempting to beat them to it.

Annika grips my arm hard, her voice wavering as she lets out an uneasy cry. "Wait, wait, wait—"

Before Noah, Tāne, or Viktor can even turn around, wolves swarm the event hall's doorway to view my pregnant body up close. They cram against one another, pushing back in irritation until not a single wolf can fit through the hall's mouth. The Lunas and I scramble backward, terrified by the sight of flailing limbs ready to pounce.

"Oi, get a hold of yourselves!" Waimārie's voice quivers as she grips Annika and me tight, pulling us back until our backs hit the furthest wall.

Talia scurries behind us, her shoulders raised to her ears as her scent omits a sour, stinging fear. "Sorry! I'm so sorry!"

"You okay, Anni?" Viktor shouts from deep inside the event hall.

"Stay back!" Annika's voice quivers. "Don't be tempted to shift!"

Annika's right: if anyone shifts into their wolf while the collective energy is already this aggressive, all hell will break loose. I pull Annika and Waimārie closer, my eyes darting to the porch doors for an escape route. The porch is wide, but not wide enough for shifted wolves. There's always a staircase we could run down to the porch's right, but wolves love to chase.

We're stuck here. Forced to see what happens when they all come barreling for us.

"Settle down. Hold still," I shout, knowing from my preschoolers that I can't say "stop shoving." All their instinctual brains will hear is the word "shove."

And their primal side has truly unlocked; everyone squirms against one another, desperate to both be freed and to beat everyone else to us.

"Back up," Noah shouts.

A few wolves peel off the doorway pile-up, likely due to Noah, Tāne, and Viktor yanking them away, only for them to scramble right back; our Alphas' desperation to reach us is riling up every other Alpha with their agitated pheromones. As Alphas break into fights, growling and snarls echo through the lobby loudly enough to force us to yell just to hear one another.

Waimārie clutches me tighter. "Oh, Lunas, I think it's best we leave. *Now.*"

My breath catches: one wolf in the front is ready to wriggle their arm through, turning to their side. Following Waimārie's advice, I grip as many petrified Lunas around me as I can, scurrying toward the porch doors with them as I watch it all happen in slow motion.

But it doesn't happen how I expect. One wolf squeezes through, and the rest come scrambling over one another—until Noah barrels his way past them. I'm tempted to stay put and wait for Noah, but as irritation rises between the Alphas shoving one another, they grapple, crashing into other wolves. Those wolves grow frustrated, hitting back, and so on, until they form a writhing mass of angry bodies, brawling on the floor.

We're forced to run from the incoming stampede, the Lunas obeying my ushering arms with unblinking, terrified eyes. Waimārie races ahead to the nearest glass door, fumbling with the doorknob until she frees us onto the porch. Noah, Viktor, and Tāne try to catch up to us with shouts over the brawling wolves, but releasing themselves from the doorway jam didn't bring them close enough; wolves stream onto the porch from every door in the lobby, trapping not only Annika, Waimārie, Talia, and me, but multiple other Lunas who dashed to our side in fear—pressing us tight against the railing as Alphas scramble over each other.

"What do we do?" Annika's rapid breath pants against my shoulder, her fear evident in her shrieking scent.

The Lunas cower behind me. Waimārie's tangible fear tugs at my heartstrings; for the first time this Summit, her smile erases from her cheeks. "Tāne's trapped behind everyone too." She keeps her voice low beside my ear—and she needs to, with how desperately Talia and Annika shake behind us.

Eyeing the nearest empty space, I herd us to an even wider section of the porch, hugging the railing on our way over as I keep our group safe behind my outstretched arms. It buys us enough room to lessen the density of the crowd, but wolves trail after us, no matter how many times our mates and other ally Alphas yank them back.

Once I have them protected between myself and a column, Noah finally bursts through to the front of the crowd. He stations himself in front of us, allowing me to breathe.

"Thank the Goddess," Waimārie hisses, gripping his shirt alongside me.

"S-sorry, Alpha and Luna Greenfield. I just got so excited—" Talia lets out a startled cry as Noah holds his palm out, fending off a few excited wolves like he's guarding us on the outskirts of a mosh pit.

"It'd be fine if everyone wasn't so fucking aggressive about it," Noah growls. "Have you all lost your minds? Back the fuck up."

Alphas in the front push back against Noah, agitated by the Lunas' fearful scents. It forces Noah to create a wall with his body, pinning us behind him.

As Noah's growls only agitate the angry Alphas, Annika huddles into me with a frantic grip. "Luna! I'm scared. What if they crush us?"

"Come here, mama. I've got you." My voice softens, maternal instincts exploding from me. Annika's shaking shoulders loosen beneath my palms.

"Luna!" Leaping over the porch railing in the distance, Tāne races over until he's in the bushes behind us. Arms outstretched, Tāne hoists Waimārie over the railing, cradling her to his chest the second she lands in his embrace. She grips him back in desperation, letting out sharp, heaving exhales. Judging by the dazed shock on her face, I assume Waimārie won't want to part from Tāne's side for the rest of the Summit.

But Noah can't help us escape, too busy fending Alphas off, and neither can Annika's mate, no matter how heavily she dissolves into panic in my arms; Viktor's head swivels toward us from the back of the stuffed porch, cussing out a few Alphas in Swedish. "Move, skitstövel. Listen to your King."

Even Reid can't help us as wolves crowd all remaining standing room, shoving back against each other at random.

While Noah remains unmovable, I turn back to Waimārie and Tāne, relieved to see their arms outstretched to help us over the railing too. But when Waimārie meets my eyes, looking at Talia, then back to Annika and me, I nod.

"Take Talia first. I've got Anni covered," I say.

Waimārie and Tāne waste no time in grasping Talia, convincing her to climb up the railing to leap for them below.

Blowing out a slow breath, I allow my back to remain turned from the chaos for a whole two seconds—which is why an Alpha twice my size takes his chance to grab Annika by the elbow, yanking her from my grasp.

18

Annika shrieks, heightening my senses until every other sound, smell, and sight disappears, my wolf locking in on the Alpha closing in on Annika.

My primal mind gathers information in rapid, fleeting flashes: Annika's terrified Omega scent calls for her Alpha mate, Waimārie and Talia cry out alongside her, and the tension in my muscles warn me of danger, each sensation heightening my urge to fight back.

But as time slows, one thing in particular stands out to my wolf: the opportunistic look in the Alpha's eyes.

I know that look. That's a look no man will get away with in my presence again, so long as I have the power to stop it.

Within a millisecond, colors dull and my chest heaves, my wolf taking complete control.

I can't shift without creating further chaos. I know I can't.

But I still have fangs.

My extended incisors snap at the Alpha's sleeve in a blink, ripping the shoulder off his suit. He jerks back, his eyes widening.

But that's not enough to satisfy me.

My jaws ache to clamp down on the hands he laid on Annika. Digging in with all ten claws, I yank the Alpha's arm toward me, just like he yanked Annika's. Then I sink my fangs deep into his flesh.

The Alpha yipes in fear and pain, releasing the Queen Luna. As wolves dart from the cowering Alpha and me to give us a wide radius, I spit his filthy blood from my mouth, growling deep as

I stare him down. He scrambles back on the hardwood porch, gaping at me from the floor with wide, frantic eyes.

Smashing Annika into my chest, I envelop her as much as I can as my Alpha musk explodes. My words come out as a snarling bark. "Don't you dare fucking *touch her!*"

This Alpha's ego must be bruised. He's clearly petrified, his lips quivering as they curl, but he still dares to snarl back.

I only catch a glimpse of Noah's eyes flashing a vivid yellow above me before he picks the Alpha attacker up by the back of his suit collar, dumping him over the porch railing.

My jaw drops. Thankfully, the porch is a mere four to five feet off the ground, the Alpha crashing into thick bushes below us. All I see are legs popping out of the top, the Alpha squirming to stand.

Turning back around, I'm met with a sea of bulging, frightened eyes across the porch, darting between Noah and me. Viktor must've arrived just in time to see Noah's takedown, standing strong despite the undulating crowd around him. But he seems to be frozen. Staring.

When I finally get a good look at him, a chill runs down my spine. Viktor's eyes aren't on Noah. They're glaring at *me*.

With Annika still cocooned in my arms, the King Alpha snarls, and I receive his message loud and clear: he's preparing to fight me for his mate.

Flexing his arms, Viktor's black eyes shine a vivid green, his wolf extending his scent as he stares deep into my soul. Growling through a low, velvety voice, Viktor speaks a single word.

"*Mine.*"

Fear envelops my heart, freezing every inch of me. Are we going to die here?

Noah grips Viktor by his jacket collar. "She's protecting Anni, not claiming her!"

But Viktor doesn't seem to see anyone else but Annika and me, his fangs glistening with saliva as he flashes them at me. "Get the fuck off my mate, Luna."

My eyesight grays as Alphas erupt back into action around us, in a frenzy at the clashing, violent scents. Noah's teeth bare, his arms rippling with their full force—shoving Viktor back again and again as the King tries to reach me.

But this only sends Annika into full-body sobs, her knees buckling beside me. "N-no! Please!"

"I've got you! It's okay!" I cradle her head like I would for my preschoolers, but nothing can soothe her now; my fury builds too as Alphas escalate into near-blows.

All at once, my frustration spills over.

"Just fucking *stop!*"

Echoing past all the raging wolves, my shout puts the entire Summit into a standstill—including the King Alpha.

Between all the petrified eyes on me, my form deflates.

I need a moment to myself to be stunned. Awestruck by how they all just listened to me, and confused by my influence. Was that just a fluke?

But my agitated wolf's focus is yanked elsewhere—Annika struggles to breathe beyond raspy, quick gulps of air.

I suck in a pained breath. "Oh, Goddess, Anni—"

She clings to me, her teeth chattering as tears cloud her eyes. "H-he almost— Almost got me—"

My sugary, nurturing Omega scent clouds the porch, instincts urging me to whine over her. "Slow your breathing, sweetheart. We've got you, sweet Luna. He's not messing with you again. Slow your breath."

"Oh, Goddess—" Reaching through the railing, Waimārie smooths Annika's mussed hair off her clammy forehead, her features just as contorted as Annika's.

"Help," Annika rasps.

"We've got you," I whisper. "Slow your breath as best as you can, bit by bit."

The Queen Luna whimpers as I massage her sternum, trying to help reset her nervous system with a grounding touch. She fists my jacket sleeves like I've shocked her back into reality, laboring through harsh breaths in an attempt to slow her air intake.

"There you go. Look at Vik for me, okay? Your mate is right here, ready to protect you with us now. Breathe slowly and deeply. You're just having an anxiety attack."

Viktor seems to blink from a haze, jumping into action. "Fuck. I'm right here!"

The second Noah releases Viktor, Annika bursts from my arms, diving into her mate's chest. Viktor coos over her with soft-spoken comforts, rubbing her all over until she melts into his embrace, finally able to catch her breath.

And I want to dissolve into the atmosphere.

Noah, can we please leave this 'bonding' day from hell?

We're not escaping. They're leaving. Gathering me against him, Noah growls at everyone else. "I hope this is a reminder not to fuck with a mother wolf. Everyone off the porch before I fucking lose it."

As requested, the wolves dash back inside—except Viktor, exiting down the porch stairs to soothe Annika in the lodge's front garden.

Noah's wolf is still in full force, puffing his chest into me until I'm smushed against the railing.

I bare my neck for him, my wolf whimpering through me. "A-Alpha, you're—"

When his gaze finally lands on me, Noah gasps. "Oh, my poor Luna." Noah cups my cheek, turning me every which way to make sure I'm unscathed. "I'm so sorry for making you fawn. My wolf is going nuts."

Pressing a hand to my racing heart, I groan. "You almost shifted, didn't you?"

"Yeah, but I managed to keep him down so things wouldn't get even worse. I just have to shelter you like this for a while until he chills out. I'm sorry."

"No, it actually feels good to have Little Wolf protected between us. Thank you."

Noah's hands stop on my belly, a soft whine escaping him. "You scared me."

"I-I'm sorry, I—"

Noah's frightened eyes strike panic in my core.

Oh, God. He's relying on me to protect our pup, and I put us in danger—challenging a violent Alpha without a second thought.

I grip Noah's hands, urging him to cover more of my belly.

"I-I didn't mean to snap. I know I'm pregnant, but Annika was terrified, and everyone was crowding us, and—"

"Shh, my love."

Stooping over me, Noah licks my mark, sending a sudden explosion of tingles up my spine. It's meant to soothe me, but the strength behind his tongue activates nerves so deep that I can't even moan, pleasure escaping my lips as a broken-up huff.

Noah purrs, flattening the full length of his tongue in an even deeper caress of my scent gland. I sigh in relief; his protective scent dissolves my fear, teasing out my pheromones with every sweep of his searching fingers down my sides and back.

"You're right, I'm sorry. I didn't mean to blame you. You did such a good job protecting our pup and our allies." Noah cuddles me into a deep kiss, pleading whines escaping my lips as Noah's Alpha musk gushes. My knees widen, and Noah readily slips his thigh between both of mine.

"O-oh, my *God*—" I huff, my legs quivering. Whether our fear heightened our emotions or it's Noah's wolf remaining at the forefront of his mind, his musk's urgency overwhelms me, fluttering my eyelids.

But I'm just as desperate to reconnect with Noah. I don't even know how to speak the words I want to say to urge him ahead; the way he's kissing me hits just right, spiking my heart rate. My hips rock, bumping his thigh until he drags his lips down my neck to suckle my sore, freshly-scarred mark—reminding me we're bound by the soul, and therefore, never alone in our fear. I muffle deep, pleased moans into Noah's bulky chest, clinging to him.

But Noah suddenly pulls away, leaving me panting.

"Fuck, I want you. But not here. I don't trust anyone else right now." Noah kisses my mark much more gently, fighting to restrain his hungry wolf in our bond.

I shut my eyes, breathing as deeply as I can to reground myself in my rational mind. "Okay. Yes, you're right. Let's not get too frisky out here."

Noah groans. "Sorry. I didn't mean to get so riled up. Tomorrow's hanging over me, and I think the pressure's getting to my fucking head. I'm all wolf today."

"It's okay, Alpha. Just breathe with me." I nuzzle my forehead into his chest, soothing his wolf with slow rubs down his arms.

After breathing each other in, my heartbeat slows, and the desperation within our bond softens.

The second Noah takes a step back, I sigh. "Is it always like this at the Alpha Summit?"

Noah hums, gazing into the distance. After a few silent seconds, his golden, shifted eyes meet mine. "Actually, yes. This isn't too bad so far."

"Oh, Goddess," I hiss.

As I take deep, calming breaths to soothe my anxiety, a shaky voice appears behind Noah's body shield.

"Alpha? Can I slip into your wolf's bubble a little to thank your Luna?"

Noah grumbles, leaning away just enough for one of my eyes to see Annika. Her mascara is still streaked down her cheeks, her big, beautiful eyes rimmed in red.

I reach for Annika past Noah's back, grasping her hand. "Please, don't thank me, Luna. It's in my instincts to nurture and protect, but I got so angry that I caused even more chaos. I'm sorry."

To my surprise, Viktor steps into view, easing his hands around Annika's waist. "You didn't. It was a misunderstanding on my end, and my Luna needed someone to step in to save her from further abuse. Goddess, I'd die if he took her while I couldn't reach her. Thank you."

Viktor's words are kind, but something in his scent still screams of jealousy.

Noah tenses, his wolf edging on snapping.

Patting Noah's chest, I put on my calming teacher voice. "Hey, it's almost dinner time, right? Let's head back inside and continue our night with some delicious food. And Vik and Anni, please don't worry; there are no hard feelings. Noah and I are so grateful to have you in our circle as both allies and dear friends—we keep talking about it."

Viktor's eyes land on Noah, and for a second, I'm afraid things could turn sour despite everyone's attempts to repair our allyship.

But after a long, tense silence, Noah releases me, relaxing at my side. "I really do admire your fire, King. Your wolf is a force to be reckoned with, so I'm lucky you're on my side."

Viktor chuckles, rubbing the back of his head. "Whatever, man. I'm sorry for charging at your mate."

"Well, my feisty Luna is a force to be reckoned with too, so I can't say I wouldn't do the same in your position." Noah stretches his neck, rolling it side to side. When his gaze lands directly on Viktor's, a subtle tension tightens all of our shoulders. "But my Luna's also fucking brilliant, and she's right. Let's let this all go—including what I left unsettled last year."

Noah's soft-spoken words might lack in volume, but his irises blaze as he stares Viktor down—Noah's wolf confirming his sincerity.

Viktor tenses. Annika's eyes dart between both Alphas, her knuckles turning bright white as she grips Viktor's arm.

Noah's straightened back doesn't budge. "I'm genuinely sorry, Vik. Let's settle our score, once and for all, in the King Alpha competition this year. I'll attack you so hard, you won't even have to question if I'm holding back."

My heartbeat races as I analyze every small flit of Viktor's irises. But with Noah's declaration, Viktor warms into the brightest smile I've seen on him yet.

"Fuck yeah, Alpha. That's all I ever wanted, man." Viktor scrubs Noah's hair as he passes us, urging Annika back inside. "Then let's get ourselves well fed tonight so it's a fair competition, yeah?"

We follow Viktor to the open porch doors, but Annika stumbles, catching herself against the doorframe.

"Luna!?" Viktor hoists her to his chest, carrying most of her weight with panicked, wide eyes. "Are you still lightheaded, my love? Your cheeks are bright red."

"S-sorry, I'm just—" She fans her cheeks, stealing a quick glance at us. "T-there's a lot of delightful pheromones on this porch, and I tried to ignore them, but... I couldn't help myself. I was squeezing my knees together while you all talked, and— I-I'm about to—" With a soft mewl of pleasure, Annika's grip tightens on her mate.

As she buries her face into Viktor's chest, my jaw genuinely drops. *O-oh, my God, Noah... Is she seriously saying she's about to have an orgasm in the doorway?*

With confirmation from Noah's flushed stare dropping to his feet, there's no question as to what Annika means.

I gasp as Viktor lunges for Annika's throat, licking her mark so hard that she warps into heaving moans.

"Ah! Alpha!"

Viktor growls, his hand skating past her breasts to smooth down her dress's puffy skirt—slipping between her legs. His circling palm rolls her clit until her legs shake, her hips bucking outside of the rhythm of his arm.

My groin aches with hers as I'm unable to tear my gaze away from the unbelievable sight in front of me. As Viktor's arm pumps outside of her dress, fabric bounces around his wrist. Squirming against him, Annika grows louder, her moans echoing across the empty porch—until she comes with a hearty cry, her thighs clamping around Viktor's hand. Viktor drinks up every whine Annika buries into his suit jacket, grinning with pride as her claws poke holes in his sleeves.

Annika falls still with happy purrs, rubbing her head all over her mate to scent him with her pleased gratitude. Viktor's hand slows, but my heartbeat still pulses between my legs, my grip tight on Noah's forearm as we continue to gape.

Viktor's low chuckle gives me goosebumps. "That better, baby?"

With flaming red cheeks, Annika lifts her head from his chest, tilting her face up to Viktor with slow, blissed-out blinks. She smiles like he's her source of sunlight. "Y-yes... Yes. Thank you, Alpha."

After sloppy kisses against the doorframe and a lot of purring, the two head back inside as if nothing happened at all—leaving Noah and me on the porch, stunned speechless.

Slowly, Noah and I meet eyes. I find his stare just as wide, and his cheeks set ablaze.

"Shit, Noah! We make wolves super horny!" I rasp through a whisper. "We have to control ourselves better than this."

"Fuck, I know. I'm sorry." Noah grips his forehead, turning from me. *I've never seen Annika lose her cool like that before. How did we even release enough pheromones to rile her up that badly?*

As Noah gulps down lungfuls of cold air over the porch railing, I chase after him, whispering. "W-well, I have to admit, I *really* liked it when you pressed me against the railing, so—"

With a whip of Noah's head in my direction, his desirous purr shocks me back into our surroundings.

I cup my hand over my mouth, my eyes widening by the second. *Oh, God, sorry! I didn't mean to say that outside of mindlink—*

But it's too late. Noah backs me against the railing once more, his hands sweeping up my sides until his purr rumbles through me. "You liked it that much, huh? That's what you want me to do, later tonight? Mate you against the bathroom door?"

I choke out a harsh, desperate breath, gripping his arms as I nod. "W-well, honestly, I'd *love*—" When Noah glomps onto me just as heavily as his wolf tackles mine in our bond, I burst into laughter. "Oh, no, not again! I shouldn't have said anything!"

I pry myself from Noah's grip, leaving him with his arms extended. He chases after me on the porch like a sad puppy, pushing a hearty laugh out of me as I back towards the open doorway. *We're just going to make things worse at tonight's dinner.*

Yeah, I know… Noah drops his arms.

But the agonizing distance between our bodies provides just enough tension to ignite an idea.

I slip my arm into the nook of Noah's elbow, allowing us a single step past the door's threshold before mindlinking him again. *Maybe we should challenge ourselves tonight. See how long we can hold it in for?*

Noah halts. His wolf bristles with excitement in our bond as he eyes me, an eager smile spreading on his face. "Goddess, help me."

❧ 19 ❧

Our allies lost their opportunity for a massage, the six of us hurrying back to our rooms to dress for tonight's formal dinner. Every global pack leader will be all dressed up to celebrate this special night: the night before the King Alpha competition begins.

After challenging Noah to a game of staving off our lust for as long as possible, we've re-entered the lodge's event hall biting back playful smiles, giggling every time we meet eyes at the elongated, cluttered dining table.

But before I realize it, my challenge morphs into a different game entirely. Noah's wolf hasn't retreated from behind his shifted eyes, his sly gaze washing over me between every bite of dinner. Just as I think I have him fooled that I'm "not watching" him either, sneaking glances when his head is turned, his mindlink straightens my spine.

Watch it, my feisty Luna. You're going to get yourself in big trouble if you keep looking at me like that.

My mate tilts his jaw to gaze down at me, spiking my heart rate. He meets my stare beneath half-hooded eyelids, presenting a clear challenge for dominance; he knows my Alpha side is still more active than usual tonight.

I squeeze my thighs together, my heartbeat pulsing through my groin. After Noah teased me earlier, I have to squirm the ache away—applying just enough pressure to stave off my craving for Noah's touch.

But shuffling in my seat only escalates my mate's teasing stare. His grin heightens my every nerve, flooding my skin with goosebumps. *You don't want to lose your own challenge, do you?*

I clear my throat, cupping my scent glands with both hands as I tear my gaze from him. *No. I'm not going to lose. Just watch me, Alpha.*

Luckily, the pregnancy-nose-safe food Annika special-ordered for me consumes my focus in a single bite. But as I shovel mouthful after mouthful of buttery mashed potatoes, Noah leans in close, as if he's whispering in my ear.

Instead, he breathes me in, followed by a hearty purr. *I can smell how wet you are for me, Luna. Are you sure that's just from earlier?*

I have to fight to swallow my potatoes, aroused shivers creeping up my spine.

When my hand slides up Noah's knee, giving his upper thigh a hard squeeze, his back stiffens. From the corner of my eye, I spot his cock twitching in his pants.

Don't play with fire, Alpha. My wolf is feisty today.

He purrs again—hardly able to help himself. *She is, isn't she? That's why you're enjoying me challenging you.*

Are you sure I'm not the one challenging you? Preparing myself to top you again? I take another bite, giggling as Noah readjusts his pants in my peripherals.

But when I turn back to my food, Noah's hand on my back slides up to my neck. A sigh escapes my lips.

Noah pauses, joining me in glancing around the room to see if anyone noticed.

But the conversation carries on as usual, and I shudder: Noah's thumb glides beneath my hair, pleasure trickling down my spine as his touch ghosts over my mark. With his thumb's gentle pet on the sensitive gland, Noah turns my panties from wet to soaked, my pussy flexing with each circle he runs over me.

I cross my legs, hoping to hide the scent. We reapplied my topical scent blocker before dinner, but my scent glands erupt with pleasure—enough for me to smell *myself*. With a few slow, focused breaths, I stifle all scent seeping from me once more.

Noah grins, his eyes flashing brighter. When he leans in, just his hot breath against my neck makes my heart race. "You really want to be called a good girl later, don't you, Luna?"

I stiffen. *That wasn't a mindlink!*

But I don't have to tell Noah; with one look into his

supercharged eyes, he knows exactly what he's doing, and his glimmering smile couldn't look more smug. I shiver, my crossed legs squeezing my clit with the movement.

My breath hitches in delight.

The Luna next to me perks up, and I freeze in place.

Noah straightens. *Shit. Sorry, I took it too far.*

Wrapping his palm around the back of my neck, Noah covers my gushing scent glands at my jugulars with his wide hand, allowing me to enjoy a gentle massage as my groin pulses faster.

But that doesn't stop Noah's scent from erupting into desire.

I clear my throat. *Noah, I can smell your rut forming.*

I know. Give me a second to stifle it before—

A clatter of dishes toppling to our left snaps Noah from his trance, his yellow eyes zipping straight to the source.

A few seats down, an Alpha's tongue is deep in her Luna's mouth, purring against her open lips in a heavy makeout.

My eyes widen. *Oh, shit! Did we cause that?*

Noah shrugs, clearing his throat as he turns back to his food. *I-it's hard to say. This… happens too.*

Ah, okay.

I glance at the other wolves around us for any signs of distress. My shoulders relax as most wolves dig back in—laughing, talking, and eating from one end of the table to the other.

But with every few breaths, my core still flexes with desire. *Noah, I… I still want you. It's starting to hurt.*

He squirms in his seat. I try my best not to feed into his fire, reining back my wolf as tightly as I can.

But Noah's heels bounce. *Fuck. We might have to leave, Omega. I've held my wolf back all day, and he wants to pick you up and mate you on the table.*

My eyes widen as they catch on Noah's tense hand on his thigh, barely hiding his flexing bulge.

Alpha, you're so… My whisper comes out shaky. "…thick tonight."

When his focus lands back on my breathy lips, a burst of his Alpha musk burns my eyes.

Swallowing hard, Noah readjusts his hot fingers on my scent

gland. Tingles swirl throughout my pelvis, and I can't help it; the horniest whimper I can imagine escapes my lips.

I clamp my hand over my mouth, muffling my words. "Oh, Goddess. I failed the challenge."

"Shit. Fuck, I—" Noah can't continue his thoughts, his focus consumed by the crash of dishes across the table.

After hoisting the New York Luna onto the table, flooding the white tablecloth with red wine, the New York Alpha licks his mate's innermost thigh—a clear sign he's preparing her to mate.

All I can do is stare.

But he's not the only one.

Over half the room is kissing. The other half have reverted from just making out to foreplay and beyond, moans erupting from every corner of the room.

"Noah, is this normal too?" I hiss, clutching Noah's suit jacket.

A low, growling purr tickles my ear. "No. It's not."

I gasp, finding myself face to face with Noah's primal mind. With his wolf in charge, his hands roam my extra-sensitive breasts, applying just enough pressure to send a jolt up my aching core.

"O-oh! Ah—" With my cries, wolves burst into heavier touch all around us.

The Lunas we protected earlier occupy their mates' lips, diving into their Alphas' laps—if their thighs aren't already wrapped around their mate on the floor, against the wall, or on the table. Tāne hoists Waimārie into his arms, carrying her with handfuls of her ass resting in his palms—the couple struggling to find their way out the door between heavy kisses.

"O-oh, my God," I breathe. "This is *not* the polite dinner I expected—"

As I fawn for Noah's eager tongue on my mark, my thighs shake with pleasure.

At the head of the table, Annika and Viktor's full-body makeout grinds deeper with every growling breath. My body pulses with Annika's every whimper, her dress barely disguising Viktor's flexing arm beneath her skirt as he pins her chest to her dinner plate.

But then he very clearly enters her from behind, the sound of her mating whines digging straight into my groin.

My hips raise in need, drawing Noah's attention. Within seconds, his hand is up my skirt too. "O-oh, my— Um, Noah—"

Viktor purrs into Annika's neck, licking her mark as she squirms over his cock. My knees spread wider for Noah, aching for him to do the same as he rubs soft moans from me.

"I want another pup—" Annika gasps from the head of the banquet table.

Viktor chuckles. "Greedy Luna."

His pace quickens until he plows into her, igniting the entire room into a musk so strong that my eyes water. As an orgasm builds low in my belly, my poor chair creaks in distress from my hips rocking into Noah's hand. But my lungs tighten into panic: Noah's incisors are on full display, my mate ready to drop into a heavy rut. Knowing Noah, he'd *hate* experiencing a rut in a crowd of potentially unsafe wolves.

But as he drools, opening his jaws to nibble at my mark, I grip his tie tight, holding him in place. "O-oh, my God, Noah! We really have to go!"

Dashing from my chair, I keep my hips far from Noah's reach. Latching onto both his arms, I figure I'll have to physically force him from the room, taking a few slow breaths to sober myself.

But with a gentle tug, Noah pops to his feet. I blink a few times, testing out what happens if I let go of him, backing up a few steps. Noah takes a few steps too, his wolf's tail pointing to the sky in our bond.

Biting back my smile, I speed-walk backward. His wolf happily chases me out the doors, purring into my cheeks with courting caresses down my torso as we rush down the hallway.

I sputter out a laugh. "Alpha, you're so sweet, even when you're rutting."

Noah purrs, grabbing hold of my hips from behind. With one lick on my mark, my knees dip in the hallway, desire pulsing through me so strong that my thighs quiver. I can hardly blink through the musky haze Noah drowns me in, his scent begging me to drop to the floor with my legs spread wide.

But we're still ten doors down from our suite.

Catching me before I crumble, Noah growls into my mark. "Mate, what do you need? You're in distress."

As if weights are tied to my knees, I groan, straining to move my legs. "Either you have to take a few deep breaths, or we're stuck with solving your rut here. I want you so badly that I can't walk another step."

Smushing me against the wall, Noah flicks up my skirt, revealing drenched panties. My moan echoes down the hall as he slips beneath the fabric, twirling his fingers across my throbbing labia.

"You can't walk, huh? Then tell me, Luna: can I mate you right here, in the hallway? Or should I carry you back to our room?"

"Right here, please." I shakily unlatch his belt, freeing his bobbing cock.

But before I can drive him wild, Noah stops my hands. He purrs, his nose skating down my neck as he peels my panties from me. "Alright, Luna, we've gotta skip a few steps before one of us comes. With how soaked you are, I don't need to warm you up."

I whimper, rubbing my clit against his tip until he lets out a hungry hiss.

"That's what I thought. Hold on tight," Noah whispers.

When his arms swoop around the back of my thighs, lifting me until I can hook my legs around his hips, I moan at the press of his thick cock between us. He grinds me into the wall, coating the base of his shaft in my fluid, my ass in his hands.

"N-Noah! I—" I moan, my knees squirming beside his torso as desire blooms in my belly.

Noah growls, slowing his heavy suckling of my mark. *Not yet, Luna.*

He draws his hips back, shushing my whines with gentle kisses against my lips. My jaw drops as he eases himself inside me, his starved stare not leaving my flushed face for a single second.

I can't stop myself from crying out, my aching core fluttering around his shaft as it fills me to the brim.

When Noah bottoms out inside me, my back rolls against the wall, delighted by how gravity sinks Noah deeper in this position.

His growl rumbles against my throat. "Fuck, Luna. You're hotter than any wolf here by miles. Let me hear you filling up this hallway with your gorgeous voice."

The slow rock of his hips draws a whimpering moan from me

regardless, pleasure shooting up into my heart. Noah purrs, his thrusts deepening until I have to gasp in delight with every breath.

"Good girl. Keep telling me what you want."

"M-more! I'm about to squirt—"

Noah flattens my writhing body into the wall, pounding faster as pressure builds in my core. He mates a rush of fluid from me, his cock stealing the attention of every nerve in my pussy.

"*Alpha*—" I breathe.

All I'm met with is a delirious growl, Noah's rough grip on my ass spreading my labia over the base of his engorged shaft—the start of his knot swelling.

I grip his hair, my inner muscles unable to squeeze him with how thick he grows as he bounces me over his shaft. All at once, a tingling bliss overcomes me, my skin bristling with sparks as he drives the orgasm out of me.

Noah smashes his lips into me as I come, pounding out more fluid as the thud of our colliding hips echoes down the hall.

When my legs fall slack around his hips, Noah growls, slowing into deep, luscious thrusts.

I skate my fingernails over his dress shirt, grazing his nipples until he shivers. "Alpha, it still feels so good. Don't stop for me. You can knot me, right here."

"W-well, I-I can't, um—"

I nuzzle Noah's burning cheeks, his frustrated breath making my pleasure-soaked body shudder. "What's wrong, Alpha? Is it not as good for you?"

"No, it's fucking glorious… But I can't let go around these wolves. I don't trust them."

Still in control and hungry for more, my wolf pulls her mate into a tender kiss, purring against his lips. "Then let's go back to our room. I'll ride you until you get me pregnant again."

Noah blinks once. Then twice. "Holy fuck."

With a desperate groan as he slips from me, Noah picks me up, whisking me to our room.

The second we lock the door behind us, Noah kneads my lips with urgent kisses, sweat dripping down his temple. His whimpers draw out the side of me I've been suppressing since I snapped to protect Annika.

My wolf asserts herself with a deep purr. "On the bed, Alpha. Flat on your back."

Noah moans into my mouth, flicking off his pants as I chase him to the bed. With no time to whip off my dress, I gather my skirt in my hands, pulling it up and over my hips as I climb over Noah's thighs.

Seating my bare pussy over him, I drag myself over his pulsing cock until he's coated in fluid.

"L-Luna—" Noah's flushed, open-mouthed bliss sends a flurry of chills up my torso.

As I slip him into me, Noah tips his head back into the pillows, surrendering himself to indulgence as I ride him. Just as I'm tempted to sputter out words of delight, relief flooding my chest at being able to treat Noah again, he moans beneath me.

"Luna, p-*please*, it's so—"

A luxurious, saccharine scent fills my nose, fluttering my heart into my throat.

I can't believe I'm making him feel like this—*again*. It's the first time Noah's let his Omega side back out since we arrived at the Summit. Like he said, I make him feel safe. Every inch of me trembles, unable to process the tenderness developing deep in my heart; his trust is twice as meaningful after witnessing firsthand what he's up against. What we're up against.

My eyelids droop at the genuine moans escaping Noah, each cry squeezing my heart muscles. I want to draw these beautiful sounds from his lips, over and over again, for the rest of our lives.

As a gorgeous, hyacinth sweetness erupts from Noah's scent, his pleading hands massage my thighs, softening my muscles enough for me to drop my ass flush to his hips—just how he likes it.

I choke out a gasp. "Oh, *Noah*, you're extra thick—"

Noah whimpers, no longer able to let me do all the work. As he bucks faster and faster into me, I roll my hips over him, rubbing my clit into his thick thumb.

His swelling cock tightens me over him, forcing his breath to hitch. "O-oh, *fuck*—"

Just as Noah explodes, unleashing a seeping warmth into my core, I arch over him, riding him as fast as my exhausted, pregnant body will allow before coming over his hips with shaking thighs.

Noah hugs me to his chest, rocking me with heavy, pulsing grunts. "Oh, *Luna*— Goddess—"

Dropping my head against Noah's shoulder, I allow my eyelids to laze shut as Noah purrs through our buzzing bond alongside me. His fingers send ticklish sparks over my skin as he caresses my breasts, belly, and exposed neck.

As we melt into a post-orgasmic haze, we stroke each other's hair, dropping into the deepest kiss we can. The gentle caress of Noah's tongue against mine makes me shiver all over, Noah's soft, open-mouthed moans soaking me in love. "You're beautiful, Aliya. So beautiful."

Our noses trace each other, slow kisses taking us from sex to an all-encompassing cuddle.

All I can do is moan. "I feel so good, Alpha."

"Good job, gorgeous Luna." He purrs into my ear, tracing slow arcs down my back. My hard nipples press into his chest as goosebumps trail his touch. "I'm so in love with you. I didn't think sex would feel this comforting."

"Me neither, Alpha. I love you with every inch of me."

After an hour of gentle caressing, cleaning each other's bodies, and returning to snuggling in our cuddle ball, I fall deep asleep in my mate's arms.

In the morning, our bodies remain loose and cozy, tangled up in how large our bond has expanded. With how deep our love has grown, it feels like we could contain the whole earth in our internal universe.

And I know Noah feels the same. It's in the way he gently mates me again in the morning, his slow, deep kisses sending waves of delight through my heart. It's in the way he caresses my womb in the shower, allowing me to close my eyes in bliss. It's in the way he smiles across the massive Community Center event hall, sharing his happiness with me, even with other wolves' pups crawling all over him.

Viktor's oldest daughter, Mikaela, scrambles from her dad's arms, dropping on all fours in front of Noah with a tiny growl. "Alpha Noah, scare me!"

Noah laughs, his cheeks darkening. "What? I'm not going to scare you, kid."

The seven-year-old pouts, her thick black curls bouncing as she crosses her arms, hard. "Please!"

Noah suddenly hunches, prowling with his fingers splayed across the ground.

With this alone, Mikaela screams—running in a circle before erupting into a contagious belly laugh from behind Viktor's leg. "Too scary, Alpha!"

Noah's eyes widen with his smile. "I didn't even growl!"

"Still too scary!" She giggles.

Noah's resulting laughter flutters my heart down to my belly in my hands.

I bite my lip when Noah looks over, his smile softening as he glances at my swollen abdomen. *I might be too scary for that pup in there too.*

No, Noah. You're the biggest sweetheart I've ever seen. If I wasn't already pregnant, there's no way I wouldn't want to be, after today.

He drops his chin with a shy smile.

I can only indulge in his giddiness for so long before Beta Johannes enters the Community Center, announcing there's only an hour before the first battle in the King Alpha competition.

My heart sinks as Noah's smile vanishes, leaving a scowl in its place.

Viktor, Tāne, and Reid seem to feel the same, meeting Noah in the center of the room with hushed whispers.

I look to Annika and Waimārie for answers, but Waimārie hasn't returned yet, holing herself in the bathroom for at least half an hour, and Annika herds two of her pups from the Community Center, carrying the third close to her chest with a weary smile. "See you there, Luna."

So I'm not the only one dreading today.

As Noah parts from the Alphas to rejoin my side, my stomach gurgles with anxiety.

"You okay?" he whispers.

"Yes, but—" I eye the wolves around us, painfully aware they're eavesdropping on our every breath this week. *Are you nervous?*

Noah sighs, leaving a longer pause than usual before answering me. *Not for the reason other wolves might be.*

Well, that's ominous. Just as my gut sinks, Noah's hand settles on my lower back, drawing me close as wolves filter out of the Community Center to prepare for the competition.

You don't have to worry about my safety, Luna. I really meant it when I told our Elder Alphas I'm always ready to defend our pack. I know the competition sounds scary, but I'm confident today's preliminary rounds will be easy to pass.

Checking behind himself with a lungful of air, Noah must believe we're alone enough now to speak beneath his breath. "Reid, Viktor, Tāne, and I are upholding a pact to divide and conquer—until we face off on the New Moon."

I exhale through a nod. "Okay, that's good to hear… I think. But you seem upset."

Noah growls beneath his breath, kissing the top of my head as we exit the Community Center. "That's because today is my least favorite part of the Summit."

My stomach flinches. "Because it's dangerous?"

Footsteps appear at our side. Noah glances at Viktor as he approaches, but to my surprise, he continues our conversation. "No. It's because it's really hard to avoid permanently damaging these Alpha-domination assholes."

"Since they make you so upset?" I whisper.

"Since they hold their top Alpha rank through fear tactics, not actual physical muscle."

Viktor claps Noah's shoulder, leaning in with a grin. "It's actually since a single one of your Alpha's claws is stronger than twenty average wolves, combined. Imagine trying to tone that down."

As Noah brushes off Viktor with a playful shove, I swallow hard, seeing Noah's massive shoulders in a new light.

Viktor only knows the held-back version of Noah. How much of his physical strength has Noah been withholding?

I think I'm mated to the strongest wolf the Summit has ever seen.

But I get the feeling he doesn't want to be.

20

The world's top Alphas line a sweeping, grassy field behind the Community Center, their boasting pheromones forcing spectators to cover their noses. Front and center are Noah, Viktor, Tāne, Reid, and six other huge wolves—last year's top ten Alphas.

A golden crest plate hangs over Noah's chest to signify Greenfield Forest's heritage, its emblem flashing in the afternoon sun. Just like the massive trees encircling the field today, embossed evergreens frame a shining full moon and a howling wolf's head on the crest's front—a long-standing signifier for Greenfield Pack's prominence in the Pacific Northwest.

Noah's broad form holds an elevated regality to his every breath in his traditional garb, but Noah doesn't seem to agree; he rolls his shoulders for the tenth time this minute. When my concern spikes from his eleventh shoulder roll, Noah deflates. *Sorry. This stupid chunk of metal is uncomfortable.*

No matter how hard my hands shake, I force myself to smile when we meet eyes across the field. *It's an heirloom, love. It means something to more wolves than just your mom.*

Well, it makes me look ridiculous. And it didn't even fit my dad.

I bite back a laugh as Noah stands even taller in defiance, his glowering making a few Alphas lean ever-so-slightly away from him. *I don't think anyone was built as big and strong as my Alpha in the old days. Not even your dad.*

Noah's wolf bristles with pride in our bond as he steps forward, Johannes introducing him as the Greenfield Alpha. My heart pounds; Noah's stare remains pinned on me, his flaring affection for me only agitating him further.

But to protect his body and Greenfield's status, he needs to be riled up—within reason.

I think it's time to give him something to look forward to. *Good job, Alpha. Keep it up, and you just might get your surprise tonight.*

As Viktor's announcement finishes, Noah breaks into a knowing grin, sending a shudder down my whole spine.

Are you sure you're ready for your surprise, Luna? I might have too much fun teasing you with it, myself.

Neither of us tear our eyes from each other as my wolf spills my secrets, rolling over to be mated. I cross my legs, pretending I'm massaging my neck with both palms over my scent glands. Good thing Noah took a rut suppressant this morning, or else this competition would turn into another accidental orgy.

Johannes announces today's preliminary battle pairings, the Alphas fighting until only ten undefeated wolves remain for tomorrow's semi-finals.

So wonderful.

The second the Alphas are released to battle their first pairings, Noah rips off his family crest with terrifying speed. Multiple Alphas flinch, and a few Lunas giggle in delight at my shirtless mate. Scowls crease their jealous Alphas' cheeks, but Noah doesn't care to notice. He's too busy eyeing me up and down, his chest puffing as the Alpha musk in the wind draws his wolf to the surface.

But I'm sweating too much to keep flirting. I'm nervous as hell. I know Noah can sense it and can't keep his eyes off me, determined to protect me, but in a way, his concern benefits us: wolves are petrified by him, not even paying attention to their current competitors as they section off into the field with their heads turned toward my mate.

"Hey," Annika mutters, taking her seat beside mine. For the first time since we've met, she's not smiling.

My stomach gurgles. "Hey."

"I hope Waimārie can join us soon, but she's worried sick—quite literally. I feel awful for her."

"Goddess, poor Luna. I feel her pain. Your pain."

Annika grabs my hand, but it's not enough. I huddle into her side, my eyes trained on Noah's rippling back. As his first competitor shifts into a snarling brown and black wolf, my stomach drops. *Why aren't you shifting?*

Noah doesn't answer, his human shoulder blades gliding over his back with every deep, focused inhale.

When the starting bell sounds, Noah grips his competitor's wolf by the snout.

The wolf rolls over in a heartbeat, submitting in forfeit.

I bite back a laugh as Noah's wolf prances in our bond, clearly proud despite Noah's irritation with the event.

He glances at me just long enough to roll his eyes. *It's going to be a long day.*

I chuckle. *Well, you look hot.*

Noah drops his head to hide a smile. His next competitor takes the opportunity to shift, aiming to catch him off guard.

Just like the Luna that slithers into the row of chairs behind Annika and me, poking her head between our shoulders until we're forced to separate. "You're the Greenfield Luna, right?"

From her mocking tone alone, I recognize her: the Illinois Luna from Brightville Pastures Pack. Annika shoots her a glare, but I simply nod in response to the Luna's question, my eyes returning to their focal point on Noah's back. He takes the second competitor down the same way, his dominant scent alone weakening the Alpha's knees.

"I've heard about you. A lot about you, actually," the Illinois Luna says.

I stiffen, suddenly aware I know next to nothing about her, beyond that her mate is a huge jerk. Guilt floods my senses; I hate when people only know me as "Noah's mate," and here I am, doing the same thing.

"I'm so sorry, I'm a little foggy from the Summit excitement so far." I attempt to seem open as I turn to her with a polite smile, hoping she doesn't automatically hate us as much as her mate does. But I'm met with a judgmental, lifting eyebrow. "Can you remind me of your name, Luna? I know we sat a few seats apart at the dinner, but there wasn't a lot of... talking."

I'm the only one who chuckles at my joke. The Luna's returning smile loses all authenticity, stripped of emotion despite stretching further. "Clarice. Clarice Brightville."

My palm covers our baby on instinct. "Nice to meet you, Clarice. I'm Aliya."

I'd rather not waste my time on a random woman glaring at me, so I turn my sights back on Noah. He's downing the fourth Alpha, this time having to use physical force.

"Hey, I have a question." Clarice stands, her hands bumping our spines as she leans on our chairs and causing poor Annika to jump.

I glance between the two Lunas, unsure by their frigid expressions if gossiping is yet another unsavory tradition at the Summit. "Oh, um… Okay. I'm a bit busy right now."

Clarice lets out a sharp laugh. "It'll be quick. And don't take this the wrong way, but—" She leans in, her wavy brown hair brushing my shoulder as she lowers her voice to a sharp point. "What are you, exactly?"

Heat blasts my cheeks as I rub my belly.

I know I shouldn't be embarrassed of myself since there's nothing wrong with being a hybrid, but she said that as though I smell like something is seriously wrong with me.

Noah thrashes the fifth competitor to the ground a little too hard, the poor wolf letting out a yipe.

Fuck. He must sense I'm upset.

But I'm angry too. If this is how wolves plan to treat our pup, I better set some boundaries before they're born.

Flipping my hair over my shoulder to look Clarice in the eyes, I straighten my back. "What am I, Luna? I'm my pack's first hybrid Luna. And possibly your future Queen, by the looks of it. Which could make me the first hybrid Queen Luna."

Clarice blinks a few times, gaping. Then she places a hand on her sternum, letting out an exasperated breath. "Why, I never. Calling yourself the Queen, right in front of our current Queen Luna too?"

Annika leans into me, keeping her volume loud enough for Clarice to hear. "Ignore her. Everyone who truly cares about me knows I don't care about titles. You and I both know it could've been possible for either of our mates to be King last year—just like many years before it."

Clarice scoffs, crossing her arms. She straightens behind us, busying her focus with the crowd, and I hope that's the end of her tirade.

The three of us flinch as Noah slams another Alpha into the grass.

"A hybrid Luna, huh?" Clarice mutters.

I finally return her stare, my eyes boring into hers with no mercy left inside me. "Do you have a problem with that?"

Clarice laughs, attempting to hide the annoyance I can smell. "Not at all! I'm just relieved to finally understand why you smell like that."

My belly aches beneath my palm. No matter how confident I am, my heart tears a little for our baby. Are they going to have to hear this their whole life? All because I'm their mom?

Guilt burns throughout my chest cavity. In the distance, Noah lets out a vicious snarl.

When Waimārie shows up a second later, her forehead contorts her washed-out skin—losing its usual warmth after what I assume has been an afternoon of illness. I open my mouth to ask about how dreadful she must feel, but I'm startled speechless by her fury, her eyes latching onto Clarice before she even acknowledges us. "Oi, you— What's all this about?"

Clarice laughs, opening her mouth to speak.

But Annika whips her head around. "Are you done now? I think you are."

Clarice reddens. Jabbing a finger at me, she grits her teeth. "She didn't even answer my question; she just dodged it with another shocking truth about how much the West Coast has devolved. I meant what *are* you—an Omega? Alpha? Beta? No offense, but I'm not used to wolves like you being so… ambiguous."

As Clarice's eyes sweep down me, her lip curling higher in disgust, my cheeks blaze hotter by the second. Annika's hand tightens around mine, and Waimārie presses against the back of my chair to join her in defending me, but it doesn't stop my eyes from watering.

And it's clear this bigoted Luna plans to double down. "There's a lot of talk around, wondering what's different about Greenfield. Alpha Noah is… You know. *Shy*. Especially for an

'Alpha.'" Clarice laughs, stoking a fire in my gut. "Are you sure he really has a ballsack?"

Annika shrinks beside me as I revert from shame to absolute rage. I don't know why our wolf sexes are so ambiguous either, but I don't think that means something is wrong with us. Especially not my sweet Noah.

My fangs flash without my permission. Annika dives behind my back, scrambling past our row's chairs to huddle into Waimārie's side, and Clarice whines.

"Do I need to sit you down with my four-year-old preschoolers, or can you find it in yourself to remember what's appropriate to ask strangers?"

My musk attracts a swarm of every Alpha in the vicinity, already heated and volatile—including Logan Brightville, heading straight for me to protect his mate.

But my wolf is still fuming. Instead of letting it go, I growl at Logan. "Stay back!"

Logan bursts into a sprint. His bustling power charging for me shoots defensive pheromones from my neck.

Shit. I've fucked up beyond repair. Running will only make Logan chase me, but a fight with an Alpha twice my size is a death sentence.

But a commanding voice erupts from behind me. "Hey!"

Relief floods my chest when I spot Reid Nordskov, the Idaho Alpha's focus locked on Logan as he races toward us.

Wolves around us dart away, Annika and Waimārie included, but I dash to Reid's side. That doesn't stop Logan from cracking his knuckles, restarting his prowl. My growls peter out with my fear, even with Reid's warm palm on my back.

But Noah parts the crowd with his Alpha musk alone. As he peers down at me with yellow eyes, my eyes water from everyone's stinging scents. Noah mistakes it for tears.

His rumbling growl vibrates through my chest. "Who the fuck forgot to not mess with my Luna?"

Reid steadies his voice. "Hey, hey, hey. *Breathe.*"

Noah grips Logan by the jaw, making the bulky man's shoulders raise to his ears in panic. "You didn't learn your lesson on the porch yesterday? She bites back."

Reid's hand on Noah's chest finally snaps him out of it. Noah drops Logan, who promptly shoves Noah.

Viktor catches my mate before he stumbles, the King Alpha's hunting eyes in full force as he rights Noah on his feet. As Viktor speaks into Noah's ear, Noah nods, his wolf slowing from deep snarls to a soft growl in our bond.

I grip Noah's wound fist. "I'm okay. We're okay."

Reid keeps his eyes trained on Noah, even as Noah softens into my touch.

But Viktor's shoulders loosen. "Hey, there you go. You good, bro?"

Noah swallows hard, nodding a few times. "...Yeah."

Viktor pats Noah's chest. "Sweet. Get back to it, Alphas."

Wolves disperse across the field, some already pairing back up with their next opponent.

But Noah hugs me tight, forcing his irritated competitor to wait. "What happened? Were they rude to you verbally or physically forceful too?"

My gut churns once I remember I mainly snapped in defense of *Noah*. The last thing he needs to hear are degrading rumors about him. He needs to stay confident.

"Let's talk about it later. Please don't worry so much about me."

"I can't help it. I hate this event."

I nuzzle into Noah's chest with a sigh, and he gives me an extra squeeze. But his wolf paces, desperate to head back into the action—and giving me an idea.

With a laugh at his precious wolf, I hold Noah tighter, batting my eyes up at him. "*You* might hate it, but who is that Alpha I see strutting around our bond, all proud of himself for not even having to use his claws yet?"

Noah groans, tipping his head back.

"Hey, look at me."

Noah peeks at me with a sigh.

I plant a soft kiss on his lips, keeping our stares locked. "I'm not scared of you."

Noah's wolf puffs his chest even higher, indulging in every second of my wolf's nuzzles and licks.

"Let him take over to fight for you. He wants to," I whisper.

"He's aggressive."

"And what does he always say about needing to be ready to protect the pack? His aggression isn't needlessly violent, Noah. Out of every Alpha here, *your* aggression keeps the peace."

Noah's focus flits between my eyes.

Then his jaw hardens. "You're a fucking Goddess-sent angel, Luna, I swear. And you're the only one here who can tame me."

My heart flips as he whispers those last words into my ear, their meaning holding a lot more weight as wolves surrounding us scurry from his single footstep. By Noah's fifth step back from me, his chest expands, fur sprouting from every pore as he bursts into his black bear of a wolf.

Except his fur stands at full attention, turning him from a giant to a Titan.

Holy shit. I knew he was huge, but so are most Alphas here—especially compared to the average wolf. They're the most powerful Alphas in the world, but Noah's beefy wolf makes every shifted Alpha look like a lanky teen.

Multiple Alphas roll over in defeat, even before Noah has a chance to be paired up with them.

I press my fingertips to my lips, preventing myself from breaking into inappropriate laughter; Noah's wolf looks just as annoyed as his human side, giving an irritated grumble at the bellies facing the sky in a heap around him.

Hey, look! Now you don't have to fight as many wolves today.

But just as I mindlink this thought, Logan steps forward to face off against Noah, baring his fangs in his human form.

At least not wolves with a conscience, Noah mindlinks.

"I heard from Mason Hart," Logan says.

I squish my palm tighter against my mouth, afraid I'll get sick.

Noah bristles, but his wolf doesn't budge a single other muscle.

Logan crosses his arms, his nude body in full view. "Everyone's heard the rumors by now. You smelled like an Omega as a pup, didn't you?"

Noah's huff from his snout is sharp, dirt clouding around his paws. But the shame in his side of our bond makes my knees shake.

What's this Alpha talking about? I've never felt Noah's confidence take such a deep hit.

"It's time you learned your place—from a real Alpha." Logan shifts, his spotted brown paws landing in a threatening sprawl. He flicks his tail at Noah, his ears jutting toward the sky with his angry snarls.

But Noah doesn't hesitate. With one swing of his paddle-like paw, he bats Logan to the ground.

I wince as Logan yipes. But he bursts from the ground twice as furious, lunging for Noah's throat with his claws extended.

Oh, my God, no—that's not allowed!

It happens faster than I know how to react. All I can do is scream, afraid I'm about to watch my mate die.

But this time, Noah's batting paw hits Logan so hard, I hear a loud *crack*. I gag, turning my back before I have to see what I just heard. I know exactly what that sound was from an unfortunate playground incident at my old preschool: the sound of bones snapping. The imagery alone has me struggling to keep my lunch down, shaking as I grip the edge of the planter boxes behind our spectator seating area. But as Logan's wolf bleats in pain, wolves stream over in hordes, and I know I have to help Noah with damage control among our packs.

Attempting to still the panicked wolf, multiple hands stabilize Logan's body before he breaks his leg further; it's dangling like a snapped branch in the wind.

Once again, Viktor is forced to mediate, stopping at Noah's side with an angry shove. "Dude, what the fuck?!"

Noah shrinks despite his massive size, his ears pasting to the sides of his head.

This single, minor flash of guilt causes Alphas to perk up across the field, seeking their chance to dominate Noah.

I dart into the midst of the Alphas without thinking, gripping Noah's fur as he whines over Logan on the floor.

But when he realizes I watched it all, his wolf's huge puppy-dog eyes aren't the only things that make an appearance.

I-I'm sorry, Luna, I didn't mean to hurt someone like this— I— His wolf whines, crouching lower and lower at my feet. Submitting himself to me in regret.

I gasp. *Noah, don't! Get up!*

The more wolves circle us, the more my Alpha musk shows itself.

Luna, I don't know what's wrong with me this year. Please, don't think differently of me—

My wolf pushes to the surface, stealing the color from my vision as she prepares to defend Noah.

Oh, Goddess, help us. Something must've severely triggered Noah's trauma. He's in a purely primal panic state, and his Alpha scent is fading.

Viktor turns to Noah with a deep growl. "Why the fuck are you groveling? Shift back and apologize."

As Viktor towers over my mate, the last thread of control over my wolf snaps.

I step closer to the King Alpha. "Are you serious? Do you want him to go all out, or not?"

Viktor faces me head on, staring me straight in the eyes in a true challenge. To my surprise, he doesn't appear offended about me holding his stare, meeting me face to face to challenge me back. "I do want him to go all out. With *me*. He knows this is too far, Luna."

"So now you're shaming him for showing remorse? Maybe his dangerously cocky opponents could learn a thing or two from it. They should also realize when it's time to protect themselves and accept defeat when they're outmatched." I gesture to the crying Alpha on the ground, howling as wolves fasten his leg to a thick tree branch. "And isn't lunging for a throat kill not allowed? If Noah didn't guard himself, our baby and I could've died with him!"

Viktor's eyes widen, turning his sights to the shattered Alpha on the ground. "Did you go for his fucking throat, Alpha Logan? Claws or fangs extended?"

Logan groans, not daring to meet Viktor's eyes.

Clarice strokes her mate's fur, tears streaming down her cheeks as she stares between us, wide-eyed. "M-maybe Alpha Noah isn't even an Alpha! He doesn't smell like it."

My fangs ache, extending further. "His paw just shattered another Alpha's leg. Omega or Alpha, you can't deny he's powerful. And I'm proud of who he is."

Noah gives out a soft whine, finally meeting my eyes again. Our bond erupts with his gratitude.

But my breath shakes. Circling Alphas stare at me in a new light, and Lunas cower from me.

Clarice sharpens her stare, her voice lowering. "Are you sure *you're* not the Greenfield Alpha? Why do you get a free pass from the fight?"

A laugh rumbles behind us. Before I turn around, chills race down my body, but when I see who it is, my stomach coils. Matthew Hillcrest, Florida's top Alpha, steps behind Clarice— likely the only time he'll side with an Omega, since his pack's volatile stance toward Omegas has him on our yellow list.

Sandy blonde hair over a jacked chest, Matthew sets his wolven glare on me, raising my wolf's hackles. "You want to know why she gets a free pass? Because she's yet another irrational, violent mother wolf. And you all complain about us Alphas being out of control? Well, look at her. She's a pregnant, hormonal Omega who reeks of fake Alpha. Where the fuck would we place someone like her?"

My mouth opens and closes, my eyes flitting from one wolf to the next. Some are disgusted by me, others terrified.

Waimārie scoffs. "Compared to tantruming grown men like you, placing a mother wolf should be a simple task."

Tāne snorts, crossing his bulky arms—and forcing Matthew to shut his mouth before he even tries to retort. But when my focus lands on Annika, in particular, cowering behind Viktor, my heart overflows with shame.

What if there really is something wrong with me?

Noah leaps to his feet, widening the circle of wolves around us.

His Alpha musk returns in full force, but the ache in our bond is undeniable. It physically hurts my heart.

Things are different now. Our status with other packs might not ever be the same again, now that everyone knows Noah and I are... Well, "like this."

No one relaxes, even when Noah shifts back into his human form. He hugs me into his side, inhaling my mark before giving it a gentle kiss.

"I will *never* be embarrassed by who you are," he breathes.

My chin wobbles through fresh tears.

When Noah turns to the crowd, they all flinch. But his voice comes out soft and even.

"I'm sorry for using excessive force. That was not my intention." Noah steps away from me, his open demeanor allowing the surrounding wolves to relax their taut arms. "As a traditional peace offering in my pack, I'd like to offer my help in healing your wounds."

Reid hums in agreement with this idea, and multiple wolves seem to feel the same, a crowd of heads bobbing in unison. My clenched fists soften, leaving me to rub out the stinging impression my fingernails left in my palms.

Noah stoops over Logan's leg to aid the healing process with his tongue.

But the half-shifted wolf shoves him away. "I don't want an Omega's pity."

I suck in a sharp gasp. All I can see are Noah's frozen shoulders, still hovering over the cowering Alpha.

But in Noah's heart, I know he's absolutely gutted, a knife-like pain jabbing the depths of my core.

Viktor growls. "Alright, Brightville, you don't want pity? I've lost it all for you. You're disqualified from all foreseeable Summits."

Logan's eyes bulge. "W-what?!"

"You fucking heard me. You went in for a kill strike; you're out. Everyone else? We're taking an hour break. Go cool off."

Noah doesn't waste a second in taking my hand, guiding me away from the crowd. As I chase after my mate, his soft sniffles tear at my heart.

$$\mathcal{O}\!\!\sim\!\! \text{21} \!\sim\!\!\mathcal{O}$$

We dash past bushy forest trees, but I can't run very far, my feet dragging.

Noah doubles back for me, his frustration rising when he sees me gripping our baby. "Fuck, sorry, I'm so fucking inconsiderate—"

"Hey." I place a hand on his chest, stopping him where he stands.

Then I strip my top. Noah's jaw drops.

I laugh. "Shift with me, gorgeous. It's a wolf-out type of day."

He softens, giving me space to shift into my nimble, pearly wolf.

Soon after, Noah's black bear of a wolf drags his paws after me, his head drooping and ears slicked back.

I let him sulk.

Our wolves weave through Kiruna's forests, reminiscent of home despite its sweeping hillsides. Soon, our paws fall in line, our wolves courting by leaning against each other's sides as we pad ahead.

Noah's emotions settle into a hum, sadness looming beneath his anger. When his wolf nudges my cheek with his big nose, I follow him without question.

He guides me to a stunning inlet on the lakeside. Daylight caresses the water's surface with its soft glow, illuminating a shady canopy of trees.

Noah's dragging wolf comes to a halt. *This is where I go to think, whenever I visit Sweden for Summits. I've always wondered if I'd have a chance to bring my mate here, someday.*

My pulse rises, ignited by Noah's amber eyes gazing deep into mine.

When we're wolves, it's like he's seeing a more intimate part of me—even more so than when I'm naked in his arms. And despite how upset he is, he overflows with love, looking at me in this form.

But from everything I know about Noah, I'm willing to bet he needs to hear where I stand.

No one can change my opinion of you, Noah. Especially not wolves with completely different values than us. I only see beauty in you, Omega, Alpha, or even Beta. If you smelled like any single one of them in the future, you'd still be my one true love.

Noah's wolf whines, its high pitch piercing my heart. *A-and so are you, Luna…*

But do you know what I see when I look at you? I nuzzle his side, circling his wolf as his head hangs low. *You're selfless. A peacebringer. An honest leader. And a gorgeous sweetheart of a softie. I see my mate. The one I'd choose, over and over.*

Noah's ears twitch in thought, but they remain flattened. *Y-you don't care if I… If I don't always smell like an Alpha?*

I've already seen and smelled those sides of you, my love. And just the same as those times, I still love you. No matter what.

But how do you feel?

I told you, Noah: I love you no matter what.

Noah softens his shoulders, rolling them as he pads forward. Nuzzling into my fluffy chest fur, he gives my neck a soft lick, washing me in a tingling warmth. *Not about that. How do you feel about yourself? When those assholes mocked your Alpha musk, you felt so much shame… It fucking crushed me.*

When my gaze lands on Noah's legs, my heart splits in half; his massive wolf is quivering, each paw vibrating in the sand.

I whine, nuzzling Noah's ear in an attempt to convince him to unbury his face from my fur. When he refuses with a deep grumble, my wolf nibbles at his neck.

He grunts, flopping to the ground and rolling himself in the sand. Some of it flicks up at me, and my wolf sneezes.

Noah!

No matter how tightly his sad ears are smushed to his head, his tail wags at my irritation.

Soon enough, we're both flopped on the sand, smacking it everywhere with our tails.

You goofball, I mindlink.

I fucking love you, Luna.

I love you so much.

Noah freezes, his focus switching between my eyes. *There's something different about us.*

My wagging tail slows to a halt. *I know.*

Noah can no longer look at me, his wolf busying himself by sniffing the air for anyone that could barge into our private alcove. With a soft whine, he settles his cheek back onto the sand, verifying we're alone. *For me, it's something I avoided about myself since I was a pup.*

My wolf whines without my permission.

Noah sulks even lower, burrowing his nose into the cool sand with deep sniffs. *But now I feel like an ass. I don't want you to be ashamed of yourself for being different, especially not just because I'm ashamed. I've got my own shitty biases about myself, and I don't even agree with them. Not when it comes to other wolves. If you look at me close enough, I'm a fucking hypocrite. A-and I'm sorry you had to see it.*

I huff, accidentally spraying sand into Noah's face. He bats me in playful retaliation, his paws poking my chest fur, but I can't find the humor in this conversation.

I'm a hypocrite too, then, Noah. But maybe we all are.

He grunts, jumping to his paws to claw an angry hole in the sand.

I allow him his moment, my wolf admiring his ability to dig in deep with such speed. A burning instinct within me craves for him to build me a makeshift nest, right here and now. Does his Omega side give him similar nesting urges, or is his Alpha side too in control of his instincts?

Or is it that his Alpha side simply covers up his internal Omega—just like Noah once divulged to me about his Grandma Greenfield, the Lycan who mastered masking herself using her scent?

Do you think— I pause, nerves stealing my thoughts. Shit, this might be an insensitive question.

Noah stops digging, staring back with alert ears.

I don't want to offend him, but we have to be honest with each other.

Noah, do you think you really are an Omega, at heart?

Stock-still, Noah grows more rigid by the second. A long silence stretches between us.

When he finally mindlinks me, my stomach lining stings like it's raw with stress.

What do you think I am? Noah asks.

My heart throbs; I'm unsure what the right answer is.

That's when it clicks. We're seeking certainty where there is none, just like OCD does to my brain.

There is *no* right answer.

I inch closer to Noah, keeping myself low to the sand without putting pressure on our pup. *Listen to me closely.*

Golden eyes meet my stare, Noah's focus unwavering despite our bond fluctuating with intense emotion after emotion.

My lungs quiver as I take short, tentative breaths. *Noah, I think you're an Omega, like me.*

His breath tenses, and ironically, his Alpha musk explodes.

I pop upright on all fours. *And I think you're* also *an Alpha… Like me.*

Noah's ears lift.

I take another step forward, tilting my head to meet his gaze, snout to snout. *Why do we have to pick one?*

Silence consumes the forest around us. Noah doesn't breathe, let alone blink. I gaze at my mate, breathing through the rollercoaster for him as a flurry of emotions in our bond rises, rises, rises…

Then our emotional bond crashes, hard.

Noah huffs short, quick bursts of air from his snout against my chest fur, sending a shiver down my spine. His inner turmoil fluctuates too rapidly for me to grasp each complex shard of it. Otherwise, he still hasn't moved.

My teeth chatter with anxiety, but not because I'm doubting what I said. This is also the closest I've ever had to an answer about *myself*—all my "weird," "unladylike," and "improper" traits that caused me to bury my truths, and then bury them again once I realized I was an Omega Lycan, supposedly designed to nurture pups. But if this Lycan fluidity could be true about Noah, it could be true about anyone. About me. Beneath the surface, I thought something was still wrong with me, but all I had to do was add "Alpha" into the equation.

But one of the only certainties in life, change, is terrifying. Noah fights through this change, processing it like I am—stuck in the raw silence. When our bond settles into an emotional melody I've never felt from him before, Noah's wide wolf eyes still haven't left my stare.

I've never seen Noah so centered. I almost don't recognize the sensation floating between us, shaking our fears free, but as soon as I land on the description I'm seeking, my whole body settles into acceptance.

Peace. That's what I see staring back.

My wolf pants as powerful, gutting emotions overwhelm me; I think I just witnessed my mate's entire world perspective shift. I think I watched a part of him be set free.

Noah's chest tenses. That's all it takes for my confidence to plummet, fear striking deep into my bones that I've spoken way too far—filled in my perspective of Noah's identity for him, which I know is out of line. My wolf rolls onto her back, submission overcoming me.

Noah's ears flick back in adoration. *Well, you look like an Omega right now. But I can't fucking believe it.* He sucks in a deep breath through his snout, shutting his eyes as he raises his chin to the sky—as if in preparation to howl to the Moon Goddess.

But he doesn't howl. His heart settles before my eyes, lowering the tension in his fur.

I gaze in awe. I never realized his wolf was fluffy because he was *tense*—not until his form softens into true neutrality. He's still bulky, but his fur takes a new sleek, softened edge, dropping its guard to leave him bare before me, a picture of sculpted muscle beneath silky, smooth fur.

Noah blows a slow breath from his snout, the frigid air clouding over his jet black nose. *I think I'm mated to an Omega-Alpha. And I'm an Alpha-Omega.*

As Noah mindlinks these raw, vulnerable declarations, I've

never been more proud of him. Excitement floods my veins, making me shudder. *You're beautiful, Noah. So beautiful.*

That's all I can think about you as I feel more and more of your heart each day. Thank the Goddess you're carrying our pup. Noah drags his chilly, wet nose down my belly, placing a soft lick over my uterus. I whine, unable to store the overflowing love in my heart. *The three of us might be the only ones who ever understand the full truth of who we are, Aliya.*

I stare into the honest, vulnerable eyes hovering over my belly, and I know he's right.

But my ears soften. *I don't care if they don't understand. We don't need to understand everything about ourselves yet, either. All that matters to me is that you grow to love your Omega side, Noah. It hurts me to watch you hate a part of you that I absolutely treasure.*

Noah carefully rests his forehead against my belly, his silky coat tickling my skin beneath my abdomen's wispy, thinner fur.

I get it. I fucking get it. And I don't want you to hate your gorgeous Alpha side either. Noah's ears droop. *B-but… This is rooted in something dark for me, Luna. I'm going to have to work on it. Possibly for a long time.*

My heart sinks.

This is it—the root of Noah's PTSD. I don't know how or why it began unless he shares the details someday, but I can feel it in our bond: the sickening, inescapable type of horror that I feel when I think of Steven.

I understand. Which is why I'm so proud. Just acknowledging all sides of yourself is life-changing. And as you take your time to process this change and work on self-acceptance, I'll be there through it all with you.

Noah whines, his aching heart shattering mine twice over.

You won't have to go through it alone. Just like I'm never alone when I'm with you. Extending my claws, I cling to his plushy fur. *You can do this, Noah. You already took the biggest step by telling me your truth. I believe in you.*

Noah doesn't respond, but his heart aches in deep, overwhelming understanding; he not only heard every word we've just spoken, he's also absorbing them to his core.

As we curl up together in the sand, our wolves fit like they always do, my chin perfectly slotting over his back.

But rather than tucking himself in too, Noah gazes at me with slow blinks, his nose pressed to the side of my snout. *You're the most powerful, loving wolf the world will ever know. I mean it.*

I whine, snuggling into him as his scent flows freely. He smells heavenly—his sweet Omega scent mixed with a doting, protective Alpha, creating the most delicious cinnamon spice. I can't get enough of it. Our hour-long break is coming to an end, but I don't want to let him go, our wolves nuzzling each other's noses back and forth every few minutes with soft licks on each other's cheeks and nibbles beneath our ears.

But as his Omega scent strengthens, it sinks in: I'm mated to an Omega too.

And he's the most powerful wolf in the world.

My fur stands on end, goosebumps coating my skin as reality dawns on me. Noah lifts his chin off my hip, his ears perking up. *What's wrong?*

I huff, unable to withstand how gorgeous he is, his jet-black fur shimmering against the light sand. *Can I tell you something, Omega to Omega?*

Noah hesitates before his puppy-dog stare hits full force, a secret excitement in our bond hiding beneath the surface—as if he's desperate to be included as an Omega, but petrified to be.

Yet, he's listening—waiting—in silent acknowledgment of who he is.

My heart flips as glee races through me. *I had a revelation.*

Noah tilts his head before giving my cheek a soft boop with his nose. *Oh? Let's hear it.*

Don't you think there's a silent agreement between all wolves that Omegas are actually the ones to be afraid of?

Noah's eyes widen, his ears perking up. *What? No, I don't.*

I know, I know, not on the surface. But let's put all the expectations aside and look at everyone's actions.

Okay, I'm listening.

I didn't start hearing this until I was pregnant, but now everyone's calling me a 'mother wolf.' Except it's like they're afraid I'm a bomb about to go off, disrupting their pack order.

Noah's snout sucks in a sharp breath against my cheek.

Is he seeing it too? *You said Omegas don't receive the same training Alphas do, right?*

Right, he says. *They're not even considered for it, whereas Alphas are all encouraged or even forced, if their family is very traditional.*

I swallow hard, my ears pointing to the sky as it all sinks in. *Okay, that's what I thought. Noah, this is blowing my mind. Traditionally, Lycans think of Omegas as future or current mother wolves, right?*

Noah's wolf grumbles. *Right. I always feel bad for Omega men and non-binary Omegas who have carried pups because of that, not to mention that plenty of Alphas and Betas have been pregnant too. It not only leaves them out, but stereotypes Omegas as baby-making machines.*

It is awful. I whine. *For argument's sake, we're thinking like your average cocky Alpha. And beneath the surface, even Alpha-domination men have been acknowledging that Omega mother wolves are something to be afraid of. But mother wolves aren't trained to fight, if they're Omegas. Yet you all agree Omegas are born with a frightening defensive power to protect our pups—whether we become 'mother wolves' or not. Doesn't that mean everyone agrees Omegas are strong, even without the training Alphas get?*

Noah's ears slowly rise, his breath coming out in short, quick huffs. But a desperation creeps through our bond that I've never experienced before—almost like Noah's emotions are clinging to me, begging me to save his life.

So I keep going, my wolf trembling with excitement. *In our top leader meeting with just the six of us, you all said I was an even stronger asset now—as a mother wolf. And that's before we admitted I'm also an Alpha, right? Omegas are powerful. Doesn't our very existence as Omegas break the logic behind Alphas' 'Goddess-given power?' What if they're not just scared of losing control over us, but they're even more scared of the day we realize we have power too?*

I pause, gazing into Noah's wide, shocked stare. A shiver races beneath my fur, Noah's golden eyes emitting power and focus.

Noah, what if they're not afraid of you because you're a powerful Alpha, but because you're an Omega, *period. An Omega who wasn't held back by social confines, and learned how to fight alongside Alphas.*

You're an Omega who broke through every mold they expected of us, and now you're here to stop them from hurting us all, just by existing.

As Noah's eyes dance across the sand, my lungs speed into an anxious pant.

But as his ears droop, swooping back against his head, he lets out the softest, sweetest whine.

I crash my forehead against his, whining with him. *Oh, my love. I'm so sorry—*

Noah huffs, his wolf whining in deep sorrow. *I never thought someone would find my Omega-ness to be needed.*

My heart flips as Noah buries his nose into my stomach fluff, whining with every breath. *Oh, Noah…*

Breathing through his emotions, my wolf cries with him. But as we snuggle, his wolf squishing his nose deep into my cheek in gratitude, I realize he's not simply grieving the hurt he's felt for his whole life; he's relishing in how beautiful I find him. And it's true; I've never felt so awed that another person exists, and so privileged to be able to exist alongside him.

I whine the entire rest of the break from the Alpha battle, my heart bursting with love.

As Noah presses his furry head to mine one last time before facing his competitor, he whines with me. *Are you okay, Luna? You're starting to worry me.*

Sorry, I'm just— I shut my eyes, letting out another happy whine. *My heart is aching with joy. I just can't believe I'm going to get to see you raise our baby.*

Noah smushes his fluffy forehead into me harder. Then he lets out the same, sappy whine. *Fuck. That's so cute. How am I going to kick wolf ass after this, Luna? You've turned my heart into happy mush.*

My whine sparks into an excited yip, urging me to nip Noah's scent gland until a shiver ripples down the fur of his back, ending with a flick of his tail. *Show them no one will tear us down. For our pup's sake.*

Noah's fur bristles, expanding him twice his size once more. As he steps back from me, his stoicism returns full force. *Fucking genius wolf, I swear… Hey, wait. Maybe you could actually—*

With a tilt of his head, Noah doesn't finish his sentence; he turns his back to me. My wolf's chest puffs, unbelieving he'd leave me hanging like this before going off to fight.

I scamper after him. *Excuse me, mister?! Maybe I could what, now?*

Noah gives my cheek a playful nudge, his tail swinging wildly. *No, I changed my mind. I'll have to wait a few days to say this, at the very least.*

I blink a few times, so desperate to talk his thoughts through that I shift back into my human form. "Noah?! Where do you think you're going?"

With a sassy tail wag, Noah only spares me a quick glance over his shoulder. *To win this stupid fucking Summit… As your Alpha-Omega.*

I stop in my tracks, a bright smile filling my cheeks. As he leaves, I see it: he's still puffed out and defensive, but there's a sleek, steady confidence to his paws, allowing our bond to soar in peace. He might not allow it to show in his scent, but his Omega side is here too, fighting this fight just as hard.

Noah's wolf prowls onto the field, renewed energy in his paws leaving me on the sidelines to watch in awed silence. He beats every competitor, only sustaining a single claw scratch. This leaves him to battle amongst the other top nine Alphas tomorrow for the semi-finals: the night before the New Moon.

22

Noah and I skip tonight's official dinner, relieved to know Reid, Tāne, and Viktor also ranked in the top ten for the semi-finals. As we huddle up in the disastrous bundle I've made of our "nest" bed, we can't stop giggling, our excitement over each other at its peak.

Noah's hair flops over his dark brow, still mussed from sweat. I breathe him in, tracing my fingertips over his bare chest as he lays beside me, stretched out for me to see. Swallowing the last bite of my dinner, I have to gulp harder, unable to fathom how this is my mate. He looks exhausted, dark circles under his slow-blinking eyes, but he's exhausted for our safety.

Just like he said, he did it. He beat every Alpha thus far, not just as another Alpha, but also as a vibrant, beautiful Omega.

"I can't stop looking at you," I whisper.

Noah grins, his eyes softening as he plucks a stray hair off my neck. "I can tell. If I wasn't also gushing over my gorgeous Luna, I'd be borderline-uncomfortable with how much you're staring."

Sputtering out a laugh, I grip Noah's shoulder, stretching over our dinner plates to plant a heavy kiss on his mouth. As I lean into his relaxed, plushy lips, comfort fills my chest, pulling a pleased hum from my throat. Noah's deep purr in response curls my toes.

Leaning into his elbow on his side, Noah slinks his weight into the mattress. He drags his eyes up my bare legs, my ass barely covered by another one of his shirts. As Noah meets my stare, his smile widens. I grin with him, figuring we're thinking the same thing: it's only a matter of time before we throw our plates aside, putting this bed to work.

But as his warm palm trails down my side, sloping over my hip, I catch his hand. "I think you've been a good enough boy to receive your surprise now."

Noah blinks a few times before breaking into giggles. "Oh, I have, have I?"

As he reaches for me, I scurry off the bed, laughing with him as he prowls after me. "Down, boy. Stay."

Dropping his head with a laugh, Noah sighs, still on all fours. "Goddess, Aliya. I don't even know how to reply to that. But I'll be a—" Noah sighs again, softening his voice. "I'll be a good boy for you, and stay."

We take one look at each other, Noah's face beet red, and burst into laughter.

Noah flops on the bed to wait, still chuckling to himself. I can't stop giggling either, dragging my suitcase across the carpet and through the bathroom door, shutting it behind me.

But I could feel the thrill in our bond as I teased Noah. It's the last I'll torture him for tonight—well, almost. I'm certain he'll be the one torturing me into lusty overwhelm soon, but not before he processes what I'm about to do. And judging by how shy he felt just now, this surprise might be just a bit too much.

Tossing his shirt off over my head, I can't stop giggling to myself, my laugh echoing across the bathroom as I dig out my surprise. Replacing my underwear with the pink, V-shaped lingerie I bought at Celestial Couture before my Luna ceremony, I'm careful not to disturb what I've attached to the lingerie's backside. This surprise swings from the crest of the V-shaped strings, perched at the top of my ass. As I tug it on in front of the mirror, I gawk at how accentuated my baby bump looks; these panties slope beneath it, following the edges of its curve to hook over my hips.

This only makes me giggle louder.

Noah groans, calling out from the bed. "Oh, Luna… What's going on in there? Should I be concerned?"

"Nothing! Don't you worry." My eyes widen as I struggle to clasp the bra half of the lingerie. Cracking open the door, I mutter through it. "Unless you don't like seeing me no longer fitting into yet another article of clothing. Did I get even bigger since we got here?"

Noah's rumbling laughter stirs warmth in my heart. "Yes. I fucking love how cute you look, little mama."

I flush down to my neck, unable to hold my own eye contact in the mirror. As I put the finishing touches on my head and neck, I bite my lips, turning to check that everything's in its right place.

Clasping the doorhandle, my heart hammers. I exhale long and slow, steeling myself.

But as soon as I open it, I gasp. "Oh! I forgot—" Rustling through the suitcase again, I find one piece I'm missing. Clutching it tight in one hand, I step out of the bathroom, keeping my face as straight as possible.

Noah lifts his head from the blankets. "Aliya, why am I hearing tinkling sounds—"

My mate's breath catches. He gawks at me as I stride in with big, fuzzy gray wolf ears on top of my head, poking out of my long, midnight hair.

I've never seen Noah's jaw drop—just like I haven't seen him slap his palms over his eyes, curling into a ball on the bed. His voice is muffled into the cushy bedding, but I can just make out an exasperated cry. "Aliya!?"

Laughing, I flick my hair over my shoulders. Grasping the chunky clasp at the end of my pink, leather leash, I latch it onto the collar around my neck. "You're not going to look at me? You haven't even seen the best part! At least give me one eyeball."

Turning his head just enough, Noah peeks through his fingers with one eye, his palm still muffling his voice. "Aliya, holy shit, what the—"

Unfortunately for Noah, I know he's an ass guy. Turning over my shoulder, I reveal a fuzzy gray wolf tail clipped to the back of my panties. Giving my hips a little shimmy, I burst into giggles; Noah makes an undignified cry into his hands, reburying his face into the mattress.

"Noah!? Is this too much?" I can't help but laugh with him as he sputters in delirium, rubbing his forehead into the mattress.

"I feel like I'm doing something devious! Did I fall asleep? I can't be looking at you like this in front of me—"

Striding to the end of the bed, I bend over, dragging my hands through his hair. "Ah, I see. So, you like it that much?"

Lifting his eyes, Noah startles the breath out of me. Golden, sharp eyes latch onto me, and as our bond rises into urgency, I know this is the last time his hands will be off of me tonight.

As he lunges for me, I erupt into laughter, smiling against his heated lips.

"No, no, no, Aliya—" Noah's fingertips drag down my cheeks between kisses, stopping on my pink collar. "My Luna can't wear this. She's a free, wild wolf."

I bite my lip, my heart flipping. "What if she wants to wear it tonight, for you? Just you."

Noah purrs, his hands sweeping down my sides before trailing back up my arms. He swoops my hair off my back, gathering it in one hand as he tugs at the collar's latch. "Then I'll free you, myself—as I mate you."

He can barely speak these words beyond soft mutterings, spurring me into heavier giggles. Noah laughs with me, tossing the pink collar onto the bed.

I can't stop smiling. "Fine. But I'm not finished with teasing you yet. Sit on the edge of the bed for me, please."

Dropping his bashful stare, Noah flutters my heart with his sweet smile. He sits as requested, blinking his puppy-dog eyes.

He has no idea I plan to tease him until he sees stars.

Sweeping my fingertips down his bare chest, I hum once I reach his waistline. "Let's free you of your clothes too, gorgeous wolf."

Noah's stare locks onto mine with wild intensity, capturing my every minor movement. As I ease his boxers past his hips, his warm grip stations itself on my waist. But he stops me from dropping to my knees; bending over first, he gives my swollen belly a quick nuzzle of affection, flipping my heart.

"Don't go too wild tonight, feisty Alpha. You're still doing me the biggest favor of my lifetime." Noah's low purr sends tingles down my spine.

When he sits back, allowing me to stare down at his naked, bruised, and clawed body, my jaw hardens. "Don't worry, I have a burst of energy just thinking about how I'd like to treat you. You better be ready, Alpha-Omega."

Noah's breath catches.

Settling on the hardwood floor, I tug the edge of the comforter beneath my knees to cushion myself while I focus on Noah. I don't meet his fervent stare, but I can feel it burning in my peripherals—tracking me. My stomach flips as his cock twitches to life, swelling between my shaky fingers as I scoot myself between his knees.

Dragging my hands down either side of his plump shaft, I dare to meet Noah's eyes once more—just as I sweep my nose along his cock, returning Noah's affectionate nuzzle. His breath hitches, parting his lips alongside mine as I ease my tongue up the thick vein on the underside of his shaft.

Inhaling deep, Noah grips the mattress at his sides. I purr, trailing my lips over his sensitive tip until his cock flexes, popping from my mouth.

I've already raised my mate's breathing rate to a steady huff, but as I spit on his shaft, slipping my hands down it to cover him in lubrication, I can't hold back a smile; he's already squirming, and he hasn't even seen my new idea yet.

Ever since his knot has become a bit more unpredictable, I've locked onto its presence whenever it does tie our bodies together, giving me that satiating, stuffed sensation.

But his body isn't the only one playing a part in forming his knot; every time it grows inside me, my pussy clamps down over it, pulling desperate moans from Noah's lips as my body encourages his knot to expand.

So when I work my lubricated massage up and down his shaft tonight, I place my lips over his tip, allowing my hands to glide all the way down to the base—where his thick length meets his pelvis. Palpitating there, I feel it; the subtle beginnings of a knot within his shaft. As I bob my head, taking his tip into my mouth, I pulse over his hiding knot with rhythmic, tender squeezes, mimicking my flexing pussy.

Right away, Noah gives a soft, hitching moan, his hips jerking.

My heart flips. Locking eyes with Noah, I find his stare fully shifted—a gleaming golden staring back. I purr, well aware the sound vibrates over his hot shaft between my lips, and Noah moans once more. Keeping one hand around the base of his shaft, I use the other to stroke his thick length where my lips can't reach, ensuring I'm stimulating every angle of his cock. As I quicken my pace, Noah's claws prick the mattress, his lusty scent stinging my eyes.

I blink up at him. *What do you think, Alpha-Omega? Do you feel good?*

Panting through every breath, Noah doesn't respond; he's too busy watching his tip disappear behind my lips, writhing as he struggles to keep from thrusting too deeply as I massage his budding knot.

The second it swells beneath my hands, I pop his tip free from my lips with a gasp for air. Noah groans, so I must've assumed right; he was seconds from coming, even though we've just started.

But I want him to enjoy this new sensation as long as possible, craving his reaction as his hips continue to rise. Cupping my hands around his shaft, I purr, loving how tightly Noah's jaw clenches.

"Go ahead, gorgeous—move your hips," I whisper.

Gripping my shoulders, Noah widens his knees. As his hips jerk into my grip, precum spills from his tip. With how wet he's become, my palms slip down his shaft with every thrust, ending with a soft squeeze over his forming knot. Noah shudders, his breath racing as he fucks my hands. He can't seem to hold back, his moans morphing into grunts as he thrusts hard enough to jerk from my grasp.

His chest heaves as he waits for me to reposition my hands around his flexing shaft, filling the silence with soft groans. My stomach flips, each of his deep, throaty sounds burrowing into my pussy until it flutters alongside his undulating body. I stare in adoration as he leans in, pumping his hips faster; his eyes have closed, my mate allowing himself to submit to pleasure before me. His trust in me is so beautiful that my breath quivers alongside his.

And it's working; Noah's knot bulges wider, even though he's not inside me. Deepening my massage around the expanding mass, I keep one hand tight around the base of his shaft, allowing the other to glide against his thrusts. Noah's grunts dip into moans at the end of each desperate sound, his hips losing their rhythm. Leaning in, I flit my tongue across the base of his tip, pulling a needy moan from his lips—just before his hot cum splashes my cheeks.

I always wondered if Noah came harder while knotting me—the unmistakable presence of warm, flooding heat within my belly whenever our bodies lock together.

I have my answer. Fighting his bucking hips to keep my hand tight around his knot, I pulse rapid squeezes over it, leaving Noah sputtering as his claws dig into my shoulders. With every squeeze, another gush of fluid spills from his cock, splashing across my chest and Noah's thighs until I'm soaked in him.

Noah attempts to cuss, but all that comes out is a grunted whimper, his weight collapsing over me. He grips me in a tight hug—trapping me in his grasp like he can't bear any distance between us.

With my hands still stationed around his swollen, throbbing knot, I bite back a smile as Noah's awed emotions in our bond evolve into shock.

"*Aliya*. How the—" Noah pants, his hips twitching at any subtle movement; I can't imagine how sensitive his knot must feel between my palms. He grips my hands around his knot, squeezing one last drop of cum from his shaft with a groan. "*That* has never happened— With just your hands? I—"

Giggling, I wriggle my face out of his chest until I can pepper kisses over his sweaty cheek. "Are you too tired to mate me now, my shy Alpha-Omega?"

Chuckling, Noah plops a pleasure-heavy hand over my fuzzy headband. "Oh, no. *You* better be ready now, Omega-Alpha. You've drawn out my horny wolf in full force."

My heart flips. He's not lying; a residual, lusty ache roughens his voice around the edges.

Another drop of fluid spills down my thigh at the thought. As I readjust my sitting position, stretching my sore lower back, I'm stunned by how soaked I feel, the air cold against my drenched core, and it's all just from watching Noah.

As he pulls me to my feet, revealing heavy-lidded, burning eyes, my breath catches.

Noah's sly grin warns of his incoming rut, his extended incisors sending a thrill through my chest. "Let go. I need to clean you."

Releasing his knot, I bite my lip as I witness the mess I've made of him; Noah shudders through a groan, holding his shaft until I can ease it from my hand. But to my surprise, it hasn't softened one bit, still standing at attention once we've released it.

See what you've done? Holding me by the waist, Noah drags his tongue up my swollen belly and chest, washing me in chills. As he licks his cum from my skin, flustering me speechless, he purrs at my needy, desirous scent. *You'll have to give me a minute before I can mate you, even though that's all I want to do to you now, naughty Omega-Alpha.*

Bursting into giggles, I jerk away from his tongue over my sensitive breasts, leaving him with a teasing grin. "Sorry. I may have gone a little overboard."

Noah's soft chuckle coats me in goosebumps. "A little? Do you know how prepared you'll need to be for me now?"

With Noah's playful *tsk*, I swallow hard—just before he gives my waistband a gentle tug.

I let out a surprised squeak as I tip toward him, but Noah catches me. He growls into my neck, giving my scent gland a tender bite, and I shriek through a laugh, gripping his hair.

Noah purrs, licking my mark in apology, but I'm far too breathless to fully laugh, my groin aching for him. He knows it, making sharp, sustained eye contact that sets my insides on fire.

When Noah slips his palm over my ass to find my fuzzy tail, he chuckles, stroking my tail before trailing his hand beneath it. I hold my breath, waiting for him to figure out my next surprise.

As his thick fingers find the gap at the base of my crotchless panties, his breath cuts short. But as his chuckles morph into purrs, his tongue pressing down harder over my neck, my toes curl through the pressure he swirls over my bare pussy.

Flopping onto his back, Noah sighs. "Come here."

My heart flips. "Where?"

Patting his shoulders, Noah grins. "Be a good girl, and sit."

My bulging eyes spur us both into laughter, my cheeks hot as I crawl onto the bed.

I've never sat on him while he pleasured me before. I don't want to suffocate him, and it shows; my legs tremble as I walk my knees around his sides until I straddle his shoulders.

Gazing down at him, I swallow hard. "S-so, um, are you okay if I actually sit, or—"

Before I can overthink it, Noah grabs the back of my thighs, widening my knees over his face until I hover a mere inch from his nose.

My heart lurches into my throat. With my pussy on full display, Noah's pointed stare only burns my cheeks brighter.

But he lets out a luscious purr. "Don't be embarrassed. I've never smelled anything so tempting." Dragging hot palms down my shaky thighs, Noah softens his tone. "Unless you're not up to it right now?"

"N-no, I—" I swallow hard, easing my thighs down over his face. The last I see of Noah's wet, plushy lips is them curling into a satisfied smile—just before they greet my pussy with a gentle kiss.

I shiver. The soft *click* of Noah's kisses spark tingles up my torso, swirling through my chest. My thighs soften, tempted for a little more pressure between them—until Noah's rumbling purr buzzes over my clit, flexing my core against his lips. As his tongue slips over my labia, I grip his hair, my chest curling over him in delight.

"*Oh*—" I sputter through a breath, my eyelids fluttering as my hips jerk over his mouth. "S-sorry, am I crushing—"

Noah growls, his hands squeezing my ass until my pussy smushes against his swirling tongue. *Crush me, please. I'm five seconds away from going feral, so I need you ready for when I rut you into the headboard.*

Crying out, I only encourage Noah, his tongue lapping over every inch between my legs. I flush down to my neck, shocked by how heavily he's working me up within seconds. If I'm not careful, his adoring scent combined with his heavy purring against my clit might send me over the edge, the entirety of my pelvis tingling.

When my core opens wide, Noah nuzzles my clit between flits of his wide, flattened tongue. Fluid spills from me, forcing Noah to lift my hips and gasp for air.

But before I can melt back into concern, Noah dives back in, his tongue racing faster over my clit and labia. My hips jerk, forcing me to clasp tight handfuls of Noah's hair. I pant through the steady climb of my incoming orgasm, my thighs quivering.

Noah sets off a chain reaction in my nerves, pleasure buzzing up my abdomen until tingles reach my parted lips.

I drop my head back. "N-*Noah*, I'm—"

Shaking his head through a growl, Noah rubs my pussy back and forth with his tongue, his nose flicking my throbbing clit. I release a desperate moan, another gush of fluid slipping down Noah's cheeks. But as my moans heighten, Noah's hips buck behind me, startling a gasp from my lips. I don't need to check behind myself to know how swollen he is; I can feel his desperation to mate me in our bond, coupled by his breath beating against my clit.

His attention feels too good to contain. My thighs clamp around his head, my pussy fluttering over his tongue as I come. Noah rocks my hips over his face, his vibrating growls between my legs heightening my cries of pleasure until I collapse backward, releasing his face in a panic.

As I feared, Noah pants for air, his chest heaving beneath me.

I gasp, swiping my fluid off his bright red face. "Oh, Goddess! Are you o—"

Noah breaks into the biggest, proudest grin, stealing my breath. "Thank you for crushing me."

Slapping my hands over my burning face, I can only hear Noah's resulting laugh, bright enough to tighten my grinning cheeks against my palms as I burst into giggles with him.

As he sits up, forcing me backward, I yelp, gripping his shoulders for dear life. But I should've known better; thick arms keep me cuddled close, settling me gently into Noah's lap. Noah's rumbling laughter against my cheek as he nuzzles me only widens my smile, my hands dragging through his hair.

"I didn't pull your hair out, did I?" I whisper.

Pressing hard kisses into my shoulder, Noah unhooks my bra, drawing a pleased hum from my lips. "Worth it."

Biting my lip, I meet his adoring stare as he slips my bra from my shoulders.

"I love you," I whisper.

"And I love you, my sweet Omega-Alpha." His kiss heats my cheeks as much as his words, his lips still carrying my pussy's needy scent.

I flush through a rush of shyness, but Noah doesn't tease me this time. He's gentle with my body as we reorient ourselves, shuffling further up the mattress until our heads rest on our pillows. But Noah doesn't keep his distance; his prowling shoulders press me deep into my nest's heap of blankets with a glomping hug.

And his sloppy kisses against my mark remind me his rut nears its peak. The musky, urgent scent beneath his every move flutters my eyelids, heating me down to my core. As Noah's hands drag down my body, I catch his cheeks in my palms.

When our eyes meet, the mere sight of his alert, shifted irises staring back raises my heart rate. I can only press one kiss into his lips before he crashes into a heated kiss, his tongue slipping over mine as we purr in unison.

I didn't expect to be worked up again so quickly, but as my hands find Noah's flexing cock between us, he glides his fingertips down my pussy, and I let out a shocked moan; two of his fingers slip deep inside me in an instant, shooting a blast of pleasure up my spine. I jerk against his soft presses against the front wall of my pussy, far more sensitive now that he already pleased me with his tongue.

Noah's growls lose their controlled edge, his fangs extending as his chest heaves. He leaves me breathless as his fingers slip from me, my mate rising on all fours. Trailing his fingers down my spine, his touch urges my wolf to raise my ass high into the air, presenting myself to him on instinct. With each stroke down my back, Noah sweeps his hand all the way down my tail, giving me the illusion he's petting me. I'm startled by how deeply it stirs my wolf into action, colors fading from my vision.

Pleased, hungry eyes stare down at me. I pant beneath my mate, my heart bursting from my chest as he breaks into a breathy smile.

"Gorgeous," he purrs beneath his breath.

When Noah disappears from view behind my raised ass, my stomach flips into my throat. Flopping my faux tail over his shoulder, he suckles over my pussy, startling a moan from me. I wriggle my hips, my pussy aching and empty, but he grips my thighs, keeping me close. He slips his tongue over my clit, intent on teasing me until my ass bounces with my desperate thrusts in the air.

Dragging his tongue up and over my ass cheek, Noah leaves me with a soft bite. I yelp through a giggle, but as I turn over my shoulders, Noah prowls close, rubbing his throbbing cock between my gaping labia.

"I want you." His growl buzzes over my back, hitching my breath. When he combs my hair up and over my pillow, my heart flutters at what it means; he now has full access to my mark.

Gripping the bed sheets, I push my pelvis back into him. "Mate me, Alpha."

Grinning, Noah settles his weight over my back—giving himself room to seat his tip between my legs.

My heart lurches into my throat as he meets my eyes. His wolf stares back.

"Not your Alpha, tonight," Noah whispers.

As the meaning behind his words sink in, Noah presses himself inside me, drawing a gasp from deep within my belly.

His smooth, hot skin inside me releases a flood of endorphins— just before I'm surrounded by a flowery, adoring scent. I shove my hips back into him, my eyes racing across the headboard as I lean into his tight grip; this isn't my shy Alpha pressing deep inside me, it's my gorgeous Omega—and just as feisty of an Omega, at that.

All I can do is let out a delighted moan, my jaw dropping as Noah's thick shaft nudges right where I want him, slipping against my G-spot in one deep thrust. His claws prick my hips as he pulls back, only to lean in deeper—paying close attention to which angle bucks my hips up behind me.

As fluid spurts across the bed sheets between my knees, I choke out a sputtering breath, gripping his taut hand on my hip. "N-*Noah*—"

My mate no longer replies in words, breaking into tender, focused mating thrusts. As our hips collide, wet sounds fill the room, my pussy dripping with every deep, intentional thrust against my G-spot. My thighs quiver in his grasp, torn between wanting to lock themselves around him to keep him cuddled close or to spread wide, allowing him deeper.

But Noah fulfills both desires for me, cinching himself tight over my back as his arms lock below my swollen belly, burrowing himself deeper. I smush my head against his, my blinks slow and sated at how safe I feel—my Omega scent gushing from me in response to his.

Drooling onto my shoulder as he nibbles it, Noah spikes my heart into my throat; he nuzzles my faux, fuzzy ear, confirming my suspicions that this outfit drew out the wild side of him I craved. His instinctual brain is in charge, grumbling in embarrassment once he remembers that my fuzzy ears are fake. His playful nip on my earlobe to make up for it jolts pleasure down my spine, but my focus drops to my clit as Noah's hand slips between my legs. Primal, pleading moans escape me as he applies steady pressure there, amplifying the pleasure expanding in my core.

I've never seen myself like this before. Mewling, I arch my back, leaning into Noah's thrusts. As his hand slams against the headboard, catching his weight over me as he leans into rapid, urgent thrusts, my claws prick into the wood alongside his, my lips gaping as my fangs extend and eyelids flutter.

The second Noah's hot breath ghosts over my mark, I come hard around his cock, my hips jerking back. Stabilizing my hips, Noah grunts through each thrust, milking out my orgasm until my moans revert into whines. Growling, Noah loses his pace, his soaked thighs smashing into mine as he comes against my cervix. I sputter out a gasp, every inch of me bristling in sensitivity as his knot swells between my legs.

Shaking, we pant over each other, unable to stop whining as we nuzzle in close. Noah's sweeping palms down my belly soothe me just as much as his tender kiss. As my arms grow too weak to hold myself up, our heads press against the headboard, but I don't care one bit; all I want is to snuggle up to this beautiful, trusting soul behind me.

My sweet Omega didn't leave my side once while we mated. As his blissful, nurturing scent gushes from his scent glands, his eyes are just as bright, his touch just as honest.

Smiling through my watery eyes, I press soft kisses all over his gorgeous face between purring, adoring nuzzles. *I love you, Noah.*

I love you too.

An hour later—once I'm plastered beneath Noah's pleasure-exhausted limbs—Noah's soft snores behind my head squeeze my heart in delight. I'm cupping our baby alongside him, unable to sleep.

After a quick mental calculation of our time zone, I close my eyes in relief; I need to share my thoughts with someone else I trust before they explode from me, and luckily, it's still early afternoon in Greenfield.

Hi, A! Are you busy? I mindink Amy.

When a whisper of her excited, cheery energy finds mine within our pack bond, I break into a beaming grin.

Amy responds almost instantly. *Not for you, babe! Is everything okay?*

My heart lodges into my throat. Dammit, I forgot how scary it's about to be to share this with her. But my anxiety doesn't sour my smile.

Noah and I figured something out about who I am. I wanted to hear your thoughts before I tell anyone else, but it's something huge.

And you think my thoughts are going to be anything except for 'I believe you' and 'congratulations?'

Biting back a laugh, I only smile wider. *You're right, I should've known better. But I didn't know this was possible, A. Noah didn't either.* I quiet my shaking breath the best I can, hoping Noah stays asleep despite my booming nerves. *I think I'm both an Omega and an Alpha. Noah and I are calling me an Omega-Alpha.*

After a few silent seconds, Amy's energy tightens closer to mine in our pack bond than I've ever felt it, stealing my breath; it's like she's hugging my soul with hers. Tears cloud my eyes through my gushing smile.

Oh, my God, I didn't think about it being possible before either, but of course it is! Holy shit, that's incredible, Aliya! I'm so touched you wanted to share this with me first.

I droop into my pillow in relief. *I love you.*

I love you too, babe. But what made you come to this conclusion? Those assholes aren't giving you a hard time for your scent, are they?

How did you guess?

…That was sarcasm, huh.

Tightening my stomach through a laugh, I can't stop smiling. *Yes, it most certainly was. I expected them to be jerks, in general, so their negative opinion on my Alpha-ness surprisingly hasn't bothered me as much as I expected. But Annika, our Queen Luna, looked so scared of me at one point today when I had to defend Noah. My Alpha side has been coming out to protect us more and more, but it's far more potent now, so I'm not sure if she was reacting to my scent, or if she was joining the Lycans looking at me like I'm an absolute freak. Now I'm afraid to see her tomorrow and find out she's not a new friend after all.*

What makes you think she doesn't accept you? I believe you, of course, but is it possible this is another worst-case scenario taking hold?

Furrowing my brows, I breathe through the ache in my chest as Annika's wide, frightened eyes come back to mind.

She ran from me. It stings coming out.

You mean like when I bolted after the first time you showed off your Alpha side, scaring Mason away? Amy's reply spikes my heart rate.

Well, yes. That's why I wanted to get your opinion on Annika's reaction too.

Oh, babe. You didn't think I rejected you back then, did you?

My stomach rumbles. *At first. But knowing you, I trust you'll always come around to understanding me.*

Damn right. I wasn't disapproving of you, A; I was rightfully scared. It was like you sent my wolf into full primal survival mode. I submitted in awe of your badass, terrifyingly powerful scent.

My eyes jut open. Was Noah right about me? That these wolves responding to me at the Summit aren't a fluke, and I'm actually strong?

Ask her tomorrow before you jump to conclusions, Amy says. *And if her answer is that she doesn't accept you, fuck her. We all love you too much to have your time wasted on anyone who doesn't get on the same page. Don't let anyone hold my Omega-Alpha best friend down, got it?*

Even though my heart spikes into my throat at the thought of confronting Annika directly tomorrow, I smile. Amy holds my heart and mind in just as deep of love as Noah's snuggling arms, the two of them wrapping me in warmth.

Amy's right. I don't want to solely be myself tomorrow, showing up as an Omega-Alpha; I want to show the sweet man huddled up to me that he can do the same. That at the very least, the ones who stay beside us when they see our true selves are the only ones who count.

❧ 23 ❧

The following afternoon, Waimārie sits alone in the sidelines, her long black hair fluttering in the wind. Overcast skies aren't strong enough to dim her vivid smile when she spots me. My shoulders settle as she opens her arms wide, hugging me twice as close; our mates are the ones facing off first today.

"You did it," Waimārie whispers beside my ear. "You got through the worst part: daring to face the world again after sharing your truth."

My stomach flips. She's right. Noah's jaw looks tighter this afternoon as well—although, I'm sure a large portion of his frustration stems from the Alphas smacking and growling at one another across the vast field.

Sighing, I plop into my seat beside Waimārie. "Thank you for voicing that for me. I'm mainly worried about Noah."

Waimārie nods, taking my hand. I give her palm a soft squeeze, smiling when she meets my eyes.

But Waimārie tames her smile as she leans in, her scent emanating concern. "Were you worried about what I might think of you now as well?"

I drop my focus to our clasped hands. "Well… I can't say I wasn't."

"That's understandable. Are you worried about what Annika thinks?"

Checking over my shoulder, I lower my voice. "Is it that obvious?"

Waimārie chuckles. "No, darling. But I can only imagine. We may act like Alpha-domination cultists are extremists, but Tāne and I have had many discussions about how we can continue to dismantle the everyday Alpha-domination beliefs that have grown up alongside us. It's not as contained as it may seem, and it's quite rare to spot top Alphas mated to any Alpha-like Lunas. I imagine you are in quite a tough place, you and your dear Noah."

I release a massive sigh. "You have no idea what it's like to hear someone else say that. I know we don't *need* anyone's acceptance, per se, but it certainly makes us safer. Thank you."

As I dare to turn back to Waimārie with flaming cheeks, my heart softens; Waimārie beams brightly enough to crinkle her gorgeous eyes, snuggling up close to my side with an affectionate cheek nuzzle.

My eyes well at the adoration in her scent. As Noah glances at me from across the field, I know he can feel how deeply Waimārie touched my heart; his gaze lingers, our bond unwinding in relief.

I love you, Noah mindlinks.

I love you too.

Tāne makes his way over, his smile widening. "Lunas!"

"Alpha!" Waimārie throws her arms in the air, ready to accept Tāne's incoming kiss.

These two hurt my cheeks from grinning too hard alongside them. I laugh, blinking hard when Tāne's hand not only comes down over Waimārie's head to ruffle her hair, but swoops my way to give my arm a hefty tap.

"You know Florida only harassed you yesterday because he's terrified of you, eh? You're a force to be reckoned with, I reckon." Tāne grins.

My heart flips. All I can do is stare at the massive man before me, struggling to grasp how he could be claiming I'm powerful too.

As Noah strides up behind Tāne, he chuckles. "Told you."

Tāne whips his head around. "Who, me? Or your Luna?"

Blinking a few times, Noah grins through a soft hum. "Well, actually, both of you, I guess. I meant you, though. You better be ready for her to beat the fucking shit out of you at a future Summit."

Sputtering into laughter, I clutch his hand. "Noah!"

Tāne's booming laugh replaces the anxious throbbing in my

heart with another cheek ache, Waimārie joining in with him until Noah's smile reaches his eyes just the same.

Tāne sighs. "Bro, I'm about to beat the shit out of you first. Don't get ahead of yourself."

"Alright, alright, sure. We'll see."

"We'll see." Tāne mimics Noah's deep voice before releasing another boisterous laugh, soothing the rest of my worries about their fight today; with how close they're standing despite preparing to fight in mere minutes, our goofy mates must adore each other.

As Tāne adjusts his ceremonial gear, Waimārie and I settle into each other—just in time for Annika to wave at us from the sidelines. Noah remains close, giving me a quick glance.

Dammit. He must feel my anxiety returning, my limbs buzzing through every breath.

"There's our Luna!" Waimārie waves. "Come join me in cuddling our dear friend!"

Dropping his head, Noah doesn't hide his smile from me. *Goddess, Waimārie is an expert mediator, I swear. I should've had you two meet sooner.*

He's right; thanks to Waimārie's warm greeting, Annika's features soften, even though her pink cheeks grow rosier as she stares into my eyes.

After giving all four of us a hug, Annika drops into the seat beside me.

The resulting silence grates my nerves.

I try my best to sit in the discomfort of it all, quieting my breath as it speeds into overwhelm, but nothing can hide my anxious scent.

Whipping her head toward me, Annika's smile dissolves into a weary frown.

My heart hurts. I squeeze Annika's hand, blurting out my thoughts. "Sorry, I— Yesterday—"

"Sorry? No, no, Luna— A-about yesterday, um…" Annika fiddles with her skirt fabric. "I don't want to be like those other Lunas and accidentally say something rude. It's just… You *did* smell like an angry Alpha—" Noah's focus zips to us, and Annika waves her hands. "W-which is okay! I think you're wonderful,

Alpha or Omega, but…" She swallows hard, gazing into my eyes. "But I didn't expect it to be so strong since I thought you were still mainly an Omega, and I got a little intimidated by how powerful you looked. That's all. I'm so sorry if that's rude."

Thankfully, another Luna scoots past our row of chairs to reach her friends, pausing our conversation. I use it to give me time to think.

How am I going to respond to this? Noah's furrowed eyebrows likely reflect my same concerns. Without spending ages detailing the nuances involved, I don't know how to explain I'm not "either" an Alpha or an Omega, I'm *both*.

And like Noah and I talked about, no one will probably understand. Not like we do.

But I don't need them to understand. Most importantly, I want to show Noah that I'm not embarrassed of us anymore. That actually, I love who we are.

Maybe the simple truth is best.

Straightening my back, I look straight into Annika's eyes. "I'm both. I'm an Omega-Alpha."

Noah's sharp inhale is minor compared to his elation erupting in our bond.

"O-oh! I—" Annika blinks a few times, her eyes darting between Noah and me. "I've never heard of that before."

My heart sinks. I drop my focus to my lap, both hands still occupied by our ally Lunas. I'm tempted to let go.

Then Annika grabs my arm. "B-but I believe you!"

My breath catches. When I gaze into Annika's eyes, I don't find the hesitation, disgust, or malintent I'm dreading. Her bright smile stretches across her face.

"I've never heard of it, but I can smell it's true. Thank you for telling me." Annika loosens the rest of my concerns with her honest, relaxed stare.

But her head whips away from me; Viktor's vibrant voice draws Annika's attention a second before it grabs the rest of the Summit's focus. "Welcome to the semi-finals! Remaining competitors, line up."

As everyone falls silent, our Alphas give us one last hug and kiss before lining up on the field.

Tāne and Noah not only won yesterday's preliminary rounds, but absolutely obliterated their opponent's chances—many within mere seconds. Alphas scowl as our mates pass them, forced to take their seats alongside us Lunas.

Viktor's voice carries across the field in the wind. "Beside me are the top nine Alphas of this year's Alpha Summit."

He pauses as wolves howl. The spiking excitement in everyone's pheromones only adds to my dread.

"After today's first round of semi-finals, there will only be five of us left at the top. Without an even number for pair fighting, it's King's choice who gets to sit out for round two."

Viktor glances at Noah, and my stomach drops.

Noah gave me his prediction this morning: he thinks Viktor will let him have a break, leaving him with no excuses. He'll be in top condition to fight Viktor as hard as he can, and he'll have to go all out to earn back Viktor's trust.

"That leaves us with the battle we're all here for." As Viktor lowers the volume of his voice, the crowd seems to hold their breath; the only sound left is the wind whispering through the trees. "The top two, fighting to be this year's King—the top Alpha of the entire world."

Noah hasn't looked at me, and I'm grateful for it. My heart pounds hard enough to pulse at my temples, leaving me fidgeting in my seat.

"The rules are as follows." Viktor's expression darkens, his smoky Alpha musk stinging my eyes from here. "No one goes for the throat, no bashing heads, and no biting spines—or tails. Fucking hate that." The crowd laughs, but Viktor bends, glancing to the end of the Alpha lineup. "Which reminds me—"

Viktor points at Noah, his smirk rising.

Annika buries her face into my shoulder with a groan. "Oh, Goddess, I can feel what he's thinking, that big jerk. Sorry, Luna…"

"Thanks to you, Pacific Northwest Alpha, and you, Aotearoa Alpha, there's a new rule that we're shifting into our wolves at the start of every fight so this doesn't turn into a fucking boxing ring."

With Tāne's booming chuckle, Noah breaks into shy giggles

that seem out of place in a line of stoic Alphas, but I absolutely love it.

My sweet Alpha-Omega, I mindlink.

As Noah meets my eyes, his wide smile allows me to smile with him.

Annika sighs. "Okay, that was better than I thought."

"Did you think Viktor would be openly upset with Noah in front of everyone?"

"I don't know. But Vik's still angry about last year no matter what I say—as you know."

"I tried to tell Noah why Viktor was offended too. I'm sure holding back comes across as infantilizing."

"Well, it's not exactly Noah's fault. Vik has a big ego, and it gets him in trouble no matter how much I love it. If Noah didn't submit last year, Vik would've hurt himself beyond his limits, and—" She shakes her head, and my throat tightens.

So is the real story that Noah showed too much mercy? Or did Viktor basically lose, and he refused to submit?

What the hell is Viktor planning to do today, then?

"So you think he's going to say something else to Noah?" I whisper.

"I think they both have *plenty* to say to each other." Annika's expression darkens. "And they probably won't use their words."

I swallow hard. Annika's soothing scent wafts over me with her apologetic smile.

"Other than that, the main rule is—" Viktor spreads his arms, separating from the Alpha lineup with a hop in each step. "We fight to submission. Let's get to it!"

I groan into my hands, speechless from my mate's excitable wolf.

Except it's not his wolf brawling with his competitor—it's his human form.

"Every damn year—" Waimārie yelps, gripping my arm tighter as our mates lunge for each other.

Grasping a handful of my own hair, I track a furious, scowling

Johannes on the sidelines, Annika chasing after him to prevent his shouting from distracting Viktor from battle.

Noah, why in the world did you and Tāne shift back?! Doesn't this break the rules?

The rule was to shift into wolves at the start, and we did. We just happened to shift back into humans afterward—to carry out our yearly boxing tradition.

The two Alphas beam at each other, grappling face to face with claws extended.

I can't believe he's enjoying this. After complaining about this Summit all week, Noah is having the time of his fucking life.

As Tāne's cackle echoes across the field, spurring Noah into weakened laughter, Waimārie and I have to laugh with them.

Waimārie sighs. "I'm glad I have you here to endure this nonsense with me now."

Laughing, I rub her arm. "Are you kidding? I couldn't be more relieved."

At least it's nice to see that fluffy goofball happy. I just don't understand why this competition has to be so bloody.

I dare to look up again, just in time for Tāne's fist to sock my mate in the jaw.

"Fuck!" Noah shouts.

I grip my mouth, nausea creeping up my throat.

But Noah shakes off Tāne's punch, his smile spreading even wider. "That was a good one, man."

Tāne beams. "Thanks, bro. Told you I practiced."

Noah charges back in for Tāne, who can't stop grinning either.

"How long— *Oof!*" Tāne grunts as Noah flips him into the ground.

The two beasts wrestle in a ball of naked muscle, flinging mud into the sky. When they break apart, fresh blood coats their torsos.

Waimārie lets out a small whimper. "Oh, Goddess. *Why—*"

Growling through a grunt, Tāne's voice strains beneath Noah's weight. "How long do you reckon it'll be before they tell us off this year?"

Noah breaks into his giddiest laugh. But then he has to hop to his feet, both Noah and Tāne sprinting across the field at the sight of Viktor's angry Beta storming after them while swinging a broom.

Before Johannes can even finish threatening to disqualify them, the pair shifts into two massive black wolves—impossible to tell apart.

"Oh, my God, are you *kidding* me?! As if this wasn't stressful enough." I groan, not caring if everyone's staring at me, giving me a wide radius as I pace.

"I'm with you. Walk it off, and come back to it." Waimārie's voice rasps as she clutches fistfuls of her jacket.

I zip back to her side, rubbing her arm. "Oh, poor Luna. I'm staying right here. Keep breathing."

When one of the wolves hops around his opponent in playful, slippery teases, I sigh.

"Oh. Never mind, that one's clearly my mate." I shake my head. *Noah, you're out of control.*

His wolf can't stop wagging his tail, spitting out a mouthful of Tāne's fur. *I know, I know. I had my fill of fun now, I promise. It's about to get hellish, so Tāne and I had to lighten the mood a bit. Sorry, Luna.*

I'm glad you had fun, you big puppy. Just don't hurt yourself.

The closer I watch the massive black Alphas—crashing down on each other in thick, audible slaps of muscle—the more I can see that the unparalleled strength of black-coated Alphas isn't just a Lycan folktale. Yasmine shared a theory that they're bred stronger for survival reasons, living with such obvious, un-camouflaged fur. But it's clear these two also trained their way up the ranks, boosting their physical power tenfold with pure willpower. They can have fun together *because* they're evenly matched.

Which means it'll probably get even bloodier before someone submits.

Just in time for my stomach to reel, Viktor finishes off the Australian Alpha, shifting back to his human form. After sharing a deep kiss with Annika, Viktor carries a crowd of cheering with him as he strides to greet Waimārie and me.

Instead of making myself sick, I could do my best to keep Greenfield on Viktor's good side—at least until Noah and Tāne wear each other out. It could be a while, knowing my mate.

I rise on wobbly legs to greet them, hoping Annika and Viktor don't notice how badly I'm shaking as they join my side.

That was just enough time for Tāne to knock Noah's wolf across the field.

I recoil, latching onto Annika's arm as the wolves tumble. Holding my breath, I wait for Noah to stand. When he finally does, he shakes himself off in a cloud of grass and mud.

Waimārie and I catch each other's strained stares, and we have to laugh.

At the sound of my distressed sigh, Viktor turns to me. "How's it going, Luna?"

I swallow hard, recentering myself despite my pounding heart.

I have to remind Viktor why we're all friends. "That Alpha didn't stand a chance against you, Vik. Even with how hard Noah trained, I know he'll be up for a challenge."

"Is that so? You think he'll still make it all the way to the final? Both of us?"

I'm relieved Viktor's grin softens; maybe he's not as upset with us as I thought.

But then his words sink in. "Noah's not disqualified for breaking the rules, is he?"

"Nah. It's nothing new, Luna." Viktor chuckles, stooping to kiss Annika. They take their sweet time before Viktor turns back to me. "But he better be ready. I'm not letting him back out this year."

"He backed out last year? From the final battle?"

Viktor and Annika exchange surprised glances.

Laughing, Viktor shakes his head. "He really doesn't tell you much, just like the rest of us, huh?"

Annika gasps, softly smacking his arm. "Viktor!"

Viktor raises his palms, wincing. "Sorry! That came out wrong."

It still sours my mood. "Noah isn't required to tell me anything. I'm just curious what your thoughts were on it. And I'm not asking him about it this week so he can focus on fighting you, like he promised."

"So you think he'll take me as seriously as he did the first year he became top Alpha?"

My eyes widen. "You both fought in the final battle that year too?"

"Goddess, no. I didn't stand a fucking chance against him. None of us did." Viktor's eyes zip to Noah's prowling, rippling form, his voice softening. "That's how I know he's been holding back—ever since the first year he was King."

We stare in silence as Tāne struggles beneath my mate, barely able to paw to protect himself as Noah pins him down.

"No one else has ever won the King title in their first year as top Alpha, by the way," Viktor mutters.

My stomach drops.

I thought I was hearing Viktor incorrectly, but the reality of this information stabs me in the chest; Noah was forced to be Greenfield's top Alpha from the moment our dads were killed…

Then he became King Alpha of the world, on top of it all?

I shut my eyes, letting out a slow, pained breath. No wonder Noah doesn't seem happy about Alpha Summits. That one year sounds like enough stress to last a lifetime.

But I can feel it in my mate this time—the same determination coursing through him since we agreed to take on Alpha-domination cultists through this Summit, stamping out their anti-Omega campaign, once and for all.

I step closer to Viktor, keeping my voice low. "I know this is all more complicated than that. What exactly happened last year?"

Viktor sighs, stretching his neck. "Depends on who you ask."

Annika scoffs. "As in, my mate nearly got himself killed over a stupid fight and I still haven't forgiven him."

Viktor rolls his eyes. "Noah would never kill me. He's way too scared of hurting me to genuinely fight me, which is exactly what happened."

I stiffen. "Well, it won't happen again. He's intending to come at you hard in the final battle this year, Alpha."

Viktor's eyebrows shoot way up. But then they settle back down. "You're both buttering me up. I hate that too."

"I'm not. But it sounds like you're picturing things panning out differently than I am."

"Well, from what he's also been claiming, I'd like to believe he'll actually fight me seriously this time. That is, if he'll make it to the top two."

"He will."

Viktor's grin returns. For the first time in minutes, he meets my eyes again. "Oh? You're so certain he'll last until then, huh?"

"*Viktor*," Annika hisses.

I follow Viktor's nod to my mate, sucking in a sharp gasp when I find Noah struggling to stand. Wetness gleams on both Alphas' dark coats—a mix of saliva and blood.

With a hammering heart, I turn back to Viktor, my eyes hot. "You better believe me, or you're heading in unprepared. He's been planning to defeat not just you but *everyone*."

Viktor freezes.

Shit. Even though it's the truth, I thought that's what he'd want to hear.

Then Viktor breaks into a smile. "Are you just saying that, Luna?"

"No, I'm not. He wants to show the Lycan world that Alpha domination will never be tolerated."

Viktor's smile disappears, a sober nod taking its place. "Good. If that's his reasoning, I better see him actually stand behind it and fight me—to the end."

I flinch.

Annika's furious, wide eyes could pierce a hole through her mate's cheek. "Viktor!? The *end?*"

Viktor waves her off, striding away from us. "You know what I mean, Luna. To submission."

I swallow hard, allowing Annika to take me by the arm to another row of seating on weak knees.

When Viktor storms off in the opposite direction, Annika blows out a slow, angry growl. "Ignore him. He gets all obnoxious right before the last few fights."

"He doesn't want to kill my mate, deep down, does he?"

Annika freezes, gripping my shoulder. "No, Luna! Goddess, no. He just… doesn't want to lose his title. At the same time, he wants to actually earn it, not be handed it."

"That makes complete sense. Thank you."

"Of course, mama. No matter what happens, let's stick together, okay?"

"Okay. I'd love that."

I nuzzle in closer, desperate for comfort. Annika purrs, nuzzling me back.

In those few minutes I attempted to calm Viktor down, Noah and Tāne reverted to snarls. Waimārie can't sit still, no longer including us in her awareness as worry overcomes her.

I analyze Tāne for a clue on how to beat him…

But I find none.

His bites are just as vicious, thinking just as crafty, and paws just as powerful as Noah's. The only advantage Noah has is how light he is on his feet for his size.

Which must be why it seems like Noah is the one dancing around his opponent this time—just like the position he put countless scared Alphas in yesterday.

Oh, God, does that mean Tāne is forcing Noah to be on the defensive?

As deftly as Noah dances, Tāne's attack is quicker. Lunging for Noah's feet, Tāne tears Noah to the dirt.

The massive wolves end up in a tangled mess of limbs, pinching my heart with panic. Waimārie dashes back to our side, burying her eyes in Annika's chest. But I can't look away; when they come to a rolling stop, I'm almost certain Noah is the one left wriggling on the ground beneath Tāne. It's a submissive position to be trapped in.

But Noah refuses to submit. He smashes his paws against the gnashing Alpha's chest with no luck, sustaining bite after bite.

Stand up, Noah! Don't let him hurt you!

Noah bursts to his feet, sprinting in a wide arc before skidding to a halt—his classic mud spray.

I release a strangled exhale.

Don't worry, Luna. I had to wear him out a bit, but I accidentally let him take it a little too far.

With Noah's mindlink, I gasp at a sudden flood of rage in our bond.

As if they can sense it too, wolves howl across the field, a firestorm of energy covering my arms in goosebumps. I can't bear to look at Waimārie. Stepping forward, I keep her and Annika out of my peripherals; judging by the intensity of emotions in the air, one of our mates is about to take the other down.

I meant it, Luna. No one will fuck with us again.

And I can smell how much he means it, my throat burning from the pheromones he stimulates in the crowd.

From across the field, my own mate makes me quiver in submission. Nearby Lunas flock behind me on instinct; their mates are too wrapped up in the action as Noah bristles down to his tail.

Tāne faces Noah from only twenty feet apart—their wolves at a standstill. But when Noah takes one step forward, just Noah's low, rumbling growl pushes Tāne back one step.

Noah's snout crinkles over his furious snarl, blurring his features until I can't recognize my own mate. What happened to playing around with his friend?

When Noah crouches lower, prowling towards his opponent, Tāne mirrors him—ready to fight.

Except I can see Tāne from a different angle from Noah.

His tail is tucking! I mindlink.

An urge to dominate blasts through our bond. Noah lunges for the black Alpha.

And Tāne bites back.

Their bodies blur into one, rapid bites snapping so loudly that I know they're breaking skin. Waimārie screams, dousing my bones in ice.

But within seconds, Noah's jaws clamp around Tāne's snout, and Tāne rolls over—declaring Noah the winner.

Gawking, I don't know how to move. Noah didn't just defeat Tāne, he destroyed him too.

But as I meet Waimārie's puffy, red eyes, pure relief shines through her smile. "We made it!" Instead of snuggling me in her embrace, Waimārie squeezes my shoulder. "Go to him, Luna!"

I want to, but wolves shout and yip as they rush the field. Noah towers over everyone, his bristling, black form still seething as wolves lick and nuzzle him.

He's not even King, but they're treating him like he's their top Alpha. What the hell is going on?

I whip my head around, searching the field until I find Viktor. My heart drops.

Lips curling, fur sprouting from his limbs—Viktor looks ready to fight Noah to the death, for real.

Noah shifts back, a quick glare sending wolves darting in the other direction until he forms a clear path to me. My heart skips the second I see him—sweat and blood mix across his skin, leaving him stained red.

He gives me a weary smile, rubbing the back of his head. "H-hey, Luna."

"Oh, my God…" My whines overpower my voice as I dash for him. The second we touch, I frantically clean his wounds, my breath shaky and urgent.

But Noah stops me. He's still out of breath, but his puppy-dog stare has returned. "Please, don't stress. I know it looks bad, but it's for a good reason. I'm ending this as quickly as possible from here on out."

Before I can respond, Viktor storms over.

Oh, no. His ego is probably bruised with all the attention on Noah.

Noah hugs me to his side, his chest puffing. It forces Viktor to a faster halt than he likely intended, all to keep from bumping into me.

But it doesn't halt Viktor's rage. "You're sitting out the next battle. Reid is mine to defeat."

In a flash of anger, Noah grips Viktor's arm hard enough for his nails to turn white.

The two wolves lock eyes, burning holes into each other's skulls.

The entire Summit quiets to a vibrating simmer, ready to lunge into action if the Alphas break into an early fight.

But Noah keeps me tucked close. When he speaks, it's through his fangs. "You better not fucking hurt him. Not truly."

Viktor scoffs, ripping his arm from Noah's grip. "So, what do you want, then? You wanted to fight your favorite Alpha so you can submit to him instead of me this year?"

Noah takes a deep breath, closing his eyes. When he opens them, he's back to the cool Alpha I see in our Pack Safety meetings. "Vik, you're still my King. I'll fight you seriously."

Viktor's lips draw into a tight line, his musk burning with deeper anger by the second.

That definitely isn't how Viktor wants Noah to view their fight.

I know it seems like his ego needs protecting, but he actually needs you to make him lose. He knows you're stronger than everyone here, Noah. You're not fooling him.

Noah sucks in a subtle breath at my mindlink, drawing Viktor's attention.

But the second Noah reaches for Viktor's shoulder, no one dares to even breathe.

Noah's heavy hand lands on Viktor's stocky frame. Viktor doesn't budge—although he glares harder.

And Noah grins.

"I have something to prove this time." Noah steps closer, lowering his soft voice so that even Lycans have to strain to hear. "You're misunderstanding my intentions last year as pitying you, when really… I was so fucking tired. I wasn't fit to be King, and I trusted you to be the one to take care of us."

Viktor gapes. His jugular pulses at his throat, his eyes dancing over Noah's face. It's as if Viktor never anticipated this reasoning, at all.

Noah nods. "But this year is different. I have a kickass Luna that changed my world, a growing pup I'd already die for, and there are forces beyond our reach that I want to stop before they grow even larger. It might be the first year I'm choosing to be King."

Excitement ripples through Viktor's angry musk, stirring my heartbeat.

Noah chuckles, but no one laughs with him. Then his smile drops. "You won't even know what hit you."

With a small shove, Noah knocks Viktor back way farther than any of us expect, forcing the surrounding wolves to catch him.

Viktor's eyes bulge. He scrambles back to his feet, and I grip Noah, afraid of what he's done.

But the King Alpha smiles, his incisors on full display. "In that case, I hope you enjoy the pre-show tomorrow."

I slip my arm back into Noah's as Viktor turns, ready to storm off.

But when our focus shifts to the last semi-final battle standing, my stomach plummets to my feet; Reid doesn't win against Matthew. Crumbling beneath the Florida Alpha, Reid yipes as Matthew slashes his chest—bringing Reid to a submissive position on his back as medics rush the field.

As Noah's body tightens into rage beside me, my blood pressure drops, spinning my head. Viktor and Noah grasp me at the same time, righting me on my feet as Tāne and Waimārie rush over.

"What do we do?" Tāne rasps, still out of breath from his fight.

Waimārie's eyes bulge in fear beside him, a reflection of how I must look too; with the lineup our mates carefully crafted, we counted on Reid winning against Matthew, preventing any Alpha-domination leaders in the yellow zone from ranking in the top five. Not only did Matthew win, he bursts with agitation, eyeing us with Reid's blood splattered across his cheeks.

"Fuck, never mind," Viktor mutters. "You're fucking up Matthew tomorrow for us, right, Greenfield?"

With a deep growl, Noah nods. "Hire a few more medics."

I have a bad feeling about this.

24

Noah won his fight against Tāne today, but I wouldn't know it by looking at him: deep scowl lines have embedded themselves into his cheeks as we walk the Kiruna Pack halls. This frown has remained plastered to him ever since he returned from Reid's side in the medic hall.

I have the feeling he doesn't want to talk about it.

While tonight's win ended in celebration, I'm all too familiar with how any large emotion can register as distress to the mind, including happiness or relief—especially in minds like ours that have been physically altered by trauma.

But when Matthew gave us a taste of the violent reality we're facing, and in such a sudden, shocking way, the rapid succession of events may have been a toxic cocktail for Noah's PTSD. I have emotional whiplash too, my stomach sour and sloshy.

When we come to the end of the hall before our room, Noah stops, staring at the door.

His breath heightens. I brush his hand, and Noah flinches.

When we meet eyes, there's a split second my mate is unrecognizable. Wild, alert eyes stare back, roaming across my face like it's the first time he's seen me all day.

Then Noah snaps out of it, jerking his focus from me to hurriedly unlock the door. "S-sorry…"

I sweep my fingernails across his back. "Are you thinking too hard, gorgeous?"

Noah simply nods.

My insides curdle. I follow Noah into our suite, waiting until

I've locked the heavy door behind us to soften my voice. "I love you for who you are, okay? You're safe."

Noah wraps his arms around my waist, nuzzling into my neck. After a few minutes of slow rocking in each other's arms, Noah sighs.

"I'm so tired."

I guide Noah across the room, rubbing my comforting scent on his arm as we walk. "Get in bed, my love. I'll come join you after brushing my teeth."

Noah's drawn eyebrows hurt my heart as he tosses the duvet back. He drops into bed with a heavy bounce like he's too exhausted to hold his own weight. I drape the covers over him, kissing his cheek, but Noah grabs my hand just before I leave.

"Thank you."

I lean over him, brushing the hair from his forehead. Each kiss I plant there slows Noah's blinking—until he finally shuts his eyes.

A stabbing pain strikes my heart; the underlying panic still hasn't left Noah's face, the space between his brows crinkling in distress.

We haven't had a single moment to talk about it since everyone arrived, but in the back of our minds, a looming chaos remains. Any second of any day, a stray pack of furious Alphas could show up to attack, and there's nothing we can do about it. With how loyal wolves remain to one another, we have no leads—no clue of what's coming for us or when.

Which is exactly why Noah needs his rest. I better hurry and cuddle him to sleep.

Padding to the bathroom, I shut the door as softly as I can. I hand-comb my hair as I pee and brush my teeth, struggling to stay focused with the unease in my heart.

Then I freeze.

Fuck. Our bond swings in a way I've never felt before—like a speeding pendulum. Hurrying off the toilet to wash my hands, I scoop water into my mouth, swishing as quickly as I can to rinse any remaining toothpaste. But it's happening too rapidly; our bond is spiraling, descending.

By the time I lift my head from the sink, my eyes widen back at me in the mirror with Noah's plummeting emotions.

His pain is so severe that it feels like someone is hurting him.

I sprint from the bathroom to find Noah lying perfectly still in bed.

But our bond screams just the same. I grip the hem of his loose, black T-shirt I threw on as pajamas, unable to keep my lungs from tensing around each breath.

"Noah?" I whisper.

No response.

I take another step, attempting to get a clearer view of him.

"Noah? Are you awake?" My voice shakes, but not as heavily as Noah's shoulders.

His back is still to me. But now that I'm frozen in place and holding my breath, I can hear his rapid pant.

And my own fears explode.

What if he's having a health crisis?

Time slows. My foot inches off the ground, taking forever to complete a single step forward to reach him. Once I'm a few steps closer, I find his eyes staring deep into the wall.

I gasp. "N-Noah? Are you dissociat—"

Noah jerks toward me the second he spots me—like he's ready to attack. I yelp, stumbling backward.

Wild, furious eyes stare back at me from the bed. "Shit! Don't sneak up on me."

Hugging our baby, I pant in pure panic. Who is this I'm looking at?

I inch closer, desperate to ease the fear from his tightened features. "I-I didn't, I was calling out—"

"Stop! Don't move!" Noah growls.

I come to an abrupt halt at the end of the bed.

Noah grips his head, sucking in rapid, laborious breaths. "Fuck, sorry. I'm freaking the fuck out. I don't want to hurt you like I hurt my mom."

I bite my lip, wavering on what to do next.

Noah isn't dangerous, especially not simply because he has PTSD. But he has a point: I hurt him badly during a flashback too. The scar on his forearm lightened from how much I've tried to heal it, but it still makes me sad. I don't want Noah to feel more guilt.

Except I'm not seeing or smelling an angry Alpha.

Right now, there's a shivering, hurt, Omega-scented wolf in our bed, fighting to the edge of his life to seem like a threatening Alpha. Not because he's part Alpha, but because there are many days he's an "Alpha" as a protection method.

Anguish burns my body, reverberating down to my bones. It takes everything within myself to steel my voice. "What do you need?"

"I don't know."

"Then, can I hold you, love? My instincts are dying to protect you."

Noah lets out a short, pained groan, turning his back—as if avoiding the sight of me would protect me. "N-no. I'm scared of hurting you."

"Okay, then I'm coming closer to the bed to talk, but I won't touch you until you feel comfortable with it. Is that okay?"

After a long pause, Noah nods.

I kneel at his bedside, sweeping my palms over my belly with slow, steady breaths. Noah grips his forehead, flopping onto his back. His chest struggles through every breath as he gazes up at the ceiling, his eyes racing back and forth.

I soften my voice. "Are you seeing something repeating?"

He takes in a shuddering breath, contemplating my words. Then he exhales. "I think s-so, actually."

My stomach sinks. I've never seen him in this deep of a trauma response, but from how horrific I know it feels, my whole being aches for him.

Luckily, this hell is temporary, and it's a hell we both have experience in surviving.

Okay, wolf, let's think about how to help our mate. When we first arrived at the Summit, Noah mentioned he forgets things around his traumas, so despite his hesitation on what's happening to him tonight, I'm fairly certain he's having flashbacks. And since Noah's first instinct was to walk me through my last severe flashback episode, that must be what works for him too.

"Tell me what you're seeing, love," I say.

Noah groans. "I don't know. If I try to talk, I can't remember what I'm so stressed about, but it's there."

"That's okay. Just tell me if you see anything. I'm here to walk through it with you so it doesn't keep looping. Mindlink it if you have to."

Silence stretches throughout the room, but my heartbeat thumps louder by the second.

Until Noah's breath hitches like he's reflexing against a hit. "Oh, fuck—"

I jump up, protecting my belly with both hands as Noah's scent warns of extreme danger.

"There you go. You're remembering it now. If you can't start at the beginning, pick any part of it. Let it out. You're remembering it because it's a *memory*. It's not the present, where you're right here with me."

Noah's still covering his eyes, but his teeth chatter as his body shakes harder. It breaks my heart.

"H-he—" Noah's swallow is so thick that I stoop over, struggling to breathe through the shared pain in my chest. "He wasn't that bad at first. He was actually nice sometimes. That's what's embarrassing."

I slump. "I'm not embarrassed by you. And 'nice sometimes' doesn't stop someone from being abusive. I believe you, Noah." Gripping my own arms, I struggle to steady my voice. "And I believe your body. It's telling us it experienced trauma, and what it's feeling is *real*."

Noah's stressed huffing reverts into tight, held breaths, Noah struggling to suppress tears. "W-well, eventually it was traumatic, I guess. A-and I… I couldn't stop smelling like an Omega to make him stop hurting me. I tried so hard to stop."

My heart sinks, dread burns in my bones…

And Noah's terrified, Omega scent floods the room.

He has never made more sense to me than at this moment. His every hidden inflection, his arguments with his Omega mother over traditional Lycan gender roles, and the way he's fought for Omegas like hell; he knows the consequences of being born as one.

So when Noah still decides to show me his truth, despite all this hurt that was done to Noah's Omega side, my Alpha musk explodes, begging me to act. To protect my Omega, always and forever.

I clench my fists at my sides. "You're doing so great, my love. I'm right here, ready to support you."

Noah suddenly reaches for my hand, his breath heightening.

I cling to him tight, letting out a happy sigh. "There you go! Can I hold you?"

The second Noah nods, I climb onto the bed. My wolf frantically squishes the comforter, primping my nest until we're surrounded by a fluffy barricade.

Then I drag Noah beneath the covers like it's our den. "I've got you, Noah. You're safe."

He shudders in my arms, gripping the fabric on my back. I nuzzle him, my wolf eyes in full control as they adjust to the darkness beneath the blankets.

To my surprise, Noah fawns for me. But when I realize it's from a trauma state, I whine.

"My sweet mate..." I cup my hand over his scent gland, protecting it for him. My every heartbeat releases a wave of soothing scent until Noah's eyelids flutter. "Good job, sweetheart. I'm right here."

I surround Noah with my whole body beneath the covers, cuddling his head into my chest. Thankfully, he snuggles in.

"I-it's still happening," he whispers.

"Okay. Then tell me anything you see, and I'll be there with you this time. Imagine me helping you through it."

He whines like I've never heard him, alighting my nerves with his fear. "I don't want you to have to hear it."

"Because you don't want me to know?"

"N-no. Because I don't want it to hurt you too."

Immersing my fingertips into his hair, I press his forehead to mine. "It's my choice to listen, and I want to know what you've been through, like you've been there for me. Let me hear you, love. Just me. Let my Alpha hold your Omega through it."

A piece of our bond tightens, drawing our wolves closer. Our connection strengthens by the second as we breathe together through Noah's pain—until his raw whisper breaks the silence.

"He'd praise my Alpha… And he hates Omegas."

My stomach drops. Noah just said "hates." Present-tense. Does he still know this man?

"But I couldn't hide my Omega around him. He was ma-ad he had to train me to be the next potential top Alpha when I wasn't a pure A-Alpha. He w-wanted to prove he was dominant over me, but I was a scrawny kid. It was obvious enough already." Noah's voice strains, soft and pleading. "It was obvious enough already."

My wolf nuzzles Noah all over, my face buried in his hair as I stroke my mark on his neck.

He's shaking so hard. He must be a really little kid in his flashback. It's killing me.

I swallow the lump in my throat. "Good job, sweet Omega. Keep going."

Shit, that slipped out before I could think it through. I've never called Noah an Omega as a pet name before.

Noah's breath tenses, and I fall still.

Oh, no. Maybe I did say the wrong thing.

But Noah breaks into gut-twisting tears, his pained cry tearing at my soul as he nuzzles closer. "I didn't know what the Alpha-domination stuff was. I thought he was telling me the truth about how the world worked. That Omegas are weak and owe everything to Alphas. Subservience, children… Sex."

This strikes my heart deep. I squeeze my eyes shut, cuddling Noah even closer. That sounds just like what Steven thought about women. What he used as his reason to assault me.

"I've got you, gorgeous, and I hear you. You're doing so well. Follow the rest of the flashback through."

"I-it… It changed over time. He switched from verbal to physical, and I couldn't fight him. I was too scared. Too Omega. Then he—"

Noah shakes his head, hiding from the rest of his story as he groans into my sternum.

"You're okay. I've got you right here," I say.

"Then it got s-sexual."

Noah's gutted cry makes me sob with him. All I can do is stroke his hair, riding the waves of his anxiety as his side of our bond burns in pain.

"He said, if I'm r-really an Alpha, I'd fight him back. But I fawned. It's so embarrassing, Luna."

My blood boils to unhealthy levels. Shielding Noah in a hug, I breathe through it with him, stroking his wet cheek. "My sweet Omega… I didn't know how much you really understood me. I fawned too, love. It's not your fault, *at all*. He was an adult. We're all taught to submit to adults, but especially as Lycans who are taught to submit to *Alpha* adults, and I'm sure he fucking knew it. He knew exactly what he was doing, and you didn't."

All Noah does is whimper.

And my wolf takes over. "I'm going to protect you for as long as I live. Is he in our pack? Is he here, at the Summit?"

"N-no. My dad almost killed him before kicking him out. I'm so afraid he'll come back. That I'll freeze again, and I won't be able to protect our pack."

"Whether you freeze or not, it doesn't matter. I'll fight him for you. He's never coming near you again." My voice shakes with rage, but thankfully, Noah isn't afraid. He burrows against my scent gland, dousing himself in my protective musk.

"L-Luna…"

"Who is he, love? Are you comfortable with telling me? I want to protect you."

Noah swallows hard, burying his face from me until his voice is muffled against my shoulder. "You know w-who he is. The whole pack does. Older wolves that remember think I just couldn't handle m-my training. Some think he only hurt the other Omegas, and I was too weak of an Alpha to protect them."

My gut fills with too many emotions to bear, washing waves of nausea over me. "You're not talking about Mason, are you?"

"No. Mason is a year older than me and wasn't in my year's training." Noah's breath rattles as he readjusts his grip on my back. "I'm talking about Mason's dad. Jack Hart."

$$\sim\!\infty\!\sim \quad 25 \quad \sim\!\infty\!\sim$$

Jack fucking Hart.

Thoughts flicker past my mind a mile a minute, instance after instance of Jack's name piling up. This explains so much. Why the Elders acted odd about Noah's anger around Jack and Mason. Why Lilian was so scared when Mason stalked us. Why a man finally faced a consequence for abuse—Alpha Ritchie kicking Jack out to protect his son.

But most of all…

I jerk upright. "Jack has a *serious* homicide motive, Noah!"

He holds his breath.

"This is the clearest proof we've ever had. He could've killed your dad! Our dads."

My body burns with the thought, so Noah's resulting silence stings.

But when he bursts from the covers to face me in the light, he's dark red and grimacing like I've never seen him—a picture of fury.

"Jack is too proud for that! He'd challenge my dad face to face like a 'real' fucking Alpha."

I'm so shocked by Noah's fierce tone that I can't speak. Not only his tone, but how ridiculous it was of me to think this was appropriate to blurt out. What was I thinking?

Noah's chest flexes, his rib cage stiffening in distrust. "I know because that's what he used on me. Do you not believe me either?"

"What? I'm on your side! Of course I believe you." As tears prick my eyes, Noah's face falls blank.

He jumps off the bed, his breath coming out in short bursts as he staggers away from me. "Ugh, I'm such an asshole. I shouldn't have yelled at you. I'm so fucking sorry."

I swipe my tears away, wishing we could go back in time to our cuddle ball. "I don't like being yelled at, but no, I really screwed up, just now. I shouldn't have said something so drastic, especially not throwing that on your plate while your PTSD symptoms are heightened. Our dads are an incredibly sensitive topic too, so I shouldn't jump to conclusions. It makes sense you'd be mad, and you should be. I'm so, so sorry."

"No, I don't care if it's a symptom. I shouldn't yell. I just broke my fucking pact with myself to never do that to my mate, and I—"

Noah groans, scrubbing his face hard until he meets my eyes with a bright red face—his swollen eyes overflowing with hot tears.

His voice crackles. "I just don't want to be this way anymore, Luna."

My heart breaks, pushing a sob from me. "My love, it's just PTSD making you agitated. It's not you."

Gripping his hair, Noah squeezes his eyes shut tight. "I don't want to have PTSD! I don't want to have to tell anyone what happened. I don't want to think about him… I don't want to…"

Noah rubs the base of his palms into his eyes for a while. When he finally stops, the exhaustion digging beneath his eyelids ages him.

His stare drops to my arms wrapped tight around my stomach. "You look scared. Did I hurt our pup? Did I hurt you?"

"No, my love. I just feel for you. I want to listen, and you probably wanted to share this for a while."

"Did I? I feel like there was still something I was about to say… What were we talking about?"

My heart flips. "Wh— What?"

Noah's wide eyes roam up and down my form. "N-no, I'm seriously asking. I don't remember what we're talking about, Luna. I'm trying really hard to pay attention."

I stare at my mate for a while in pure confusion. All I can find is honest, equal perplexity staring back.

Oh, my God… Noah just blanked everything out.

His brain must really feel threatened. All it could do was reset, preserving our conversation for later processing when it felt more equipped to tackle such a dangerous subject.

For now, I open my arms. "Please, come back to me. Let's cuddle and sleep. We can talk about it tomorrow."

"No, I… I want to know what I did wrong to make you look so upset. Please, I'm dying to fix it."

"You didn't do anything wrong. You just had a flashback, and now you look really tired. My heart is hurting for you."

Noah drops his head and cries. It's nothing like his sobs from a moment ago. Exhausted, weepy tears drip to the floor. "Look what I'm doing to you. You're so stressed, and you're pregnant. I'm awful—"

I let out a pained cry. "You're not!"

Noah holds his breath, shaking his head.

I shrink. "Oh, God. I'm not mad at you or meaning to raise my voice either. But I understand what you meant now, every time I've talked about my ex. I'm angry that someone thought they could get away with hurting my mate. I'm *furious* no one helped you before it was too late. I'm really fucking mad someone made us both understand abuse like this. I don't understand why he got away with it, but I can only imagine why, with this world we live in. No matter how much proof the cops had, Steven got away with it too, so I'm not surprised with all these Omega-haters in charge—no matter how much I hate it." I swallow hard, catching my breath. "I'm mainly just heartbroken that I wasn't there to help you through it, either."

Noah peeks up at me, his expression contorted with tears.

After a sharing long, uncertain look, my stomach knots from the tense silence. "Please, tell me what you're thinking."

Noah swallows hard before releasing a shaky breath. "I'm thinking I l-love you. I love you so much."

"I love you too."

"And I didn't forget what just happened between us, even if I can't remember what triggered it. I won't pretend to forget how I acted." Noah drops his head. "So I-I remember you wanted to hold me during my flashback, but…" He huffs through fresh, quiet tears, meeting my eyes once more. "C-can I hold you instead?"

My shoulders droop. I nod, desperately biting back tears.

We rush across the bed and grip each other hard. No space is left between us as we burrow in, a mess of tears and snot.

I sigh. "Good thing this happened now instead of next week; my belly is still small enough to plaster myself to you, but not for long."

Noah huffs out a chuckle over my shoulder, petting my head as he keeps my cheek smushed into his chest. "Please try to relax. I can't stand thinking about how much I stressed you out with that pup. Breathe, Luna."

I pull back just enough to see his face. "Only if you relax with me. We're both under too much stress."

Locking eyes, we stroke each other's cheeks, arms, and sides for what feels like hours. When Noah's eyes laze shut, my shoulders finally loosen in relief.

I'm still trying to relax, but I can't stop thinking. Noah isn't in a good place to talk about it, but I wonder if he'll come around to seeing Jack had a motive.

Either way, I might be a horrible person like I've always been afraid of.

The next time I see Jack Hart, I might be tempted to… hurt him.

Noah's eyes laze back open after seemingly being asleep. It snaps me out of my rage.

"Shh. Quiet that beautiful mind, Luna." Noah strokes my forehead, lulling my heavy eyelids closed. He purrs. "There you go. You're right: we're safe. We're here to protect each other. Thank you for protecting me tonight. And I'm sorry."

"Don't be, please. You've helped me through so much, and this is just one moment in everything we've shared. I'm so happy you felt safe enough with me to tell me."

With a deep kiss, I squeeze Noah even closer, tightening our cuddle ball until we have no choice but to spoon again, allowing us to become a unit while giving Little Wolf their space.

Immersing myself in Noah's body heat feels so good that the next thing I know, I'm sprawled across the bed in the early morning sunlight, stealing the whole mattress for myself. My hand is already holding my belly—and so is Noah's.

Noah's also crying, hurriedly wiping his tears when he sees I'm awake.

I gasp. "Oh, my love, are you okay?"

"Y-yeah. I'm just feeling so lucky to have you. Both of you, now."

No matter how much my eyes sting from crying last night, fresh tears cloud my vision.

Noah scoops his big hand behind my head, drawing me in for a full-body cuddle. His lips press deep into mine, pleased nerves awakening across my body with my heightened emotions. My breath grows heated as I slip my tongue into his mouth, salty tears mixing on my lips.

Noah holds all of me with his wide form, his kisses deepening until he's massaging me into the mattress.

His voice comes out breathy between each kiss.

"Thank you—" With full lips gliding through our kiss, Noah rolls his hips over me. Lust leaks from my scent. "No one has held my Omega like you did last night—not since I was a kid."

Noah's fragile voice tears at my heart, a desperate whine slipping past my lips. I scoop his head into both hands, urging him to kiss me harder. Faster.

"I love him, Noah. I love your Omega, your Alpha, and every other piece of you."

My body lights up with his resulting elation in our bond. As we kiss harder, my tears smush across Noah's cheeks.

Propping myself on my elbow, I hover over him to gaze into his eyes—his hands still roaming my back. "But right now, I want to protect your Omega's precious heart, in particular. I want him to feel loved."

"Wait—" Noah pulls back.

I freeze, my heart kicking up the pace as Noah's nerves heighten.

But despite his anxiety, he doesn't drop my stare, cupping my cheek. "I remember everything we talked about now. And I need some time to keep processing this, but—" He winces. "I was just scared about that possibility. That he could've killed our dads."

My heart pangs. "Oh, love—"

"I'm so sorry for how I reacted. When we get back home, I want to go back to therapy. And since we have all morning, I want to finish talking this through with you."

Cuddling him close, I huff out the pain in our hearts. "I'm so proud of you, Noah. I'd love to support you in getting as much time as you need in therapy. But let's not talk through this yet—not today. My timing last night was awful. We'll solve who did this to our families, I'm sure of it, but it's just like you said: with time."

Noah sighs, rolling his forehead against mine. "Okay. Okay."

We massage our tears away with deep rubs across each other's bodies.

Noah kneads just the right spot on my achy back to melt me into the mattress. My sniffles soften into desirous hums. Noah's next kiss is slow, multiple breaths stretching through the silence as we hold our lips together. When we release each other to catch our breaths, Noah's eyes laze open, their soft teal staring back with enough adoration to flip my heart.

His voice comes out as a pleased purr. "Well, I want to take care of your heart too, and especially today. Can I treat you with your surprise?"

I pull back, surprised he brought it up. "Don't you need to rest before facing Matthew tonight? Not to mention you'll likely be facing off with Vik tomorrow."

"That's exactly why I want to spoil you—before I'm too exhausted to." Noah's shoulders ripple as he rises above me, his elbows sinking my shoulders deeper into the mattress. "And I have a feeling my pregnant Luna needs some rest and recovery."

Reaching beneath the bed, Noah fetches something wrapped in a towel—a bulky object long enough to extend past his entire palm.

My heart pounds as he places it on the bed beside us. A million guesses erupt as to what this surprise could be.

Then my eyes bulge at the tip of a massive dildo Noah accidentally reveals, the towel still hiding the other toys.

I slap my palms over my heating cheeks. "O-oh, my God, that's too much solo attention while you're feeling bad—"

Noah gathers my hands off my cheeks, hugging them to his chest as he kneels beside me. "Hey, hey— Don't worry about me, Luna. I offered this. You're not forcing me."

"Oh…" I giggle, biting my lips. "I guess you did, yeah."

Noah's grin returns for the first time since last night. I didn't realize how much I craved it until my heart overflows with joy, exciting Noah's wolf into perking up in our bond.

"So, do you want me to show you what I got you? Or are you not up for it right now?" Noah asks.

I swallow hard. I've never thought to ask Noah to use my toys on me since his body feels so much better than most toys. But now that he's offering, I bet he'd drive me wild.

It burns my cheeks to admit it aloud, but I nod. "Thank you for asking, love. If it's something you want to do too, I actually think it could be fun."

Noah bites his lip, but he's unable to hide his giddy smile. "O-oh. Good. Close your eyes for me, okay?"

I giggle. "Okay."

Closing my eyes, I slow my shaking breath long enough to notice the aching desire in my core. Without my vision distracting my focus, every sensation heightens as I anticipate his next move.

Noah's low purr coats me in goosebumps. "I won't use anything on you that you don't want, so please, don't feel obligated. I just thought—"

"No, I—" I sigh. "That's not why I'm hesitating. I'd like them too much if you were the one in control. That's why it still feels a bit unfair to be the only one."

Noah shifts his weight beside me, his breath inching up my neck until his deep voice rumbles beside my ear. "I wasn't lying when I said this is as much of a treat for me as it would be for you, Luna. I might even enjoy it more."

I keep my eyes closed, amazed by how much stronger limiting one sense amplifies every other. Noah's hand on my upper thigh warms my skin with soft, tickling pressure, inching closer to where I want him. His gentle, focused breath brushes my cheek, gliding over my lips. The warm spot he left behind on the mattress heats my bare back as he sits up, easing my panties off my hips. There's even more depth to Noah's voice—his tone soft but deliberate as he purrs through every word. "So, I'll ask you again: is this what you want right now?"

I swallow hard, my heart picking up the pace as excitement swirls in my core. "Yes. Thank you."

"You can thank me after I turn you into a happy puddle."

With my resulting giggles, Noah's smile is evident in his breathy words.

"Tell me where you want some attention. We'll start slow."

Noah's fingertips ease past my clit, drawing a slow circle around my labia until skating back up again.

I purr alongside him, shimmying into his touch as tingles crawl up my belly. "Mm… Anywhere except my chest. It's sore today."

"Anywhere else? Then give me one of your beautiful hands."

I bite back my smile as I hold out my palm, keeping my eyes closed.

"Alright, Luna, let's give you a sample of each: pick a letter between A, B, or C to start with."

I giggle. "Oh, wow. Um— Hmm…"

OCD takes over, at first insisting I *must* go in alphabetical order, then launching into a deeper worry that if I avoid going in alphabetical order in fear of OCD, I'll be doing a compulsion in fear of doing a compulsion, and, therefore, allowing OCD to ruin my life. Blinking through my rapid-speed catastrophizing, I laugh again, deciding to torture OCD back.

"Then, how about A?"

Noah chuckles with me, but that's not all my ears lock onto: the soft click of a button whirrs one of the toys to life.

"This is A," Noah mutters.

I jump as it touches down on my palm, and Noah quickly lifts it off me. "If this is too much—"

"No, it's—" I squirm a little, the vibrations buzzing through my palm, across my thigh, and echoing to my clit.

I can picture it in my mind's eye—the velvety little egg packing a delightful punch. Just the thought of feeling it stronger up close, and in Noah's skilled hands, upticks my breathing rate.

"I like it already," I whisper.

"Okay, good to know."

I bite back my amusement as Noah clicks the toy off, my palm feeling oddly empty without any vibrations there.

"B or C next?"

I smile. "B."

I'm tempted to hold my breath at the delicate shuffle of sheets between us as Noah sets toy A down, fetching my second choice.

Smooth silicone weighs down my palm, pressing my hand into my thigh.

"This is B," Noah says.

My eyebrows furrow. I'm unable to stop myself from tracing the object in my palm with my other hand, feeling over unfamiliar ridges on the toy. "What's going on with this one?"

"Don't open your eyes." Noah scoots closer to plant a gentle kiss on my cheek, guiding my hand over a protruding lump from the toy.

I quickly form an image of its familiar shape in my mind. "O-oh. It's a rabbit."

"I-I know you said your old ones weren't big enough…"

I sigh. "Thanks to you, you big wolf."

"U-um, either way…" Noah clears his throat, and I laugh at the mere sound of his flustered breath. "This one also moves, so…"

I freeze as Noah turns it on, the shaft flexing in my palm to make a thrusting action. My cheeks burn red hot.

After a long pause, Noah clears his throat. "Fuck. I'm too shy for the next one."

I burst out laughing, opening my eyes to find Noah's cheeks darkened. "*You're* too shy for it? Then how am I going to feel if it's being used on me?"

Noah's eyes widen as he erupts into giggles, scrambling to cover the last toy with the towel. "D-don't— Don't look—"

I can't help but gape at the toy in his hand anyway, my eyes bulging as Noah fumbles the thickest dildo I've ever seen in my life, accidentally flopping it against my thigh with a thick *slap*.

Noah gasps. "S-sorry—"

"Oh, *my*—"

Noah only burns darker. "I-I know. But you wanted bigger, so—"

I want to laugh, but my giggle comes out breathy and cuts short, especially as my eyes catch on the larger base—another familiar sight.

My smile stretches as I track Noah's eyes. They flit across the bed sheets, avoiding me as the truth becomes clear. "I've never seen anything like this before. At least not available to humans."

"Y-yeah, it's— It's a wolf thing they only have at the Alpha Summit. It— Um…" Noah's thumb presses into the bottom of the bulging sack. The engorged base of the shaft expands twice its size, stealing my breath. "Vik warned me I could stop knotting as often when my body realizes you're pregnant, and I thought you might miss it, so…"

My heart hammers, but my core flexes with need.

Noah's breath speeds as he finally dares to look me in the eyes. A spike of anticipation floods our bond, followed by immense affection for each other.

"Let me treat you?" he asks.

"Noah, before that—"

I cut myself short, distracted by his earnest eyes—his puppy-dog expression shier than ever after turning me on with mere suggestions.

I grin. "You have a spicier side than you ever let on, my shy Alpha-Omega."

Noah drops my stare with a giggle. Just the sound sends a wave of relief through my entire being.

I tilt his chin until he's looking straight at me. Capturing his lips, I hum into his excitement in my bond. When I release his lips, I break into a beaming smile at his precious, elated stare. "That's not entirely what I wanted to say: I just want to thank you before we go any further. I love your surprise, but I love how thoughtful you are, most of all. You're so sweet to me, Noah."

He kisses me again.

Then again.

By the third kiss, they're no longer kisses, but heavy makeouts, his tongue slipping across mine in a teasing dance.

"I want to make you feel good," Noah pants against my lips. "I'd love to, if you'd like me to start."

"I would," I whisper.

Noah's Alpha musk washes over my senses, his stare darkening into a newfound mischief. "Then how about this: we can use them all, building them up, one by one?"

I erupt into giggles. "*All* of them? At once?"

He shrugs, grinning wider. "Why not?"

Sputtering out laughter, I rub his arm. "Okay, wild wolf. Show me what you have in mind."

His giddy grin softens his eyes, stirring my heart.

Noah hooks my thigh over his bare lap, spreading my legs. My breath stills alongside his. Gazing deep into my eyes, Noah ghosts his hand up my inner thigh, sending a shiver up my spine. As he traces circles between my legs, goosebumps coat my skin. I shiver.

"Sensitive?" Noah whispers.

"Very. Ever since you got me pregnant."

Noah's playful stare softens, a shy smile overtaking his features.

He leans over me, planting a weighty kiss on my lips. At the same time, his fingers circle my wet core. Our lips chase each other, Noah's thumb brushing over my clit until tingles spread throughout my pelvis. I suck in a hitching moan against his lips, my back arching. Noah purrs in response, rubbing deep, slow circles into the swollen nub.

Then he clicks on the vibrating egg, slowly introducing it to my body by gliding it up and over my hip. I shudder, gripping his wrist to urge it lower.

Releasing my lips with a heavy breath, Noah's free hand sweeps my hair off my forehead. Tipping my head back with thick, massaging fingers, he gazes down at me. "Patience, feisty Luna."

Noah's tongue slips into my mouth, our kisses capturing each heated exhale as his thumb moves off my clit—his touch replaced by a gentle buzz.

I suck in a sharp breath through my nose, my legs twitching as Noah's circles deepen.

Then my lips unlock, my body urging me to take heavy, needy breaths. "N-*Noah*—"

"Fuck, you sound gorgeous." His hand trembles as he flicks open a fresh bottle of lube.

With his fingers coating my labia in fluid, Noah rocks the egg up and down over my clit.

My chest hitches in delight. Moving on their own, my hips chase his movements, but Noah's eyes on me are what make me tingle all over. Their usual teal is only half-shifted to green, but considering I haven't touched him at all, a fuzzy warmth fills my belly at how pleased he looks, just watching me. My thighs widen for more attention between them, each rock of his hand rolling the egg faster and faster until my pussy makes wet, suckling sounds.

Then Noah reaches for one of the penetrative toys. My eyes catch on his twitching cock, dripping against my inner thigh despite never being touched once.

"Which one's next, Luna?"

I swallow hard, catching my breath. "How about we continue going in order?"

Noah grins. "The rabbit, then the dildo?"

I nod, flushing down my chest.

With a quick splash of lube onto the toy, Noah circles the rabbit's tip at my entrance. But between Noah's horny musk and his hot breath on my neck, it slips right in.

My moan escapes me as a throaty, pleased purr.

Noah's wolven stare traces my face, spiking my heart rate. But I'm not nervous: instead of making me feel self-conscious, those green, eager eyes make me give the rabbit a heavy squeeze.

Noah glides it back and forth a few times manually before pausing to click it on. To my surprise, it doesn't thrust just yet, lighting up and awaiting another button's instructions.

"How does it feel?" Noah asks.

I smile. "It's nice… But still small, after a certain someone taught me how good it feels to be filled to bursting."

Noah chuckles, his eyes shifting from emerald green to a grassy golden. "Then how about we turn it on? Tell me which setting you like."

He flips through the settings until my lungs expand, my eyelids fluttering.

"Th-there."

Noah lifts an eyebrow, listening in. The uneven thrusting rhythm catches my nerves off guard in the best way.

"Does that mimic the real thing?" he whispers.

"Almost."

Grinning against my cheek, Noah purrs. "But?"

I giggle. "But you definitely mate me heavier."

Reaching between my legs, I search for a second, separate button than the thruster. Noah's eyes glow yellow with hunger as I take matters into my own hands, clicking the button. When the protruding nub vibrates over my clit, I suck in a tight breath, my hips rocking on their own accord.

Noah strokes my hair back, his eyes sweeping over my writhing form. "Oh, there you go. Beautiful."

Having memorized the thrusting pattern, Noah angles each thrust with his hand, rubbing up on my G-spot.

"O-oh! Noah, you make it better—"

"Fuck. I want to thrust that knotting toy manually, instead. Can I, Luna?"

I can barely get my words out, my chest heaving as the vibrations tease my clit until I ride on the edge. "Y-yes. Please—"

Noah clicks the toy off, leaving me breathless and desperate for release. I collapse into the mattress, my toes curling through residual aftershocks of pleasure.

But Noah makes quick work of switching the toys, the massive dildo lubed and ready at my entrance. After rocking the thick tip between my labia, Noah bends to kiss my inner thigh, sending my heart into my throat.

"Breathe, Luna. This will take some work."

I relax my thighs, nuzzling my face into the cushy blanket nest surrounding me. As Noah's forearm flexes beneath my palm, I help him control the amount it slinks into me, widening my knees as I provide counterpressure. But the damn thing is massive, its domed tip struggling to fit past my pelvic opening—until it slips in with a sudden pop, my muscles granting entry.

A cascade of pleasure washes down my chest, my jaw dropping. After allowing me to take a few heaving breaths, Noah sinks the toy's thick shaft deeper. Heavy, blissful pressure mounts low in my belly as the toy steals any and all room inside me, pushing a groan from my core at its thorough massage.

The second I relax, my mate pumps with soft, slow thrusts.

I choke on desperate pants for air, my hips bucking at the sight of Noah's veined arm flexing into me. "O-oh, yes— That's more— More like—"

Noah purrs, pulling the flexible toy back before plunging its thick shaft even deeper.

"Ahh! Oh—" I gasp as Noah clicks the vibrating egg to life

against my clit. My hips rise off the bed. "Oh, my God! It— It feels like we're mating—"

Noah thrusts the toy faster with each of my heaving moans, my hips twisting out of my control in desperation to come. My jerking pelvis scoots the vibrator faster, amplifying Noah's heavy pressure on my G-spot until tingling pleasure shoots up my belly.

Crawling closer on all fours, Noah stations his thighs below my ass, angling my pelvis for better access. "Fuck, look at you. You're taking it so well for me."

His words push a rush of fluid from me, splashing across Noah's lap. All I can do is moan louder, Noah angling the toy's flared tip into just the right spot.

"Shit. You like that, huh? That's what I thought."

Noah rocks the vibrator, at the same time working me deeper with each jerk of my hips.

"Ah! Ah— N-Noah—" My back arches and my knees drop open on their own, forcing me to cling to my thighs for leverage. "H-how did you know I'd like these?"

"Beyond seeing your bedside drawer, I just know my Luna." Noah breaks into a sly grin. "But I was actually talking about how I know my gorgeous mate still has a praise kink."

I open my mouth to disagree, but as my pleasure only heightens, I flush hot. "O-oh, my God, I think you're right."

He laughs. "That's my good girl. I hope you know it's not for show. I mean every fucking word."

Flustering me speechless, Noah circles the vibrator over my clit, clicking the button another time to increase the vibration's intensity.

My voice rasps as I cry out, my moans louder than ever— whether I want them to be or not. "Oh, my God, it's— It's strong!"

"Too strong?" Noah chases my clit with enough stimulation to raise my eager hips high off the mattress. "Oh, no, that looks like it feels *good*."

Growling, Noah circles my clit over and over again, watching me arch higher into the air. At the same time, he massages me on the inside, my claws extending into the bedding as my body begs me to ask for more.

Then my wolf whines for her mate. "Noah, please—"

"Please, what, beautiful?" Noah slows his pumping arm, but it's torturously good still—slackening my jaw at how delicious his tender attention feels.

I groan. "I want you in me. Just you—"

Gaping, Noah stops everything at once—until he pulls the toy out of me. I cry out, shuddering as Noah mutters frantic apologies, but he's still fumbling with his boxers. Which means he's left my hips rolling on the sheets, my body trapped on the edge.

"Alpha, *please*—" I breathe.

"Fuck. Fuck—" Noah scoops up my hips in both hands, readying his dripping cock at my clenching entrance.

But I jerk upright at the intrusion, grasping his wrists. "Ah! You're still big—"

"Fuck, sorry—"

"No, it's good. It's just so—" As I grip the mattress edge above my head, I push my hips down over him.

Thankfully, Noah stimulated enough fluid from me to coat us both. Applying warm, soft pressure to every inch of my inner muscles, Noah's flexing shaft glides all the way in with one deep thrust.

With how sensitive he made me, my whining moan is loud enough to echo across the wide ceiling. Tingling warmth boils over in my core, rocked over and over again by Noah's smooth skin inside me.

"Oh, Goddess." Noah squeezes handfuls of my ass to add to his internal massage, thrusting deeper by the second.

My limbs writhe across the sheets, my claws scratching the headboard, sheets, and Noah's back. He doesn't seem to have a care in the world, engrossed in my every movement as his chest heaves.

"Fuck. Just watching you has me— Oh, I'm—" Shifting my hips to one arm, Noah fetches the abandoned, buzzing vibrator.

As he smashes my hips flush to his, he flicks the buzzing toy across my clit until I scream. "Noah!"

I come in a flurry of lights behind my eyes, my pelvis jerking as tingling pleasure extends to my face. Noah pounds against my urgent flexing over his shaft, his breath trembling as my body squeezes every last drop of affection from him.

My moans soften, relaxing into pleased hums as Noah slows into gentle thrusts, soft purrs escaping his lips. I drag my hands across my belly, breasts, and face, blissed out with a fuzzy warmth that traces my body. Noah purrs at the sight, leaning over me to kiss my mark. His careful, caressing lips give me butterflies.

Shuddering again, Noah rocks himself tighter against me, fluttering my eyelids. "Oh, what a good girl. You did such a good job."

I hum through the leftover pleasure, endorphins flooding my heart as I open my eyes to Noah's blissful gaze.

His eyes drag down me before returning to my huffing lips. "You look like you feel so good, Luna."

"I do. Especially because I love you so much."

"I love you too." He smiles, his engorged shaft sliding back before giving me another gentle thrust.

Gripping Noah's shoulders, I moan. "Ah! God, it's still nice— But you didn't finish? You're still moving."

"I-I did finish. But Vik was right. You smell so pregnant that my body stopped knotting."

My cheeks flush as we break into giddy smiles.

But Noah's mischievous grin takes over. "Which also means that whenever you want more, I can keep working you without stopping."

My heart flips. "Oh, Goddess, Noah. I'd love to, as long as you're okay that I'll have to lay here like a lump. You really did turn me into a happy puddle—"

Purring, Noah licks my mark—hard. I moan at the pleasure it echoes between my legs, my sensitive core squeezing his shaft with every slow pulse of his hips. After stimulating a flood of my scent from me, Noah breathes me in, letting out a hungry growl.

I shiver. "Oh, shit. Never mind, I'm awake again, and I want as much as you'd like to give me."

Chuckling, Noah drags his lips over my throat, tracing my mark with kisses until warmth floods my groin again. When I squeeze his shaft faster, I'm met with urgent, pulsing flexes in response.

Noah groans. "I can feel that. But we can still catch our breaths. Take a minute, Luna."

I sigh, running my fingers through his messy hair. "Noah?"

"Hmm?"

"I want to mate you face to face like this, as many times as we can, before our baby gets too big." I rub my hands along my belly, drawing Noah's stare between our linked bodies.

As he strokes my abdomen, Noah's loving smile fills my chest with a buzzing excitement. "Okay, my love. I'll be nice and gentle this time while cuddling you as we mate. I'm not putting pressure on you there, am I?"

"No. But I am worried about your arms getting tired if you have to hold yourself up all morning."

Noah grins. "Don't be. I feel way too good to care. But do you need anything? Do you want your bread?"

I gasp. "Oh, fuck yes."

Noah laughs. He leans over for my secret pumpkin bread stash in the bedside table drawer.

But my jaw clenches, my wolf genuinely infuriated as Noah takes a huge bite of pumpkin bread in front of my face—until I see he's simply holding it between his teeth.

When he stoops to drop the bread into my mouth, I open up like a baby bird.

Noah lets out the brightest laugh as I moan at the sweet spices hitting my tongue, my legs squeezing his waist. But Noah only waits for the bread to disappear behind my lips before he smashes his lips against mine in a heavy kiss.

Cinnamon crashes through our kiss, Noah's sweet pumpkin lips urging me to lick them clean. His deep, delighted purr curls my toes, my knees widening for him to drop more of his weight across my pelvis.

Burying one arm beneath me for a full-body hug, Noah has slow, cuddly sex with me. Every nerve buzzes with his skin gliding over mine. His gentleness allows me to indulge in every minor pleasure before coming anywhere near a climax.

But it's more than just sex. We whisper our affections, grip each other's hair, massage each other's bodies. And while we're doting on each other, adding layer upon layer of blissful sensation until we rise back to the edge, I notice something different.

Our scents flow freely. One second we both smell like

Omegas, the next we smell like Alphas. And the rest of the time, we alternate between Alpha and Omega, free to express ourselves as we kiss each other senseless.

Then Noah whispers something I don't expect, his breath hitching just before he comes. "A-*Alpha*—"

Noah's pleading moan beside my ear makes me come so hard that my hips buck into him between heaving gasps. He doesn't seem to notice what he just said—filling me with another burst of warm fluid without a single worry in the world, allowing himself to submit to pleasure—but I'll never forget it.

By the time we're in a tangled, satisfied pile of limbs, Noah melts into the sheets in a deep sleep with me.

When I wake up a second time in the afternoon, pleasure-soaked and lazy, I open my eyes to find Noah reenergized, stretching in his ceremonial gear across the room with a bounce in his step.

I thought today would be a nightmare after last night, but Noah seems happier than when we left home. It's a relief, and at the same time, it guts me.

All this time, he just needed someone to listen to him.

I sob, pregnancy hormones getting the best of me.

Noah whips around, his eyes wide. "Oh, my poor Luna. Did you have a sad dream?"

I shake my head, reaching for him. "I'm so proud of you."

Noah's emotions spike with love and sadness to mirror mine. He leans over the bed to squeeze me in a tight hug. "You're more of my hero than ever, Luna. Thank you for taking care of me."

"Thank you for taking care of me too. I feel all refreshed and safe."

Each slow kiss we share soothes my aching heart. Noah's big palm behind my head makes my whole body feel protected—but I can't help but worry about the fight.

I groan, pulling back as a wave of nausea stings my guts. "Are you feeling ready after all those triggers? Do you need to withdraw?"

Noah nuzzles my cheek. "Don't you worry a second longer about anything except carrying this one, here." He places my palm over our baby before layering his hot, massive hand over mine. "They could be anyone, and I can't stand the thought that another King could make this world less survivable for them. I'm going to fight for you and that pup today, Luna. And I'm going to win."

❧ **26** ❧

Only two hours later, I cover my mouth over the toilet, my body shaking. I'm struggling to keep my dinner down between "morning" sickness and anxiety, fighting as hard as I can not to vomit: I know if I do, I could pass out during the fight. I'm already lightheaded enough, and I need every last bit of nutrients I can get with how rapidly Little Wolf seems to be growing.

With the death glares we've been getting from Alpha-domination cultists all evening, I need to look ready to be the Queen Luna, not like a puking mess. But when all I can see is Matthew slashing into Reid last night, I'm struggling to slow my raging heartbeat.

I step back from the toilet, plastering my quivering body against the bathroom wall as I steady my breath.

Okay, I don't think I'll throw up after all. Hopefully it'll be safe to change into tonight's outfit now.

My mind blurs as I go through the motions, hoping I look acceptable enough with what energy I can afford to expend. Noah tries his best to help sort me out, braiding the last bit of my hair in case I need to hold it back.

I head to the field on shaky knees.

Despite Noah's confidence in tonight's competition, my stomach won't stop flipping, forcing me to empty its contents just outside the field.

Pinning my braid behind my head, I cough into the bushes, guilt crushing me into another bout of nausea. My body shakes and sweats until it's sure I'm empty. "Ugh, *fuck…*"

"Oh, Goddess, my poor Luna…" Noah kisses my clammy

forehead as my head spins. He holds me tight to his chest, his heartbeat against my ear like a grounding drum. Closing my eyes, I listen in, counting each pulse until my breath settles.

As soon as the world stops spinning, Noah guides me to the nearest bench. "Rest for me, Luna. I'll get a medic to help you."

I sigh, waving him off. "No, I'll ask Annika when she meets me here. You need to focus—"

"*You* are my priority." Teal, focused eyes capture my gaze. I stare back, speechless.

Noah flags down a medic without an ounce of uncertainty.

His confidence has skyrocketed. This isn't what I was expecting at all. He's assertive, calm, and focused, his back straight and shoulders at ease.

But I don't smell only Alpha musk. I smell his spicy cinnamon sweetness everywhere, soothing my rocky stomach.

He smells like an Alpha-Omega.

Noah's Omega side is here to compete today—out in the open. The thought flips my heart, tempting me to hope for the best outcome.

I just can't shake what I also know to be true; dangerous men like Matthew will strike without mercy, especially once they smell him. Like I warned our allies, men like Steven don't have rules.

Annika rushes over, the front of her dress covered by a wrapped, white fabric I can't seem to figure out.

"Sorry, um… A small fistfight broke out on the sidelines, and Viktor had a lapse of judgment and overestimated an Alpha-dom cultist's strength. He may have—um—knocked out another rude Alpha. All medics are occupied."

Noah rubs his temples. "Shit…"

Annika laughs sheepishly, her shoulders raising. "Yeah, I'm sorry, but… Hi, Luna. Can I help, somehow?"

The second I see her cautious, fearful face, reminding me of the danger ahead, my heart rate spikes, and I gag again. Thankfully, all that's left is air.

Annika stabilizes me as I reel over the bushes, groaning. "Oh, Goddess, someone needs to get you some wolf-strength tinctures for nausea! Let me mindlink them."

I shake my head, clinging to her arm. "Pregnancy made me

hate that herb's smell, so I always puke the second it's in front of my nose."

Annika's eyes brighten. "Ah, wait! I have an idea—"

At first I think she's turning to leave, but she untucks the wrapped fabric from her dress, propping up something heavy behind her.

Annika beams. "I know how to soothe both an Alpha *and* an Omega!"

She wasn't wearing a wrap; a tuft of tight brown curls poking out of her fabric bundle tells me she's actually carrying a little sleeping wolf.

Gripping my heart as it throbs with delight, I let out an uncontrollable coo. "Oh, Goddess, Anni, you brought your youngest! He's *beautiful*."

Annika shuffles his sleeping body from her back to her chest, giving me a better view of her pup's sleepy, squishy face. Her infant stays sound asleep through all of it, so cozy that his quiet purr only intensifies as she repositions him against her chest.

"This is my little Omega boy, Markus. He's almost seven months old, but still such a sleepyhead." Annika giggles with pride as I gaze at him, my heart exploding with affection.

"Oh, what a sweetheart. I'm so happy for you and Vik."

She beams. "Would you like to hold him, Luna? Here—"

The instant Annika plops Markus's warm body into my arms, a rush of doting hormones ooze from me.

"Oh, Goddess—" I swallow hard, not having held a Lycan baby since Noah got me pregnant. Markus is extra warm, and just like Noah's sleepy wolf—loose and unbothered, no matter what happens around him.

But as Markus settles against my chest, I'm startled as his eyes open—not only because they're a gorgeous, deep brown, but because for the first time, I feel a light fluttering in my stomach.

Shifting Markus to one arm, I gasp, gripping my belly. Was that just my upset stomach? But no, it's there once more: a delicate pittering stirring within me.

"What? What is it?" Noah zips to my side, his eyes racing over my form.

I gape at Annika as Markus stirs, nestling himself closer to me with gentle purrs. Yet again, I feel the same, featherlight sensations in my stomach.

"M-maybe it's a gas bubble in there, but—" My eyes widen as I stare at Noah, his eyebrows shooting up his forehead as the biggest smile forms. "Noah, I— I think I just felt—"

Placing his hands over my belly, Noah gazes into my eyes, holding his breath with me. But as that fluttering sensation stirs within me again, I grip Noah's arm, releasing a trembling exhale.

"Did you feel that?" I whisper.

Smiling up to his eyes, Noah drops his forehead against mine. "Not yet. But I felt every second of your emotions with you through it, and it's beautiful enough to make me cry."

Sure enough, Noah's eyes spill over despite his vivid grin. I laugh, swiping him free of tears as I shake my head. "Oh, *Goddess*, I can't believe this, Noah. It didn't feel like gas, it felt like—" Looking back up from my belly, I do a double-take at Noah's shining, elated eyes above me. I burst into giddy laughter at his rapt attention. "My sweet, curious, Alpha. It felt a bit like this…"

Placing my free hand on his abdomen, I cover his skin in light, fluttering taps with my fingertips. Noah's grin widens.

"Oh, *Aliya*, that's—" His eyes close as he holds my stomach. "I can't believe how beautiful your excitement feels in our bond."

My heart twirls, bringing joyous tears to my eyes.

But Markus coos in my arms, wriggling. When I look to Annika for her response, I'm surprised to find her overflowing with smiling tears. "Goddess, that was so, so sweet. Let me take him so you can continue to enjoy the moment."

Annika scoops her slim hands beneath Markus's bundled body. But Markus releases a shrill cry, refusing to return to his mother—snuggling back up to me with tight grips of my dress instead.

Annika's eyes widen with a touch of hurt. "He's never—"

But as our pup stirs in my belly once more, I blink, still in disbelief.

Except when Markus lets out another pleased coo, I'm stunned further; his timing fell almost perfectly in line with Little Wolf's fluttering.

I cup Markus's sweet head, my heart flipping. "Wait, Luna… Do you think Markus can sense I'm carrying another little wolf?"

Annika breaks into the widest grin I've seen on her yet. "Oh, my goodness, wait, you're right! It's on the verge of a fairytale, but I've heard stories of pups sensing other pups in the womb, especially if they're destined to know each other. Do you think that may be the case with our little ones?"

My stomach flips. But meeting Noah's eyes, I sputter out a laugh; he's speechless, his stare darting between my belly and the baby in my arms.

Not ready for that, Noah mindlinks.

All I can do is laugh, shaking my head. "I have no idea, Anni. This is all so surreal."

Shaking, I skate my nose across Markus's squishy cheek, allowing myself to rub soothing pheromones over the pup's head. Could I be holding a special pup to Little Wolf?

My heart flips. Noah's right; that's thinking way too far ahead of ourselves. Only Little Wolf can tell us the answer, once they grow up.

Markus gives me a satisfied, sleepy coo, and my lip wobbles with fresh tears at how innocent his happy scent smells. He's so pure, existing simply to love, and be loved. Is this what Little Wolf will smell like too?

I gasp, tilting my chin to the sky. "Oh, no— My tears are going to drip on him—"

Noah's sleeve comes to the rescue. His breathy chuckle stirs warmth in my heart. When I look up at him blotting my tears, I melt at his red, weepy eyes.

This is the most beautiful thing I've ever seen in my life. I can only imagine what you'll look like, holding our pup.

"Oh, Noah—" I laugh. "You're making it harder to stop crying."

Noah lets out a wet laugh, swiping his tears away.

Annika rubs my arm, beaming at us. "Look at you, mama. You're definitely part Omega."

Before I can respond, she releases a rush of sweet, delicious scent that makes my eyelids flutter. My shoulders relax, tension falling away with every inhale.

"There you go. That's some Omega scent to soothe your Alpha

self too." Annika giggles as I purr uncontrollably, smashing my head into my mate's chest. "You feel good now, don't you?"

I bite back a smile, stroking Markus's fuzzy, dark brown curls as he nuzzles against me. "Yes. Enough to distract me from what's scaring me shitless all morning."

Annika laughs, rubbing my arm. "Trust me, I understand. Let's go find our lovely Waimārie and sit on the sidelines together."

I sigh. "Okay."

At the edge of the field, Noah separates from me with a kiss. "I'm keeping this short because I want it to be a 'be right back' for you and not a goodbye. That's all it is, okay?"

Swallowing hard, I nod. "Okay. I love you."

"I love you too, gorgeous Luna. You look so cute with that pup in your arms."

I can't smile; my heart aches as we separate, Noah's soft smile peeking over his shoulder as he crosses the field.

It's even worse on the sidelines, knowing I have to return the happy baby in my arms. I try not to show it, giving Annika a warm smile. "Thank you so much for your help, Luna. Markus is such a sweetheart that it's hard to let go of him."

"Oh, mama, you can keep holding him! Actually, I want you to."

My heart flips. "What? Are you sure that'll feel okay for your wolf while you're under so much stress during Viktor's fight too?"

"Yes, actually. I trust you to protect him as well as I can. Probably even better with your tough Alpha side. Which reminds me, Luna—" Annika presses to my side, speaking as low as she can. "I want you to know that I trust you, in general. That if you do become my Queen Luna, I'll protect you just like you've protected and honored me. You're a true ally, mama."

Too touched for words, I nuzzle Annika's head on instinct.

I'm surprised by how much she purrs in reaction, inspiring a fresh smile despite my anxiety. Wolves really do love affection.

Including me. I rarely used to touch anyone, but my body feels so content now despite puking my guts out a bit ago. Annika knew exactly what I needed, just like a mother wolf.

"I want to be just like you for our baby," I whisper.

Annika squeezes my hand, her chin dropping to her chest. "Oh, Luna. That's too sweet."

As we join Waimārie and Tāne relaxing on the sidelines, I attempt to share their warm greeting. But as Waimārie and Annika huddle on either side of me, whispering soft reassurances, I track every Alpha in the vicinity, watching for who supports Matthew the loudest.

They must be watching me too; I can't seem to track who does what, most wolves keeping their voices hushed and remaining as far as they can from Noah and me—likely anticipating our wolf hearing to be above average too.

Johannes gives his official announcement for the second round of battles in the semi-finals, pairing Matthew with Noah, as expected. Viktor will face off against the Thailand Alpha afterward, leaving the Brazil Alpha to battle whoever wins Viktor's round.

With that, the top five Alphas strip, preparing to shift into their wolves. As the rest of the Alpha Summit wolves erupt into howls, Noah finally glances at me, his chest bare.

His cool, collected demeanor is nothing like his emotions in our bond, boiling with excitement. *I love you, okay? It's going to be okay.*

I stand, rocking the little Omega in my arms. *Listen to me for a second, Noah.*

He eyes me in acknowledgment, forcing Johannes to wait to start the battle as Noah slowly peels off the last of his ceremonial gear.

My heart hammers; I'm not sure what he'll think of this, but I have to try.

Your Omega is powerful too, I mindlink. *I don't think your power is sectioned off into just your Alpha side. Your Omega has faced everything head-on, no matter who attacks him. He's brave, he's beautifully vulnerable, and I'm so proud of him. Let him show everyone he's someone to be proud of too.*

Noah doesn't say anything, but when he launches himself into his wolf form in a swift jump, electricity charges every black paw.

Don't worry, Luna. You've inspired me since the day we met.

Whether it's this year or next, I'm going to be the first King Alpha-Omega, just like you're our first hybrid Luna.

My breath hitches, and Noah's wolf bounds across the field, teasing the crowd as they dash away from him. I have to laugh.

And just like you transformed our pack for the better, we'll all be better wolves for it if we rule the global pack. They'll be lucky to have you as their Queen Luna, and the first Omega-Alpha to do so, Noah says.

As my mate approaches Matthew's nude, human form, my heart pounds into my throat so heavily that I can't swallow.

When Matthew shifts, I feel even sicker; Noah's black wolf is only marginally larger than Matthew's stormy-brown wolf. If this is the strongest Alpha-domination pack leader we know of, I have a terrible feeling about the damage he could accomplish if Mason follows through with my ambush theory.

The second Johannes announces the start of the fight, Matthew's paddle-like paw swipes for Noah.

But my mate is already leaping, punting Matthew into the dirt with a vicious snarl. He clamps his jaws over Matthew's snout and body-slams him, preventing the Alpha from wriggling free.

They're not going to touch us this time, Luna. None of them.

My heart speeds into a sprint, my wolf pacing faster in our bond as Noah's fury riles me up.

In him, I see the defender I needed when Steven broke down my door to get his hands on me.

Hot, angry tears stream down my cheeks as Noah's claws hold no mercy, pinning the whining Alpha to the ground.

But despite having no chance, Matthew bites back. I can read the cultist's intentions from here: there's no compassion behind his angry, batting paws.

Matthew is driven by the belief that he's owed more than Omegas are—a belief Noah shatters by existing. He hates Noah. Not just for who he is, but what his life stands for.

Shit, Noah was right. It's not just about winning the King title anymore.

I know how this story goes. If we let them get any stronger, they'll hurt more wolves than just Omegas.

No one we know will be left unharmed.

∽ 27 ∽

One second, Noah has Matthew pinned to the ground. The next, Noah flies across the grass, launched by all four of Matthew's paws.

I scream without meaning to, waking up Markus. His plushy cheeks warp before my eyes—until Markus bursts into full-blown tears.

I cup his quivering head, my heart shredding. "S-sorry, sweet boy! Oh— Oh, no, sweetheart—"

"Åh, stackars liten…" Annika scoops up Markus, nuzzling into him with soft-spoken Swedish.

Letting out a sad whimper with Markus, I rub Annika's shoulder. "Oh, I'm *so* sorry, Anni, it just came out."

"I understand, mama. I feel like screaming too." Annika's somber, pale expression guts me.

"Poor Luna," Waimārie whispers, holding me close.

I can't bear to be distracted a second longer, my focus flipping back to Noah. I've never seen him get tossed like that in my life. No one usually matches up to Noah's strength.

But Noah has already popped right back up, shaking his fur off.

Matthew stalks closer, ready to strike, and Noah's tail stands on end in excitement.

I'm almost annoyed he seems so thrilled to kick Matthew's ass. This competition is fucking ridiculous.

Like the wolves they are, they pace for a while—before lunging back in with wicked, rapid snaps of their jaws, snarling and vicious barks echoing across the field.

My breath catches, each bite shaking my entire body. When

they move this quickly, it's increasingly difficult for me to process what's happening at all, spiking acidic fear into my throat.

When the wolves break apart, Noah's fur is too dark to tell if he sustained any wounds.

But their bloody fangs sink my stomach down to my feet.

"I can't tell who's bleeding. My wolf is losing her shit," I whisper.

Annika simply squeezes my hand.

Judging by Noah's little sneeze, I can only guess he got one or two knicks on his snout. They restart their prowling circle, estimating how to strike next.

That's when I spot a subtle limp; Matthew is carrying himself differently after their last bite clash.

I almost forgot I have an advantage: I can figure out what's wrong from a distance, mindlinking Noah with a hint.

Focusing on Matthew's massive paws, I find each step perfectly calculated. The back paws take the place of the front, the brooding Alpha sneaking through his own footprints. When he leaps for Noah, his movements are sharp and fleeting, snapping back just as quickly. He's agile, and he's deceptive about it.

He's clever.

Putting myself into Matthew's shoes, I scope out his fighting tactics. It's clear he only wants to allow quick, passing bursts of aggression between him and Noah, likely betting he has a better chance to wear Noah down without overexerting himself all at once.

But I'm certain there's a reason for Matthew's subtle shift in behavior. That something has altered his strategy, even if I don't know what yet.

Racking my brain for answers, I think about what Yasmine taught me: never show them your back. Always stay on your feet, if you can. Evade, evade, evade.

Each of these tactics put me more on the defensive—a far more common strategy for surviving wolves, rather than the attacking beasts they're painted as in folklore. If we really went around killing one another, we'd never have enough energy to protect ourselves. By instinct, we're too good at defending one another's lives, hunting only what we need for food.

But here at the Summit, Alphas are forced to exert their wolf bodies to the max if they want to win against the best of the best. Which means they have to act on the offensive, draining their wolves faster than they would during the average territorial fight.

So I analyze Matthew's angles of defense and offense— looking for patterns in how he approaches Noah.

Almost immediately, I notice it: he only shows Noah one side.

I perk up, my heart lurching. *He's protecting his left flank!*

Noah hops in a zig-zag around Matthew, and sure enough, the brown wolf won't let Noah see his left side.

Genius, Luna! We're unstoppable together with your observant mind.

Even though my teeth are chattering, I laugh at Noah's goofy tail wag, his supercharged ears pointing to the sky.

When Noah's jaws snap at Matthew's left side, it forces the Alpha into full defense mode. Each bite seems to shrink Matthew further into the ground, only making Noah bristle larger.

Good job, Noah! Keep overwhelming him!

Matthew can hardly keep up with Noah's relentless lunges to fight back.

His tail droops.

Matthew tucks his tail tight between his legs…

And rolls over in submission.

Towering over the cultist, Noah's bragging, puffed-up wolf gives one last irritated sneeze, and I burst into laughter.

His alert ears rotate to me before his head, and I laugh even harder. "You adorable, powerful goofball! Come here!"

The Lunas flinch beside me as Noah's enormous wolf scampers over. He flattens one ear in apology—before shifting back to be stark naked in front of all of us.

But my only concern is Noah's wounds. My skin washes in an icy chill, my eyes skating down his clawed-up chest, blood mixing with sweat everywhere I look.

I grip my heart. "*Goddess*, Noah—"

The second we meet eyes, Noah tightens his jaw, barely restraining his rising desperation in our bond. We dart forward at the same time, crashing into each other's arms. As my wolf whimpers through me, forcing me to lick her mate's face clean,

Noah whisks me away from the crowd, tucking me behind the garden entrance to the field.

"Shh, Luna. It's all okay, gorgeous." He nuzzles over my whimpering lips, stroking my hair back with soft, shaky sweeps.

"Are you sure you're okay?" My eyes water even worse from his sharp Alpha musk, his scent potent enough to force any Omegas at the edge of the field to cover their noses.

"I'll be fine, but… I heard you scream earlier. I felt so bad." Noah's voice breaks as he kisses me all over. "Please, tell me the truth. Is this too much for you? Say the word, and we'll leave."

I swallow hard, rubbing my belly in an attempt to stifle my rolling emotions.

But the tears come anyway. "I want our pup to have their dad."

"Oh, my sweet—" Noah curls me in his embrace until I'm marinating in his scent. This time his musk is even stronger, but it's laced with such a heavy sweetness that goosebumps cascade down my limbs, drawing a sigh from my lips.

"That feels good," I whisper.

"There you go." Noah tilts my jaw until I reveal my mark.

With slow, tender licks on my scent gland, Noah replaces every discomfort with delight, his scent seeping down to my bones.

Noah purrs. "Good girl. I'm right here."

I smush my forehead into his chest, drenching myself in his adoring scent. But no matter what, my heart aches.

"Listen closely, okay? If I come anywhere close to being hurt badly, I'll submit," Noah says.

I freeze, gripping him tighter. "But you said you'd only submit to—"

"I don't care what I said. As far as I'm concerned, it still would only be submitting to you. Because you're right: you and our pup are my priority."

My eyes water as Noah's fingertips skate over my stomach.

"I want to come home to watch you be the mom you've always dreamed of. I want to live to hold our pup with you. And I want to protect our pack by your side for years to come. I'd do anything to witness you in action." He softens his shaking voice, pulling me closer as if he's telling me a deep secret. "Every time I look at you, I see the only wolf here who should be King."

My heart soars higher than I expect with those words, unlocking a beautiful vision within me—as much as it terrifies me.

I grip Noah's arms, my eyes tracing his. "If you win this competition and become my King, then I'll be—"

I swallow hard, terrified to say something so extreme out loud.

But the look in my mate's eyes dares me to—begs me to—his claws extending in anticipation of my next words.

"If you'll be my King Alpha, then I'll be yours," I whisper.

My heart hammers into my throat as I watch my words erupt behind my mate's eyes, brightening them into sunshine.

Noah grows more alert by the second, his wolf's chest puffing as high as his human form.

Cupping my cheeks in his palms, Noah gazes at me in pure awe. He eases his lips against mine, dragging a wave of pleasure down my spine. Then his voice rumbles deep.

"Feisty Luna."

He's dead-serious. I freeze, unsure what he'll say next.

"One day, you're going to change the entire world with nothing but your own paws, I know it. You *will* be King."

Noah pulls back. Determination radiates from him as he steps away—the ability to achieve anything set into his tight core.

But I grasp his hand, bringing him to a halt. "Wait, Noah, I need to tell you something else before you dive back into Summit chaos."

Vigilant eyes flit all over me—as sharp and wolflike as they can be outside of his wolf form.

I grit my teeth. "I'm afraid if you don't win tomorrow, the whole world won't be safe. Look how strong these Alpha-domination wolves have become. How frequent they are. Entire packs follow *all* of them. It makes me so sick to think how many there must be."

He growls, his half-shifted eyes roaming the field with detest.

Then I see it—the same wolf in him that I needed in my worst moments. The leader the world needs.

It ignites a fire in my core. I grip his biceps harder.

"There he is. I felt him out in the field, just now, too. The one who I needed to defend me."

Noah sucks in a harsh breath, holding it. He meets my eyes, agony creasing his forehead.

But I hold my grip strong, even as my voice quivers. "Remember this feeling. Chase it, Noah."

He blows out a slow, fiery breath. "I will. I'll show them all it's time to protect Omegas and Betas too, and that doing so protects all wolves."

"Good. Go out there, and express yourself. Including your Omega side that needs protection too. He deserves it."

Noah's growl comes to a halt, but his piercing stare shifts into something so strong that I have to look away.

Holy shit, he's catching my insides on fire. I'd never want to have to take him down. Not in a million years.

But that fact doesn't terrify me.

He gives me hope again.

I struggle to catch my breath as Noah stalks away from me, ready for his next assignment with fury in every step.

Viktor's latest opponent—already humiliated from submitting—dives away from Noah's mere stare. As Noah strides to Viktor's side for Johannes's official congratulations of this year's two top Alphas—and tomorrow's competitors for the King title—wolves howl across the entire field in celebration.

But Viktor's eyes are glued to Noah. Locking onto my mate, Viktor stiffens, jealousy overpowering his clenched jaw.

My stomach rolls, weakening my knees.

I don't know how I'm going to get through this.

But I have to. For Noah, and for the safety of all wolves.

$$\infty \quad 28 \quad \infty$$

Thankfully, Reid's wounds healed faster than expected with the best medics in the world available at the Alpha Summit. But that means Reid and Noah have been strategizing all morning, sparring in a secluded, nearby field, preparing Noah to face off against Viktor tonight. They're startlingly aggressive with each other, pausing only if the other bleeds a bit too much—which, unfortunately for my reeling head, has already happened twice.

My wolf is having none of it, her tail twitching in a last attempt to keep from snapping at her mate. Logically, I'm aware Noah's PTSD is still at its peak, heightening his upset around aggressive Alphas, but it doesn't stop his agitation from riling me up too.

It's time to step away from this nonsense, Little Wolf. With a hand on our baby, I walk away from my mate at the edge of the field, settling myself onto a nearby boulder—my back to their snarls.

Even from back here, my stomach won't stop flipping. Vivid images of every horrible thing that could happen spill across my mind.

What if my stress makes Noah and Viktor actually hurt each other during the battle?

The second I create an opening, darkness floods my mind.

Good point! What if Viktor goes on a rampage? Or what if Noah does? He could turn around and lash out at you right now!

I flinch at the thought, picturing Noah scarring my arm—just like I scarred his.

Gritting my teeth, I struggle to keep my focus on the present. How could I even think something like that? Noah wouldn't hurt me.

Or, what if you go on a rampage, and you accidentally kill every wolf here before you realize what you're doing?

What? That makes no sense. I'd *never* do that.

You're right! I meant Noah. What if Noah kills Viktor by mistake and your lives are over? Your pup will grow up fatherless!

I suddenly recognize my thought pattern, snapping me out of my head.

Dammit. My intrusive thoughts are out of control, and I'm feeding into them way too far. That must be why I feel this familiar vague, never-ending urgency that something horrible is about to happen.

I take a deep breath, focusing on what's actually happening in front of me: maybe Noah will get hurt tonight, or maybe he'll make sure he's safe for our future pup, like he promised. I can't control him. That's all I know.

My stomach settles just enough for me to sit without feeling worried about getting sick.

Then my phone chimes in my jacket pocket. It's so unfamiliar these days that it startles me.

Everyone important to me is in our pack, so they'll just mindlink me instead of texting or calling. What if it's urgent?

No, wait. Is that another intrusive thought? I need to focus on the present moment.

I try to focus on the soothing breeze ruffling my hair, but the feeling gets worse and worse as my phone chimes again. Then again.

Okay, fine. I'm giving in and looking.

But when I check my notifications, my heart rate spikes so high that I struggle to breathe.

My panic is strong enough to whip Noah's attention off his practice battle. Shifting back into his human form, he takes swift, determined strides toward me, calling out. "What?! What's wrong?"

His golden eyes are so vivid that they nearly glow. Reid shifts back after Noah, his brows furrowed at Noah's heightening alarm.

All I can do is stare at my phone, blinking over and over again as if it'll make the notification disappear.

When I open the notification, I find a direct message from

a new social media follower I've never seen before. But the username "stbarrett92" leaves little doubt in my mind of who it is.

Steven.

Noah stoops to my eye level, gripping my shoulders. "Tell me what's wrong, Luna."

I shake my head, unable to speak as my eyes trace Steven's messages, again and again.

> ***stbarrett92:*** Hey, I know I'm not supposed to contact you but I thought you should know something I heard
>
> ***stbarrett92:*** I was at the bar last night and another hunter was bragging to my buddy
>
> ***stbarrett92:*** This old dude was fucked up and said he accidentally shot someone 5 years ago and got away with it.
>
> ***stbarrett92:*** Do you think it could be your dad?

I drop my phone, scrambling away from it like a poison. It lays face up on the forest floor between me and my wide-eyed mate. His severe focus hardly allows me to catch my breath; I don't want to have to witness his crushed reaction when reading these messages too.

Noah picks it up, and my heart drops as he reads the message. Then he reads it again. And again.

Until I let out a sob.

When Noah's eyes flip up to mine, there's a split second where pure bloodlust hazes his eyes over.

Then he melts for me, his forehead warping in agony. "Luna... My poor Luna."

Noah tugs me tight against his chest, whining over me.

But it doesn't help. With all the chaos of tonight's battle, every scent, sound, and touch clutters my mind.

"Please, take me back to our room," I rasp.

Glancing at Reid, Noah hoists me to my feet. "Thank you for the warm-up."

"Don't thank me. Go," Reid says. "You still have an hour and a half. I'll come get you if it's getting late."

My stomach jolts, pushing a panicked whimper from my lips. How can anything in the world feel okay enough for Noah to fight for our lives in an hour and a half, let alone for us to function as a potential King and Queen? We dart back to our room, not a single word more shared between us as dread seeps through every inch of our bond.

Once we're locked behind our door, my knees wobble. Noah hurriedly guides me to my makeshift nest, placing me at the edge of the mattress as he stands before me. His hands are outstretched and shaking, ensuring I don't topple over.

The sudden silence is stifling—especially when I find Noah gazing back at me with eyes just as wide.

For a while, we say nothing. But as Noah's panic rises in my mind, I grit my teeth, and Noah lets out a shaky breath in response.

"He could be lying, Aliya."

I flip between rage, grief, and terror all at once.

Then I finally settle on the same sense of doom I've felt all day.

"He's not lying." The words sting like acid coming out, forcing me to grip a fistful of my skirt. I suck in a desperate breath. "He's terrible, but not that terrible. He thinks he's a good person—by his standards."

Noah bites the inside of his cheek, struggling to keep his breath in check. He breaks our stare, lifting his head toward the ceiling with one hand on his forehead. As he frantically paces, I grip the bed sheets, barely able to tether myself to the earth.

"No matter what, he's fucking with you. What asshole would drop that on a grieving person?" Noah stops dead in his tracks. "And without any details! What's the drunk fucker's name? Steven said the dude was old, but that's it? What a fucking dick."

My stomach sinks lower when I realize exactly why Steven did it this way.

"It's because he wants me to reach back out," I mutter.

A sudden calm falls over Noah as he freezes in place, but the way he's gazing at me unsettles me. Like he has an idea—one I'll hate.

My skin crawls. "W-what? What are you thinking?"

Noah flashes his incisors—halfway between a grimace and a snarl. "I'll call him with your account!"

"What?!"

"And with access to his new account, I can finally track him. He probably doesn't know his photos can be traced." Noah reverts to mindlink. *Dave, this is an urgent lead about Steven Barrett; track the username "stbarrett92" and get back to our Luna and I as soon as possible, please.*

On it, Dave says.

I choke out a gasp. "Noah! Finding Steven isn't important right now."

"Yes, it is! For all we know, he's the fucker who killed them! He already hurt you!" Noah growls. "And why is he forcing his way back into your life *now?* Attempting to weaken you today, out of all days? What if he's here, acting as a spectator wolf with a fake-ass name or something?"

I groan as I curl over my burning chest, unable to bear sitting upright. Noah rushes to my side, smoothing my hair out of my face.

He softens his voice. "I don't have to call him now. But if I do, I can record everything he says, then I can tell him to leave you alone."

I sigh. "He won't talk to you. He'll only talk to me."

"Fuck. Well, then calling isn't an option."

I blink a few times, adding up the pieces. "No, you're right. I should call him. I *need* to—"

"Shit, no—" Noah groans, but I reach for my phone. "No, I shouldn't have put that idea in your head—"

"My love, please, just listen for a second."

Noah freezes, fear creasing his forehead.

"You're right. But I know him best, and thanks to how much he manipulated things, I know exactly how to twist our conversations back to safety, like my life depends on it."

As expected, Noah's frown darkens. "Because it did."

Placing my hand over his taut forearm, I soften my voice. "Here's what I need."

Noah swallows hard, his wolf pausing in his pacing in our

bond. He stands, enraptured with me, just like Noah's human eyes staring deep into mine.

I can't bear to hold his gaze; if I look too closely, I'll see too much of our shared pain.

Rolling my shoulders back, I steady my voice. "I need you to sit with me, and I'll call him. You can't say anything or he'll stop talking—trust me."

"Then can you at least use me as a threat?"

"I can't threaten him. It's illegal in the human world."

Noah takes a breath to speak, but I shake my head.

"Even with physical fucking evidence of him invading my body, the police never protected me, Noah. They only protected *him*. They always will."

Noah closes his eyes, pain stinging our bond. "I know."

His fragile voice nearly breaks me.

I suck in a hitching breath. "He won't listen to my fears or cares, anyway. I'm a woman. He probably *likes* when I suffer. Finds it amusing."

Noah grits his teeth, leaving us in silence. We sit in limbo for a solid minute, wavering over the possibilities.

Until Noah's voice fills the space between us, his voice soft and even. "Alright, if he needs a man to put him in his place, I'll step in at the end—after we have our information."

I swallow hard, feeling a bit safer with this plan.

But Noah's jaw can't stop clenching.

"I'll let him know he'll never be able to hurt another woman again without paying for it." His voice comes out just as delicate, but this time, it leaves a chill in the air.

My heart pounds into my throat, face to face with Noah's blaring emotions. They're too much to process beside my own. But with an overload of overwhelming sensations, my PTSD symptoms kick in—numbing me out.

Finally, all I hear is silence.

Noah's eyes widen as my crying comes to an abrupt halt. "L-Luna?"

He's looking at me, waiting for reassurance that I'm okay.

I don't answer. I can't.

"Omega? What's going on?"

Noah rubs my shoulders, arms, and cheeks, kissing each one with no response.

"*Aliya.*"

My eyes zip to his, not used to him calling me anything but his nicknames for me, unless he's really trying to make a point. But I don't know what else there is to say. I have no thoughts left, only vague whispers of terrors licking at my soul like escalating flames.

"W-what are you thinking?" Noah whispers.

"I'm thinking…" I tilt my head, distracted by the unfamiliar sound of my own voice; not only is it deadpan, but it's also echoing in my head like it's at the other end of a long tunnel. "I want to call him."

Noah shuffles where he stands. "N-now?"

"Yes. If I have to live another second not knowing who might've killed our dads, I don't think I can handle it."

Veins bulge across Noah's temples. "Okay. I'll be right here."

My thumb shakes as it hovers over the voice call button. When I finally tap it, my mind goes blank.

There's silence.

Then there's the first ring.

"A-are you going to be okay?" Noah whispers.

"Yes."

Another ring.

Noah huffs. "You don't look okay. But I can't feel you. Did you shut yourself out of our bond from how afraid you feel?"

I glance at Noah. The call is already on its third ring.

"No. I can't feel anything. At all," I say.

Noah's eyes widen.

His rubbing on my arms doesn't even register, but it's rapid enough to catch my stare. Noah takes a breath to speak, right when Steven picks up.

"Hello?"

His voice is so familiar that I sit frozen in place—my mouth agape.

I'm tempted to fool my brain into thinking he's just an old friend; the truth is too horrible to bear. I just called my abusive ex. He's talking to me.

Say something, Luna, Noah mindlinks.

When I don't move, Noah's wolf nips my wolf's neck in our bond, and I jolt upright.

"Uh, hello? You there?" Steven asks.

Come on, brain, speak!

But what the fuck do I even say? The last time I saw him, he was—

My wolf tightens in defense, ready to rip off that face I see above me in my budding flashback.

I want to seem tough—to be angry.

But when I finally speak, all I can sputter is a soft, "H-hi."

Noah's eyebrows arch in sorrow at my strained voice, coming out squeaky and small.

"What? I can't hear you," Steven says.

"Hi," I blurt out, filling the eerily silent room. "Hi, Steven."

His laugh chimes through the receiver, surprising Noah and me both. Noah sucks in a tight breath. I see him analyzing me in my peripherals, but I can't bear to look at him. I'm afraid if I do, my protective mask will fall, and my true emotions will show Steven where to strike.

But Steven is still chuckling. "This is awkward, isn't it?"

Steven breaks my mask anyway.

I jump to my feet. A flicker of unbearable rage pierces through the numbness blanketing my mind. Noah chases after me, sticking to my side with his phone already recording.

"I don't know what could be funny about someone possibly bragging about killing my dad, asshole." I'm startled by the snarl in my own voice, but it only adds to my anger. I don't sound like this. This isn't me. I hate how much he's changed me, again and again.

"Jesus, woman, calm down. You know I laugh when I'm nervous."

Noah's rage spikes.

His low growl startles me. But Noah softens when he sees me jump, hugging me close in apology.

Steven's voice chirps from the speaker. "Uh, what the hell was that? A dog?"

I take a few hot, shaky breaths, clinging to the strings of our conversation before Steven derails it, like always. "Steven, you're going to tell me what you know right now, and then we're never speaking again."

He blows out a slow breath. "Okay, fine. What do you want to know first?"

I blink a few times, struggling to process; I didn't expect him to give in so quickly. What do I even start with?

Whipping open my messages with shaky fingers, my eyes land on one word:

hunter

"What did the hunter say, in his exact words? Tell me the story, from the beginning," I say.

Steven hums, pausing for about ten seconds. "Yeah, I told you pretty much all of it already: the dude was drunk, bragging about something fucked-up that sounded familiar."

"Then tell me again. I need to know as many details as possible."

Steven sighs, wind rushing through the receiver in his silence. "Are you outside?"

"Yeah. I didn't want anyone in the office to hear me. It's just twisted, you know? With how the cops basically cold-cased it, I wanted to tell you first."

I drop to our bed, Noah's emotions flip-flopping faster than mine as he halts in front of me, our knees brushing.

Finally, I allow myself to meet Noah's eyes. As I feared, they're steeped in horror.

But so are mine.

Yet Noah is here, braving this pain for me.

As my heart opens up to him, Noah's posture softens, and my thoughts slip out.

Steven is being surprisingly empathetic… It makes me anxious.

Noah cups my cheek. *I'm right here.*

"Aliya? Are you still there?" Steven asks.

I blink a few times, struggling to push the words out.

My voice comes out soft and emotionless. "Just tell me what you know. Please."

"I really did tell you everything." Another whoosh of air muffles the receiver. I'm suddenly reminded of how much of a fidgeter Steven was, like he was always afraid I'd see straight through to his rotten core if he stayed still for too long.

Rolling my eyes, I open my mouth to urge him ahead, but to my surprise, Steven continues.

"I was sitting a couple stools down from him at the bar, and he had too much to drink. He was slurring, but we all got dead serious when he sobered up a little and said he got away with killing a dude once."

I cover my mouth, nausea creeping up my throat.

"He said he could've sworn he saw bears, so he shot them. Turns out it was two big, bulky guys."

By now, Noah is restless and jumpy, gripping the back of his neck as he shakes his head. I can't contain myself either.

"And you just let him go on and on about this without doing anything about it? *Everyone* did? What the fuck?"

"No, Aliya, we *did* do something about it—of course we did! But not before I dug for more information for you! I thought you'd be relieved."

I roll my eyes, biting back every cuss word I want to scream at him. "Then what else did you ask?"

"I asked him how long ago that was. He said five years. Almost six."

Noah and I lock eyes. Their death anniversary is next month.

"Either way, my buddy and I told the cops once we sobered up today," Steven says. "They said they'll look into it, but they also suggested Jack was just drunk."

My heart flips. "Jack? The hunter's name was Jack?"

"Uh, yeah. It was Jack…" Another whoosh. "Jack Hart, I think?"

Panic tightens my chest.

But it's ten times worse as I look at Noah in front of me. His eyes fall flat in defeat.

Without having to ask, I can feel it in our bond: neither of us are surprised.

But the thought of Jack killing my dad still turns my heart inside out.

To my surprise, Noah dives to his knees in front of me, rushing to embrace me, chest to chest. *You're doing great. Ask him to tell you anything else about the act itself, in greater detail.*

I squeeze my eyes shut. Nuzzling into Noah, I allow his presence to soothe my skyrocketing nerves.

When I first saw Steven's message, something within me hoped it was finally the answer we've needed.

But not if it's Jack. I believe Noah over Steven; Jack would've much rather killed Ritchie with his own fangs.

My voice wavers. "Do you remember any other details about the act itself? Did he say he acted alone? No one else saw this hunter kill someone and get away with it?"

"Well, he didn't mention anyone else in his story, so I don't know."

"Was it even the same murder, then? They've always said there might've been at least two hunters since the bullets were different."

"That's right, shit…" Steven is silent for a moment, leaving me on the edge with my heart pounding through my ears. "Well, I wouldn't be surprised if someone else was there. People rarely hunt alone by your parents' place. It's too overgrown and difficult to navigate."

I stiffen. "I remember. You refused to go hunting with my dad, let alone meet him. Then he died, and you lost your chance."

Steven has nothing to say.

Noah boils, barely containing his heated breath. I squeeze him tighter to my chest, our baby protected between us, and he drops his forehead against my shoulder.

Ask him about Mason. If Jack spends a lot of time with anyone.

"D-do you know if he has any friends he hangs out with? What about his son?"

"His son?"

Steven is silent for a while.

Noah lifts his head, meeting my gaze. We hang on every word, Noah's chest stiffening like he's hardly daring to breathe.

"I didn't even know he had a son. He acted super lonely and sad while he was drunk," Steven says.

I deflate, shaking my head at Noah. *I thought that would give us another clue.*

Jack was estranged from Mason as a kid for what he did to me and other Omegas. It was a long shot, but… Noah's brows furrow, his focus dropping to the bed sheets beside me. *Mason just sounds so much like Jack lately. I've wondered for a while if they'd team up someday.*

Steven's voice cuts through our mindlinks. "Hey, wait… How do you know so much about this old dude, anyway?"

My back stiffens. "How do *you* know him, Steven? I heard he hurt a lot of people—that's how. Why are you hanging out with a guy like him?"

"It was a hunters' event at the bar! Why would I tell you his fucked-up secrets if he was a friend?"

My heart drops when I realize something important. "T-the bar? Which bar?"

"The one in Westview."

I grip Noah, barely able to catch my breath. "He's in Westview? Like, our Westview? Next to Greenfield?"

"I mean, I guess? People travel from all over for these meetups, so who knows where the dude actually lives."

Noah hisses beneath his breath, but it's forceful enough to shift my focus.

Dammit. It's over now. Steven won't tell us anything else.

Steven waits for me to answer—to cover for Noah—but I can't think. The only sound is my own rabbiting heartbeat, throbbing in my ears.

When Steven speaks again, he's lost his "charming" lilt. All that's left is a dark, treacherous depth to his tone.

"Are you not alone?"

I grip Noah's arm, swallowing a spike of panic. "N-no, of course I'm not alone! I'm freaking out! I'm with my—"

My breath shakes.

I'm so petrified that my wolf had no choice but to step forward for me—so much so that I almost said "my Alpha."

Closing my eyes, I erase the panic from my voice. "I'm with my husband."

Steven breaks into laughter. I wince, the sarcasm in his tone threatening to tear me apart; that tone means consequences are incoming. "You're fucking *married*? Since when? Did you get knocked up, or something?"

My heartbeat pounds harder and harder, rage bubbling to the surface.

I break away from Noah, standing at the edge of the bed to clench and unclench my fists—unsure what to do with the fury in my veins.

"Seriously, Aliya, I never imagined you to be the type. The last I heard, you were still in that cottage—"

"Fuck you, Steven!" My voice echoes throughout our suite. "You don't deserve to know anything about me! You're a sick fucking stalker!"

Steven is silent, but I've unlocked something within myself I've kept trapped for a long time. And she's not going back into her cage.

When I look into my mate's eyes, the horrified ache overpowering his rage makes it all spill out of me.

"I wasn't the type to get married after I broke up with *you*, only because you— You—" Despite my best efforts, my voice catches with emotion. "You hurt me!"

There's a beat of silence.

Then Steven's voice comes out soft. "You hurt me too."

Sobs break through my anger, and I huff in frustration; he'll never take me seriously, now that I'm crying.

He has no idea what he really did to me since he thinks I owed him my body. He thinks I took his property away from him by dumping him, when really, he took everything from *me* that day he broke in.

So many times, I've wished I could shake the reality into him, screaming the truth of what he did to me to his face. But just like every time he's knocked me down, I sputter through my fear of what he'll do next, unable to spit a single word out.

Steven sighs. "After everything I've done for you, you still fucking hate me, huh?"

My lip quivers as Steven laughs.

Noah's hand grips his chest, grimacing as I cry my ugliest cry.

My shoulders droop. "You never used to be this cruel. Why do you have to keep treating me like this?"

To my surprise, Steven doesn't reply right away. When he does, he's quieter than ever. "I don't know. I just don't understand why you hate me so much, I guess."

With this, Noah doesn't allow me to continue to see his expression. He buries my head into his chest like he's protecting me from the pain. His heartbeat pounds into my ear. *I love you. I've got you.*

I love you too, Noah.

You don't have to deal with this a second more.

"Anyway, I, uh…" Steven sniffs. "I'm sorry. For how badly I hurt you."

My eyes widen in shock.

But a fuse snaps in Noah, freezing me in place as he opens his palm.

Before he even asks aloud, I place my phone in Noah's hand. My eyes trail up his arm—the whole length bulging with veins as his blood pressure skyrockets. Finally, I meet his eyes. Luckily, he's not looking at me. If he was, my wolf would cower on instinct; cold-blooded hatred seeps from Noah's golden stare.

Gripping the phone close, Noah cuts through the silence, his voice deepening into a growl. "It's too late for apologies, you pathetic fuck."

❦ 29 ❦

Noah's voice cuts through the air like he's clawing through meat, leaving my wolf to shiver—enraptured by his every miniscule movement.

"The trauma you forced onto Aliya will follow her for the rest of her life, no matter what she can do to heal."

Steven scoffs. "Trauma? What—"

"Shut the fuck up. I'm going to find you and show you how I really feel."

"So you're threatening me now?"

Noah laughs, but its icy, piercing tone sends a shiver down my whole body.

"Threatening you? Like how you threatened Aliya, you mean?" As Noah hugs me tighter, all I can do is stare. "How is this different from you bombarding her on a new account despite her repeatedly blocking you? How is this worse than breaking into her fucking house and putting your hands on her? Aren't you asking me to give you a real reason to stop?"

Steven is silent.

"Either way, there's nothing I can physically do to you that will hurt you as badly as you've hurt her." Noah closes his eyes, gripping his head. "Unless I rip your balls off—since you seem to care about them so much."

Despite my anxiety, I'm tempted to laugh.

But Steven does first. His laugh is so disingenuous that my mouth sours, nausea burning my throat.

"So this is all about the supposed 'break-in?' She probably didn't tell you what actually happened. She wanted me to—"

Noah takes the phone off speaker, raising it to his ear with his eyebrows knit and jaw clenched.

Fuck. Even if Noah protected me from hearing it, I know exactly what Steven is saying.

Steven doesn't agree that breaking in and raping me was non-consensual because we were in the middle of a breakup. While we dated, he convinced me he owned me. His twisted viewpoint on that day distorted my thinking for years. He had beaten my mental health down so much that I blamed myself for something I never asked for. Jenny and Amy had to drag me out of his distortions before I gave up on life.

Someone's finally getting to witness how Steven really treated me. And I trust Noah to be the one who understands me.

My forehead warps; Steven is also why I understand Noah too, after what Jack did to him.

Steven's voice prattles on into Noah's ear, but Noah cuts him off with a low hum.

"Are you done?"

Steven replies, but Noah cuts him off again with a barking laugh.

"You really think I'm going to believe your bullshit ideas about what you did to her after all the lies you told her today?"

This time, Steven is silent.

Noah puts the phone back on speaker again, crossing his arms.

"I have no fucking clue what you're going on about," Steven says.

"Alright, let's start with something real fucking obvious. It's Friday, and you're in Westview, supposedly. Why would you be outside 'the office' in the middle of the night?"

I freeze.

If I were in Steven's place, it wouldn't be hard to come up with a lie; he could claim he's working overtime. Maybe he has a big project due tomorrow, but he's taking a walk. Maybe he's on a business trip in another time zone, and not actually in Westview tonight.

Steven doesn't say a single thing.

Noah's jaw flexes. "What's the name of this hunter event last night? Do you have proof it happened? I bet you didn't even talk to the cops."

Steven sighs. "Look, man, I don't know what you want me to say. It sounds like you'll never believe me, even if I defend myself."

"Uh huh. Whatever. If you're not going to try, I'll just keep calling your bullshit out. I've got more."

My gut flip-flops, unsure what to believe at all now.

Maybe Noah is right: I feel so confused and disgusting inside. It's how Steven wanted me to feel all those years. Confusion kept me trapped—made it easier for him to blame me. And if he convinced me everything was my fault, I became all the more manipulatable.

"Dude, seriously? The hunters' event was a private event hosted by the Westview Hunting Club. If you look it up, it won't show up. Since, you know, it was private, and all."

Noah rolls his eyes. But then we both pause as we're mindlinked by Dave and Yasmine.

Yas and I dug for more info on 'stbarrett92' across various platforms. He only has two photos, and the caption from his last photo says he was in Westview yesterday, Dave says.

Bullshit, Noah says. *He knows we're tracking him and is faking his location. He claimed he met Jack Hart in Westview last night, so we better keep an eye out for Jack, whether Steven is lying or not. This level of effort to frame Jack for murder makes me think they've been in contact locally—enough to become enemies.*

Yasmine mindlinks, *What if he's trying to distract us? Wasting our resources to find Jack while you're gone and Steven plans some sort of coup?*

Good point, I say. *Noah just called him out for lying about being at his Westview office job, and he didn't defend himself.*

It's still possible Jack pissed Steven off recently, even if it wasn't at a Westview Hunting Club event last night. Or that Jack killed them, but it wasn't a solo job. Steven is trying to pin this murder solely on Jack, and when you're guilty of something, the closest target to pin the blame on would be someone else involved, so... Noah's mindlink trails off, leaving me gutted.

"You don't think...?" I whisper.

Noah hangs his head, unable to meet my eyes as he shrugs. "I don't know."

"Hello?" Steven says. "If you're going to whisper to each other, I'm just going to hang up."

Want me to look up that event too? Dave asks.

Sure. Thanks, cuz. Noah sighs, shaking his head. "Alright, Barrett. Maybe you are at the office at two in the fucking morning. Maybe you did go to a private hunters' event. Even if you told the truth about all that, there's one thing I can't believe."

Running a frustrated hand through his hair, Noah somehow makes his hair even messier.

"Are you fucking kidding me, man? You expect us to believe *Jack* would attend a hunters' event at a dive bar? What the hell is your motive? Frame that asshole for what you really did? Did you fucking kill my dad? Or did you kill Aliya's dad, and let Jack take mine out?"

My fists wrinkle my skirt, clenching hard enough to make my fingers ache.

It's just a millisecond of silence, but it punches me in the soul; I don't like how long Steven waits to respond. That was a guilty silence.

"Steven, really? *No—*" I choke out, just before the phone speakers garble Steven's words from his shouting.

"Dude, what the actual fuck?! That's fucking crazy as hell! Seriously, don't listen to him, Aliya. It's so fucking far-fetched that I'm not even going to answer that," Steven says. "But doesn't that mean you're the one who knows too much about Jack? Who said he'd never attend a hunters' event?"

Noah pauses, and my heart skips. But he doesn't budge when I grip his forearm.

"Unfortunately, I was close to Jack. I was forced as a child to hear all about his beliefs on hunting, and to know why he'd never show his face in Westview unless he's looking for a fight," Noah mutters. "But you know exactly who you're talking to about this, don't you? That's why you brought Jack up to my wife. And why you didn't think to ask me who my dad was when I accused you of killing him."

My head spins, blood draining from my face. Steven takes a breath to speak. A beat of silence forces me to hold my breath, waiting for Steven's next move.

But with Noah's words about our fathers and Jack, something rings clearer than it ever has. A possibility so simple, yet so terrifying, I never considered it plausible.

My voice shakes as I whisper. "Mason, answer the question."

Noah's eyes bulge further than I've ever seen them, his grip growing limp on my thigh as he gapes at me. *Mason?*

"I tried to warn you. He's back in Westview," Steven says.

Noah's breath races as fast as my raging heartbeat. *Holy fucking shit. You think he's…?*

Oh, my God, Noah, he didn't even register that I called him a different name. Did he not hear me, or did he find the name 'Mason' so normal, responding to it for most of his life, that he thought nothing of it?

We stare at each other, frozen—unable to fathom the possibility Steven just unlocked.

"You can take it or leave it," Steven continues. "Your loss."

Despite fighting through rapid, frantic blinks as we both spiral into panic, Noah does his best to play the part of my pissed-off husband with a scoff. "Oh, fuck off. When we find *you* in Westview, you'll hope you listened to my wife and never showed your face there again."

My nails dig into Noah's arm in fear of Steven's response.

But with a soft chuckle, Steven hangs up.

I can't catch my breath, sputtering through harsh gasps of disbelief. Noah guides me to the bed and sits me down.

Grasping him all over, I can hardly gain my bearings. "W-what just happened?"

"He confirmed it," Noah hisses, shaking his head. "Mason is Steven."

I choke out a breath, gripping my forehead. "I can't think, Noah. Are we sure that's true? He didn't directly confirm it."

"I… I don't know. We'll have to capture Mason, and get him to—" Noah's breath hitches. Closing his eyes, his jaw tightens around his words. "Fuck, that makes so much sense why he's hiding his fucking smug-ass face from us. Because it wasn't just us he's hiding from—it was *you*."

Numbness crawls over my limbs, my jaw stuck hanging open as my mind glitches over this possibility. The possibility Steven not only lied about who he was, but continued to stalk me, warping everyone around me into believing he was just another jerky Alpha-dom wolf with no power. Not only that, but he destroyed my life, down to possibly killing my father.

Nothing can be said to truly process this. Noah and I huff out our anxiety together, at a loss for words as we stare into each other's wide, sunken eyes.

"How the hell did we manage to put this together? What made you guess Steven knows who you are?" I whisper.

Steadying my shoulders, Noah stares deep into my eyes. "Because I believe you. I believe you about what you've been through with every piece of my heart."

I freeze. My lip trembles, a burst of emotion rushing up my spine.

Noah grasps my hands. "I believe you; he's a stalker. It's easy to suspect he knows who I am. And I believe you; he's a rapist. When he said otherwise, I knew to search for what else he was lying about."

I drop my forehead into his chest, letting out a relieved sob.

Noah strokes my hair, but then his musk heightens. "Goddess, I let him near you, I—"

Grasping Noah tighter, I steady my voice. "No, listen to me."

Noah halts, but his chest heaves between us, his eyes racing around the room.

I cup his cheeks. "*You* didn't let him near me; *he* forced his way in. As we've both said, this is entirely his fault."

Noah chokes out an exasperated groan, burying his head against my shoulder. "Knowing this much, he *has* to be Lycan. It makes way more sense why he's impossible to find. Packs will protect their own with their lives."

"But if Steven has always been a wolf, what about all his hunting friends? Was he lying about that while we dated?"

"Many wolves still hunt for their food with their closest pack members, so 'hunting friends' is a human-sounding coverup."

"Oh. *Oh…*" I deflate, shaking my head in disbelief. "So is that why you don't think Jack would be at a hunting event for humans?"

"The whole reason I met Jack was because he trained Alpha pups to fight. To hunt hunters and protect the pack. He'd joke that human hunters are free meals—even off-the-grid ones that hunt for food only. None of us ever thought it was funny."

My guts churn. "So if Steven really is Mason, why would Mason frame his own father? Do you think Jack hurt him too?"

"Oh…" Noah opens his mouth, then closes it. "I don't know. I didn't think of that possibility… Either that, or Steven—*Mason*—really is the one who shot our dads."

My head spins hard enough to make me wobble. Noah steadies me, an aching concern infused into his musk.

"I feel sick," I whisper. "Is this all my fault? M-maybe I pushed back against him too harshly, and—"

"No. Absolutely not." Noah scoops me into his lap, cuddling me to his chest. "I've blamed myself too. Do you remember what you just told me?"

I grip Noah's shoulder, huffing into his collarbone. "We couldn't do a damn thing. It was completely out of our control."

"Yes, my love. But you know what? Now we're experts at spotting abuse. It doesn't have to repeat." Noah kisses my forehead.

I sit up, cupping his scruffy cheeks in my palms. All I can do is sigh at the sight of my sweet mate. No matter how worn his poor heart feels, he's ever-present with me, as usual.

And he's right; if Mason shows up in front of me in the future, I won't let him hurt a single soul more. I'll do everything in my power to capture him, binding his hands so they'll never have an opening to hurt anyone again.

Noah rasps out a haggard breath. "Fuck, this is fucking crazy. If you weren't a badass mastermind, what if I never realized—"

I groan, kissing Noah's forehead. "*You're* the mastermind who led me there, Noah. And I know you want to be King and change the world, and I think you already are succeeding in that… But are you sure you can fight today? This is a lot, and…"

I trail off, gazing into my mate's vibrant, teal eyes. He's more present than I thought.

I'm amazed by him. He looks so solid—angry, but righteously so.

Maybe this is exactly what he needed to remember why this "King Alpha" title isn't as superficial as it may sound. The King's power influences how all packs treat one another—an opportunity I trust Noah will run with.

I drag my fingernails through Noah's hair, giving his scalp a thorough scratch. "Sweet, sweet Alpha-Omega."

Noah's shoulders soften. He tugs me closer, and my lips ease against his, massaging my love into them. His big hand encompasses my lower back, pressing our baby tight to his stomach as my tongue slips against his.

I feel so safe with you. Thank you, I mindlink.

Thank you. *I can't believe I get to spend my life with you.*

Huffing through the loving ache in my heart, I dive back in for as many kisses as I can squeeze in, our desperate lips colliding with delicious pressure. I want nothing more than to be wrapped up with Noah, forgetting about this stupid Summit for a moment.

But someone pounds on the door.

Noah gives me one last reluctant kiss before heading for the door. I'm still sorting my dress with shaking hands when Noah finds Reid in the hallway.

Reid's brows are furrowed. "They're waiting to start the final battle. You're not planning on backing out of the fight, are you?"

"Fuck," Noah hisses, spinning in circles to search for his crest. "I didn't warm up. But I may as well have with the fucking cardio I just did."

Reid grips Noah's wrist, halting him in place. "What happened? You both look devastated."

Noah deflates, his stare dropping to his feet. He must have his puppy-dog eyes on. "My poor Luna has been through hell. We just got a tip from her ex that Jack might've killed our dads. And it turns out her ex was lying about who he was, and he's been Mason Hart this whole fucking time."

Reid blinks rapidly, his jaw tensing. "*What?*"

"We haven't seen Mason's face to confirm it. But either way, I think her ex is a wolf. And even if Steven is still a separate person, he could've killed our dads just the same."

Reid grips Noah's shoulders. "Breathe. We'll find him, and stop him—them. I promise you."

Noah groans. "Fuck, man. All that I know for sure is that this can't fucking happen again. I won't let it. These Alpha-domination fuckers need to be stopped before they start believing they're too invincible."

Reid nods as I approach them. Gazing at their profiles, I find Reid's expression is just as solemn and furious as Noah's. "Vik's ego is his main focus tonight, which means it's also his weakness. He doesn't have a higher motivation like you for the greater good. Use it. Become our King. My King." Reid meets my eyes. "Her King."

Noah's heart lifts out of every dark fog Steven draped over it today, inspiring me into a full grin. I grip my heart as Noah crashes into Reid's arms, met by just as heavy of a hug. Relief floods our bond, Reid's soothing presence reminding us we're not by ourselves in this.

God, this is exactly what Noah needed: a loving Alpha's father-like reassurance. I'm so grateful.

Reid sighs. "I know you think this is your fight, but you can always count on me. Don't you dare wait to call me if you need me."

Noah chuckles over Reid's shoulder, and his shaky breath melts my heart.

I meet Reid's shy glance and break into a smile. "Thank you, Alpha."

All Reid does is break into a soft grin, but I can smell his pride from here. He loves Noah too, ready to fight for his lifelong friend.

As Noah speeds to the field for the fight, Reid and I follow at his sides.

"What's going on? You're not focused," Reid says.

"Yas and I are discussing Jack and Steven/Mason. If there's a chance they'll ambush Greenfield, we need to double our security. But not enough to leave anything vulnerable in case it's a diversion tactic."

My rib cage tightens. "Will all of this distract you from focusing on Viktor?"

Noah stops at the edge of the field, his chest puffing higher by the second. "No. It's only reminding me why this is so fucking important."

He cups my cheeks in his hands, planting a soft kiss on my lips. I grip his shoulders, begging for another. With a low chuckle, Noah scoops his hand behind my head, immersing his fingers into my hair to kiss me even deeper. His Alpha musk seeps into my bones, allowing me to relax despite the pressure we both feel from every angle.

"I love you. I'll be right back, okay?" Pulling back with a sly grin, Noah's wolf comes out to play—a flash of his incisors greeting me in his smile, just before he turns his gaze away from me.

My heartbeat catches. "Wait!"

Noah's eyes widen as I grip his arms, not allowing him to pull away.

He's under so much pressure. I want to give him a fun incentive to win. Something that appeals to his playful, mischievous wolf.

The one who's about to become King.

I draw Noah closer, kissing his cheek before whispering into his ear. "When you become King, and we confirm we're safe from harm, I'll lay myself down for you on the field to mate me in any way you'd like. If you're too tired to move, I'll mate you in front of everyone—" Gliding my hand up his chest, I stir my wolf into action as Noah's lungs inflate in anticipation. "And show them how much I love you with a fresh mark on your neck."

When I trace my scarred bite mark on his scent gland, Noah shudders. I capture his heavy breath with a kiss. Noah hums against my lips, his scent flourishing with a hint of lust as his hands wrap around my waist.

But to my surprise, it's not Noah's Alpha musk that presents itself. Drawing me closer, Noah breathes through our kiss, his heart racing beneath my palm as his cinnamon sweet scent brightens into the hyacinth I smell in our bond. Huffing through our kiss, I pull back, dazzled by his eyes flashing golden for me. In my heart, I see it; he's going to do this. He will be King Alpha— and he'll achieve it with his Omega side, alone.

Keeping my voice as low as possible, I give Noah a gentle nuzzle. "Your pup and I will be waiting for you, my sweet Omega."

Sucking in a tight breath, Noah freezes, his eyes flitting between mine as I step back. As he breaks into a flustered smile, Noah's wolf bristles in our bond, and his human form rushes to cover his bare groin. I giggle as Noah glances at his ex with flaming red cheeks.

Noah grins. "Protect my feisty Luna for me, will you?"

With Reid's nod, Noah shifts into his hulking wolf.

My black fireball bolts onto the field, forcing wolves to dart out of the way. Energy ripples from every strand of silky black fur, standing on end to make him tower over Viktor.

Waimārie and Tāne wave at us from across the field. They're by Annika's side as she clutches Viktor's shifted wolf, the King Alpha nuzzling baby Markus on Annika's back.

Since we're so late, a massive crowd spans the spectator seating, blocking our path to our allies. I'd like to support Annika through this battle too, but with the anticipatory jitters in the air, my wolf urges me to stick close to Reid's side, not trusting the crowd enough to cross it.

And I need to keep my focus pinned on Noah; it's almost time for the final Alpha Summit battle. Towering over Annika, Viktor's beast of a wolf licks the tears off her cheeks before he turns to my mate. With a bloodthirsty snarl, Viktor's glare sends most Lunas into hiding. I quiver along with them, a whiff of Viktor's musk carrying on a gust of wind.

Viktor's motivations aren't the exact same as Noah's, but he cares about stopping the Alpha-domination cult too, and his ferocious wolf looks dead serious. Did we push him too far?

Before I can panic, Reid settles in at my side, his soothing scent extending as his eyes track my mate. The steady faith in his gaze raises my hopes.

I return my focus to Noah. *You're going to crush this, gorgeous. Stay focused.*

I will, Luna. Six months from now, this will all be resolved and we'll be cuddling our new pup on the couch together.

Biting my lip, I cup my belly. I'm tempted to melt, but I can't.

It's time. Noah tenses into a crouch—ready to pounce.

The world's top wolves stiffen, a hush falling over the field. Only the wind whistles past my ears.

It's curious: the field was split into sections before, allowing us to spectate in rows of seating along the field's edges. But now there's only standing room, and a wide radius between the battle's starting location and the crowd.

I lower to a whisper, afraid to disturb the silence. "Alpha Reid, why are they so far away? I feel like I can hardly see my mate, and he's huge."

The quiet Alpha nods. "You'll see them closer in a second. I'll help you, Luna."

My eyebrows furrow. "Help me? What do you—"

The split second Johannes shouts the "start" signal, Noah lunges into a fierce sprint. His claws tear into the dirt, sinking in deep before erupting from the earth—each pulse of his paws launching him faster, faster, faster—until he crashes into Viktor with all four paws extended, clamping Viktor's massive wolf down to the earth with a *thud* that echoes through the trees.

Reid pulls me out of the way—just in time for a mass of wolves to dart away from the tumbling Alphas.

But I saw it; Viktor's ears drooped, just before Noah landed on him.

I was wrong. Noah isn't a forever-puppy. He's a predator who prefers to play around until he gets sick of it. I've never witnessed a wolf this terrifying in my life.

But is this fear I'm feeling? My body shudders as Noah's fangs flash beneath the Swedish sunlight. The first drop of Viktor's blood stains his lips.

A thrill zips through my veins.

With what Noah has contemplated the last few days, it's like he's letting his inner monster out, finally telling everyone to fuck off.

And I want to see more.

Hope surges through me so deeply that I can't stop shaking, unaware how to process the depths of it. Someone is fighting for us. Someone is *finally* fighting for us.

We're fighting for us. Together.

With my excitement rising, Noah's movements sharpen. Quick, untraceable snaps of his jaw set Viktor on the defensive, and it's only been thirty seconds since the fight began.

But already, something is becoming clear to me about Viktor.

He wriggles from beneath Noah's clenched paws until he bolts free, dashing for the treeline. His chest is already heaving, paws splayed at his sides.

Now that Noah isn't holding back, Viktor is genuinely shocked.

And he's unwilling to appear submissive around Noah, even a little bit.

Noah, keep Viktor off his feet, I mindlink.

Rather than sticking to random nips or lunging attacks, Noah focuses on smacking Viktor to the ground with wide paws, forcing the current King to scramble back to his feet as quickly as he can—avoiding seeming too submissive.

It perks Viktor's ears up; Noah's ability to knock him around in a flash sets Viktor on edge, blurring his decision making.

Yes! Good job, Noah!

Noah breaks into a sly pant, his tail giving a soft wag.

Okay, I take that back. He *is* a huge puppy, even when he's a monstrous one.

But now he's pissed Viktor off. The air shifts with stormy pheromones as both massive, black wolves come to an abrupt halt.

I stifle my breath alongside every wolf in the vicinity, stilling with the hulking beasts. The only sound is Markus's soft crying.

Just when I meet Annika's petrified eyes in sympathy, our mates break their standstill.

Loud, vicious snapping of their jaws riles every wolf into angry protests.

I can't breathe. It's happening so fast that it's difficult to tell who's biting who, but I can see the blood staining their white fangs from here.

They rise onto their hind legs—snarling giants towering twenty feet tall. I've never felt so small.

I shudder through each breath. "I-I don't like this, Reid!"

He tucks me tighter against his side, his lungs flinching with each clash of Noah's and Viktor's fangs. They're not allowed to bite each other's throats, but they nip each other's necks below the ear—dangerously close.

I cry out as Viktor grazes my mark on Noah's neck, piercing me through our bond.

Reid growls, tucking me closer. His torso stiffens against my cheek.

Noah breaks free with a bounding leap, turning over his tail and splattering a few Alphas with a mix of mud and blood.

Logan snarls. "Hey!"

When Noah stares straight at me, my heart drops to the floor. *Sorry, Luna. I didn't mean to let him bite me there.*

Please, just focus! I don't want to feel you hurting.

But Noah is too close to us—and the rest of the crowd.

We both realize it in the same second: Viktor darts in a wide arc, and with how fearsome Noah is, Viktor's coming in fast and hard. With the crowd blocking his escape, Noah has no choice but to take Viktor's strike.

There's no mercy in Viktor's snarling, loud strike of his claw, hurling Noah across the field. My mate slams into a tree with a sickening crack. The hundred-foot tree splits in half, crashing down over him.

Even before I know what fully happened to him, I crumble to my knees from the blast of pain in our bond.

All I can do is scream.

◡⚬ 30 ⚬◡

"*Noah!*" I've never heard myself scream like this. Rabid, panicked shrieks escape my lips, extending seconds into ten times their length.

There's no movement I can see beneath the collapsed tree, and no reaction within our bond.

But with chaos unfolding across the field, Reid doesn't give me time to scream Noah's name twice. He hoists me off the ground— just in time to dodge the stampede of angry, thrashing wolves.

My claws extend beyond my control. "No! I need to get to Noah!"

"Not until you're safe. The global pack's hierarchy has been thrown off," Reid shouts over the noise.

My eyes widen as bodies clash, threatening to shift and break all further control. Does this mean Noah was the one keeping it all stable, even more than we realized?

But as Reid keeps me high in his arms, fending off anyone coming too close, I have a better view of the field from up high.

Viktor slinks toward the tree in fear, his ears slicked to his head. That's when I realize I'm still screaming at the top of my lungs.

"Noah! *Noah!* Get up, *please!*"

Reid hitches through the end of his breath, clutching me tighter. "Oh, *Goddess*, Luna…"

Just when I'm ready to jump out of Reid's arms, the fallen tree rustles over Noah.

Everyone freezes, craning their necks.

Viktor nudges the fallen tree trunk out of the way, freeing Noah's wolf.

Please, Goddess, let him be okay. Let him stand up.

But Noah doesn't stand up; with the tree no longer crushing him, he *leaps*.

With a roaring snarl that drops hundreds of wolves to the ground in fear, Noah tackles Viktor's face.

But a tackle isn't enough for Noah. As Noah sinks his teeth into Viktor, Viktor's screeching wolf pierces my eardrums, splitting my heart with pain for him. He's terrified, pinned to the ground beneath Noah's angry teeth and claws.

Even though Viktor manages to squirm free of Noah's jaws, my mate rips out fur as Viktor struggles to defend himself.

Noah's wolf snarls through our internal link, shocking me out of my stupor. *No one can make my mate scream like that again! He could've killed you with me!*

I wriggle out of Reid's arms, my eyes zipping straight to Annika's shiver-inducing scream.

"Vik! Vik, *run!*"

Oh, God, she's just as scared as I just was.

I dash for Annika, reaching my fellow Luna just in time to catch her as she stumbles to the ground, nearly dropping Markus in her panic. She's bawling and shrieking in Waimārie's arms, and Markus screams with her.

Turning toward the field, I can't stop my voice from coming out wracked with panic. "Stop, Noah! Don't kill him!"

But Noah's wolf has stolen full control, his side of our bond blazing with rage. *He almost killed my mate by killing me! He's a threat!*

He's not listening.

Covering Annika's eyes, Waimārie and I hold her, her youngest tucked between us as Tāne envelops all four of us in his embrace. I hold them all tight, extending my protective pheromones until my surroundings are flooded with my Alpha musk.

Mustering every ounce of power in me, I shout. "Noah, *stop!*"

Whether it's from my command or an unspoken body language between the massive wolves, they both come to a complete stop.

Noah's fangs ooze over Viktor's neck, his jaws wide open…

Hovering over Viktor's throat.

Viktor is frozen, his bright wolf eyes as wide as they can stretch.

I gasp, hugging Annika even tighter. Noah won't kill Viktor, but if it was a real fight, he *could*, judging by the position Viktor's in.

Which means Viktor just lost, even if he doesn't want to officially submit.

Unfortunately, it's not over—not if Viktor refuses to admit he did, in fact, lose.

But as every wolf hangs on the stretching silence, we tense as a collective global pack. Each wolf is as shocked as the next as Viktor relaxes onto his back, baring his belly to Noah in submission.

I sputter out a breath in disbelief. Annika breaks free from my hands, cradling her baby's head to her chest to see the outcome for herself. As soon as she breaks into a relieved smile, I let out a weepy, giddy laugh.

Annika meets my eyes with an exasperated groan. "Thank the Goddess it's over!"

She crashes into my arms, laughing in near-delirium with me as Noah pops up, shaking himself off in a cloud of black fur. Noah's big head towers everyone as wolves flood the field, howling and prancing around the two Alphas.

But when Noah's head dips down into the global pack, obscuring him from my view, my heart urges me to find my mate. To somehow reach him past the crowd of rowdy wolves, pulling him back to safety to never participate in this stupid shit again.

When he slowly rises, I realize he's helping Viktor back onto his paws with gentle nudges and licks on his wounds: a loving nuzzle in truce.

Annika grips me, turning to me with a big smile. "My new Queen."

My breath catches. "Luna…"

Nuzzling Markus's cheek until his tears slow, Annika can't stop sighing between every breath. "I wholeheartedly believed you, Luna, but I'm happy to report your prediction hasn't come true. There have been no aggressive wolves sighted at our borders today."

Waimārie cheers, diving into her mate's arms. Tāne nuzzles her into a deep kiss, sweeping her off the field into the forest.

Their celebration makes it real; it really is over. We're okay. We're safe.

Drooping in pure relief, I heave out a slow, raspy sigh. "Thank the Goddess."

Annika and I huddle close as our mates lick each other's gashes with gentle tail wags—a symbol of solidarity between two old friends.

Until Noah's wolf tells everyone he's had enough with a quick, irritated sneeze. Wolves scurry away, clearing a path. As Annika dashes to Viktor, Noah pads toward me, dipping his big head to meet my gaze with golden eyes.

Luna. My gorgeous Luna.

I laugh, extending my arms for him. *I want to run to you, but now that Annika told me there are no ambushes to report, my body decided it's done walking for the month. My legs are like wet noodles.*

My poor Luna. Stay there. These wolves won't bother us now. Noah slinks down to crawl to me, easing his huffing snout into my arms once he's finally close enough.

I whine over him, kissing every scratch on his silky face. "My *King*."

Noah freezes. The next thing I know, I'm covered in a wriggling ball of fluff, Noah hardly able to control himself until he crashes back into the mud, his excited huffs fanning my lap. My heart fizzles with warmth as I burst into laughter.

Noah purrs, his big tongue giving my belly the softest lick he can manage.

I roll over onto my back on instinct, and Noah shifts into his human form, melting over me with soft, desperate whimpers. "I love you. My Queen."

At the sight of Noah's breezy smile over me, I finally allow myself to laugh. Wolves howl as our lips crash together, Noah's overheated, bleeding, and naked body draping over me. Slipping my braid over my shoulder, Noah gives my exposed neck such a heavy lick that my legs tremble.

The intensity of my pleasure startles us both, but Noah hums in a pleased growl. He cups his hand behind my neck, pressing his tongue deeper into my mark.

I release an uncontainable, breathy moan. Wolves howl even louder, heavy courting erupting into action all around us.

"Oh, my God, Noah, we're doing it again. Everyone's about to mate."

He chuckles, switching to heavy suckling on my neck until my hips rapidly buck into the air for him. "Good. You like it, don't you? The thrill of everyone's eyes on us. How we drive the wild side out of them."

A shiver races through me, my fangs extending at the thought of us marking each other again.

"Yes. But especially because I'm doing it with you. My wolf is rolling over for her King."

He chuckles. "And mine is drooling. Let's let them have their fun."

Tearing off my coat, I hike up my dress, baring my bottom half to my mate. He happily slips between my thighs, ready to grind a few moans out of me.

But when his full weight presses against my core, he freezes. "Fuck. Are you not wearing any—?"

Noah's breath hitches; I smash my bare pussy in heavy circles over the underside of his cock.

I laugh. "I told you I'd treat you as my new King. My King Alpha-Omega."

A spike of emotion crashes into Noah's heart as he stares into my eyes, trusting in my smile; he knows I want him. All sides of him. Noah growls, his claws pinching my ass as he thrusts his shaft along the outside of my entrance, coating himself in time with each of my needy moans.

As he lines himself up to enter me, I can barely keep my hips still for him.

Noah grins. "You want me to mate out all this stress I put you under, huh?"

"Noah, please—"

He nips my earlobe, stilling my hips with a tight hug until my knees drop open for him. "What a good girl. Hold still for me."

I whimper, struggling to calm my clenching core. He circles his tip over my entrance, swirling faster and faster, until he sinks into my dripping pussy with a hungry growl.

A pleased cry releases from my chest, butterflies filling my belly. Noah pumps a few times, each thrust sending a jolt of pleasure to my heart. I raise my hips, helping my mate hit deeper and deeper until he meets my cervix with a slow, massaging thrust.

"Ah— Alpha!"

Noah purrs, our kisses growing sloppy as we work each other faster—too impatient to last longer than a few minutes.

My head drops to the side in bliss, giving me a clearer view of the mating chaos around us. Annika and Viktor hump heartily in the dirt. Her white dress is coated in mud, caking her breasts, forearms, and left cheek as Viktor mates her into the earth.

My grip tightens on Noah's ass, hugging him deeper as I lock eyes with Annika.

She cries out, her moans stealing my breath. Lust clouds her face as she gives me a weary smile, replaced by a sated drop of her jaw as Viktor slips his hand down her belly to give her clit a hearty rub.

As Viktor knots her in front of us, Annika's airy moans make it difficult to breathe through the fluttering in my belly.

My chest flushes hot. "Noah, I need more—"

Noah regains my full attention, bottoming out inside me. As I turn back to my King above me, desperate to indulge in every inch of him, his pelvis kneads my clit with each bump of my cervix. My back arches, rapid, heaving moans escaping my lips as my inner muscles clamp down over his cock. It sucks the orgasm out of us both, Noah filling me with hot fluid as my legs jerk in pleasure beside his hips.

I laugh through the haze, unable to fathom how this is my life. That the wild, love-drunk man over me is my mate—and I'm having his baby.

Propping himself over me with one hand, Noah holds my head with the other, soaking in my every breath. Every whimper. Every subtle flick of my eyes.

He doesn't need to say anything to tell me he's beyond smitten, those sweet eyes cherishing me all over just as deeply as I cherish him. All I wish is for him to feel this loved, this happy—forever.

Noah's eyelids flutter as my fingertips trace down that sweet spot on his neck.

"Can I re-mark you, my love?" I whisper.

His eyebrows arc. But he breaks into a soft, grateful smile. "Please."

I tease him with soft kisses along every ripple of his scar, amazed by Noah's shaky, breathy reaction above me. My wolf craves to hear more, her desperation buzzing through my incisors as my fangs extend.

By the time my tongue strokes his flesh, he's rock-hard inside me again, his hips bucking on instinct.

I massage his scalp, combing his hair in reassurance as I widen my tongue over his mark with every lick.

His breathing deepens in pleasure, breaking into soft, pleading moans. "L-Luna…"

That sweet, aching pull in his voice stirs my Alpha side into action, warping my vision as she takes control. I purr, locking my ankles behind Noah's pulsing hips to drag him deeper.

As we slow into lengthy, tender thrusts, my toes curl with the explosion of love in our bond. *I want you to feel how much I adore you, Noah. Every little bit of you. Including this sweet Omega coming forward, showing me how powerful he is to brave existing in this world.*

He whimpers, tears dripping onto my cheek as my licks turn into slow, hard suckling over his old mark.

Noah bucks harder now. I give little moans with each thrust, my core bubbling with pleasure. He cradles my head to his neck, his body shuddering.

"I can't believe how much I love you, my Luna… My Omega… My—" Noah's breath hitches. "*Alpha…*"

It's just a whisper, but it sets my heart on fire.

I'm no longer suckling. Fast, heated nips prickle his skin as I mate myself over his cock.

Noah pants, squirming over me as he stretches my swollen pussy to the limits, riding me on the edge.

I growl, craving to tease out every last drop of his pleasure. *I love you, Alpha-Omega. My sweet, shy King.*

My fangs sink into his flesh, a flood of sticky heat coating my tongue—followed by a burst of euphoria in our bond.

Noah moans loudly enough to draw every wolf's attention, our clashing, wet bodies making enough noise as it is. Our bond surges as he pounds into me. Overwhelming bliss lifts me up and over the edge as I lap up his blood.

On an impulse, Noah's fangs scrape my mark. I bare my scent for him without hesitation, allowing my mate to mark me a fourth time. It restarts my orgasm at the tail end of itself, mixing with Noah's intense pleasure to turn us both into quivering mush.

Ethereal colors cross over my vision, numbing me to the outside world. I already recognize the vast fields when I arrive: the field where our wolves reside inside our bond.

When my consciousness skates toward our wolves in the distance, my heart skips. There's something I've never seen here before: an object glowing beside my wolf.

As my mind zips behind the eyes of my wolf, she's focused on Noah's bleeding neck, healing it with tender licks. His wolf whines, nuzzling himself all over me, but beside us, there's a faint glow nestled into the grass.

Then I see it's a glowing mass. It's fuzzy around the edges, a faint outline of fur tucked into a little ball.

Noah's ears perk up with mine as I unlatch from his neck, taken with the sight of this little glowing ball. We stare at the odd mass, our wolf heads cheek to cheek as we continue to court. Noah's curiosity vibrates through me as he tilts his head, making my tail wag. I don't know why, but the little glowing mass feels special to our wolves. It's something they're keeping tucked away and safe.

My mate purrs, and the mass twitches like it heard him.

That's when we see a tiny ear poke up to the sky.

Both of our wolves whine in unison, our bond bursting with a type of love I've never experienced.

Pup, I mindlink.

Pup. Noah's wolf yips, urging me to my paws.

Our wolves frolic together through the field, overjoyed by not just our re-strengthened connection, but at how fast our family is growing.

As my wolf rolls over for Noah's, allowing him to snuffle hot, loving caresses over her expanding womb, I know my wolf trusts Noah with her whole soul.

When I come back down into my human body, it physically

pains me to have to leave the comfort of our bond. But then I remember who I'm nestled under, a content sweetness overflowing from my scent glands as Noah cuddles me.

I'm happy-sobbing against Noah, his blood dripping across my collarbones and down my chin.

"Oh, my gorgeous mate—" Noah's voice is so breathy with love that I whine even harder, crashing against his lips.

The remnants of our bond's world fades into my subconscious. Rustling wind roots me back in Kiruna, Sweden…

But that's all I hear.

It's dead silent in the field.

Shifted wolves surround Noah and me, but they're no longer facing us. All I can see is a circle of prickling, alert tails, tense bodies defending us as they tighten their circle.

Something is very, very wrong—and it's something that only occurred within the past minute.

While Noah and I were absorbed in our bond, almost all top Alphas and Lunas shifted into their wolves. They form a barrier around us, their tails facing us as they keep their eyes locked on something else. On the barrier's innermost section, smaller and less experienced wolves huddle in, hiding behind our Alpha allies.

What could make even the strongest Alphas and Lunas so afraid?

Noah separates his body from me quicker than intended, making me wince.

"Fuck, sorry." Noah stumbles to his feet, still dazed and bleeding from his fresh mark as he assesses the wolves around us. He doesn't even look at me as he helps me to my feet, calling to the wolves. "Let me through. I'll need room to shift."

Wolves shuffle to create space for Noah, but only on one side. The front half remains tight, keeping something out.

I grip his arm. *Noah, what are they defending us from?*

I don't know. But with how serious they are, I have a sinking feeling that you were right, and it's my worst nightmare come true.

Regardless of his fears, Noah pushes through the crowd of wolves, and my heart pinches. I *need* to follow him.

I scurry after Noah in his footsteps, using his broad form to slip through the gap he creates in the crowd of wolves. When we reach the perimeter, we're face to face with a horde of uninvited wolves. Noah's shoulders rigidify.

How did they get here? Annika said we were safe.

Were our allies in on this?

Whipping my head around until I spot familiar faces, I'm horrified, but not because we've been betrayed; there's no mistaking the raw, petrified fear in Annika's eyes as she meets mine, screaming for help.

Waimārie and Tāne emerge from the brush, dashing straight to us with wide-eyed horror. As I clutch Waimārie's hand, Reid pads to Noah's side in his massive wolf form, as well as Viktor in his human form, the previous King panting in near-panic.

It's dead silent. Why is no one saying or doing anything?

Luna, please stay near me. I need to be with you before this happens, Noah mindlinks.

Why is he making it sound like it's the last time we'll see each other?

As I huddle up to Noah's side, he hugs me even closer, his Alpha musk exploding.

But it's not just Noah's musk. I have to cover my nose, my eyes watering on impact of an offensive, gut-twisting scent blowing across the field.

These aren't just random wolves facing off with us.

They're a massive pack of *only* Alphas.

And with one look at their snarling teeth and agitated tails, I can guess why they're here. Especially when I recognize who's leading them.

Stepping to the front of the invading horde is Mason Hart.

You were right, Noah mindlinks.

My stomach plummets to the floor. *I didn't want to be.*

∽ 31 ∽

I'm supposed to be the Queen Luna, but as we stare at the horde of wolves with unknown plans, I don't know what to do. Nothing I can possibly think of could protect the wolves behind us, relying on us. Not even speaking up is safe; a single wrong breath could send the Alpha mob charging before we can defend ourselves.

But someone has to do something. Say something.

Mason is here, but I'm thinking this looks much bigger than what he could've gathered alone, Noah mindlinks. *It looks like we all were right about the super pack, so we'll have to treat them as such. But I'm not sure what's best to start with. What do you think?*

I don't know yet. I need time to strategize, even if it's thirty extra seconds, I mindlink Noah.

Okay. If I talk to Viktor, they're not going to like that, so all I can do to stall is talk to them directly, Noah says. *I want to say something first, or else they'll think we're backing down. But do you think that's too risky?*

Swallowing hard, I try not to focus on the heavy pressure in my chest, knowing what I say next could cost the lives of the living, breathing wolves behind me.

I mindlink my opinion anyway. *Go ahead. I trust your judgment.*

Straightening, Noah breaks the silence. "You really want to do this, Hart? This is a much different game if you're challenging the world's top pack leaders."

Mason's wolf stands rigid—still refusing to shift. And now that he's no longer in our pack, he can't mindlink with us to respond.

When multiple Alphas slip through from behind us, joining

Mason's side, Noah's confidence plummets. I've never seen him lose faith in his leadership like this.

Fuck, Luna… Nope, this really isn't just Mason's offshoot pack—

Logan is the last to limp to Mason's side, everyone's eyes on him as he drags the leg Noah broke. "You sure *you* want to do this, Greenfield? It's not too late to change your mind. Admit you're all weak as fuck against Alphas. Since you clearly aren't one."

More negative attention is drawn to my fresh mark on Noah's neck than ever before, Mason's pack showing their teeth.

Even if Noah was 100% Omega, he just triumphed over every Alpha here. It makes no sense to keep denying his strength.

But this isn't about strength. This is a show of power.

Mason meets my eyes just before I look behind us—seeing who's still faithful to Noah as King Alpha. My stomach drops, realizing we only have 50 pairs of wolves left, whereas Mason's Alpha-domination pack must have at least 400 angry Alpha men and a small grouping of subservient top Lunas.

When I turn back to the Alpha-domination Super Pack, Mason is still staring at me. His glare slithers up my spine.

Could that really be Steven? And if so, does he realize what I made him disclose mere hours ago?

It's true that these Alphas have extra muscle mass, but I feel gross admitting their physical capabilities when that's what they want. At the same time, I can't deny we're in major trouble with a pack of only Alphas; like Noah said, Omegas rarely receive the same training, and Betas aren't as socially encouraged to train, unless it interests them. Viktor's pack is large, but if we're mainly counting on his young, able-bodied Alphas to protect us, we may only have a slight advantage. We're also facing off against a handful of the top Alphas in the world that just joined Mason's side—and Alphas who don't give a fuck about fighting by the rules.

Wolves might be designed to defend their loved ones from other wolves in short scuffles rather than wasting energy taking another wolf's life, but I'm certain these Alphas have different intentions. As Mason continues to glower at us, it's clear he came to kill.

Viktor whispers to Noah, and Mason bristles.

"Don't talk!" Logan yells. "This isn't a conference between packs. It's a takeover by the rightful leaders."

"No, it's not. I recognize every single one of you: you're on our Alpha-domination cult blacklist. But where's Jack Hart? Is he your true top Alpha, or are you all just shitty Jack copycats?" Noah says.

Mason releases a fierce growl, inching closer.

I grip Noah's arm, numb to my raging heartbeat beyond its pressure in my chest.

Breathe, Luna. I'm stalling while Vik calls his pack for backup, Noah says.

Try not to instigate them. They're on the verge of snapping, and I'm too confused to know what to do.

Confused? Noah asks.

Yes. They should've attacked us while we were mating. And we know they're not honestly trying to talk this through—compromise isn't an option for them. Why are they also stalling?

Fuck... I don't know. I didn't realize that until you said it. That's... Noah's hope drops in our bond. With it, my skin erupts in fearful goosebumps.

I have to figure this out—to save this pup I'm carrying, my loving mate, and the future of every Lycan. I *need* to.

Their behavior just doesn't make sense.

But that's exactly what they want me to feel. They aren't playing by Lycan rules; they're playing by abusive ones.

This is a game I know how to survive.

Hope rebuilds in my chest. With it, Noah's shoulders settle beside me.

But Matthew grimaces at us, his incisors flashing. "Your way isn't working, Greenfield. Without our power, promised to us by birth, Alphas are facing severe neglect. We're banding together in the name of the domination we're owed. We'll show everyone how the world is supposed to work."

Noah's fists tighten. I can hardly breathe, OCD and hypervigilance tag-teaming as my eyes zip from Alpha to Alpha, searching for a clue, tell, or any other warning of what's to come.

"No matter how strong you are, we can't allow a single pack to dominate the whole world," Noah says. "We'll never let you.

There's a reason why super packs go against the instincts the Moon Goddess granted us. It only ends in death. You'll kill one another for power and break into hundreds of packs, soon enough."

Logan glowers. "You really think Alphas can't rule together? That we're all violent, thoughtless beasts? How do you know Alphas who have been violent in the past weren't just acting out of suffering? Our true, natural order is ignored unless Alphas are shown the respect we're owed."

Viktor lets out a sharp, sardonic laugh—more like a deep and menacing snarl. "So we're all just supposed to roll over and submit to you while you abuse wolves you think are weaker?"

"We're restoring *order*, allowing naturally weak wolves to be protected. They can't protect themselves," Matthew says.

Tāne crosses his arms. "They can't protect themselves? Think for themselves? Decide for themselves on what happens to their bodies and loved ones? Sure sounds 'safe,' bro."

"I'm sure you'd never understand with a weak-ass Omega as your 'King,'" Logan hisses.

With how intensely Noah's emotions waver in our bond, I wrap my hand around his, squeezing tight.

Their bullshit is expected, but it doesn't change the fact that they *did* band together. And with how violent they sound, I don't think they'll be taking prisoners. I think they came to kill more than just a few leaders. I think they came to kill *us*.

But how will they achieve that? Especially if they've also given Viktor extra time to gather wolves from neighboring packs?

I look to Noah, whose eyes haven't left the Alpha-domination Super Pack. Dozens of global leaders stand at our side, but a third are cowering Lunas, hiding behind us for protection.

Even if Viktor's wolves come, they're not all beefed-out, volatile Alphas. And with how remote Kiruna is, Viktor's neighboring allies will take at least an hour to run here.

But there's one stark difference between us that gives us a fighting chance.

Noah, your true strength is your ability to rule with compassion. Your heart is in everything you do, which I know is a major reason why you detest Alpha domination. Besides it feeling totally unjustified, it goes against your core values—the ones that make Greenfield a unified front. All these Alphas share is a hunger for power, no matter the destruction necessary. You're right; they'll destroy one another soon. But that also means our unity is how we can win.

You're right, Luna. I know you're right. Which means I physically, mentally, emotionally can't let this happen. You know what that means, right?

My heart drops.

I can feel it in our bond, but I can't bear to mindlink the words.

This is a cause Noah is willing to die for. If he doesn't fight, the guilt could kill him just as well.

And I'd never forgive myself if I didn't fight by his side, no matter what he says to keep me safe.

Noah's panic rises with mine the longer I take to respond, so I tell him the truth.

Yes, I do know what it means. And I understand why you feel this way, even though it terrifies me more than anything.

I'm so fucking sorry, Luna. But I can't let you or our pups live in a world like theirs. I love you with all my heart.

I love you with all of me too.

Noah lets out a low growl, a deep-seated anger boiling in our bond as tears slip down my cheeks.

That felt like a goodbye. It can't be. Please, Goddess, no.

"So, your shitty plan is to wipe out the leaders of the strongest packs in the world so you can swoop in with yours?" Noah's voice deepens into a shiver-inducing growl, sweeping down my skin.

When the Alphas don't say anything, continuing to stand their ground, I can only assume Noah guessed right.

Noah shakes his head, his fangs extending with every breath. "If you go through with this, then you're a bunch of fucking fascists. And we won't surrender first. You'll either surrender or rot in our confinement dens, Hart."

With Mason's growl, Noah's chest puffs.

But then Noah freezes. I get the sense that if I move, even a little, we'll all be attacked.

Not attacked. Killed.

Luna, I have a secret to tell you, Noah mindlinks.

Wolves tense, crouching deeper and deeper into the earth— slow, shaky forms ready to blast into action.

What?! Now?

Yes. I need you to know what I see in your wolf because I already know you're planning on joining the fight.

My chest puffs with his, my own musk extending to the surrounding area. *You assumed right. If you die, we both die, and Little Wolf will die with us. There's no point in me sitting out.*

I hate that, but it's true. Which is why I need to tell you: you aren't just my strongest wolf. You're my strongest Alpha.

My heart skips. The small gasp I take zips Mason's focus to me, his wolf crouching and ready to pounce.

We haven't trained long together, but you don't need to be physically large to be a serious threat. Just your scent scared off Mason and many top leaders here, countless times since we've met. You could be King, if you wanted. I wasn't joking.

As my Omega side sinks into the background to continue strategizing, my Alpha side bristles, her ego boosted to the max.

The second I shift, I need you to pretend you're running. Take any scared Lunas to shelter. Then I need you to be my assassin. I'm a lumbering beast. I can take quite a few hits, but I'm not sneaky at all. You're slippery, quick-witted, and agile, and your bite is deadly as fuck. If I gave you openings to swoop in… They'd never see you coming. Noah's breath slows, but it shakes alongside mine. *We could protect each other. Keep you from being noticed while I'm less distracted by working with you. Do you want to team up with me? Stick by my side, so we always know where the other is?*

Noah, my wolf will protect you, always. If anyone comes close to hurting you, I'd do anything to save your life. You are our pack's future. Our pup's. But I also don't want to do anything I'll regret.

I understand. You don't have to hurt anyone, Luna, and you definitely don't have to kill anyone—no one on our side will.

B-but that's the thing; I'm afraid, but I want to defend you and everything we stand for anyway. If anyone comes close to hurting you, I don't think I could stop my wolf from hurting them first.

That's my feisty Omega-Alpha. Just do me a favor: don't focus on attacking as your number one priority. Focus on weaseling out of the way like you always do until you have a safe opening. Promise?

By now, not a single one of us dares to breathe. The only sound across the field is a gust of wind rustling through the forest leaves, not even the birds daring to peep.

The collective scent rises into urgency as Noah breathes faster.

Mason's muscles twitch in his full crouch, ready to pounce.

My heart throbs so hard that I'm dizzy. Am I going to be able to do this? What if I fail us all?

Maybe I will, maybe I won't.

I promise.

The second I mindlink my promise, Noah gives my hand a soft squeeze. He releases it, slipping from my fingers. My heart jolts, terrified we just held hands for the last time.

Mason tenses, anticipating Noah's incoming wolf, any second now; and once Noah shifts, Mason's probability of survival is slim.

But Mason is still standing there.

This doesn't add up.

The second I allow my intrusive thoughts to the surface, I realize they're not like my usual intrusive thoughts at all. They're knifelike observations, protecting me from active trauma. The danger is *here.*

And I see something hidden in the bushes.

There's no time to mindlink my spiraling thoughts, not as the first ripple of Noah's fur sprouts from his skin, his face elongating. He's crouching, preparing to leap, when I see it's not just an odd rock in the bushes. It's a long, black, metal pole, catching the smallest glimmer of light as it locks into position.

No, not a pole. A barrel.

Noah doesn't see it. No one does.

This is it; the reason they're stalling.

They're going to shoot us to death, just like our fathers.

32

It's happening faster than I can think: Noah leaps, shifting into an enormous, snarling black wolf mid-air, forcing wolves to lean away as they prepare to run. Meanwhile, the loaded barrel in the bushes raises, millimeter by millimeter, lighting my insides on fire.

I stop thinking. My wolf takes over, and she *moves*.

One breath, I'm standing in petrified horror. The next, I'm all fur and teeth, tackling Noah to the ground. A bang sounds off before I can register it, striking hot, acidic fear into my heart.

But we're unharmed.

I trust Noah to get back up and defend himself from Mason. If we all want to live, I'm forced to set aside his well-being for now; I've locked eyes with the gunman. A chill digs beneath my fur at the merciless disgust in his eyes.

He's furious. I've warned everyone of his vile intentions, creating a stampede of wolves bolting across the field, and moving targets limit his ability to aim.

So I take to the shadows. Leaping to my paws, I cut across the field into the brush. As more shots are fired, it's clear there are multiple gunmen along the forest's edge. Chaos unfolds, the Super Pack peeling back from the firing zone as our wolves scramble. Fear crisscrosses with anger in my chest, tightening my jaw as I keep low to the ground at the sound of Noah's barking commands on the field.

When Noah charges in—his brutal smack across Mason's chest spilling the first blood—it isn't logical for the Super Pack to waste their time tracking me as I disappear deeper into the forest.

Or so they think. I silence my paws, weaving through the forest with eyes on my target: the first gunman I saw, rising to his feet for a better view. He and his friends create so much intentional distress—chuckling as they watch us scurry—that they don't think to search for hunters on their trail. Making a wide arc, I come at him sideways, silent as I fly through the brush.

He doesn't have a chance to pull the trigger again.

My jaws come down on bone, a vicious *crunch* twitching my ears. Spitting the Alpha's sour blood to the dirt, I don't stop when I hear him screaming behind me; I'm already burying his friend into the brush with me, crushing his trigger arm too.

Noah, six gunmen were hidden at the edge of the forest. There are four more; I already took down two. Someone still needs to confiscate their weapons, I mindlink.

I feel Noah's panic in our bond, but I'm grateful for it—it means he's alive, likely having to fight off the Alpha-domination wolves who stayed to fight in wolf-to-wolf combat, as we originally expected.

Meanwhile, I'm now a major target. Not two, but three gunmen scream at the top of their lungs, rolling on the forest floor.

I thought I'd be disgusted with myself for hurting them, but I'm too horrified by their actions to process my own yet: they reek of Alpha pheromones, boasting of their "innate strength." And yet, they know they can't defeat Noah face to face, so the cowards tried to shoot him to death. They almost did.

My guts twist at the thought, forcing me to the ground. I rub my white fur in the mud, shimmying to camouflage myself in the shadows as I catch my breath. Pausing allows me to track them closer, my ears rotating every which way to focus in on their conversation between picking up on every thrashing wolf on the field. As far as I can hear and smell, my count is still accurate: three reeking gunmen remain. They yell at one another in an attempt to find me, but it's more like slinging insults for not being Alpha enough to shoot an Omega. Their volume allows me to move faster, not having to put as much emphasis into keeping my shaky paws silent.

"Where is that bitch?" The man closest to me snarls beneath his breath, showing me his back.

It's too late for him. When he finally spots me, turning over his shoulder, my snout parts the bushes behind him. In two nibbles, I've ruined his ability to shoot too.

Noah meets my eyes across the forest—just as three more sneaky Lycans on our side burst from the brush beside me, teaming up to take down the remaining gunmen. Johannes dashes in to gather the weapons, bolting as fast as he can back to the lodge. With all guns officially out of sight, my jaw loosens, allowing me to pant in relief.

When all gunfire and human yelling stop, only the sound of snarling and yelping wolves remains.

Shifted Lycans immerse themselves deep into the woods with us, and the game of hunt changes; now we're on an equal playing field.

I'm supposed to protect our Lunas, but now that the immediate danger has left, an adrenaline crash hits. With paws as heavy as my whole body, I'm forced to quiver in the brush, huffing with my tongue out as I recover my energy.

And my eyes don't want to leave my mate yet. Noah throws himself at Mason, over and over again, with deep, wet snarls. Except it's not just Mason he's attacking; he's having to juggle fending off Mason on top of multiple other Alphas—all targeting him, specifically. Our allies join his side, and for a moment, I freeze, stunned by my mate spilling more blood, his claws gashing every wolf's pelt who dares approach.

Violence unfolds unlike anything I've seen before, new injuries and clashes spinning my head every second. Thankfully, top leaders on our side are doing their jobs of keeping the focus off the Lunas who can't fight—who have hopefully entered the lodge by now.

But as I shake my coat free of leaves and debris, ready to jump back in to help, a prowling wolf catches my eye. Rather than entering the fight in the forest, he's exiting the brush—replacing one paw after another with his eyes locked onto a horde of wolves nearest the lodge.

My heart drops. Are those the Lunas who can't fight? Why are they still outside?

The attacker Alpha sneaks back onto the field, his snout trained onto the scared wolves behind Annika, Waimārie, and a few other Lunas I recognize—their wolves holding the line with protective snarls as they inch backward to the Community Center.

My wolf bursts from the brush, cutting across the field and overtaking the Alpha's speed to beat him there. Leaping in front of the huddling group, I lick my bloody fangs, keeping my paws splayed. With the deepest growl I can manage, my hackles raise, every inch of my skin disgusted by this Alpha's intentions.

The Alpha hesitates, skidding in the grass. He dashes to the left in a wide arc, avoiding crashing into me just in time before sprinting back into the woods. I want that to be the end of his confidence, but as I turn to Annika, I spot the Alpha prowling in the brush, waiting for another opening to attack.

And I see why the Lunas weren't running; the wolves behind us have entered the "freeze" state of trauma, staring with wide, tracking eyes at the Alpha, no matter which herding method Annika and Waimārie attempt. Before the Alpha can realize we're extra vulnerable, I let out a sharp yip, and the wolves jolt, breaking out of their petrified trance. I leap in a zig-zag around the scared wolves, herding them back faster.

Since I can't mindlink them, I'm surprised by how well they obey, just from my urgent scent and body language. They huddle in close, allowing my wolf to guard them at their flanks as we dash from the field.

When a different straggler Alpha spots our susceptible group, sneaking up on my tail, I put on my meanest snarl, whipping around and slashing my claws at him without a second thought.

The Alpha yipes, his tail tucked as he scampers back to the field with petrified yelps.

I didn't even touch him, but I must look terrifying; my wolf's fury has left me shaking and panting, burst after burst of adrenaline firing my nerves at their peak.

But not even the sight of a scared Alpha makes me feel better. This should've been a day to celebrate my mate's victory and to recover. By this point in the Alpha Summit, we've spent nearly all our energy on surviving the dominance challenges, and I bet that's exactly why Mason showed up now.

I don't even need to go home, if that's too much to ask of

the universe. All I want is to at least go back to a couple hours ago—when my main worry was Noah losing the title of King Alpha. Now I'm just hoping I'll get to see Noah hold onto his life for another minute.

My stomach somersaults, never feeling heavier as my aching back strains over our growing baby. I don't want to be forced to do this without Noah.

Using her teeth, Annika yanks open a hidden cellar door in the garden behind the lodge. Her gray-and-ivory wolf guides our group underground—into the Community Center depths.

As we silence ourselves, Annika slinks through underground tunnels, guiding us in the dark with soft pants. When my eyes adjust to the lack of light, I spot Markus in his blanket cocoon, hooked over Annika's bottom fangs. Even her pristine wolf looks shattered, her ears slicked back to her head in agony. Yet she's still guiding us all to safety, not giving up.

Once the wolves pile into an innermost chamber in the basement, Annika shifts back into her human form—followed by Waimārie. The other scared wolves must not feel safe enough to shift back, cramming their massive forms as deeply as they can into the back of the room in a quivering cuddle pile. All that can be heard is soft panting, silencing ourselves as best as we can in our panic.

But in her human form, poor Annika breathes so raspily that I'm afraid she's having an asthma attack, my heart twinging with her every wheeze.

"Darling, we're okay—" Waimārie steadies Annika's hands, helping her light a match from a hidden, dusty stash in the wall. "We made it, love. Breathe."

The second Annika lights the fire, resettling Markus safely in her arms, she turns to me. Wide, shattered eyes stare back, candlelight flickering in her fair irises.

I whine, reflecting in her agony as I ask the same question: how did we get here?

"Goddess, *Aliya*—you saved—" Annika erupts into desperate cries, gripping my fur. "You saved our mates from being shot! I couldn't stop it. I saw the barrel aim at us too, a split second before you leapt to—"

Annika can hardly choke out her words as she collapses against me, multiple Lunas erupting into whines as she bursts into loud, frantic cries, expressing the sorrow in the air for all of us.

My ears flatten back as tightly as they can press. But as I allow myself to take a deep breath, I'm terrified: I can finally feel how hard my legs are shaking. What if I have no energy left to help Noah keep us alive? It's far from over. What's it like out there now—is it worse? And who died already, despite our efforts?

Waimārie snuggles me with Annika, wiping the blood from my chin and chest as she sobs into my fur in gratitude. Multiple wolves stream in to copy her, licking me clean as they wrap me in their loving warmth.

But my wolf pants and whines in distress; I need to get back to my mate.

Giving them each a soft nuzzle in their hair, I ease my paws back, sending a clear message of my intentions.

"Luna, wait—" Annika pulls a crushed lunch sack from Markus's diaper bag. Even before she opens it, my wolf drools onto the tile from its scent; Annika reveals three slices of smushed pumpkin bread. "Please, Luna. You need your strength—"

My wolf snatches the bread into her jaws, swallowing it whole—paper sack and all.

A burst of cinnamon and pumpkin swirls at the back of my tongue, alighting my wolf in pleased bristles.

Annika blinks, a weary smile lifting her cheeks as she gazes up at me. All at once, the Lunas around me burst into giggles and tail wags, lightening the heaviness in my chest.

Waimārie gives my ear a deep scratch, urging me into a pleased grunt. She smiles even wider, inspiring a burst of energy within me. "Oh, good girl, Luna!"

Annika giggles despite the tears still cascading her rosy cheeks. "Please, stay safe. You're dear to all of us."

I give Waimārie and Annika soft boops with my nose before sprinting out the door, anxious to get back to Noah.

I don't need Annika's guidance to find my way out of the tunnels; my wolf remains on high alert, following the clearest scent trail I've ever tracked: the rotten, urgent scent of our distress from when we entered. The second I reach the door, I sniff the cool air blowing in through the cracks. Once I'm sure no one is around, I hop from the exit, my body bursting with a second round of adrenaline as I bury the door in dirt with a few kicks of my back legs.

My wolf weaves through the garden, sneaking through the bushes with rapid, expert dodging of rose thorns.

I'm a little stunned that pumpkin bread gave me so much energy. Between my snack and my wolf's pride of returning to Noah's side after protecting our Lunas, I feel like I'm flying.

But I spot an Alpha sniffing in the distance—his nose pressed to the garden's stone path.

He's probably searching for Luna scents, looking for easy targets to distract our Alphas.

But he doesn't notice me prowling. Watching him.

My swift paws make no sound as I hunker into the earth, speeding my run into a hunt.

The Alpha yelps at the claws lashing his face, my wolf sending him cowering into the ground. He scampers back onto his paws with bloody jowls, bolting away and leaving behind a trail of pee.

He better warn everyone not to come back here. Instinct takes over, and I pee on top of his pee, warning any Alphas who dare come close that I'm coming for them too.

I sneak to the field's entrance, curling against the frigid stone as I pant away my stress. Glancing around the corner, my heart drops; the smell of blood lingers in the air, but there are no wolves to be seen.

They're all fighting within the forest. While we can use its cover to our advantage, so can they.

The closer I get to the snarls, howls, and whines in the distance, the deeper the pit grows in my gut. Charging back onto the field, my stomach rolls, threatening to lose my pumpkin bread with how terrified I am of what I might find.

I'm on my way back, Noah. Are you okay?

We're faring… Vik's pack is kicking ass now that we're in his forest, but Mason has even more wolves pouring in. This has to be thousands of Alphas who joined the Super Pack.

Oh, God. I'm on my way to help you.

Stay low. Do you remember Viktor's only rules before the Alpha battles?

No tail biting or other dirty tricks?

Yes. Every single one of those are exactly what I want you to do. Play as dirty as possible, and please, above all things, do not let yourself get caught.

I won't, Alpha. You and our pup are my world.

Noah's heart aches with mine, and I'm certain I understand the dark path his mind just traveled to.

Noah, I'm not letting us die. We're getting out of this alive.

He doesn't respond as I dash deeper into the forest—not until the sickening smell of fear and blood ices my veins over.

…I love you, Noah finally mindlinks.

That's when I spot him: a flash of black in a sea of scampering, terrified wolves.

I love you too, my gorgeous beast. I'm coming up on your left.

Okay. Stay clear of these terrified ones. Fear bites are the most dangerous.

I slip through the trees, skirting around the insecure, flinching Alphas until I find Noah in the center, facing off against a far larger beast than my tiny wolf.

Rage bubbles in my chest at the sight of the stranger Alpha attacking my mate with his full heart, standing by everything he believes in with violent tenacity.

I slip through the less confident Alphas, using my Alpha musk to blend in with their equivalent rage.

Lying low in the brush, I wait.

Within seconds, I see it; I have an opening, but only to grab a tail or an ear.

My Alpha wolf is different from my Omega; impulsivity pushes me to act without as much contemplation. The second the stocky gray Alpha nears my hiding spot, I tear out a mouthful of his fluffy tail, making him let out an embarrassing whine.

Before the other wolves can see who did it, I scamper back off into the trees.

Adrenaline crashes through my system. My fur raises at the thrill of possibly being chased by the Alpha's angry, golden eyes; *I dare you to fucking catch me.*

But when I sneak a quick glance behind me, I find Noah taking his opportunity to strike at the Alpha's turned back, leaving a flash of blood to streak through the air.

I know Noah's okay, but his anger horrifies me.

I feel like Noah's going to kill him because of me. Would he?

After the Alphas tumble in a jumbled mess of snarls and cries, there's a brief silence. My limbs sting with fear.

Then the surrounding wolves dart away in whining, shaking horror.

Oh, Goddess. Did Noah just…?

Noah's black wolf slowly lifts his head, blood dripping from his lips as the massive Alpha lies at his feet in an unmoving heap.

I shrink, imagining how the Alpha's family must feel, especially after being in their shoes.

Noah's ears fall flat, sensing my extreme discomfort. *H-he's not dead! I'm bringing this one back for questioning. B-but Luna, if I don't hurt them enough, I don't know if they'll—*

He's right. The Alpha was only biding his time, his golden eyes whipping open as his muscles flinch to strike my mate. His claws slash up in the air, right in line with Noah's throat.

$$\backsim\!\sim\!\backsim \;\; \textbf{33} \;\; \sim\!\backsim\!\sim$$

Launching myself at the massive Alpha, my every claw digs beneath his coat, drawing blood, no matter our stark size difference.

He can't shake me off. My teeth meet the injured Alpha's muscles again and again, my bites as rapid as the Alpha's surprised cries. He twists to nip me off his flank, but before the Alpha's fangs can reach me, Noah's jaws clamp on his shoulder with a heavy crack. The Alpha collapses, limp and yowling.

An eerie stillness falls over the forest—no other wolves in sight. As the Alpha continues to cry in pain on the ground, Noah nudges me into a less open forest clearing.

Before I have time to process what could be coming for us, my agitated wolf spots someone darting for Noah behind his massive form.

Tracking my line of sight over his shoulder, Noah bares his teeth, prowling at the wolf approaching. No, *wolves.*

Luna, hide now.

Dashing into the bushes just in time, I wince as Noah is ambushed by Matthew's stocky gray wolf and several other large Alphas. I sink further into the leaves, sensing more wolves coming straight for us in the distance.

Except this time, they're on Noah's side.

Viktor's pack streams in, more and more Lycans joining the fight by the second—not allowing the Alpha-domination Super Pack to continue their rampage.

When Noah shakes his coat to rid himself of Alphas like little pests, Matthew flies into the nearest tree with a reverberating thud.

But as our allies' support frees Noah's focus, Noah's eyes lock onto something else—his tail rigid, ears pointing to the sky, and teeth bared. I follow his glance, only to find Mason Hart, his form obscured by the shadows beneath the trees.

Mason can't see me, but he certainly sees Noah.

They stalk each other, pressing low to the forest floor as their allies clash in violent ripples of bloodied fur to their sides. Mason is already bloody as it is, his gashed chest still dripping from Noah's claw marks at the start of the battle.

If this really is Steven, what was his life like before I knew him to turn him into this predator I see before me? His agitated form appears rabid—tense, corded muscles sending him off-kilter, even when he's frozen, mid-prowl.

The Mason I know could've been hurt by Jack, like Noah. While Mason's past doesn't excuse his actions, Jack's influence explains why Mason treats violence as his first course of action.

But the more I picture Steven in Mason's shoes, the less I can tell their stories apart. Steven couldn't bear discussing his parents often, blaming his mother for kicking his dad out. Like Steven, Mason must've grown up estranged from his father.

What if Mason's coping method was to become spiteful toward his mother for "allowing" his dad to be expelled from the pack by Ritchie? What if he resents his father too, envisioning Jack as too "weak" of an Alpha to win against Ritchie, and therefore, Mason feels abandoned by Jack? Would this abandonment make Mason hate Jack enough to frame him for murder?

I know it firsthand; if Steven feels abandoned, there are no limits to what he might do to hurt someone he "loves."

Oh, God. What if I really am looking at my ex's wolf?

What would Steven gain from this? If he kills Noah, he'll kill me too, yet he stalks me relentlessly as if my suffering feeds him.

Why is he so desperate to hurt me?

Noah's paws lift inch by inch, one by one, stalking Mason in a slow circle. *We have to get Mason to submit. If Viktor or anyone else kills him, the Super Pack will only get more agitated, and another Alpha will take Mason's place as pack leader. That, and I have quite a few questions for him about how far this Super Pack reaches.*

Okay, you're right. We also need confirmation of who he really is— if we're right about why he's hiding his human form.

As Noah's rage upticks, I huddle deeper into the bushes, catching my breath as silently as I can.

When Mason makes a sudden jerking motion, lunging into a full sprint, my heart drops.

This isn't the usual Mason. He's not relying on psychological attacks today; he's going in for the kill. And no one else is covering my mate.

Fear pounds through my body as the wolves tumble. For once, Noah's deadly clobberings don't deter Mason. He's clearly trained hard with strong Alphas since he left our pack. Even if he can't kill Noah, Mason won't stop unless Noah destroys his ability to move.

But I can't help from here. If Mason sees me too soon, he could mindlink someone from the Super Pack to stop me. That would distract Noah and leave Mason a chance to strike.

There's no more time to strategize. Multiple Alphas creep in the distance, inching closer by the millisecond to gang up on Noah.

Stained with blood and mud, my snow-colored paws don't make a sound as they blast through the earth. Zipping through trees, I weave between any and all wolves in my path. None of them have a chance to catch me, my wolf far too agile for their delayed, fumbling reactions.

Within a second, I'm on Mason's back, tearing out his fur.

My wolf snarls louder than I've ever heard her, ripping Mason to shreds with my claws and jaws, my entire heart behind each fang. Mason hasn't even realized what hit him yet, yipping and squirming to pry my small, vicious wolf off of him. My ears twist as I continue to gnash, catching onto the sound of Noah tearing into the surrounding wolves with equal fury.

But then our bond dips in alarm.

One's coming! Noah mindlinks.

I bound off of Mason with a wide leap, dodging one of the last supporting Alphas before scurrying back into the bushes. Noah's subsequent snarling occupies every wolf's attention in the vicinity, a few Alphas darting away with their tails tucked so tightly that their asses drag in the dirt. It'd be funny if I wasn't panting my lungs out, my heart lurching rapidly at the thought of what just happened—an Alpha nearly got me. This almost ended in the worst way, and now all attention is on us.

But I refuse to give up.

As I draw a wide loop in the forest, I hunker back into a sprint, ready to back Noah up. I dart from bush to bush, careful to make as minimal sound as possible as I zip closer to Noah and Mason's violent clash.

No one has spotted me—probably because Mason has tripled his aggression.

And Noah has had enough. His rage kicks into overdrive, each bite strong enough to crush Mason's bones—if Mason wasn't scurrying out of the way.

But Mason is barely able to keep up. He stumbles, letting out stark whines between frothing snarls—a constant whiplash of fear and hatred coursing through his vibrant yellow irises.

Noah finally latches on. He bites like he's starved, the white of his fangs no longer visible between rapid, devastating clamps of his bloodied jaws.

Then I see it: the fear Noah warned me about. The fear of a cornered animal clinging to his last hope for survival.

Mason lunges, his fangs gnashing at Noah's throat.

I charge so hard at Mason, I can't even feel my impact. Instinct overwhelms me, eating up every trace my senses give me as I act on them without any thought. I thrash over Mason until he's cowering deep into the dirt. The stench of his fear burns my nose, but it only makes me angrier. Does he even know how afraid he makes others feel?

Mason attempts to roll over.

I don't let him.

Pinning him to the floor, I bite harder, spitting his stringy fur over my shoulders. His cries echo through the forest, desperate pleas for life.

I swear I hear snarling, whining, and howls all around us, some even begging me to stop, but I don't give a fuck. No one can hurt us like Jack and Steven again.

Mason's wolf screeches, his body quivering beneath mine, but it's not enough.

Luna, he's submitting! Stop! Noah mindlinks.

No! He almost killed you!

You don't want to hurt anyone like this, Luna! Don't abandon yourself because of him!

Noah's words don't make any sense to me.

Mason stands for everything that's scarred us. And deep down, I know he's the closest chance I'll have to destroying Jack for what he did to Noah.

It's only when a sharp pinch on the back of my neck yanks me off that I bite someone other than Mason, twisting as far as I can to nip the giant wolf lifting me like a pup.

Luna! It's me!

I fall limp in an instant, allowing Noah to set me at his feet. He curls me beneath his massive wolf, plopping his huffing torso over me to use his body as a shield.

But no one comes to attack us.

I heave through pants, unable to stop whining. Dragging my snout from beneath Noah's, I glance at our surroundings. Lying mere feet in front of my nose, Mason's broken body quivers so badly that he can't even hold himself up with one paw, let alone escape, forced to wriggle in the dirt with distressed whines.

As Viktor, Tāne, and Reid approach, poking him with their noses in confirmation of Mason's defeat, it's over, and Mason knows it. He offers no resistance to their prodding, giving up.

Viktor grabs Mason by the scruff, dragging him through bloody leaves. He's flanked by dozens more wolves by the second, a massive army of beat-up, furious Lycans howling and snarling in agreement at their hunted catch.

Every Alpha-domination wolf in sight is either tracked down, submitting, or too injured to flee.

But as Noah licks my bloody cheeks, calming my shaking wolf with soft whimpers, I only whine more.

It's okay, my love. It's over. You did so well.

Noah, all these pack leaders… My wolf gives a soft, despairing howl as we gaze out at the still forest together, horrified by what the day has become. Wolves whimper and howl throughout the forest, cries of pain echoing from every direction. My paws and lips reek of Mason's blood, only heightening my heart rate.

Noah drops his head over mine, attempting to cover my eyes with his snout. We burrow into each other, shaking in silence.

It's not until I'm smothered under Noah's secure embrace that it finally sinks in: Mason's sharp blood on me smells familiar.

Colliding within my skull all at once, images flash before my eyes.

Noah nuzzles me, nibbling my mark as he whimpers with me. *What's going on, Luna? You're panicking.*

Panting, I whine sharper with every breath. *It's all coming back. That was him. That was Steven. I remember the scent of his blood beneath my nails.*

Noah freezes.

Then he seethes, vicious growls colliding with gutted whines.

Wrapping his paws tighter, Noah cradles me beneath his massive wolf, every strand of fur raised on end.

Opening my mouth, I pant harder in the face of Noah's horror, my wolf's tongue lolling to the side. *I know why he didn't kill me that night. I completely forgot I clawed into him—until now. He tried to strangle me, but he must've also wanted to mark me. And I... I became the wolf backed into a corner. He couldn't hold her down anymore—not like he had been doing for years, belittling me until I was a quiet, shaking shell. But she was not quiet. She came out to kill him first, even as she shook, and he ran. He never came back... Not until you found me to finally take me home.*

Noah's anxious panting settles with mine. To my surprise, he purrs, licking my mark with slow, steady strokes. Nothing about it feels sexual, even though it buzzes warmth throughout my belly—he's thanking me. Not only for allowing him to mark me after Steven's brutality, but for surviving the brush with death that Steven attempted to force upon me. I can feel it in the weepy gratitude beneath each of Noah's purring whines, no human words capable of describing the bliss in our bond at the thought of us now remaining entwined, forever.

When I'm finally ready to stand, Noah's coat brushes against mine the whole way back to the Community Center lodge. Neither of us mindlink a word.

Instead of following Viktor's pack to their confinement den—where they keep their most violent prisoners—Noah's wolf nudges me down the hall to our room. I'm too weary to question him, padding after Noah in my wolf form, even when he shifts back.

Ducking into the door, my wolf can barely squeeze inside our suite after Noah's human form. Noah doesn't persuade me to shift back, easing the door shut behind my wolf before burying his face into my coat.

I whine, hugging him tighter to me with my chin.

Noah lifts his head, and my heart drops; tears streak his cheeks. Cupping my big snout in his hands, it's the first time I've felt so big compared to him—and yet, I feel smaller than I ever have.

Sweeping his palm up my snout, Noah eases my eyes shut as he kisses my wet nose. "Sweet, sweet girl. You're safe now, gorgeous Luna. I have you here, and no one else is with us. You don't have to shift back yet, but when you do, I'll be right here to hold you, okay?"

His gentle hands spur deeper whines from me. It's not until then that I finally allow myself to shudder hard, shaking out the trauma of what we just witnessed. But the second Noah's features warp in guilt, I shift back as fast as I can, collapsing into his arms. He buckles to the floor with me, pulling me into his lap.

Doubling over me, Noah presses me tight to his chest, cradling my head over his shoulder as I cry. We sob together, sweat and dirt sticking our bare bodies together as we grapple each other as closely as we can.

Nuzzling his cheek, I can't lose the primal edge to my pounding heart. Luckily, Noah seems to understand what I'm seeking, turning his head to crash against my lips. We sniffle through harsh, tearful breaths as we kiss, our desperate fingers unable to let go of each other's backs.

After a few minutes of kissing and cuddling, Noah's slowing breath soothes me back into equilibrium. He guides me into the shower, rinsing every last bit of grime from my hair. When his soapy hands swipe over Little Wolf, Noah pauses. Staring down at my small belly, his features warp into heavy tears.

"Oh, my *love*." Lifting his chin, I press my lips into his once more.

Our foreheads rub as we hold our pup together, breathing out

the fear of what tonight could've looked like, if we missed just one swipe of a claw coming at us to take our lives.

Noah carries me to bed with soaking wet hair, unable to let go of me more than a second or two. "I love you. Please be okay."

"I love you too, Noah. I'm okay, but only because you're still here. I could barely stop you from being shot. I almost lost you."

"You didn't, Luna. I'm right here."

He curls around me, burrowing me into the nest of blankets I created at the start of the Summit—what feels like a month ago. I've never clung to Noah so hard.

But after a few minutes of Noah's steady, comforting rubs on my back, I sink deep into the mattress. Before I can recognize the sadness refilling my chest, it spills over, flooding my pillow with tears. Noah huddles closer with gentle kisses, but nothing can remedy how deeply my heart hurts.

"They wanted to kill us. They probably did kill some of us, didn't they?" I whisper.

"I…" Noah swallows hard. "I don't know. It's possible."

My forehead warps. "Which means so many wolves are hurting tonight, just like we did when we lost our dads."

"I know. It's monstrous. And, fuck, Aliya, I think—" Noah's horror in our bond deepens enough to steal his breath.

"What? What is it?"

"The way they came in with guns, and how Mason morphed into a carbon copy of his dad, over time. I can't help but think—" Gazing into my eyes, Noah shakes his head, disgust creasing his features. "I'm wondering if you really were right about Jack."

My heart lurches into my throat. "Or did Mason do it to make his dad proud? Especially knowing his distant girlfriend would also lose her support system from it, allowing him to dominate the gap?"

The soft gasp on Noah's lips guts me; I watch him struggle through the terrible possibilities, none of them softening the gut punch in our bond.

"Fuck, Aliya. Fuck." Noah groans, shaking his head. "I guess we can ask him, now that we have him, but—" Noah swallows too thickly to finish his sentence, likely as nauseated as I am.

But he doesn't need to say anything more. Holding each other in the silence, I feel it too; this might finally be our answer.

The truth feels surprisingly quiet. Noah's shoulders settle, even with the rising sadness in our heated breaths.

"I'm so sorry," I whisper.

"I'm sorry too." Urging me to turn back around, Noah snuggles me tighter, his chest pressing against my back with every inhale as we breathe through the ache in our bond. We hold Little Wolf together, our four hands encompassing the full surface of my swollen belly.

I'm grateful Noah hasn't told me it'll all be okay; what happened isn't okay, and I'm relieved to not be alone in feeling this tremendous despair. His honesty nourishes me, allowing me to keep living through one minute of my grief to the next.

"I want to help everyone heal, but I'm so tired, Noah."

"Go to sleep, my love. We'll all take care of one another. All you need to do right now is trust your wolf's instincts on what you and Little Wolf need."

The second Noah rubs my belly, I melt into him. But my eyes flush hot. "I can't sleep. I wanted to be wrong about the Super Pack. I wanted to celebrate you. You saved us, Noah, just like you promised—my King."

"Aliya…" Noah nuzzles into my hair, his breath hot with shared tears. "You have no idea of the depths of what you did today, do you?"

All I can do is weep. "It wasn't enough."

"No, my love. I love you, but you're so wrong about that. You really have no idea…" Kissing my mark over and over, Noah strokes me until my lungs slow, my body sinking into our nest. "Let's put this aside for now. I'm going to stay with you, all day and night, until you feel okay again. I'll be by your side, for the rest of my life. Okay?"

Turning towards him, I press my forehead to his. "And I'll be by yours. By the Moon Goddess's blessing, please, let it be long."

As promised, Noah remains plastered to me for hours, not budging an inch, even as wolves enter our room with soft-spoken questions about global decisions to make. Neither of us sleep, instead spending the entire night debriefing our pack and whispering about what we've just witnessed and experienced—refusing to allow their forced trauma to seep into our bones.

Processing my thoughts with the love of my life, I bounce between emotions with him: rage, grief, terror, and agony spinning us in a rapid cycle.

But after a full twelve hours, Noah's soft smile finally meets his eyes. My shoulders loosen—we're going to be okay.

Noah kisses my forehead. "My love, I have to do something important before the ceremony tonight. Can you sleep for me? At least for an hour?"

My smile fades. But I nod. "Come right back. Not because I won't be okay without you—I will, thanks to you. But if I can do anything, I just want to make you smile again. I can't let them take your joy from you. I won't."

One leg off the bed, Noah freezes, gazing down at me. His side of our bond wavers with emotion, his chest laboring through each breath as if he's awestruck by the very sight of me.

Stroking the hair off my forehead, Noah softly kisses it. "They won't. As long as you're right here, I can survive anything."

His voice is soft but deep enough to send pleased shivers down my spine. I curl around his pillow with a smile, nuzzling into his scent and obeying his request—falling into a deep sleep.

I awaken to soft, soothing whispers of two women in the corner of our bedroom. It's not what I expected to hear, but something about the warmth in their near-inaudible tones sets me at ease, allowing me to stretch my arms above my head before prying my heavy eyelids open.

Annika and Waimārie are nestled into the chair in the corner of the room, the cushion just wide enough for the sweet Omegas to cuddle up together. Their relaxed shoulders and breezy smiles shrug away my concerns; with the Super Pack dismantled to such a severe degree, everyone seems to be calmer than I've ever seen them.

Waimārie meets my eyes, breaking into a beaming grin. "Good morning, gorgeous!"

"Hey, you two." My groggy voice scrapes my throat as I hoist myself upright, cupping Little Wolf. "I'm still so relieved you're both okay."

Like a true mom, Annika stops at my bedside, handing me my water glass from the nightstand. "How are you feeling, mama?"

The gentleness to Annika's tone brings it all back: the horrifying past two weeks and the terrible way it all ended last night. I groan, gripping my lurching stomach.

"That bad, huh? Ah, well, for now, I bet you're desperate to pee, eh?" Waimārie says.

I break into a weary laugh. "You would be correct."

While I drag my achy body to the bathroom, Annika and Waimārie shuffle around outside the bathroom door. I'm too tired to care, throwing on one of Noah's discarded shirts I find on the tile floor so I don't have to walk around naked.

"Don't worry about brushing your hair or anything, and I mean it!" Annika calls out.

"Oh?" I laugh, setting my hairbrush down beside the sink. "And why not?"

Annika's voice chimes closer. "We want to pamper you!"

Opening the bathroom door, I gasp; Waimārie and Annika stand with a fluffy white robe and a breakfast tray brimming with my favorite food cravings.

"What's all this?! That is so sweet!"

Annika drapes the robe over my shoulders. "We really do want to pamper you. Get back in bed, Queen Luna."

"Ah, I see. So this is the queen treatment?" I laugh as I shuffle back to my blanket nest. "I'll get back in bed, but I don't want to be treated like I'm above anyone else for being Queen Luna. Winning the Summit competition was Noah's victory."

Waimārie pulls the covers back over me, smoothing them over my lap before laying the beautiful breakfast tray over my thighs. "What if we *want* to treat you? You saved our lives yesterday, along with countless people we love."

My heart jolts. They look so earnest.

But I can't bear to hold their kind stares. Glancing at the

delightful plate of food in my lap, I sigh, picking at my thumbnail; no matter how hungry I am, I can't stomach the thought of eating while gory intrusive thoughts flood my mind from last night—which also means it's extra difficult to see their point. I don't feel like there's anything to thank me for, considering the damage that was done by the Super Pack anyway. As far as anyone told Noah and me before I finally fell asleep, there were over three hundred injured wolves, at least forty-three of them critically injured, and counting.

Even if no one were injured, just the fact the Super Pack got this far sears a wound in my heart; this many Alphas decided it was okay to destroy our safety, no matter the cost. Unlike a physical wound, an ideology can't be erased. How can something like this be repaired?

But I try my best to smile for the kind women in front of me. "Okay, fine, especially because this food is absolutely beautiful and so thoughtful, so thank you. But don't call me Queen, or anything. Aliya or Luna is fine."

Annika and Waimārie share a sneaky smile, raising my eyebrows.

"Was that insensitive? I'm sorry," I say.

Annika grins. "Not at all. We'll accept your request on what to call you. We still want to mom you, though, especially before the King Alpha ceremony tonight."

I drop my stare, my heart twisting. She remembered how much their maternal kindness meant to me, earlier in the Summit—knowing I don't have a mom to confide in.

The thought of Mom's reassuring hugs stings. Cupping my belly, I ache for her more than ever. How scared must she have been, pregnant with me and immersed into this Lycan world, but with no way to shift and defend herself like I can? How did she get through it without having her mom nearby?

Drawing my hand into her lap, Waimārie massages every bone in my hand. "Not hungry?"

"Just a little woozy after last night," I mutter.

Annika copies Waimārie on my other arm, squeezing up and down my sore arms until I droop into the pillows, letting out a huge sigh.

Annika giggles. "There you go. Relax, Luna. The worst is over now. You've provided the whole Summit with a sense of true, quiet peace."

My heart flips. I lift my head, surprised to find both women staring back so lovingly. Annika isn't exaggerating; even as the Lycan world weighs us all down, Waimārie and Annika wear carefree smiles, their gentle voices carrying far more genuine, relaxed tones.

Annika's smile falters. "I do want to deeply apologize to you, though, Luna. We thought we had vetted everyone protecting our borders, but one quiet, older Alpha within our pack snuck them in one or two at a time, allowing them to assemble up in the mountains."

Waimārie groans. "One single Alpha traitor, enabling all that damage. Can you believe it? How can you even vet against something like that?"

"All it takes is one," I mutter. "And Waimārie's right; it's not your fault what they decided to do to us, Anni."

Dropping her head, Annika bites her lip, her touched, watery eyes leaving an ache in my chest.

"Did anyone—" I swallow hard, my heart hammering. "Did anyone die?"

I can hardly bear to whisper those terrifying words.

The last thing I expect is for Waimārie to break into the warmest smile, her dark eyes shining in the soft lamplight. "No, Luna. *No one* died. We stopped them in time; not even anyone in the Super Pack had to die."

My lip wobbles before her words fully hit. Gripping my exhausted heart, I close my eyes, releasing a heavy, relieved sob.

"Oh, *sweetheart…*" Annika gives my arm a deeper rub, swirling soothing pressure over me until I lie limp, only my chest shuddering through tears. "You have the kindest soul."

As the Lunas massage my arms, shoulders, and legs in silence, humming a soft song together, they allow me to cry, only stopping to hand me tissues for my runny nose.

When my tears run dry, I find myself smiling, my heart lighter than ever.

"How did you manage to heal everyone? I really thought we could lose so many by the morning," I say.

Waimārie sighs. "We did too, at first. But thanks to your fast action, no bullets hit the mark—leaving grazes, if anything. Claw and teeth marks are something our saliva can handle, and with how much camaraderie the incident inspired, you wouldn't believe the result. Top leaders were lining up to heal one another, all night long, taking turns licking everyone's wounds whenever someone got tired. Thanks to their expertise and genuine teamwork, we worked miracles together. I've never seen such a large group of injuries heal so rapidly."

As my heart swirls, I shake my head in disbelief. After all the hatred and violence we've witnessed this weekend, is it really possible for us to care for one another? Is it possible that this many Lycans believe what Noah and I know in our hearts to be true? That each and every one of us is precious?

"Is Noah with everyone?" I whisper. "Has he seen this?"

Glancing at each other, Annika and Waimārie smile even wider.

"Yes," Annika says. "I'm sure you both will have plenty to talk about. It's not all good things, of course, considering we have all these captured Alphas to decide what to do with, but for today, the good far outweighs the bad."

"Especially because we're together," Waimārie says.

As the women move to my hair, combing it out, inch by inch, I sigh in bliss, my heart fluttering. I'm tempted to be moved to tears again. While that violence is the reality our pup may be born into, they'll also be born into the one currently melting me into the bed. Rubbing my belly in slow circles, I hold Little Wolf as Annika and Waimārie hold me, our quiet chat healing the hole in my heart.

They also remind me of all the loving people in my life, choosing to spend their short lives taking care of me as I take care of them.

Amy, I miss you, I mindlink.

We're not blood-bonded like Noah and I, but I swear I can feel it; the instant I mindlink her, a faint giddiness crosses through my soul, Amy's happiness warming me up from halfway across the world.

I miss you dearly. I heard what happened, and I can't believe it. I'm so unbelievably proud of you, Amy says. My heart lifts into my throat. *But I also have to scold your wild wolf ass when you get home. How dare you put yourself in danger like that, especially without me there to kick Alpha ass with you? I need an auntie, an uncle, and a baby cousin for Lexi to grow up with, so you better not do anything like that again. I'm mad at you.*

Breaking into a smile, I dry the last of my tears, refocusing on the present. *Sorry, babe. I'll be back soon. Kiss everyone for me.*

Within minutes, Annika and Waimārie have me laughing my heart out, allowing me to devour this heavenly plate of my favorite foods. With my belly full, Little Wolf gives me faint, fluttering kicks in shared excitement. Holding them in pure awe, I whistle out my breaths; they're okay. We really made it. I find myself sighing every few minutes, still unable to believe today is real.

When Waimārie hands me a mirror, I gasp. They've managed to comb my bedhead into order, two delicate braids wrapping around my head like a crown while the bottom half falls around my shoulders.

"Oh, my gosh! Thank you both so—"

The door to our suite opens, and my breath cuts short. Noah stands in the doorway, his eyes racing over me. I'm still lazing in bed in his shirt and a plushy robe, but as his chest swells with a heated breath at the sight of me, my belly swirls at the sight of him. Whatever he's thinking about me, he must not realize how stunning he looks—clean black slacks elongating his legs. A casual dress shirt stretches over his wide shoulders, adding a regal elegance to his effortless, dark hair.

Noah opens his mouth to speak. "You—"

"You look gorgeous," I blurt out. Noah blinks a few times, and I laugh. "I wanted to say it to you first."

Dropping his chin, Noah doesn't manage to cover his beaming smile in time; I already saw it stretch all the way across his face, crinkling up to his eyes. "Luna…"

I giggle, opening my arms. "Welcome back to our nest, my shy Alpha. Where have you been?"

Noah's eyes soften. He settles beside me, wrapping me in his arms. "Thank you for waiting for me. I had some things to figure out before the ceremony, but on my way back, I visited our injured and our captives."

"We told her everyone was okay," Annika says.

Meeting my eyes, Noah smiles. "That's the good news. My bad news isn't the worst, either. Everyone's pinning this all on Mason, which I'm thinking is just to lessen their consequences."

I sigh. "Probably. And Mason? Have you seen his human form yet?"

"Guess." Noah rolls his eyes, and I'm tempted to laugh. "Everyone's already scheduled for extensive rehabilitation in their home countries."

I nod. This is a Lycan protocol; following through with compassion and empathy development once crimes have been committed, allowing perpetrators an opportunity to learn and grow.

Waimārie scoots closer, softening her voice. "Are you okay, Luna? We heard he… That Mason might actually be Steven Barrett. I can't imagine having to decide what to do now."

Biting my lip, I look to Noah for answers. Like me, he's uneasy, his stare focused on the hardwood floor, rather than my face.

"I think I'm just a bit concerned. I'd do the same for my preschoolers, even if they caused physical harm, so I agree with the principle. That's why I'm torn." My throat thickens. "What if…"

When I can't bear to speak, Noah's quiet voice deepens. "What if we can't fix him, no matter what we do? Yeah, I've learned that lesson the hard way too. When someone adopts it as a personality trait to hurt other people like this, I don't have much hope for them, either."

My heart twists. Grasping my hand, Noah gives me a soft smile.

"What if he's not ours to fix, and he's his to fix?" Annika mutters.

I blink a few times, absorbing her words. When our focus turns to her, she smiles.

"You said it perfectly when you got here. We can give him the opportunity, and it can be his choice whether or not to take it. If he doesn't, he'll be trapped learning and re-learning the same lesson for the rest of his life."

My shoulders soften. "You're right. Maybe this isn't our problem to resolve for him anymore."

"You get this too, don't you? What it's like to have to make this decision?" Waimārie whispers, stroking Annika's hand.

Annika doesn't answer, ducking her head.

Tracing Annika's pained stare, I hold her hand too. Noah and Waimārie follow suit, the four of us creating a web of comforting touch until we burst into giggles together.

Before I can ask more, a sharp knock on our door straightens our backs. Noah shifts his weight to get up, but the door flings open, startling Annika, Waimārie, and me into a gasp.

Viktor grins in the doorway, excitement racing through his eyes. "He shifted back, the minute you left!"

My stomach drops. "Mason?"

Noah rises, his eyes wide. "What? What'd he—"

Viktor's groan cuts Noah off. "Greenfield, you better deal with that asshole before I break him in half. He's the most fucking annoying creature I've ever seen!"

Biting my lips, I'm tempted to laugh. Noah and I meet eyes, just before he fetches his suit jacket with a groan. "Here I come."

But I catch Noah's arm. "I'll go with you. I just need to change."

Noah's eyes darken. "You feel up to it, Luna?"

"Well, there's no better time than now, I guess."

Noah nods, striding to my suitcase to dig through it. Despite the dread creeping up my throat at what we'll find when we finally see Mason, my shoulders soften; Noah really is treating me as his equal, accepting my decisions like we're two top Alphas, leading the pack together.

Once I'm clothed, an army of our allies walks at our sides, Reid, Tāne, Viktor, Annika, and Waimārie following us to the confinement dens. But the closer we approach, the faster Noah's breath races.

"Hey." Reid's hand settles on Noah's shoulder, rubbing him as I massage his hand.

But Noah turns from us, gripping his hair. "I can't. I'm sorry, Aliya. I have a really bad feeling about you going in there."

"Bro, she's ready. Look at her." Tāne's hand on Noah's back makes him flinch. But as Noah and I meet eyes, my stomach churns.

He's not okay.

"It's not just my badass Luna I'm worried about. It's Anni

and Waimārie, and—" Noah's voice catches, and my heart lurches through the blank space left in his words; he's been gravely hurt by both Harts now.

I soften my voice, easing Noah's clenched fist open. "Let me ask you something. Is this a trauma response, or do you think there really could be something dangerous he's planning by luring us in to look at him?"

Noah's eyebrows warp as he thinks it through, his eyes racing across the tile. "I don't know. There's no way to know."

Breathing out a sigh, I nod. "Okay, so maybe, maybe not. Since I trust your wolf, how about this: you and Reid can go in first to assess, and the rest of us can join you afterwards."

Gritting his teeth, Noah drops his head. With a shrug, he sighs. "I'm probably going to need Tāne and Vik in there together to calm me the fuck down while I know Reid can protect you out here. Otherwise, that sounds fine."

Stroking his back, I smile. "Okay. See you soon."

Bouncing on his heels, Noah finally lifts his head. Haunted eyes stare back, strained to the point of sinking further into his skull.

My shoulders droop. "Oh, Noah—"

Rushing for me, Noah clasps me tight to his chest. I embrace him just as tightly, scrunching my eyes as if it'll squeeze the fear from the sweet heart hammering against my ear.

His soft voice buzzes against my cheek. "How are you not freaking out?"

I sigh. "I'm sure it'll hit me once I see him. Otherwise, I'm strangely done with him."

Noah groans. "Still."

"Still, yes. It'll always be hard. But I have so much to live for now, my love. I think he'll see it on my face, and he'll never want to fuck with another soul."

Sucking in a sharp breath, Noah freezes. Pulling back, he stares deep into my eyes. Whatever he sees hardens his shoulders. Planting a heavy kiss against my lips, Noah huffs until his fear morphs into determination—and our friends cheer at how thorough our kisses grow.

Releasing his lips with breezy laughter, I finally manage to pull a hint of a smile from Noah.

Slipping from my fingers, he strides down the hall, forcing two massive Alphas to tag on his heels. Glancing over his shoulder at me one last time before he turns the corner, Noah flashes vivid yellow eyes. *See you soon, Omega-Alpha.*

◆ **34** ◆

Mere minutes pass before Annika, Waimārie, and I jump; a furious shout echoes from the confinement den's depths, dousing my skin in goosebumps.

The Lunas grip me tight, turning to meet my eyes; that wasn't either of their mates.

"Shit," I whisper, glancing at Reid's tight frown above me.

He's guarding our row of chairs—only a hallway and a spiraling stone staircase away from the basement's high-risk confinement den.

What's going on? I mindlink Noah.

Noah doesn't respond at first, but I can feel his emotions whirring.

I grip Reid for stability, keeping a protective palm on our baby. "I need to go in there, Reid. But I don't want Mason to look too closely at me."

Reid nods, gripping the back of my chair to bring it in with us.

Waimārie rubs my back, her voice low. "Would you like us to come with you, darling?"

I sigh. "It's up to you both. He has a mouth on him, and I'm sure it could be triggering."

As I suspected, Annika pales. "I-I'm sorry, Luna, I—"

My heart drops. Gripping her hands, I stare Annika in the eyes. "Never apologize for what someone did to you. You should always have the choice whether it feels safe to confront this. I'm not offended that you need to stay safe—not in the least." Turning to Waimārie, my chest puffs. "Will you stay with our dear Queen Luna, Waimārie—"

As Waimārie breaks into a smile, I blink a few times, realizing my mistake; Annika isn't Queen Luna anymore. I am.

Annika breaks into breathy giggles, her shoulders loosening. "Thank you, Omega-Alpha Aliya—who is absolutely not our Queen. We'll both be here when you're done."

I'm surprised I still have the ability to laugh at a moment like this, except I also know who I'm looking at—what their kind presence stands for. This is a different world of our own making. Someday soon, it could be one where Mason/Stevens will no longer thrive.

Either way, nothing can prepare me for the face I'm assuming I'll find on Mason's human form.

Descending the stone staircase, dim lighting does little to warm the basement's stinging chill. I'm grateful there's a hall leading to each cell in the confinement den, preventing us from having to be seen by any captured Alphas we don't want to associate with today; their murky hatred clings to the air as it is, chattering my teeth with nerves.

When we enter the confinement den, Noah's angry brows lift, revealing his underlying panic. "Luna, what—"

Viktor rushes over, grabbing the chair from Reid. Multiple wolves follow him, instinctually protecting me from the dangerous figure locked into his cage.

I huddle into Noah as he guides me from Reid's side. With everyone's help, I'm stationed with a chair facing Mason's cell.

But I don't sit. I cling to the back of the chair, using it to cover my belly.

"Does this work?" Reid whispers.

"Yes, thank you, I—"

Noah growls. "No. He's not safe to be around yet. Not only is the fucker still trying to shift back, he's manipulative as fuck, and a waste of our Queen Luna's time."

"Noah." I gaze up at him, stroking the back of his tense hand. "It's okay. I want to experience everything with you—good and bad."

Noah's heart aches with both love and despair.

Then I hear a curdled cry.

"Stop! This is inhumane!" A figure scrambles to the back of Mason's cell, keeping his head obscured from view.

I almost don't recognize Tāne's voice, losing its shining intonation as he growls through each word. "Hate to break it to you, bro, but it's not a civil right to abuse others. We're not letting you shift tonight—not until there's no one nearby you can hurt."

My eyes widen when our wolven allies step out of my view, revealing a cage full of Alphas and Betas pinning down one cowering Alpha.

Mason struggles, his claws extending and retreating in a failed attempt to shift. With Tāne grabbing a better hold of Mason, Johannes injects him with more Alpha rut suppressants, his rusty brown fur sinking back into his human skin. Mason's back remains turned, the Alpha hunched into himself until he looks like a small mound on the stained stone. I can hardly see a human form, let alone his face.

A part of me wants to feel pity. But that only makes me angrier.

"Mason, that's enough," I say.

He sucks in a heavy breath, then freezes.

Everyone's expression contorts in confusion.

"He stopped struggling. It's the first time today," Viktor mutters.

"I don't like this." Noah's breath speeds up beside me. "He fits your profile, Aliya. And I know you have to be the one to confirm it, but I can't fucking stand it—"

All thoughts escape me when Tāne attempts to turn Mason's head towards me with a handful of Mason's hair. "Let's get this over with then, eh? Is this who you think it is, Luna?"

I catch a glimpse of short, dirty blonde strands in Tāne's fist. If that wasn't enough, I spot a little mole above Mason's eyebrow— the one I always used to kiss.

My heart threatens to stop.

The more his body struggles against furious hands, the more I recognize his gait. The way he carries his shoulders. How he shifts them out of the way, tilting one up to bend his body to his advantage rather than wasting energy by jerking around.

My very first thought is odd: I always thought Steven was too agile to want a desk job out of college.

Then all his other lies come crashing down, one by one.

It's true. Noah's suspicions about Steven being a wolf, the lies Noah and I picked apart on our last phone call, my suppressed memories that came flooding out of me last night, all of it.

I'm looking at Steven Barrett.

Steven is Mason.

Even after all this time in therapy, and no matter how tough I want to appear, my shaking body admits the truth: he still scares me.

At first, disappointment creeps in—a bitter piece of me spitting at the thought of him still soiling my mind. Logically, I know I have new reasons to be scared after his Alpha-domination stunt, if my initial traumas weren't reason enough. But that's not what I'm truly afraid of.

This secret is too huge. Is this the extent of the damage he's done to me? To *everyone?*

What else do I not know?

Then denial kicks in. I blink, expecting to stop recognizing his face. When my eyes verify it, over and over again, reality bends until I can no longer feel my hands.

I thought I accepted this as a possible truth, but now that it's here, I'm too shocked to speak, my gaping mouth desperate to shout, scream, or even cry. All I can do is gasp for air.

Until a raspy whisper escapes me. "Why did you even lie about your name?"

Noah's head slowly turns, recognizing my fear in our bond.

When I glance at Noah's eyes, they're already yellow.

Then he's no longer at my side.

In a flash, Noah enters the cage. He rips Mason from the wolves' hands like he's stealing a floppy piece of cloth, chucking Mason to the stone ground.

I cry out when Noah strikes, a sickening crack of bone on bone echoing throughout the den.

Mason—*Steven*—screams.

But Noah screams louder. "Shut the fuck up! I'm gonna fucking kill you!"

I know I should stop Noah—this isn't what we agreed upon either, and Mason holds so many truths—but I can't move or speak. It's happening in slow motion, each of my breaths more labored than the last as Mason's cries are muffled by his arms protecting his head.

Then I think back to our last phone call. I didn't get to share what I really wanted to: to speak my truth to his face.

As Mason cowers beneath Noah's fist, I realize I might never get the chance. Panic strikes my heart.

"Wait!" I say.

Everyone freezes. All eyes are on me, but my stare locks onto Mason. He's still alive, wheezing on the ground in a whimpering heap. Despite bleeding down his lips and chin, he keeps both elbows folded around his face, not allowing me to see him beneath the cover of his arms.

But I can even recognize his busted lips.

This is real.

As I come back to my senses, my emotions come crashing down all at once—as do Noah's.

My eyes zip to his, and for a second, I don't even recognize him. His strained gaze is almost rabid. "He tried to kill you last night—*again*. How could you stop me?"

Noah's upset looks like it's directed at me, but I know what he really means. If Jack was right here, and it was after a long night of attempting to kill Noah, I wouldn't understand either if Noah stopped me from hurting Jack. Especially when, like Noah said, no matter what I could physically do to Jack, he's still scarred Noah for life.

There are so many things I could say. Instead, I just shake my head.

No one dares to speak another word until I do. But my voice quivers, echoing throughout the den. "I've always wanted a chance to explain to him how badly he hurt me."

Noah's expression warps, pain rippling across his features until he looks a decade older. "He... He won't listen, Luna... I'm *so* sorry to have to say that, but—"

Despite my quivering lip, I smile. "It's okay. I need to do this, anyway."

Noah glances back to Mason, still limp in his grasp. Now that I can take a closer look, I'm surprised Mason isn't hurt worse.

Some part of Noah knows we still need to question him. Force him to help us find Jack and any other leading Alpha-domination figures that escaped, or else this Super Pack could reunite with twice the fury.

Even still, Noah's rapid breath tells me letting this go is one of the hardest things he's done.

"Everyone, please leave us," I say.

Wolves evacuate from the room without a second thought.

Noah's stare shifts into wide-eyed panic, thinking that means him too. I give him a weary smile.

I know it's a big favor to ask of you to watch me in pain, but I've needed to do this for a long time. Will you please stay here and stand by my side, my love?

As all the pain and sadness I've held onto for years brings me to tears, Noah's lip wobbles with mine. *Okay. I love you so much.*

I love you too.

Noah releases Mason.

We both hold our breaths; we're the only wolves in the den that are ready to strike if Mason decides to defend himself.

But he remains motionless beyond his labored breath.

So I take a breath too. And another.

"Steven?"

Mason flinches.

Fuck. With no plausible denial left to keep me afloat, the truth rolls through me in nauseating waves, forcing me to white-knuckle the chair to keep from toppling over.

Noah grips his hair, his breath rapid and uneven. His rage boils in our bond, driving my heart rate higher. *He not only lied to you about who he was, he fucking stalked you this entire time, making you believe he was far away!*

I-I know, it's… I don't even know how to describe it to Noah. Despicable, sickening, and petrifying aren't dark enough.

But now that we're here, the anger I've carried for Steven subsides to reveal its true form, bringing me to grieving, gutted tears.

I have so much I want to say.

But am I ready?

I look to Noah, my limbs shaking. *This is finally my chance, but… I'm scared.*

Noah's head droops, our bond screaming in agony. *I promised you, he'll never have a chance to do anything to you again. And I stand by that. I don't care how much we need him, if he hurts you more, I'm not afraid to break him.*

I shake my head, my heart sinking. *You were right to stop my wolf from hurting him beyond repair to begin with. I've never wanted to hurt anyone, and I still don't. Not even Steven.*

Noah deflates.

But my words inspire a revelation. *Wait, Noah— That's exactly why Steven hurt me so badly.*

Noah's eyes widen, his breath just as shaky as mine as he stares at me for answers.

I know exactly what I've always wanted to say.

Hobbling on shaky legs, I grab a discarded towel on a nearby table beside empty Alpha rut suppressant syringes. Gathering as much saliva as I can, I spit on the towel.

Steven glances over his shoulder, terrified of me coming closer. But I simply pass the towel through the cage door.

Neither wolf inside takes it.

So I step inside.

Noah's chest puffs, but I grip his arm. "Trust me, sweet Alpha."

After a tense silence, Noah relaxes enough to step back, giving me room to enter while remaining within arm's reach.

I drop the towel in front of Steven's face.

At first, his scent warns of fear and overwhelm. Then he croaks out a dry, sarcastic laugh. "So you're playing nice now? Being the good girl you always acted like you were?"

Noah's growl hums throughout the cage, heightening all of our emotions.

But Steven only strengthens my resolve.

"Steven, you—" I take a deep breath, and speak my truth. "You think I tricked you. Forced you to hurt me. Hurt others. All because I was your girlfriend, and I never gave you a chance to debate it when I broke up with you."

Steven's mouth closes like I spoke for him.

Then he gives a weary, bloodied smirk. "So you agree with me, deep down? This is even more fucked up then. Letting your mate beat me to death, all for nothing?"

"No, stop. I just know exactly how you think, and what you want to say," I snap. "Because I took time to actually see you. Listen to you. You never truly saw me, and you never wanted to."

I swallow my shaking voice, but no matter how confident I want to seem, the pain he inflicted forces my entire being to keep quivering.

I continue anyway.

"All that time, I was there. You saw a kind, obedient woman, and thought it fit your mold of how life was supposed to look. But I had no other choice except to obey you. I never had a choice."

Steven shakes his head against the stone wall, not even sparing me a glance. "Oh, come on. Clearly you did, otherwise we wouldn't be here after you broke my fucking heart in the most humiliating way."

"I told you the truth! You didn't give me what I needed in the relationship, and I was leaving you out of fear! But even if you think that was cruel, why didn't you give me any other choice, then? In your fucked-up world, where a man deserves power over everything a woman says and does, wasn't it your job to grant me that choice to stay? To protect me instead of hurt me?"

Steven takes a breath to speak, but I stand, my claws extending with my heightening volume.

"Maybe I did hurt you back. I broke your heart, breaking up with you when you expected me to remain loyal for life. But no matter what, you hurt me irreparably that night you broke in. You saw a grieving, scared, and alone woman, and you did everything you could to make me feel weak!"

I let out a heavy sob, hardly able to catch my breath. Noah recoils with me, tempted to join my side. But I shake my head no.

And Steven scoffs. "If you understood me so well, you'd know exactly why I did that. You started acting like an Alpha, when you're really an Omega. You needed a reminder where you stood—"

I grip Steven by his shirt collar. The blood dripping from his nose and mouth sticks the fabric to my sweaty fists. "If you truly believe men should feel nothing, then fucking *look* at me as I'm talking to you!"

For the first time since we've started talking, Steven's eyebrows flinch in visible fear.

But he still won't look at me.

"I would've talked it out with you! Instead, you took my health and safety from me! You claimed ownership over my body, and you hurt it in ways it'll never heal from! Do you know what that was like to experience, right after losing my family? You were part of the family I lost too, and after you emotionally abused me, I grieved the person I thought you were—even before you hurt me worse! Then I had to grieve myself!"

Noah whimpers now, shuddering through angry tears.

But Steven's eyes finally lock onto mine.

When I'm tempted to back away in fear, my wolf pushes to the surface, showing me she has my back now too.

"I couldn't even hurt you back to stop you because I still cared about you! *That* was real love, Steven. You took everything from me, but I was never yours to take!"

The resulting silence scares me more than anything Steven could say. Both men have their eyes on me, and I'm still holding Steven with shaking fists. I drop him in a hurry, afraid to make a hypocrite of myself.

But as Noah rushes to my side, Steven finally snaps out of his petrified stupor.

"You did hurt me. I had to run for my fucking life."

My skin erupts in goosebumps. I didn't imagine it; my wolf came out to protect me.

And Steven's suppression of her was intentional.

As my heart races faster, the hatred in Steven's pale, empty eyes chatters my teeth. "So, because I had Alpha in me, and I was supposed to be your obedient Omega, you beat the shit out of me and raped me?"

Steven growls through a half-there laugh, thinly veiling his fear. "This makes no fucking sense. I was just trying to cheer you up after he died, but you blew up on me, all because I asked to have sex. You were my girlfriend, so, naturally, I thought—"

My teeth clench, my rage blasting in full force. Steven stops at my wild eyes alone.

"I know what you believe, but you're fucking *wrong!*" My shout echoes throughout the den. "After all this, all you still care about is that I wouldn't keep fucking you? Get over yourself! My body is all that will ever be mine, and you scarred it in every way you could, even taking my family from me! I just wanted to love you!"

Steven scoffs.

But I scoff louder. "I wasn't done."

Steven freezes. Noah shuffles in the corner, his breath heightening with mine.

"If you couldn't have me, then no one could, is that right?" I cough, my voice scraping in disgust at the reality of his actions. "Even before breaking in, you shot my dad to get back at me for pulling away from you, didn't you, Mason?"

If I thought Steven's eyes were cold, Mason's ice over. Gritting his teeth, he drops his head. "That wasn't the plan."

Horror races through my veins. He didn't deny it.

"You sick fucker," Noah hisses.

But does this mean it really was an accident, or was Mason aiming for Ritchie and he hit the wrong target? And who else shot our dads alongside him?

Mason's eyes sink into his skull, gaping up at us like a skeleton. All I see staring back is honest, soul-destroying guilt.

Worst of all, I know that guilt isn't for what he did to us. It's for how he's destroyed his own life, unable to fathom how he's let himself down so severely by finally getting caught.

My head spins. "Oh, my God, Steven. You did do it."

"No, I wasn't lying to you on the phone!" Mason sputters. "It wasn't my fault! Jack planned it all out, and your dad wasn't supposed to be there. I don't know what happened, I— The rifle went off on its own."

Shaking my head, I clasp my hand around my mouth, my heartbeat pounding in my skull.

"On its *own?*" Noah grits his teeth.

As my blood burns, Mason's eyes haven't left mine. I never want to see his twisted face again, yet I can't stop gaping at him, unable to fathom how I let this monster into my home to help me grieve over the crime he committed.

Mason blubbers on the ground at my feet. "Aliya, I didn't— Takahiro wasn't supposed to be there. I knew he was busy, otherwise I would've persuaded Jack to pick another time."

I back away from him, but the second his words register, my eyebrows arch, sorrow striking me in the gut.

"Because I had to skip lunch," I whisper.

Noah lets out a strangled cry, grasping me as I reel. "Goddess, Aliya… Fuck."

Meeting Noah's eyes, I see the same pain reflected. That's right; Ritchie took over Noah's perimeter run shift too. But instead of dissolving back into his old guilt pattern, Noah straightens at my side, staring Mason down.

"So it's his fault? Aliya's fault? My fault?" Noah's voice scrapes out, gutting me further.

"*No,*" Mason croaks. "It's— It's Jack's. It was just supposed to be Ritchie. When the rifle went off, Takahiro came for us, Jack had no choice but to save our lives, and—"

Squeezing my eyes shut, I grip Noah tight as our souls twist in agony at the thought.

"What the fuck? What the fuck," Noah rasps beneath his breath, gripping his hair.

But as horror shifts into numbness at the sight of the sniveling, fake man beneath me, I can barely mutter out my words. "So even now, it's everyone else's fault, huh?"

Mason's eyebrows furrow. "You're not listening! I swear, Aliya, I didn't—"

Noah's voice deepens into a snarl. "You *both* fucking killed them. Who the fuck cares if the job was accidentally done too early? Do you think that really fucking changes anything? I don't even care if it turns out you weren't even holding the gun; you planned it, and that's that."

At first, there's silence, the terrible reality behind Noah's words echoing through my mind on repeat.

Then it clicks.

"So, with all this fighting at the Summit, you've just been trying to finish the job," I mutter. "Because in your mind, it wasn't

Jack's fault he got kicked out. It wasn't Jack's fault he abused the children around him and left you behind, and now it's not your fault that you're continuing to cause chaos either. Because you were trying to kill Ritchie, yes, but you were also trying to kill *Noah*."

Noah freezes beside me. My hands quiver as I grasp Noah's hand, terrified to let go. I really could've lost everything and more that day. As Noah chokes out a furious growl, my chest puffs.

And Mason's voice thins out. "*Aliya*— No, don't look at me like that, *please*— It wasn't supposed to happen like this. You were supposed to be my—"

"I'm done with you," I say.

When Mason's waterworks hit, his perfect jawline warping over his enthusiastic tears, I'm surprised; this used to always get me. Now, I laugh. It's not my usual laugh—a darkness creeps from my core.

Noah stiffens beside me. I hold my breath, my jaw clenching tight.

But as Mason's tears halt, I stand taller, lifting my chin as I peer down at him. "This will be the last thing you and I say to each other, you know that?"

His tears were artificial at first. I know this is true, because for the first time tonight, life reaches Mason's eyes, his chest caving like he's genuinely torn in two.

Reaching for me, Mason whimpers. "No, no— Come on, Aliya, you can't—"

Noah smacks his hands away. Mason bounces on his ass, stunned that I haven't crumbled with him—not a single apology escaping my lips.

I soften my voice. "Hey."

Mason freezes, holding his breath.

"This isn't working for you, yeah?"

"W-what do you mean?" His eyebrows warp, his voice shaking harder than mine.

"You've wasted so much time chasing after me, and after Noah, but at what cost? All this time, we've been healing. Even this morning, we've been laughing with our loved ones and holding them through the pain you caused as we healed, together."

Eyes darting between mine, Mason continues to stare, his eyebrows twitching.

I grit my teeth. "I know this won't make sense to you, possibly ever, but I hope you're starting to hear what I'm saying: even if you took my life the night you broke in, it would've still been mine. You *can't* own me. I've been hurt by you, yes, and so have all of us, but you still didn't get what you wanted. I'm hurt, but I'm so, so happy. And here you are, still chasing after something that can never exist. It's sad."

With these words, there's an abrupt silence within my mind—one I haven't felt for years. As I stare at Mason frozen beneath me, I suddenly realize I don't need to hear his answer; there's nothing he could say that will ever satiate me.

But that was never the point. I finally did it. I finally spoke my truth.

Noah's palm covers our growing pup. His reddened eyes lock on mine in an unreadable flurry of emotions.

I grip Noah's hand, tugging him out of the cage.

But rather than following me, Noah scoops me into his arms, slamming and locking Mason's cage doors shut. His shouts warble with pain. "Reid, Tāne, Vik? Your turn."

Wolves come pouring into the den, but Noah hugs my aching head to his chest, rushing out as fast as he can.

Noah doesn't stop until we're tucked into a secluded hallway of the stony basement, his ragged breath echoing across the walls. All wolves are out of earshot as they get back to work interrogating. But as Noah sets me down, I realize this privacy isn't only for me, but also for him.

Noah isn't gasping for breath; he's sobbing his heart out.

I spill over with him, crumbling against his chest. Noah squeezes me all over like he doesn't know how to hold me. We settle onto our knees on the icy stone. Noah tugs me into his lap, holding as tight as he can without squishing my belly. I hold our child and mate alike, burrowing into Noah's burning neck.

His grating cry breaks my heart. "You're the bravest fucking wolf alive. I'm so proud of you, but I'm so sorry you had to do this at all. I'm so sorry he took so much from all of us. I wish I could take it away, I—"

I stop Noah with a heavy kiss, hiccupping through tears against his lips. Noah sucks back snot as he kisses me twice as hard, too stuffy to breathe through his nose. As we share frantic, breathy kisses, our love erupts just as fiercely as our shared pain until it overpowers everything else, intensifying with every kiss.

"I love you. You gave me strength to finally speak," I breathe.

"Oh, Goddess," Noah rasps. "No, you always had it, my love. I'm so sorry he crushed it. But seeing you stand up against him hit something raw inside me that I didn't know needed healing, and—" Noah frantically nuzzles his mark on my neck, whimpering through tears. "You make me feel so safe in this terrifying world, Aliya. Thank you."

As I pull back to stare into his tearful smile, it's the first time I've seen such beauty in myself.

I love it. After knowing how it feels to have someone terrify me, I love making my favorite person feel safe.

$$\backsim \!\! \multimap \quad 35 \quad \multimap \!\! \backsim$$

Every injured ally manages to join us for Noah's King Alpha ceremony. Standing before a crowd of delighted faces, my heart softens just a bit more; despite all we've been through at this year's Alpha Summit, we not only made it through, but we survived, smiling.

Although our bond courses with both of our nerves, Noah's chest remains high, his embroidered suit catching the banquet hall's chandelier light with silvery threads. Moon cycle patterns grace his arms and back, streamlining his broad form until he appears even taller. Celestia from Celestia Couture designed a coordinated silver, embroidered dress for me, thousands of finite stitches elevating me to queen status by merely slipping the handmade fabric over my head. Together, we stand as a united force—until it's finally time for Noah to receive his crown.

As Viktor lifts a golden circlet off his head, my heart races. Noah briefly catches my eyes before turning to the crowd, ducking his head low for Viktor to reach. Noah's wide form obscures his back in shadow, but as Viktor hovers the circlet over Noah's head, it catches the light in just the right way to steal my breath; Viktor fits Noah with a wire-wrapped circlet, pristine gold braided in an intricate weave that dips into a curved point against his forehead, illuminating Noah's dark hair in a crowning glow.

Noah flushes from the eruption of howling cheers.

I clutch my hands to my chest, unable to contain my gushing smile. *You deserve it, my love. Soak it in.*

Turning over his shoulder, Noah breaks into a wide smile. My heart lifts with his—until it drops to the floor.

"I have an important announcement." Noah speaks to the crowd, but he holds his hand out for me.

The crowd falls silent, but Noah's smile doesn't waver. He gazes deep into my eyes as my heart hammers, urging me to glance around the room for answers. When no one seems surprised, their smiles only growing, I tame my expression; maybe I got the order of events wrong?

I'm supposed to stay back with every other wolf on the stage, giving Noah his moment until Annika steps forward with her circlet to entrust her Queen Luna title to me. But when I glance at Annika, she's not holding her circlet at all—it's not even on her head.

Instead, Noah guides me to his side, placing me at equal footing.

My heart lurches into my throat. Everyone important in the Lycan world watches me step forward, abandoning the process we rehearsed this afternoon. Is this really okay?

Leaning in to nuzzle my cheek, Noah wraps me in his embrace. When I turn to him with wide eyes, he presses our foreheads together, softening his voice. "It's all okay, Luna."

"What's happening?" I whisper, struggling to stabilize my rocky stomach.

Noah smiles. "Keep breathing, and try your best to be open to what I'm about to say."

As he releases me, I can't help it; I'm confused beyond belief, and my warped forehead announces it.

But with Noah's softening eyes, I trust it will all be okay. He glances at the crowd, but he doesn't keep his eyes trained on them when he extends his voice for everyone to hear; his stare lands back on me, warming by the second.

Taking my hands, Noah speaks. "Everyone here agrees, Queen Luna Aliya of Greenfield Pack, that your role in protecting the life of all Lycans at this Summit was unparalleled. You may not have been a competitor, but it doesn't feel right to me to crown you as 'Queen Luna,' alone."

I can hardly breathe, looking around the room—anticipating someone to protest. But our world's leaders continue to smile back. Turning back to Noah, I grip him tighter. "W-what?"

Undeterred by my anxiety, Noah's grin reaches his eyes, his teal irises gleaming as brightly as his joy in our bond.

Johannes approaches Noah's side, presenting a royal blue velvet pillow. An elegant, woven gold circlet perches atop it, designed similarly to the King Alpha's crown.

Except this circlet has a dangling, iridescent moonstone in the center, resting above the third eye.

Noah's fingers quiver as he lifts the crown from its velvet pillow, turning to me. "Unlike King Alphas having to fight for their title, our Queen was voted in to hold a new, never-held title—which our allies agreed upon, unanimously. While she does possess every quality of Queen Luna, I believe she also embodies a Lycan 'King,' at heart, fighting valiantly for the sake of our safety and love, no matter how terrifying those may be who attempt to strip that safety from us. She not only embodies this title, but she's achieved it of her own accord. And for that, we wish to honor you, our dear Luna."

Sharp, wracking breaths interrupt my breathing, forcing me to stoop over as my knees shake. "Noah, what? This is too—"

My voice peters out, struck by the genuine smile on Noah's face. The tranquility in his eyes allows me to believe it; maybe I can accept this. Maybe it's okay to stretch outside of my comfort zone, allowing myself to be thanked too.

Noah straightens, raising the circlet above my head. "As this year's King Alpha, it's my honor to grant an honorary title to Aliya Matsuoka of Greenfield Pack, the world's first King Luna."

As Noah drapes the circlet over my head, balancing it perfectly over the braids Annika and Waimārie weaved for me, howls erupt around us. The top Lycans create such a gorgeous, authentic song of gratitude that goosebumps erupt across my whole body, coating me in touched awe. With the world of Lycans cheering for me, I'm left frozen before them, unable to process my new status.

Gazing up at Noah, my voice shakes. "This is so— This is the biggest— What am I supposed to say that's good enough, Noah?"

Gathering my face in his big hands, Noah plants soft kisses over my cheeks, smiling wider as I grip him like a lifeline. "You don't have to do or say anything. You're our very first King Luna, so there are no traditions to uphold. Just keep being you."

He's right. Drawing inspiration from Noah's tradition-shattering wolf, I loosen my shoulders, allowing myself to laugh at the rollercoaster of our lives. Diving into Noah's arms, I kiss him hard. When wolves around us only cheer louder, my smile breaks our kiss.

We haven't walked this path before, but at least we're walking it together.

It's hard to believe we've been in Sweden a mere two and a half weeks; it feels like a lifetime.

By the time we're ready to fly home, Mason has revealed further information about the Super Pack's reach, but not enough. Not to mention he confessed to killing our dads with Jack, but now refuses to say more about his father. We've decided to bring him back to Greenfield, keeping him detained in our own confinement den in the hopes he'll eventually share something about Jack's whereabouts as he's rehabilitated in his hometown.

As we say our goodbyes to Viktor, Annika, Tāne, and Waimārie, my heart is sore with far too many emotions to express.

While the rest of our dear friends chat, I pull Annika to the side. "Thank you for everything, Luna. You gave us a safe space to stay, and I couldn't be more grateful."

"And I'd do it again for you, mama. Without you, we might not be here."

I hug Annika tight.

But when I nuzzle her cheek, Annika's breath halts.

"Is everything okay?" I pull back, rubbing her shoulders.

Waimārie glances over at us, joining our side. "What's wrong, Luna?"

"I, um—" Annika flushes, peeking at us through her eyelashes. "Vik and I have a secret we've been waiting to share."

All at once, our Alphas whip their heads to us, their ears on high alert. Waimārie and I laugh, and Noah's warm arm returns around my back—just in time for me to gasp as Annika fetches a familiar piece of plastic from her purse.

Holding up a positive pregnancy test, Annika drops my jaw. "That welcoming dinner really did the trick."

Waimārie and I throw our arms around a giggling, overjoyed Annika as our whole group cheers in surprise, Tāne and Noah hugging a chuckling Viktor.

"Oh my goodness, congratulations, mama!" I laugh.

I let out a happy hum at Annika's giddy scent, suddenly understanding why she's smelled a bit sweeter the past few days.

But as I meet Noah's wide, petrified eyes, his jaw slackening, I bite my cheek, struggling to hold back my laughter.

Fuck! We really have to control ourselves better, Aliya! Is this almost exactly two weeks from the dinner?!

Viktor nudges Noah's side, leaning in close. "Hey, man, it'll uh… be weird to not have you here to spar with."

Us Lunas giggle even harder as both Alphas sink into a somber silence, leaning on each other for support. I let out a bright sigh as Noah and Viktor hug it out, a stark contrast to how they treated each other when we arrived.

But my heart belongs in Greenfield, and elation swirls through my chest at the thought of returning home. Sometimes, I still can't believe I have a pack to return to.

A few hours into our flight home, Noah buzzes with a sudden excitement.

I turn to him expectantly—just before he turns to me. When we meet eyes, he drops his stare with a grin, his flustered cheeks widening my smile.

Noah scoots closer. "I know this is a really fucking weird place to say this, but I feel so relieved we finally have one Hart in custody that I want to—" Noah stops, biting his lip. "W-well, I don't know."

I giggle, snuggling in closer. "What is it, my shy Alpha?"

"W-what if…" He peeks up at me as our bond bursts with his anticipation. "What if we pick out a new house of our own when we get home? I know you moved into my place, but what if we choose something new, together? Somewhere we'd like to raise Little Wolf?"

My whole being lights up, soaking in just as much joy as

Noah's. Before I can respond, he breaks into a beaming grin at my giddy smile.

I laugh. "I'd *love* that, Noah."

Noah studies me carefully as my heart dips. "But?"

I slump. "But… If we're going to move, I should probably sort through my parents' old cottage and decide what to do with it, once and for all. It just doesn't feel right to sell it."

Noah's brows furrow as he takes my hand. After a long silence, he softens his voice and leans in closer. "Are you sure you feel ready for that decision then, love?"

"It's been hanging over my head. But now that I've lived with you for a while, I feel ready to move forward with it somehow." I sigh. "Either way, it sounds like a dream come true to create a home together, my love."

With that, Noah kisses my forehead—hard. I giggle in surprise.

Noah grins. "In that case, I'll help you through every step of the way, and we'll figure out how we can take the stress off your shoulders with such a big decision. Maybe there's another solution, rather than just selling or keeping it."

I smile. "Maybe."

Then I straighten, clutching Noah's hand.

His other hand lands over mine. "What's wrong?"

Blinking a few times, I vibrate with excitement as the pieces fall into place. Turning to Noah, I keep my voice just above a whisper. "What if we allow a refugee parent to raise their children in my parents' home, rent-free, until they'd like to live elsewhere? I can't make it a home for our kids, not after what I know happened to me there, but that wouldn't stop someone else from absolutely loving that home."

Noah sucks in a deep, awed breath. "Goddess, that's *incredible*, Aliya. I love that. Let's do it."

As we share a deep kiss, a subtle hiss comes from across the aisle.

"Disgusting," Mason mutters.

Rolling my eyes, I grip Noah by the jacket collar, kissing him as much as I please. Noah breaks our kiss through laughter, keeping his hand over my mark.

To my surprise, I haven't retained any of the panic I felt around

Mason/Steven—not after I last confronted him, and not with everyone here, by my side.

Maybe it helps that my and Noah's glares alone have kept Mason invisibly detained the whole flight beside Yasmine—unbeknown to every human on board. With Yasmine meeting us in London, Viktor's strongest two Alphas were able to hand Mason off to our pack's custody, allowing Noah and me to keep our distance from him and never speak to him again, as promised.

I glance at him just as he shrinks into his seat, cowering away from Yasmine's bared fangs.

Yasmine chuckles. "That's what I thought."

Nestling into my mate with a grateful purr, I already feel like I'm home.

It's not until my feet touch the Greenfield grass that I realize I was wrong; we're welcomed by a giant pack of adoring, sweet faces. After all the stress we endured, they greet us gently, no matter how excited they are to have us home.

And Greenfield is my home. Not only with Noah's presence residing here, but also with everyone else by our side, surrounding and protecting the wolves I love. And soon, we'll be adding another little wolf to Greenfield Pack.

∽ **36** ∽

It takes two months for Noah and me to stop clinging to each other a little tighter, afraid to lose each other like we almost did at the Alpha Summit. Our pack celebrates me as King Luna alongside my sweetheart of a King Alpha, but nothing makes me feel more appreciated than Noah's careful hands as they comfort my ever-swelling belly each night, the two of us laying in silence as we feel our baby's kicks.

Winter has officially set in, coating the yard in a blanket of pearly white and a blissful silence. The moonlight flickers through Noah's eyes, catching their wolven reflection to remind me what a powerhouse I have beside me—especially as his soothing Omega scent coats my skin after a long day of aches and exhaustion, allowing me to finally rest.

"I have a secret." Noah's whisper is so gentle that I'm not sure if I imagined it.

When I snuggle closer, moving my head to his pillow, Noah kisses the tip of my nose. His big hand rests on my belly, right where I told him Little Wolf last kicked me. He sweeps across my skin, his thumb caressing the curve of my abdomen and loosening the rest of my limbs.

I'd be tempted to close my eyes if I wasn't waiting on this secret he has to share—and I can feel it's a big one, his stinging anxiety seeping into my chest.

"Sometimes, I feel bad that—" Noah clears his throat. "I feel bad that it's so hard on you to carry Little Wolf, and— And I'm also always curious how it feels. I wish I could take on most of the work for you, and instead I'm just… here."

I prop myself on my elbow, my brows furrowing. "You don't think you take on a ton of work for me? Noah, I really couldn't have survived this pregnancy without you already, and we're not even through some of the hardest portions."

"I-it's not just that, it's—" Noah's voice wavers with nerves, flipping my heart. When he speaks next, his soft voice comes out smaller than I expect. "I wish I could carry them too."

Thank the Goddess it's dark. I'm speechless, my heart pounding as Noah's breath speeds, reflecting the flustered, embarrassed vulnerability I feel in his side of our bond.

Stroking his hair back in the darkness, I soften my voice. "Noah, can you do me a favor, my love?"

"What's wrong? Do you need to lay on your other side to get more comfortable?"

I smile. "No, I'm okay. Can you scoot closer for me? Until we're belly to belly?"

Noah's breath halts. When it restarts, he shuffles closer, enveloping me in his body heat until I let out a happy purr. Chuckling, Noah buries his fingers into my hair, rubbing the back of my neck. I groan in bliss, and Noah lets out a genuine laugh.

"Is this what you wanted, my sweet Omega?"

"Not quite, but I do love this." I sigh, my eyelids fluttering as he massages me deeper.

Like clockwork, Little Wolf kicks me—hard. Noah's wolf jolts upright in our bond, his ears as high as they can be; they kicked him too.

I giggle. "I know you can feel them already, but I want you to stay right there. I'm going to put a little more pressure on my belly, but not enough to hurt or be dangerous, so don't worry, okay?"

"O-okay," Noah whispers.

Wrapping my arm around Noah's waist, I press us even closer, widening the surface area on our abdomens where skin meets skin. Every breath pushes my swollen belly against Noah's stomach until our lungs sync, trading off inhales and exhales in tandem to each other's movements.

I whisper as softly as I can. "Do you feel them?"

Sliding his palm around my belly, Noah's breath hitches

again when Little Wolf gives us another set of good, hard kicks. "Holy shit."

"They're strong, aren't they? They're definitely your pup." I bite my lip, staving off laughter as Noah's wolf zooms around in our bond, excitement overcoming him. "Can you get quiet with me for a second, and really try to feel into their presence in our bond? I don't know if it's possible, but sometimes, I see our inner world, just by feeling extra connected to you. Maybe we can meet there for a moment, and really focus in on this pup we're holding? I wonder if we can feel their bond to us clearer if we try it together."

Noah doesn't respond, instead falling silent as he softens his breath. I close my eyes, diving into my connection to him in the center of my soul.

As Little Wolf does a mini somersault, pressing their tiny legs into the lowest part of my belly against Noah, my mate laughs beneath his breath. "I think they're not appreciating the lack of room we're creating."

I giggle, following his hand until we cup their pittering feet in Noah's palm. "I think they might also like feeling snuggled. Lately, they seem to get sleepy and stop stirring as crazily when you hold my belly."

Joy trickles through our bond, widening my smile. But as we both grow quieter, our hands holding the base of my stomach together, I sink deep into the pillow, my head drooping until Noah's forehead presses against mine.

Laying in silence with Noah, I'm surprised how easy it is for me to venture into our inner world—even without renewing our bond with a fresh mark. Fluffy, fresh snow coats the field like a sea of clouds. My wolf is snuggled up in the center of it, her tail furled over the distinct energy I've come to recognize as Little Wolf. Their faint presence blinks brighter as soon as I nuzzle in, curling tighter around them.

But within a span of a minute, two black, fluffy ears perk up from the snow in front of my snout, startling my wolf's head into popping upright.

Noah shakes his fur, unburying himself from the snow. A bit of it sticks to his nose, but he couldn't care less; his full focus locks onto the little glowing ball peeking from beneath my bushy white tail.

His alert ears tempt me to laugh, threatening to pull me from my focus. Instead, my tail thumps wildly in our bond, smacking snow in every direction. Meeting my eyes, Noah's wolf happy-squints, his tail wagging so hard it nearly smacks his sides. Lowering to his belly, he keeps his chin low to the ground—inching closer to Little Wolf.

When we're face to face, Noah huffs in excitement, glancing between me and our pup's soul. We gaze down at Little Wolf together, growing quiet as I nuzzle them delicately. Their outline is faint, but they're certainly here; Little Wolf's paws pop into the air as they flop on their other side.

My ears pull back as Noah breaks into delicate whines, his heart bursting with love alongside mine.

In our bed, Little Wolf kicks against Noah's stomach once more, startling us both into taking a sharp breath.

I stroke Noah's arm as he rubs my belly. Softening my voice, I press my nose against his. "Noah, are you still looking at them in our bond?"

After a long pause, Noah breathes out the quietest whisper he can. "Yes. They're beautiful, like you. I always love finding your wolf holding them here."

My throat thickens with emotion. I smile, drawing my hand up his warm side until I cup the back of his head. "That's why I wanted to bring you there: they're not tied to my wolf's body in our inner world. While I carry them here, in person, why don't you hold our pup there, in our special place—keeping their soul safe for us through the rest of my pregnancy?"

The silence heightens my throbbing heartbeat, but as soon as I hear a shaky exhale, my eyelids pop open.

"A-are you sure?" Noah's words are watery.

"Oh, my love—" I huff with him, my lungs pushing my belly against his until we loosen our hold on each other, chuckling. "Of course, I'm sure. I'd love for you to be able to experience this with me."

Noah doesn't respond; he holds my head in both hands, pressing quivering lips to my forehead as his scent overflows with gratitude. I adore how tender his heart feels, my smile gushing from me. As I close my eyes once more, meeting Noah's wolf back in our bond, I find him circling in the snow behind Little Wolf. Once he finally plops down, Noah nudges our pup into place on his soft belly fur, purring as he gives them slow, careful licks.

Little Wolf glows brighter and brighter, the beauty of their soul stunning me so deeply that my eyes fling back open.

I find Noah gazing back at me, his eyes shining in the dark. "Holy shit, I feel them. I feel them in our bond, clearer than ever."

Gripping Noah tightly, I crash my lips against his, cuddling him as close as I can despite our pup blocking our cuddle ball. Noah curls me into his arms, just like his wolf holds our pup, and I couldn't be happier.

"I feel them too, Noah," I whisper. "I love them. I love both of you, so much."

Propping himself over me, Noah gives me a slow, heavy kiss. When our lips release with a smack, I sigh in bliss.

Noah chuckles, his nose stuffy as he strokes my hair back. "I love you both more than anything. Thank you for doing this with me."

"I wouldn't have it any other way, my love."

❧ 37 ❧

The following morning marks six months into my pregnancy, and Noah's presence has nestled deeper into my heart than I imagined possible. I can't absorb every single emotion he has all day—that'd be way too overwhelming—but if I wanted to, I could listen in to find every minor flicker of feeling within him.

And with how open we've become with each other, I've reached an unexpected roadblock in our lives: I've hit my limit of tolerance with Lilian's needless blame and cruelty.

We're sitting across from each other in the Community Center kitchen, having just finished prepping tonight's dinner for the pack. Noah's mother shares his sharp, deep-set eyes, and more mannerisms than I can count, but the longer I listen to her soft voice chatting with me about the near-complete Greenfield Daycare we're building together, the less I can understand why she never speaks this gently to her son.

Lilian pauses, her brows furrowing. "How are you feeling, Luna? I know you're starting your third trimester, so I hope we didn't work you too hard. You look stressed."

I swallow hard. Her words stoke a fire in my gut, intensifying my breath.

As my heart pounds faster, I cup the base of my belly, gritting my teeth. I can hardly bear to look at her staring back at me so kindly, knowing what she's done—how she's tormented Noah for *years*.

Noah should be rejoining us in a few moments, but he's likely stopped on his way out of the bathroom by excited pack members.

He doesn't say it out loud, but I know he needs her guidance right now; he's about to become a parent too.

And I don't think I can bear to see Lilian reject Noah a single time more. Not while I'm carrying his baby, knowing how deeply my soul has bonded to them already—and how deeply Lilian's soul must've bonded with Noah's too. How can she bear to break his heart?

It's too late to calm the fire in my gut. My true thoughts snap from my lips like a red-hot iron brand. "Why did Ritchie let Jack go after what he did to your son? And why are you still blaming Noah for it?"

Lilian's eyes harden. She sets down the napkin she's been fumbling with, clasping her hands in her lap. "We didn't think he'd live. Jack's mate licked his wounds until he survived, even though she still had his bruises on her face. We realized their bond hadn't fully broken, and we didn't want his death to kill her. But that was after we found Mason in the bushes, watching his father be attacked half to death. Ritchie couldn't bear to break Mason more than Jack probably already did, so no matter how pissed he was for Noah, he couldn't kill Jack."

My throat runs dry. When I speak, my voice is darker than I've ever heard it. "You're telling me my ex almost saw his father get killed, and he still shot my dad dead?"

Lilian drops her head, her forehead contorting through the start of tears.

I shake my head. I have no tears left, only rage. "I still don't get this. I love you, Lilian, and so does Noah. So why do you blame him for Ritchie's death when you know how badly this hurts?"

When her eyes meet mine, I stiffen; her irises shine a furious golden, just like her shifted wolf. "It's not your place to question how I relate to my son."

Gritting my teeth, I shake my head. "You're not turning your aggression on me. And it's absolutely my place. I won't have you treating my mate like this in front of our pup."

"Now you're threatening me with my future grandchild? All because your mate allowed mine to die?"

I can hardly breathe, my eyes widening. "No, it's because none of this has ever made sense. How the hell is it Noah's fault?

What could he possibly have done to deserve this treatment, Lilian, truly?"

"Nothing, okay?" she snaps, her face scarlet. "That's the problem. Ritchie knew Noah was stronger than him—that he could beat him in a traditional top Alpha challenge to take his place. But after all that training that hurt Noah to begin with, he let his father grow old and stressed instead of using his skills for good. My son didn't want to be top Alpha anymore."

My blood runs cold. Knowing the hell Noah has been through due to his top Alpha status, that thought terrifies me. I grip my belly with both hands, struggling to catch my breath. "What?"

"He was too damaged by Jack. But top Alphas don't usually live very long, Luna. I hate to say that to you because it killed me my whole life to know, but it's true. They're targeted until they forfeit their title, so if our pups wait to take over, we just grow weaker. Which made his dad a target past his prime."

I grip my forehead, struggling to unpack her words. "Hang on—Ritchie was shot, not challenged to death!"

"I know that, Aliya."

"And you really believe this? You believe your badass, powerhouse of a son, our world's King Alpha, who went through all of this bullshit even though you're telling me he never wanted to, *still* wouldn't have stepped in to protect his father from anyone and everyone he could? Of course he would've, Lilian!" I hiss, and Lilian's focus drops to her lap. My heart wrenches with her watering eyes. "You know what really would've happened if Noah was there? We'd never have to have this conversation because your son would be *dead.*"

As Lilian slumps in silence, I cough, my lungs aching with how out of breath I've become lately. But when my eyes catch movement behind Lilian, I freeze.

Noah stands across the room, just as wide-eyed as I am.

The second his heart drops into pain with his mother's sharp scent, I wince.

Fuck. Maybe this wasn't my place, after all.

But Lilian straightens, her shifted irises desperate as they race across my features. "I just don't want him to give up! I want him to be a top Alpha who lives!"

Lilian stands, and I scramble to my feet with her, afraid she'll blow up once she sees Noah behind her—my mate shell-shocked, judging by his unmoving form.

But Lilian squeezes her eyes shut tight, tears spilling down her cheeks. "Of course I want Noah to be okay. Noah and Rainn are the only reason I lived, at all!"

My heart tears as Noah's emotions somersault. Lilian's warped expression shifts to confusion when she sees my eyes flick to Noah, but I'm more concerned about the genuine horror on Noah's face. When he melts into grief, I mourn with him.

"Oh, no—" Lilian whips her head away from her son, hiding her tear-stained face. "You weren't supposed to—"

Noah strides across the room, reaching for her. I have to press my fingers to my lips, suppressing tears at his empty arms outstretched for her like a child.

Lilian gathers her belongings, her voice quivering. "S-sorry, I didn't mean to— I didn't think—"

Noah's expression warps further. "Please, Mom."

She tries to pull away, and it sets off my final fuse. "Lilian!"

Both mother and son freeze, staring at me.

I don't know what's come over me. I don't raise my voice like this. But as Noah's bruised heart only worsens, my cheeks flush with upset. "If you think you're going to lose your son someday too, enjoy him while he's here!"

All at once, Lilian crumbles. I expect her to turn away again, but for the first time since we've all met, she drops her forehead against Noah's chest, letting out a heavy, despairing cry. Closing his eyes, Noah shields his mother's face from the world, his big arms curling around her head as his cheek settles on top of her hair.

Drooping into my chair, I attempt to pull my gaze away from them—to let them have their moment—but as their quiet, shy voices kickstart a raw, whispering conversation, I can't help but stare. They're opening up before me by the second, reforming their relationship in ways I'm positive they never have since Ritchie's death.

As they dive into an extended series of talks, I leave them be at the table, returning my focus to cooking tonight's pack dinner while still remaining at arm's reach to mediate, if needed. Most of their conversation is calm, and sometimes it flares hot, but after an initial awkward period, I'm stunned by what I'm witnessing.

Within the span of an hour, they *laugh* together. As I witness this shift from the corner of my eye, a flurry of electricity shoots up my spine; they're not just laughing. They've scooted closer, Lilian daring to gather her son's hand in hers.

As I watch their relationship reseed itself, I slip from the kitchen as quietly as I can. Pressing my back against the closed door, I hitch through silent, hot tears, caressing our growing baby.

I didn't realize I was furious for another reason, but as Little Wolf kicks beneath my palms, I close my eyes, cherishing every second with them. I wish I could hold my mom's hand too, to hear Dad's goofy jokes about my pregnancy, and to watch them both cry the first time they hold Little Wolf. I'll never have that with Mom and Dad, but every inch of me craves the possibility for Noah. Watching Lilian throw that away insulted me to my core.

But as Noah's tumultuous heart gradually softens in our bond, he proves my fears wrong; it's not just possible, it's happening. Not only does he still have his mom on this earth, but Little Wolf will have one surviving grandparent—one whose claws can defend them from the greatest of enemies, and whose gentle tone can heal a steeled heart.

38

It's time to let go.

Not only are we selling our current cabin that originally belonged to Noah, but we're also letting go of my parents' old cottage, all for the sake of starting our baby's life in a brand-new home, organized specifically for our growing family.

That, and I've avoided digging up the past for far too long now. The cottage is cozy and sweet—far too lovely to sit here, empty. Guilt pangs at my heart every time I think of it.

It's finally time to let a new family create loving memories there—and for me to let go of the ones Steven created that tainted my beautiful childhood home. I'm bringing with me the memories that really matter in my parents' keepsakes.

I weep over box after box of my parents' things, go rigid with disgust at the flashbacks crossing my mind as I pack my room, and sigh in relief when Noah hires someone to safely transport my mom's favorite rose bush for me.

Just before we drive away, an Omega just as pregnant as I am pulls up behind us, her legs straining to hoist herself out of the car. Two little Lycans hop out after her, climbing up the porch, cheering, "Mom, Mom! Look! It's blue!"

As the exhausted Omega mother caresses the soft blue paint we refinished, her relieved smile heals a piece of me I didn't know was still so raw.

No matter what I tell myself as we back out of the driveway, I'm still hit with a stinging fear that I've made a drastic mistake. What if I failed somehow in treatment, and I should just suck it up and live with the memories in that cottage?

But as Noah and I pull up to our new home, it's all worth it.

Tall, protective evergreens coat every corner of our new plot of land, the remaining space blanketed with a rolling clover field and an empty garden for me to fill. The house is earthy and gorgeous, its stained wood warming the gray skies above the towering trees. We have a cute white porch, and dirt beds big enough to fit not only Mom's favorite rose but dozens of my own new plants and trees. There's even a perfect tree for a swing, once Little Wolf gets older.

We're moved in within a mere two hours, every friend and friend of a friend pitching in to help out—and banning me from doing anything but resting on our new porch's rocking chair.

Grateful doesn't begin to describe how I feel for all of it: the house, the support, and the love that brought us here.

I can't pretend my heart doesn't still sting, letting go of that old cottage.

In my heart, I know the logical truth: Dad literally wrote in his will that he wanted the cottage to be an investment for me and his future grandkids, and I should use it or sell it however I please to make ends meet. This is what he and Mom wanted. They'd *adore* this home Noah and I found, tucked in an even safer Greenfield Forest sanctuary, now that I'm part of Greenfield Pack too.

But the second I find Noah in the empty, extra bedroom of our new home, opening the box to our baby's new crib, my eyes burn hot. Maybe it should've been obvious, but with so many worries consuming my focus, the best part of today hadn't hit me until now; releasing the cottage also made space for something new. Someone new.

Noah does a double-take, startled by my sudden sniffles. Then he smiles, hopping to his feet to pull me into his arms. "You have to wait to cry until I'm done building it."

I blubber out a laugh, and Noah chuckles, kissing my head.

"Well, and after we've painted the clouds on the ceiling like we talked about, added that squishy rocking chair... Oh, and I can go grab the squishy rug for under our feet as we cradle this one, right here."

Sweeping his hands down my belly, Noah pulls another

giggling sniffle out of me. I nuzzle into him. "I love you. I'm so excited for your baby to arrive."

"Me too, King Luna. I love you both so much."

I can't stop smiling as I work alongside Noah, primping and prepping the nursery as I let my nesting wolf go wild.

Until there's one more nursery box.

Noah stoops over it, knife at the ready. "Do you want me to help you unpack this one while you rest? You can boss me around—tell me where to put stuff."

Glancing at the writing in permanent marker on the side of the box, I tighten in dread. But I do my best to give Noah a quick smile.

"Oh, no thanks. I'll do it later."

Noah searches my eyes, but I can't bear to look at him. I don't want to cry again. Not now. I'm afraid I won't be able to get anything else done.

As our bond wobbles with my rising grief, Noah gives me a soft smile. "Okay, sweet Omega. I'm going to see if there's anything else I can unpack in the kitchen while we wait for our food to be delivered."

I sigh in relief; Noah leaves the box untouched for me, even though I can feel his heart aching in response to mine. But I'm not ready to face that box yet. I wait until I'm alone—after we've said our goodbyes to all our generous friends, started our new dishwasher, and Noah has hopped into the shower.

Padding down the hallway's hardwood floors in my fluffy socks, I stop in the nursery doorway, patting its unfamiliar wall all over until I can find the lightswitch. A soft lamp flickers to life in the corner, its gentle glow a warm yellow that soothes my tired eyes.

Running my fingertips along the railing of the crib, my stomach fills with butterflies, imagining how soon they'll be nestled up in here—until Little Wolf stirs. I smile, swirling my fingertips around my belly until they wiggle against my palms, saying hello despite how cramped they're becoming. Closing my eyes, I rock side to side, simply holding them.

"This is going to be where you'll sleep," I whisper. "Your dad will probably love snuggling you, though, so you might not sleep in here too often."

Little Wolf settles beneath my hands, and I sigh, gripping my aching back. Without daring to bend over, I scoot the last box with my foot. Shoving it over toward the mint green, plushy rocking chair in the corner, I grip my belly, easing myself into the cozy new chair with a slow exhale.

But as I pry open the box at my feet, my heart hammers wildly.

Mom's keepsakes for baby Aliya

It's written on the side.

In her handwriting.

A hard lump forms at the base of my throat as I lift each flap of the box, afraid to disturb its contents.

But my breath catches when I find what's draped on top: a squishy, quilted baby blanket rests above a stack of photos, baby shoes, and more, all of which once belonged to me.

A piercing shard of grief wracks my chest as I stroke the fuzzy fabric. I forgot this blanket was patterned with baby forest animals.

Then I see it: a little, gray wolf, frolicking in the center square with a butterfly perched on their nose.

Tears drip onto the blanket, a desperate, hitching exhale escaping my lips. I clutch the quilt, bringing it to my chest.

It's like she left it here for you, Little Wolf, I mindlink.

My heart pounds faster as I hug the soft, silky blanket, draping the bottom half over my belly to hug it around our baby.

Looking around the room, I let out an aching breath; I wish I could share this moment with my mom. I wish she could meet Noah, see the new house, and hold my newborn with me when they arrive. I wish Dad could take them outside, teaching them all about the forest and bugs like he taught Noah and me without either of us knowing each other.

But as I hold the blanket tight to my chest, my forehead warps through a pained smile. It's like she did it on purpose—as if she knew to wrap up this box as a perfect gift for me and this baby, mailing it to our new home at this exact moment in the future.

Hoisting myself to my feet, I drape the blanket over the crib, then take a few steps back. I laugh despite my sore heart, shaking my head; even the colors of my baby blanket match Little Wolf's room, soft blues, greens, yellows, and pinks of the forest reflected in the mural we half finished on the walls before today's official move.

"Thank you, Mom," I whisper, my lip wobbling through a smile.

I stare in awe as I search the rest of the box, finding a perfect picture of my parents and me to hang up in Little Wolf's room to see who their grandparents were. Setting the photo on the white wooden dresser, I grip my panging heart, imagining Noah and me propping Little Wolf up on our hips to get a better view, telling them everything we can remember about Grandma An and Grandpa Takahiro.

But then I freeze. Something about this photo looks familiar— and not just that I recognize it from my mom's shelf, growing up. The second I remember what I found buried in Noah's hall closet while packing, my eyes widen.

Scurrying down the hall, I know exactly which half-unpacked box to seek out: the one with Noah's favorite baby picture of him and Rainn, and the *only* photo he had of his whole family of four. I cup the frames in my hands, my grin widening at Noah's precious squishy face in the family photo, his mouth wide in what must've been screeching laughter from Ritchie lifting him high in the air. To their right, Lilian snuggles a newborn Rainn to her chest, smiling up to her eyes like Noah does at his happiest. And as Noah cups baby Rainn in his lap in the second photo, his little toddler hands awkward and stiff from how cautiously he holds her tiny body, I groan; he looks so amazed by her, his face lit up so brightly that I can't stand how cute it is. He held the purest love for his baby sister, even then, knowing she'd be his buddy for life.

I'm so screwed. There's no way in hell we're waiting long to give Little Wolf a baby sibling to grow up with—not after seeing this.

Giggling, I speed-walk back to the nursery, gripping our baby as they push against me in shared excitement.

Once I have the photos propped on the dresser, adding a few of Mom's knickknacks she kept from when I was a baby, I step back, my fingertips plastered over my growing smile.

It's perfect. It's like Mom decorated it with me.

I can't wait to show Noah. To fantasize with him about what Little Wolf will think someday as they discover more and more about the world.

But then another idea strikes.

As I rummage through the kitchen, Noah stops in the hallway in nothing but boxers, his hair still dripping around a rising, mischievous grin.

"I guess I shouldn't have been waiting in bed. Are we nesting at 12:30 a.m.? And recently crying?"

I sputter out a laugh, covering what must be my bright red nose. "Yes, and yes. Can you help me find some paper? I have to write Little Wolf an important letter."

Noah perks up, his eyes brightening to match mine. Without asking a single question more, he rummages through our things with me until we gather paper and pens, reconvening at the kitchen table.

Noah clicks his pen rapidly, his nocturnal eyes glimmering in the dim light from down the hall. "So, what are we writing?"

A gushing smile spills over my cheeks, my shoulders lifting in delight. As I tell Noah the story about Mom's box, his features melt into absolute warmth, grief, and excitement with me.

But the second I finish telling him what we'll be writing down in honor of Mom's gift, Noah stoops over his paper, beginning his letter.

I do too. I jot down all my thoughts about Little Wolf's upcoming arrival, my fingers shaking as I pour my heart out over every joyous, fearful, and adoring thought I have about meeting them.

But most of all, I tell them about the depths of our love for them. About how their dad inspires me to feel more of it, every second, with how much he loves us both—even without having met them.

By the time we finish, Noah and I grip our hands tight over the kitchen table. As we meet eyes, only to find each other brimming with giddy smiles, we giggle at the same time.

Noah gives my hand a soft squeeze. "Aliya, can I tell you something before we put these away?"

I freeze. "Oh, of course."

Worry strikes my chest as Noah grows quiet. But as I straighten, Noah breaks into a hyper smile, vibrating in his chair.

I sputter out a laugh, gripping his arm. "Noah, what? What is it?"

He chuckles, scooting his chair closer. "We wanted to pick a name that they would still like, no matter who they turn out to be, right?"

"Right." My voice comes out as more of a breath, my chest too stuffed with excitement. "You thought of something you liked?"

Noah bites his lip. When he nods, I break into a wide smile with him, playfully shaking his arm.

"Then tell me already, goofy Alpha! I can't stand it!"

Noah giggles. "I will, I'm just nervous. I don't know why. I can just picture them here so clearly, all of a sudden."

I clasp his hands. "Me too, oddly enough. I was so afraid to let go of that cottage, but I feel like moving our little family here made things fall into place."

Grinning even wider, Noah's eyes flit between mine.

"Ari," he whispers.

I suck in a tight breath, unable to blink. "Ari…"

My heart leaps. As I picture Little Wolf dashing around this kitchen, forcing us to scramble after them with laughter, I can't help but smile with Noah, loving the thought of that name echoing through our new home.

As our focus turns to my belly, Little Wolf stretches right in time—likely responding to my pounding heart. Noah shakes his head, beaming at me. "You're so beautiful. I still can't believe you're doing this for us."

"We're doing it together." Drawing Noah in for a kiss, I press his hands tight over our pup. "Soon, we'll be holding them together too. Holding—"

My heart flips as a rush of shyness strikes me to the core.

But as Noah's soft smile stretches up to his eyes, I can't help but smile with him, allowing my voice to shake.

"Holding Ari," I whisper. "How does it sound?"

Noah's voice comes out fragile. "Our Ari. God, Aliya, I—"

As my mate breaks into wobbly tears, we sputter into wet laughter together. Handing us both tissues, I stroke Noah's hand over my belly until he's calm enough to speak.

Cerulean, overjoyed eyes stare back. Noah whispers, "If you love it, I love it. And I love Ari so much already."

At the sound of Little Wolf's new name on Noah's lips, I tremble with excitement.

I stroke Noah's cheek. "I *love* it, Noah."

As if they agree with us, Ari brightens our smiles as they wiggle against our palms.

We giggle, drawing closer.

"And I love Ari too," I whisper. "You've both stolen my heart."

We tuck our letters away, storing them in a small box for Ari to open in the future—whenever they're ready. Alongside our letters, we add keepsakes from each of us: photos of our dads, my mom, our best friends, and the picture of us at the airport before we left for Sweden—with Ari in the picture too as they form my first tiny baby bump.

As Noah and I tuck the box away safely at the bottom of Ari's baby dresser drawers, we stop in the middle of the nursery, just holding each other. Knowing that no matter what happens to any of us in the future, at least our Ari will have a collection of our love that reaches forward in time too.

$$\infty \quad 39 \quad \infty$$

Every single person I've talked to this week has gasped—jaw gaping and everything—when they've taken one look at my dropping belly. So when my ever-stoic mate's composure finally slips tonight after dinner, fear creasing his forehead, I sigh, flinging my legs in the air in an attempt to heave myself up off the couch.

After two tries and an added grunt from my core, Noah bursts into laughter. "Can I please help you?"

I groan, plopping back into the couch cushions. This only heightens Noah's giggles. Flinging my arms up for him to grab, I can't help but laugh with him. "Not if you tell me I look like I'm about to pop. I'm already aware."

Gripping my arms by my elbows, Noah struggles to heave me off the couch nearly as much as I did; slipping on the fuzzy rug beneath us, he topples over me, catching himself on the couch cushions behind my head with a sharp inhale. Nose to nose, we burst out laughing at the same time.

"Noah, I think I'm glued to the couch. I don't think I can make it to bed tonight. Maybe not even tomorrow night. Actually, I might just have to give birth right here."

My mate's eyes widen in horror.

With that, I'm hoisted to my feet in one smooth motion, Noah's beefy limbs doing the work for both of us. "Don't even joke with me like that, little Omega-Alpha. Not even when you're my grumpy little Alpha."

I let out a slow, shaky laugh, running my hands over our baby until I cup the base of my belly. Noah's eyes follow my touch, his brows furrowing even deeper than when I was plastered to the couch.

I sigh, turning away from him. "Don't—"

"Aliya." Noah's soft, serious tone halts me in place. "I've delegated out my workload for the week."

"What? But what about—"

"Yas and Dave will handle it. That pup has completely dropped, and my wolf is about ready to kill me for leaving your side for a single minute."

Nerves spike my core. I drop my gaze to my feet. Except I can't see my feet, my pelvis sends shooting pain up my spine with every breath, and I'm about ready to have a breakdown thinking about mustering the energy to give birth soon, let alone this week.

But before I can spiral into fear, Noah swoops over my shoulder, cupping my cheeks in his palms. "I'm sorry I decided that without you. But I want to spend as much time as possible with you before Ari arrives. I can feel how strained your poor body is, and how petrified you are, and—" Noah's voice catches, flipping my heart. The second his expression contorts into sadness, emotions steal my breath.

I cup his cheeks in my palms too. "Oh, my sweet Alpha—"

"You're so brave. But you're not alone, Aliya. You've got this, okay?"

There's no way I can keep my lips from wobbling now. Stooping over my belly to drop my forehead against Noah's chest, I breathe through the pounding ache in my back as fears crawl out from somewhere deep in my core. "Are you sure I can do this?"

As if he knew where I was hurting, Noah's thumbs settle on my lower back, massaging out my pain. I heave out a tremendous sigh, and Noah's deep chuckle hums through my forehead. My eyelids flutter shut even before he speaks.

"You can. You will. But for tonight, you're going to bed."

"I can't argue with that," I mutter, my eyelids drooping as I shuffle down the hall. Noah's bright giggles behind me tempt me to smile, even as my forehead warps through another hard Braxton Hicks contraction.

Like clockwork, Ari stirs, straining like my belly is too tight for the poor pup. Even as I soothe them, softly stroking my belly as I stretch to spit my toothpaste into the bathroom sink, they're just as active as ever.

Not even Noah's gentle touch over my stretched skin can calm them as we lie in bed.

Wolf eyes catch the light, shining back at me in the cozy darkness of our bedroom.

"Can't sleep tonight, either?" Noah whispers.

Settling my palm over his, I draw his hand far lower on my belly. We're face to face in the darkness, but the reflection in Noah's eyes shift as our baby's back adjusts against his palm, their head sending a sharp pain through my pelvis.

"Oh, sweetheart…" Noah sighs. "Ari is absolutely huge."

I let out a sleepy giggle. "Don't remind me."

Staring me in the eyes, Noah shuffles closer until we're belly to belly. Our baby pushes against him, raising his eyebrows, but Noah offloads the most delicious, soothing sweet cinnamon scent I've ever smelled, his Omega side showing himself in full force. When Noah decides to also drag his fingers through my hair, I hum in bliss, my eyes lazing shut.

Stroking from root to tip, Noah plays with my hair slower and slower, washing pleasure down my spine until my heart rate is soothed and Ari's wiggling slows. As my body loosens beneath Noah's featherlight touches over my eyelids and lips, I finally drift off to sleep.

But when I wake up sore and with a bladder ready to burst, I'm too exhausted to move. Tears flood my eyes the second I open them.

Noah, all instinct, dashes into our bedroom to find me upset, only to have his expression drop into fear alongside me.

I laugh as I swipe at my eyes. "I don't know why I'm so extra emotional."

Noah usually smiles along with me. Today, he drifts silently to the edge of our bed, taking my hand in his. "Do you need anything, gorgeous? Other than a bathroom trip."

I want to keep laughing at myself, but it comes out as an embarrassing whimper. "Sorry."

Stooping over me, Noah plants a slow, soft kiss on my forehead. My heart bursts with affection as more tears slip down my cheeks without my permission. Thankfully, Noah doesn't take it too seriously, his voice gentle and soothing as he delicately cleans away my tears. "Do you still feel up for therapy, my sweet Omega? I can call Jenny and cancel it for you."

"No, I feel like I really need it. I think it'll help."

"Okay, good. I'm going to take you soon, after we get you some water and food."

I sigh. "Okay, thank you. And I'm—"

"Nope. No more sorries."

I chuckle, expecting Noah to smile alongside me. But as I gaze into my mate's eyes, his protective wolf stands proud in our bond.

"I told you, Aliya; you're doing a favor so huge that I could never return something as beautiful and meaningful back to you in my lifetime. Don't apologize for anything you need to keep you and this baby safe. That includes after you've given birth for us and you'll need as much recovery time as you can get. Not a single second more of this guilt, okay?"

I don't think I've met anyone so sweet. Fresh tears cloud my eyes, but this time, my fear has melted away. Letting out a slow, shaky breath, I nod through a smile. "Okay. I love you."

My mate's eyebrows finally soften. "I love you too."

As Noah drives me to therapy, our hands remain laced over our stirring baby. Ari is as vibrant as ever, pushing against my sore ribs.

My sweet mate has been dragging our birth necessities bag with us everywhere, just in case, but today, the sight of it in the back seat blasts nerves through my chest. Noah counts my deep breaths with me, pointing out the beauty in towering treelines, hawks perched on the mountainside, and fresh signs of winter's chill around us. By the time he's helping me hoist myself up the two front steps leading into Jenny's office building, the part of me that's determined and ready to give birth to Noah's baby has taken charge once more.

But Noah stops me in the hallway, just outside the elevators. The second I turn over my shoulder to look him in the eyes, my heart flinches.

Redness swells Noah's features, his tears ready to spill.

My hand tightens around his. "Oh, Goddess, Noah. What's wrong?"

He chokes out a sharp, breathy laugh, covering his face from me with an elbow hooked around his eyes. Turning away, Noah forces me to waddle after him a few steps before he whips back around with a wet laugh, grasping both my hands to keep me from walking any further. "S-sorry, I don't know. I'm just extra emotional too. I've never seen someone so strong in my life."

As Noah's eyes sweep across my face, I'm unable to grasp how someone so beautiful could cry over me with his whole heart. Our eyes lock, and a tremendous love bursts inside my chest, giving me all the power I need to do this.

Gripping Noah by the collar, I kiss him in the hallway the best I can, struggling to reach his lips over our pup. But Noah meets me halfway, cuddling up to me as close as he can as he stoops over me to ease my stretch. It's a small gesture, but shines as clear as ever as I release his lips.

"You have no idea how much you're doing for me," I whisper against his lips, my racing heartbeat waking our baby until they wiggle against the pressure of Noah's body against mine. Our eyes chase each other as we huddle as tight as we can, our baby nudging Noah's belly just as heartily as my own. Noah's hands scoop beneath my womb, lifting it ever-so-slightly to ease pressure off my pelvis until I let out a heaving sigh. "I might seem like an emotional wreck, but it's only because I love your baby so much. Not only would I have lost my sanity ages ago without you, but if I didn't have you nourishing every piece of me, I don't think I'd have anywhere near the amount of courage or confidence I've found to run our pack family too. *You* are the strongest wolf *I've* ever met, Noah, and I'm not just talking about physical strength. You bring the best out of everyone you love."

Noah bites his lip. Silence stretches between us as we separate, Noah's palms slowly easing my belly back to its low drop.

Goddess, maybe Noah has a point and Ari really has dropped into position: I've never felt this much constant pressure in my pelvis, and so low in my hips. I bite my lip, staving off the pain.

Noah doesn't seem to notice; he helps me into the elevator

with his chin tucked to his chest, silent but absolutely touched. I giggle, cuddling against his arm.

In therapy, Jenny and I work on some of my most difficult harm fears about motherhood using Exposure and Response Prevention. At least, I expected them to be difficult.

I almost can't believe how easy it feels. Whether it's the strength of Noah's heart rooted firmly in my chest, or the many loving conversations I've had with our pack leading up to my giving birth any day now, it's clear how much my favorite wolves have healed my soul; I feel like I can achieve anything.

What if I can actually be a good mom?

Joy creeps up so high in my chest that it spills from me in laughter.

Jenny's eyes widen as much as her smile. "What? What's so funny?"

Picturing how odd I must look only makes me laugh more—at least, until I suck in a tight gasp. "Oh, no! I can't pee on your couch!"

Springing into action, Jenny and I have the same problem Noah and I had last night: I genuinely can't get up from her couch, leaving us laughing so hard that I have to clamp my hand over my crotch to keep from peeing on the soft cushions. Eventually, we manage to free me from the couch's grasp, and I waddle off to the bathroom.

Reentering Jenny's room, I find her still quietly chuckling to herself. "There you are! Feel better?"

I laugh. "Barely. I'll probably have to pee again in five minutes."

As I ease myself back onto the couch with an aggrieved old man's grunt, Jenny and I erupt into giggles again.

Jenny curls into her chair. "It's nice to see you enjoying yourself. I know the past month has been so tough."

I sigh through the last of my laughter, adjusting a pillow behind me to take a bit of pressure off my back. "It has been. But I've always felt like it's nicer to try to laugh through the tough times anyway."

"Isn't that the truth. What was so funny in the first place?"

I smile. "I guess it wasn't funny exactly, more like exciting. I've been so stressed that I'd never feel better, or that my OCD's anxieties would poison our baby somehow. But sitting here with you today, exhausted as hell, this was probably the simplest ERP session in my life."

The reflected joy in Jenny's eyes confirms it; she sees the strength in me too. My wolf puffs her chest out, even as her belly droops low.

I think I can actually do this. *I'm ready for you, Ari.*

Just as my confidence soars, Jenny's smile falters. "I have to say, your baby has dropped *really* low, and you've seemed more out of breath than ever today. Are you sure you're feeling okay?"

My heart flips. I blink a few times, startled by the sharp contrast in my emotions as a biting fear reenters my mind. "Yes, just the usual pain and exhaustion. Why is everyone seeming so concerned?"

Jenny sort of smiles along with me, but sort of not—just like Noah did to me this morning. "I'm not sure, I'm just sensing something a little fearful beneath the surface."

Just as soon as I've reached the peak of my confidence, I'm hit with a flood of anxiety.

I want to believe this feeling is temporary. That Jenny just pointed out old, tired fears in my head.

But the second I feel this rooted fear, it's clear this is an anxiety that has been creeping up on me. What if, now that I've reached such a critical point in my lifetime, all the joy we've worked tirelessly to cultivate could be stripped away from me in a heartbeat—just like it was in the past, time and time again? I swallow these thoughts down as hard as I can, stroking our baby as they wiggle back into action.

I want to explain this all to Jenny—my wild, fluctuating swings of emotions, and all the heavy, heartfelt feelings beneath them as Noah and I have been preparing to expand our family. But just as I suck in a breath to speak, I'm met with a whipping, air-stealing kick to the ribs.

Crying out, I can hardly breathe through the pain; a tiny foot wedges itself against my rib cage, bringing stinging tears to my eyes. "Ow, ow, ow!"

Jenny rushes over, at my side in a heartbeat. "Oh, God, are you having another practice contraction?"

I groan, stretching as far as I can in an attempt to ease pressure away from this tiny, havoc-wreaking foot. "No, nothing like I was the whole weekend. I just have a very stubborn foot in my ribs!"

Jenny laughs as I sputter through a whimper-laugh. "Oh, you poor thing. Breathe through it."

Grasping my hand, Jenny breathes alongside me, each passing second extending as our stubborn little pup is determined to carve out more room inside me. I can't help it; I squeeze poor Jenny's hand tight and mindlink our pup.

Please, my love, move that little foot. They wiggle, forcing my breath to hitch. *Come on, sweet baby, you can do it. Please, move for me.*

Whether it's luck on my side, Ari tiring themself out, or the chance that they could somehow understand my pleas through our budding bond, they unlock their little knee, curling up with a drag of their back across my belly button. I release a sputtering exhale, panting hard. "Oh, thank God."

Jenny sighs with me. "Goodness, Aliya. I am just so proud of you."

I'm suddenly aware I'm still death-gripping her hand, releasing it with a gasp. "Oh, Jenny, I'm so sorry!"

She laughs, but she catches my gaze with a beaming smile. "Aliya, I mean it. I hope you're proud of how well you're doing too."

Staring into Jenny's earnest eyes, my heart swells once more. Maybe I am still afraid of the future. Maybe I'll never stop being afraid. But just like Noah has given me strength, this woman has guided me through every single one of my deepest fears. My heart lifts as I smile wide, gratitude flooding my being for Jenny and all she's done to save my soul too.

And yet I've been lying to her about one core truth.

Jenny's eyebrows raise. As we continue to look into each other's eyes, her voice lowers. "Is there something you're afraid of telling me?"

I blink hard and fast, biting my lip. Holy shit, I let my thoughts wander too far. Normally I'd tell her near-truths, leaving out the wolf-y parts, but there's something so pure, so vulnerable about this moment that I don't know what to say.

And Jenny appears unusually concerned. She straightens,

turning towards me until her whole body faces me on the couch. "Listen, I know it can make things so hard when people around us, who we love, do things we never expected."

My heartbeat spikes into my throat. What in the world is she talking about? Does she think Noah is abusing me? Am I behaving how I did after Steven hurt me? That can't be possible, can it?

Okay, that sounds like OCD and PTSD teaming up. Refocusing on the moment, I'm left in confusion; what else could Jenny be talking about?

I freeze as a thought hits me: did Jenny actually see Noah shift, all those months ago?

Jenny pauses, her wandering eyes acknowledging my anxiety for a long time. Too long.

Fuck. Does she know that I'm not "normal?" Not *human?*

She can't know.

Does she?

Before I can settle my raging heartbeat, Jenny twists her lips. "If we were working together during your relationship with Steven, I would have loved to help you through that process of realizing something was off."

Every inch of my wolf tightens in defense. "Noah is nothing like that cruel man."

Jenny's eyes widen. "Oh, I know, I know. But if you had any worries about the community around you, any one of its participants, or your religion, I'd still want you to feel free to tell me, free of judgment of whatever situation you're in."

Okay, now I'm really confused.

"Jenny, what are you talking about? What situation am I in?"

Jutting back, Jenny frantically waves her hands. "So sorry to startle you, I'm so sorry. I just thought, with what you mentioned last week about that ceremony you had to go to, and the week before where you had to prepare for it despite nearly giving birth, that you were leading me towards something going on when you looked at me in such deep fear a moment ago. Please feel free to correct me, but I don't know how else to put it; I came fully prepared today to help you, a fully pregnant woman about to give birth, escape a… Well, a sticky religious situation."

My eyes bulge just as wide as Jenny's.

And the pieces of all my near-truths start falling together.

Holy shit, does my therapist think I'm trapped in a cult? Especially since we have all these constant Full Moon rituals? Oh my God, she probably thinks I'm in it deep for sure now!

But then I perk up: this problem finally feels fixable. I know exactly what to do. How to tell Jenny the truth, without telling Jenny all of it.

Except it's so funny that I have to belly-laugh, accidentally bouncing Ari with my cackling.

Jenny's chin juts back. "Aliya, what?"

"What I've been afraid to tell you for *months* is—"

I sputter through laughter as Jenny blinks rapidly, tempted to laugh alongside me but too wholly perplexed to understand why her client is laughing like a hyena after scaring her shitless.

Sucking in a desperate gulp of air, I attempt to center myself. "I've been trying to say that I'm heavily interested in the *occult*, not *a* cult."

This time, Jenny busts out laughing with me, her voice coming out as a near-shriek. "What?"

My cheeks burn hot. "I don't know! I've never told you because I thought you'd think I'm completely irrational!"

Jenny throws her head back, her cackle echoing across the walls until I have to laugh my heart out with her. "You thought I, a therapist in the Pacific Northwest, would even *blink* about my client believing in the occult?"

We laugh even harder, Jenny swiping away tears as I'm forced to lean to the side again, tightening my thighs.

"Oh, God, I hope I don't pee again," I rasp.

Gripping my shoulder through hearty giggles, Jenny struggles to quiet herself. "Sorry, sorry. But really, there's no judgment here. No matter what it is."

I sigh. "No, I can see why you thought that—about the cult thing. But I promise you, I've never felt more loved or safer in my community. I've just felt really guilty lying to my therapist about my other interests. Occult-y ones."

Jenny's wavering voice verges on laughter once more, and I have to bite my lip to prevent us from turning into another heap.

"What part of the occult could it be that *I've* never heard of before? Some type of alien summoning?"

I sputter. "*No!* Although, I wouldn't discount it being possible."

Jenny grins and shrugs. "Maybe, maybe not, right?"

I laugh. "Right."

Stroking my belly, I take a soothing breath. But just as my hand sweeps over my bulging belly button, a deep, relentless Braxton Hicks contraction rolls through. But this one feels different than my usual practice contractions: it tightens every muscle deep in my lower spine, taking my breath away.

Jenny is no longer laughing. "Oh, wow, are you okay?"

I nod, but Jenny helps me ease back against the couch cushions. I deepen and slow my breathing, struggling to not be too shocked by the contraction's intensity. Thankfully, it subsides fairly quickly. Blowing out my last deep exhale, I smile. "Yep, we're all good. No, what I'm really interested in is—" I bite my lips, gazing into Jenny's eyes. "What do you think of shapeshifters?"

It's no wonder I spurred on a contraction; my heart pounds hard and heavy, urging Ari to shuffle around again. I'm terrified of what Jenny might say next. What she'll ask, and if I'm making a mistake by sharing something so deep from my heart. So dangerous.

But I want to trust her. I do.

As if her heart answers mine, Jenny grins even wider. "You know, I really think Sasquatch is actually a shapeshifter."

My eyes widen—until I let out a huge laugh.

Jenny does too, but she also scoffs at me. "I'm serious! I swear, I saw this bulky, hairy, *naked* man shift into a hulking black beast, just at the start of your pregnancy—right outside my office window too."

I slap a hand over my mouth, muffling my words. "At the edge of the forest? Across the street?"

As Jenny laughs, her eyes nervously flit between mine. "Does that scare you?"

Holy shit, that's a "yes, across the street." I'm dying to answer her, but I have no idea what the hell to say.

All I can do is mindlink my mate. *Oh Goddess, Noah, she* did *see you shift!*

Noah's wolf freezes in our bond, his tail jutting out perfectly taut. I have to laugh while gasping out of nerves and fear.

But she thinks you're Sasquatch!

Giggles erupt from me uncontrollably as Noah's wolf head quirks in confusion.

Jenny grips her forehead, her smile wider than it's been all day. "Aliya, don't laugh! I'm not kidding!"

I'm near tears. By some miracle, I know exactly how to remedy this situation, shaking my head in an attempt to ease Jenny's worries. "No, no, no, I believe you! I'm just so relieved because I've seen something like that too, and I didn't know who else to tell except Noah and Amy since they're also believers."

"Aww, you could've told me! They don't call us weird here for nothing." Jenny practically bounces on the couch cushions beside me, unaware her excited scent fills the room in front of a shapeshifter's nose. "What did you see? When was it?"

I sigh, shaking my head. "Right before meeting Noah. I saw it in the woods. A big, beast-like thing watching me before another big beast swooped in and saved my life."

Jenny beams, nodding along with me. "Oh, I absolutely believe you. There are weird, unbelievable things in those woods."

40

I can't stop giggling until the end of our appointment, especially because it feels like a weight has been lifted off me.

But as I take the elevator down, I'm surprised to find Noah's parked SUV empty.

I freeze. My soul dampens before it's ripped from safety; I haven't been sensing anything from Noah for at least ten minutes. I didn't think I needed to focus on his emotions.

But the more I pay attention now, the more I realize it's because he's so petrified that he's numb.

Shock courses through my limbs. My purse clatters to the sidewalk, the sharp sound bristling the hairs across every inch of my skin.

All I can sense is my wolf.

She's begging me—urging me—to shift, right in the middle of the street. But I can't let Jenny have another Sasquatch sighting.

With my belly in both hands, I hobble as fast as I can to Noah's driver's side. Ripping open the door, I suck in a deep breath, preparing myself to do the near-impossible; I have to heave myself and my huge stomach up into the tall seat. With my back to the chair, I stretch on my toes, my arms straining behind me as they drag my heavy body toward the driver's seat. I inch higher, step by step, until I can finally collapse into the seat, a gasping, sweaty mess.

I have to both move the chair forward to reach the pedals and move the wheel back to fit our baby. But as I stretch to start the car, my breath cuts short.

Sharp stabbing in my pelvis forces me to wince. I double over myself, whimpering through the pain as a contraction tightens itself all the way to my back.

"Oh, my *God*—" I hiss aloud to the empty car. "Oh, my God." This feels far harsher than any Braxton Hicks contractions I've had thus far. Am I just stressing out my strained body too much, or is this the start of early labor?

But the longer I've taken just to get inside the damn car, the worse this instinct feels in my gut. It's different from OCD's frantic, urgent voice; it's my wolf, demanding I run to protect everything I stand for.

The contraction finally ends, and I let out a slow, heaving breath.

Noah, where are you? My mindlink comes out as desperate as my pulse hammering in my ears.

No answer.

Tuning into our bond, I search Noah out in our bond's inner world as I pull out of the parking spot, frustrated I can't try to smell him while I'm driving.

Or maybe I can.

Rolling down the window, I stick my head out to sniff the wind rushing in, even if I might look crazy.

But Noah isn't far; within milliseconds, I latch onto my most familiar scent.

Quivering as I drive, I swing onto a side street: the shortcut I used to take from preschool to my parents' cabin. The one toward Mrs. Jensen's farm.

Today is one of those Pacific Northwest dark days, appearing as if the sun has almost set when it's only morning. Mrs. Jensen's red barn appears at the end of the road, shining like a deep, bloody beacon beneath the overcast sky's blue-gray hues washing over the horizon.

The second I pull up to her farm, a chill trickles down my spine; the cows are huddled deep into their pen despite the day being young, and there's a huge, black creature hunched in Mrs. Jensen's field—about four acres away.

I don't need to see him up close. I don't even need the glaring proof his scent gives me as it rushes through the car window on the wind. I know him solely by the way he stands.

Noah's wolf.

My heartbeat surges faster as adrenaline bursts through me. Everything feels wrong about how Noah is crouched. I drag myself from the car, breathless as a hard, heavy contraction wracks my body. Curling over myself with a deathgrip on the SUV door, I struggle to catch my breath.

Noah, answer me, right now.

But all bird chirping halts, thrusting Mrs. Jensen's field into pure silence. Except the birds don't fly away.

Just like the cows, they're hiding.

My lungs heave faster, sensing someone is close to death.

It can't be Noah. It better not be Noah.

Shaking through a squat, I drop myself low to the ground, crouching in the brush with my knees splayed wide. But my belly is so big that I can't crawl forward.

I need to reach him. *You're terrifying me.*

Noah doesn't respond.

That's when I smell something putrid. I slam a hand over my mouth, stifling a sharp gag; it's the scent of an old, rotten wolf pelt.

But the rancid scent guides my eyes to the treeline at the edge of Mrs. Jensen's property. That's when I spot the rifle. A man. A fur coat.

Everything clicks into place.

In my heart, I know I'm looking at Jack Hart. And Noah isn't responding because he's 100% wolf and 100% petrified.

As this abusive Alpha who we were convinced would never sacrifice his pride to kill with a gun marches straight for Noah, I know in my heart that Mason's confession was true. This is the man—the Lycan—who joined Mason in shooting our fathers.

But only after traumatizing Noah for life. And I'm willing to bet Noah's trauma was perpetrated, decades in advance, for this exact moment: the moment Jack decides Noah is at his most defenseless, most nervous, and in one of the final days he's alive without an heir. The day Jack Hart can become the top Greenfield Alpha.

❦ **41** ❦

I grip our baby in both palms. It's my sole responsibility to keep them alive.

But as Jack aims at Noah, charging from the forest on human feet to come into range, time slows into the slowest crawl I've ever experienced. Each of my ragged breaths deepen, and instinct silences me as my fangs extend.

Noah's ears perk up. *Oh Goddess, you're here. This is my worst nightmare. You can't die.*

Don't get shot!

Noah bristles. *I can't let him shoot you instead.*

I don't answer; that's exactly how I feel.

Yasmine, we need backup at the Jensens' farm. I'm staring down Jack Hart's barrel, Noah mindlinks Yasmine and me. *Aliya, I love you.*

My heart shatters as despite his fear, Noah rears up in defense, hardening his resolve to face Jack head-on. Blood-curdling panic blasts through the numbness in our bond, along with the deepest, most rageful sadness that steals my breath.

I knew this day was possible. I just didn't want to believe it would come true.

Like his father, Noah is ready to die for his pack. His fearful, yet mortifyingly fierce form ripples, and I grieve every inch of his gorgeous, midnight black fur.

Despite our best laid plans, I race toward him. I won't let him die. I can't.

But I'm too far. I stumble closer, unable to reach him fast enough even if I were to shift.

I know Noah can feel my panic, raising up in snarling, ferocious defense. Despite our best laid plans, he charges at Jack.

That's when I see it; Jack hesitates.

That single, fleeting pause sends my wolf ripping through my human skin. My pregnant belly hangs low as she flies through the field, shifting before I can process her control over me. I haven't sprinted as my wolf like this for months, stumbling as my back legs have to widen to give our baby room. But I need to protect Noah and our baby—no, *all* of our babies.

As Jack raises his gun, Noah's snarl shreds past my pelt, the desperate sound scraping across every inch of my skin.

Jack lifts the rifle to his eye, taking aim. He's ready—steely, weathered eyes intending to rip my mate's life from his wolf's proud body. To steal the Alpha's soul, replacing Noah's title with his.

But Jack is mistaken; this pack has two top Alphas.

And I can run faster than anyone.

Before I've taken another breath through my heaving snout, I burst through the brush at Jack's side, leaping with both paws outstretched. He barely has time to flit his eyes in my direction before one bat of my extended claws slash the entirety of Jack's face and torso, sending him flying into the treeline. His rifle spins across the forest floor, over fifteen feet from where he lands with how hard I hit him.

Skidding back into the brush to hide and assess the damage I've done, I'm startled by how frail Jack felt beneath my furious paws—enough to halt in panic that I've actually killed someone this time. But Jack rolls on the forest floor, his hands muffling his screams as he cups what he can of the blood cascading down his shredded face.

Before I can push my anxious body into moving again, a ginormous black blur whooshes past me, ruffling my fur and sending a chill down my spine. My instincts process before my mind, forcing me to hunker down and take cover in the bushes; this is a predator coming in for the kill.

Noah cracks Jack's ribs beneath his paws as he pins him to the ground, his wolf's growl is more of a roar. I crouch low, sneaking in to hunt Jack alongside Noah.

But my heart rips as I see Jack's hunting pelt close up; multiple hides have been stitched into one reeking, pasted-together shape of a wolf.

Oh, Goddess, how many…? Noah mindlinks my exact thoughts, hesitating as he analyzes Jack's wriggling form. I'm gutted by the aching, horrified disgust in our bond at the sight of the butchered wolf pelts, wishing Noah never had to witness this either. Yet Noah's poor wolf huffs through heavy, distorted breaths like a snarling dragon, his claws digging into Jack's skin through every layer of hardy hunting gear.

Instinct takes over my blurred, gray vision; the next thing I know, I've gathered the neck of Jack's prized pelts between my teeth. Tearing the fur coat off Jack, I whine in agony as Noah holds Jack still for me, pinning him tight to the earth as Jack yelps. The stale furs in my mouth wring my stomach at how these wolves' families must feel. Noah whines between snarls with me, our bond aching as the hides free themselves from Jack's body with a loud *rip*. My wolf shakes her head in disgust as she spits them out, their sour taste lingering on my tongue. The furs fall into a discarded heap on the forest floor.

Exposed and cornered, Jack howls in fear—except it comes out scraping and wrecked from his bloody face, like a wolf bleating its final cry. Fur bursts from his skin, his wolf surfacing out of pure panic.

My stomach churns at the thought of Jack's primal instincts kicking in. Noah has taught me time and time again to never underestimate a wolf's willingness to survive.

If Jack is given the chance to kill first, our entire pack would be at this man's mercy.

Deep down, I know Noah trains to defend us from Jack, and Jack alone. He's fought harder than any wolf he's met, and it shows—his skill crowning him King Alpha of the world. He's strong, and everyone knows it. I know it.

I just never expected Jack to crumble so completely against Noah.

With a single flash of Noah's fangs at Jack's throat, I yelp, terrified Noah broke his own core rule. But as I blink at the aftermath before me, I'm stunned.

Jack's frail black wolf lies limp in Noah's mouth, but he's not dead; Noah holds him by the scruff like he's carrying a feeble pup, leaving Jack to whimper helplessly with exhausted, dangling limbs, his tail tucked so tightly that it nestles against his belly.

There's no question; Jack has given up. A millisecond ago, he represented the unsurmountable fear, murder, and pain he created in Noah for years. All he is now is a heap of an old wolf, stripped of his prized pelt.

$$\infty \sim 42 \sim \infty$$

Holy fucking shit, Aliya, you just kicked his fucking ass. Noah yipes with his mouth full of Jack's scruff, hyper eyes beaming back. *After all those years, we finally caught him! We don't have to worry about this freak anymore—*

A sharp, shrill wolf whine cuts Noah short. Whoever this crying wolf is, they bleat in pain, striking my chest with icy horror.

But Noah's wild, adrenaline-soaked eyes zip between mine, spiking a primal thrill through me.

Oh, that bleating wolf was *me*.

We don't have time to discuss what we're going to do with Jack next; my wolf shakes, hanging her head low as an odd sensation fizzles from the depths of me.

Holy shit, are you— Noah's fur bristles as the heaviest contraction I've ever felt rips through my abdomen, cutting my frantic whine short.

White hot fear blasts through my chest. Am I going into labor?

Wait, no—have I *been* in early labor for a while now, too distracted to recognize it?

As my body wracks with dull, aching waves of pain, I'm almost certain I've skipped a labor stage, launching us forward to the point where I can't breathe through the cramping.

Golden eyes track my every move, Noah's wolf on high alert. *Breathe, Aliya. You're not breathing.*

I can't—

The second my harsh contraction ends, I break into desperate, frantic whines between harsh panting. *Oh, God, Noah. This can't be happening. It hurts badly enough that I'm dying to shift back, but I can't if we're in danger. We finally have Jack, but what if he's calling for backup? What if they take everything from us?*

Aliya, look at me.

The second we meet eyes, I freeze; rustling blasts through the leaves from every direction. My fur stands on end. Was I right, and the Alpha-domination Super Pack is back for more?

But Noah doesn't move. *Don't worry. Just look.*

Plastering myself against his side, I'm tempted to sprint as what must be thousands of wolves approach. But when Noah settles Jack against the forest floor, howls erupt around us. At least twenty wolves snatch Jack from our paws, Yasmine and Dave leading the pack in dogpiling Jack to keep him contained.

Greenfield Pack floods the space around us, surrounding Noah and me with a symphony of victorious howling. As I stare into Noah's eyes, I whine for a new reason.

Despite how much suffering Jack caused Noah, my mate doesn't join in the howling. It's as if Jack is no longer a part of his mind. Not as he stares down at me, his golden eyes squinting and his wagging tail expressing the purest love.

We're not alone in this anymore, Luna. I've got you, you've got me—and they've got us.

He's right; forming a protective circle around us, our pack provides just enough space to keep me comfortable.

Then their howling comes to an abrupt stop. Not a second later, my abdomen tenses, warning of another incoming contraction. I'm stunned; it's like our shifted pack members sensed it was coming, hundreds of restless wolves falling silent as my breathing rate rises.

They're holding space for me.

As Noah's wolf presses his wide forehead into my cramping back, I close my eyes, leaning into his pressure until my wolf lets out a pleased grunt. Smushing himself over my sides, Noah surrounds me with his saccharine, adoring scent—carrying me the rest of the way through the pain.

When my wolf slumps in relief, Noah rumbles deep purrs over me until my hackles lower. *There you go. You can do this, Luna.*

Oh, God. Can I?

Shifting back to my human form, I caress Ari in my massive

belly, terrified. But when I catch a glimpse of my hands, my head reels.

"There's b-blood on me!" As intrusive thoughts surface about Ari getting infected with Jack's blood, I cry out, scrubbing at my skin. "No, I-I want to be in our den— In the n-nest we worked so hard to make, but we're—"

A massive, slobbery tongue stuns me silent, swiping my nude skin free of blood in two seconds. *Then we're going to our den.*

I want to collapse against Noah's fluffy black fur in relief. But poor Ari attempts to make more space for themself, pulling a groan from my lips as they stretch my belly with little feet.

Noah's ears point so sharply towards the sky as he watches our baby wiggle inside me that I have to laugh. He flattens his ears, lifting his big puppy eyes to beam at me. I reach for him, desperate to hug his snout.

But Noah shifts faster than I've ever seen him, his human form catching me in warm, thick arms. Kissing my head over and over, Noah sighs into my hair. "You're the most amazing person alive. I love you."

"I love you too. Thank the Goddess I have you with me right now," I whisper.

Yasmine shifts into her human form, and Noah reaches for her first—desperate to include her in our hug. As his best friend glomps onto him, keeping her touch delicate on my back, Noah's shoulders soften.

When Yasmine pulls back to face us, I clutch her hand tight. "Yas, thank you."

"Holy shit," she giggle-whispers.

Noah lets out a rattling exhale, shaking his head. "I-I know."

"Fuck, I'm trying to stay calm for you, Luna, but I'm sorry— I'm way too excited to meet Little Wolf. Is there anything I can do to help you out?" Yasmine's fanged smile spikes my heart rate; her excitement makes this real. Are we finally about to meet our precious Ari soon?

"Oh, my God. I-I don't know, um—" I stare at Noah in disbelief.

He breaks into a beaming smile, kissing my forehead. "We've got you, Luna. Maybe you can help us to the car, Yas?"

But a familiar voice cries out behind us. "I have blankets, Alpha!"

Mrs. Jensen dashes across her front yard, her white hair blowing in the wind and a stack of blankets up to her chin. I'm not used to seeing fear strike the gentle wrinkles around her eyes, but it's written all over her as she sees me in my disastrous state.

"Oh, *Aliya*. Would you like a nice warm shower before you go, or do you need to hurry to your den?"

My stomach churns. I can't even attempt to smile as a terrifying thought enters my mind; what if we really did skip a stage, and we can't make it to the den in time for me to give birth? That can't be likely, right?

Shit, but didn't I just have another contraction, soon after the last?

"You're okay." Noah rubs my back, softening his voice. "Would you like a nice shower, love? I can hold you."

For some reason, his sweet tone sends me over the edge; I burst into hitching, heavy sobs, my hot breath clouding in the chilly air.

"Oh, my love…" Noah swipes my tears away. "Are you in too much pain?"

Our pack pads closer, the wolves whining and people whispering gentle reassurances. Yasmine joins Noah in wrapping me in a gentle, warm hug, her calming scent washing over us both. I waver between smiling and sobbing, touched by how quiet and calm everyone has grown for my sake.

"Thank you, everyone." I manage to blubber out my words between chattering teeth. "I really want to get clean, actually."

Mrs. Jensen rushes forward, covering me with a blanket. Her calloused hands rub my arms. "It's all okay, sweetie. We'll get you all the help you need."

Noah and Yasmine have to support me by the arms as I whimper on Mrs. Jensen's front porch, the stairs applying extra pressure to my pelvis. I cling to my mate's soft voice. "Breathe, gorgeous. Take it slow. You're doing so well."

We pause in Mrs. Jensen's dim, cozy living room, wiping the grass and dirt off our feet as the old farmer scurries past us with shuffling feet. But when she dashes from the bathroom two seconds later, the water splashing in the distance as the shower heats up, she furrows her brows. "Oh, Alpha, Luna— Don't even worry about that! Half the time, I'm the one bringing the muck in. Come, come—"

Beckoning us down the hall, Mrs. Jensen soothes me with her grandmother-like energy. I can't help but feel like some part of me knew I'd be safe to start early labor in her yard, no matter how stressful the circumstances.

"Thank you so—" I reach for her, pulling her into a hug, but it's quickly interrupted by yet another contraction.

My contorting expression in the mirror strikes me—I'm not only a dirty mess, but as I watch myself stoop in heavy pain, the utter power of my body's efforts hits me all at once, drawing a deep groan from my throat.

Springing into action, Noah kneads heavy, rolling circles over my back. "I've got you. As soon as you can move, let's give you some relief in the warm water."

Clinging to both Mrs. Jensen and my mate, I don't even care that I'm butt-ass naked anymore. Sputtering through the tail end of the contraction, I can't help myself, producing low, humming groans.

Noah and Yasmine meet eyes in the mirror.

"I'll go flag down Amy when she drives up so we can leave right away," Yasmine whispers.

She dashes out without waiting for an answer beyond Noah's quick nod.

"Come on, gorgeous. I'll scrub you down." Noah eases me into the shower, wasting no time in lathering his hands in soap.

But Mrs. Jensen doesn't leave, her brows furrowing as she grips the shower door. "Alpha, those sounds she's making…"

Meeting Noah's eyes, I'm too exhausted to speak. Noah's jaw tenses above me.

"I know," he whispers. "Give me a moment alone with her, please."

As Mrs. Jensen shuffles from the bathroom, shutting the door behind her, Noah gathers my cheeks in his palms.

I grip his hands, my heart surging into a sprint. "I might need someone to check how soon this is happening."

But Noah doesn't respond; as he douses me in warm water, his focus locks onto my lips. Furrowing his brows, he cups my chattering chin in his hand. His eyebrows warp at what he finds, his eyes zipping between mine. "Oh, *sweet girl*, you have labor shakes already. I thought you were cold."

He's right; I can't stop my whole body from shaking, hard.

My chin wobbles in his hand. "Oh, no. Can we even make it back in time?"

Noah swipes my clingy, wet hair off my cheeks, giving me a sad smile. "Hey, it's okay. I've got you. No matter what happens."

Lathering me clean, Noah purrs, attempting to soothe me. But my heart won't stop pounding. Mrs. Jensen was implying I was already making productive labor sounds. Caressing our wiggly baby in my belly, I know my body can hardly handle expanding any further. Ari's cramped and fidgety—and, therefore, ready to meet us as soon as possible. But I couldn't feel more anxious about giving birth in a completely unexpected location.

Before I can catch it, an intrusive thought slips from my lips. "What if I have to squat down in this shower and push them out?"

Noah's purring stops. "Please don't."

Taking one look at his frazzled eyes above me, I burst into laughter. As Noah breaks into a beaming grin, my tension rinses down the drain. Drawing me in as close as he can with my belly in the way, Noah cleans me with careful hands.

"Bend over for me, gorgeous," he whispers. "Put your hands on the wall."

When I plant my hands on the cool tile, Noah positions my lower back underneath the running water. Warmth streams down my back and belly, pulling a pleased hum from my lips as the water relaxes my cramping muscles.

"Good girl," Noah whispers.

I flush, blowing out a slow breath; he normally says those words to me in bed, but they feel just as intimate now, when not even a drop of sexual desire courses between us. This is a different kind of intimacy, Noah remaining ever-present as I trust him to witness the worst physical pain I've ever experienced. And he's happy to, our bond trading silent thank-yous to each other as my heart lightens in his care.

I knew he'd be sweet to me when the time came to give birth, but he's even gentler than I pictured, fluttering my heart with the way he's caring for my laboring body.

It's about to be far more care than he's had to provide on a single day of my pregnancy thus far, and yet, for the first time, I'm not tempted to apologize for all the work he's doing. Instead, I lean into his big hands on my hips as he sways them from side to side, working the ache from me. Massaging my tightened neck muscles, Noah stoops over to meet me, face to face. The second I see him, I lean into his plushy lips, closing my eyes as I sweep my fingernails down his back in gratitude.

Noah's solid hands on me clear my mind, replanting me back in the present. I rest my weight against him, purring and groaning through another contraction before he coaxes me from the shower. Nuzzling into Noah's warmth, I smooth slow, loving touches over his pup in my cramping belly.

"I feel better. Less primal," I whisper, my eyes still closed as Noah towels me off.

Noah places his hands over mine, holding Ari with me. "That's my good girl. The timing between your last three contractions extended a little, so we're all good. Amy will be here with the car soon, and we'll get you right to our den."

Easing my eyes open, I'm delighted by Noah's mushy, adoring scent flooding my senses. Purring, I rub my head in his hands until he buries his fingers into my hair with a low chuckle.

I smile. "I think things sped up when I started panicking. I just can't believe we're doing this, Noah."

"I can't believe it either. My poor Luna; you must've been under so much stress that your body switched into survival mode, preparing to push Ari out as fast as possible. So, now that we're safe and together, let's reframe this change of events, yeah?" Drawing my hands back to my belly between us, Noah softens his voice. "You're about to be holding them in your arms. We're *finally* about to meet them."

Tears flood my vision, but as Noah kisses my wobbly lips, I break our kiss with a giddy, hitching laugh; he felt just as delighted as I did when he said that.

I sigh. "I can't wait to see you holding—"

Gripping Noah's shoulder, I choke out a harsh breath, another contraction hitting just as hard. But now that the vision of Ari has been planted in my mind—our Little Wolf soon to be bundled in their new baby blanket from Lilian and Rainn, the fabric hand-embroidered with chubby wolf pups in a pastel forest—I breathe through the cramping with far greater ease, rubbing my head against Noah's chest.

Okay, maybe this is still happening soon. *Soon* soon. My heart spikes into a sprint.

But Noah's touch remains slow and soothing. "*There* you go. You're doing so well, Luna."

Peppering kisses over my head, Noah flips my heart. He's right; I love his praise. Not just because he uplifts me rather than shuts me down, but because he means every word he utters, his heart spilling over with affection as he holds me.

There's no mistaking how rapidly the pain has intensified, but as I lift my chin, gazing up at my mate in pure exhaustion, all I can do is smile. "You look like a scared dad already."

Breaking into a grin, Noah chuckles against my lips. *You really aren't alone in this, Aliya. You put it the best way once; I'm scared because I care.*

I feel it; the love we're birthing Ari into is so immense, I can't quantify the depths our hearts have expanded for them.

A knock at the door widens Noah's eyes.

"Can I come in?" Amy's familiar voice inspires a fresh wave of emotion.

When Noah opens the door, the first flash of red hair softens my shoulders; I almost forgot Noah's reminder in Mrs. Jensen's yard. The two of us aren't doing this alone, either.

"A," I huff, reaching for my best friend.

"Oh, *babe.*" Opening her arms, Amy dashes for me.

But as soon as I take one step from Noah's embrace, a bucket's worth of fluid splashes from between my legs, all over Mrs. Jensen's bathroom tile—and just as Mrs. Jensen pokes her head in.

Noah's and Amy's jaws drop in unison.

I yelp. "Oh, my *God—*"

Amy meets my bulging stare, her voice wobbling with laughter. "Girl, here I was, about to ask if you wanted your underwear—"

I sputter out a shocked laugh. "S-sorry! I— I didn't pee, I—"

Mrs. Jensen beams. "Oh, don't you worry! I'm so blessed to have our darling Luna's water break in my home!"

Biting back laughter, Noah grips me to keep me upright. "Thank you, Mrs.—"

Mrs. Jensen smacks Noah's arm. "Don't laugh, Alpha! It's a beautiful thing!"

"Sorry, sorry," Noah giggles, cuddling me close. "Come on, Luna—"

Noah can't finish his sentence, hissing beneath his breath as my claws extend on instinct, digging into his skin. "Shit, are you—"

I let out a sharp cry, doubling over as Amy and Noah support my arms; if I thought my contractions hurt pre-water break, this one rips through me, bringing tears to my eyes. Clasping my tensing belly in both hands, I blow out strained, shaky breaths.

Yasmine's head pokes in. "How's it going?"

"It's hurting *way* worse." Noah's voice trembles as he speaks my thoughts. It's the first hint of fear I've heard in his tone since this began.

"Yep, we're leaving!" Amy hoists my birth bag over her shoulder, backing through the door. "I've got the minivan, Alpha."

"Thank the Goddess," Noah mutters. "We're getting you to the den, Luna."

Nodding, I huff through a surge of anxiety; I have an indescribable feeling we'll be holding Ari soon.

❧ 43 ❦

By the time everyone helps me hobble out to Amy's minivan, another contraction stops us at the doors. But with Noah's coziest black T-shirt draped around me, hugging my tensing belly along with the hands of my dearest people, I close my eyes, breathing through it. Noah pre-scented the T-shirt for my birth bag, leaving it with the sweetest blend of excitement, adoration, and calming comfort for me, but I don't need it as much as I expected to; the gorgeous, flowery blend of my best friends rooting for me smell just as delightful, ending each vicious contraction with pleased tingles down my spine.

In the back of Amy's minivan, I nuzzle against Noah's shoulder, phasing in and out of awareness of the outside world as instinct overcomes me. Kira and Amy chat in the front of the van, their voices low and soothing as they escort us safely to our den. Yasmine leaves us be for the most part, only chiming in with quiet jokes that ease the tension between Noah's brows. Noah's palm sweeps circles over my belly, loving on Ari with me.

But his breath quivers as he kisses my head.

Stopping his hand low on my belly, I laze my eyes open. Swollen, terrified eyes stare back. But for some reason, I don't lapse into fear with him.

Giving Noah a soft smile, I brush the tip of his nose with mine. "I'm in pain, but I want to be for this pup you've given me. Thank you."

Noah's chin quivers just before I kiss him, tugging at my heartstrings. As his hand immerses itself in my hair, drawing me into a deeper kiss, my stomach flips at the cushy pressure of his swollen lips; he's gentle with my body, but not my mouth, his tenderness encompassing my being with his love. I hum in bliss, urging him closer. When my belly tightens beneath his palm, Noah flinches, tempted to pull back. But I lean in, kissing him harder.

Huffing through the pain with our lips locked, I cup Noah's sweet face. Noah's tears slip down my palm, but Noah pulls me in tighter, his breath hitching as his mouth opens for a deeper, tonguing kiss.

I know you signed up for this, and so did I, but it kills me to watch you suffering in my arms when I can't do anything. I love you more than anything. My poor mate whimpers against my lips, the desperate sound squeezing my heart.

Breaking our kiss, I heave through the end of the contraction, pressing our foreheads together. *Feel into me, Noah. I was so scared earlier, but I'm in some sort of meditative, determined state now—all thanks to your love.*

Noah lets out a sharp exhale. I open my eyes to find him gushing with tears around a wobbly smile.

Caressing his wet cheek, I nod. *We're okay. And I just love you to pieces. My heart can hardly contain it already, so I can't imagine how striking it's about to be to see you holding our child. You reminded me to think of Ari, so it's my turn: let's think of them together.*

"Thank you," he whispers against my lips, giving me another soft kiss. Scooting in as close as he can in the back seat, Noah cuddles me as devotedly as he cradles Ari in our bond, his wolf panting with nerves between licking Ari's little soul with soft, adoring whines.

I stare into Noah's eyes, clinging to his hands. His unwavering faith in my strength outweighs his fear, his wolf shining through as he coaxes me through it. Every inch of me loves him. Ari isn't here yet, but I see someone new in Noah already—the sweet father of our Little Wolf. Beside him, I can manage this.

I can't bear to let go of Noah, not even after we successfully exit the minivan. It's a slow, agonizing walk, leaving me a mere minute or two to hobble forward before I stoop against a tree to shudder through another contraction. I've never felt pain to such an unbearable degree, unable to keep from screaming.

But my dearest friends aren't deterred.

"Goddess, you're fucking incredible." Noah massages me all over.

Amy rubs my back with him. "Seriously. You're a goddamn rockstar, A."

Yasmine chuckles. "I'm honestly afraid of how tough Ari is going to be."

"Dude, same, what the fuck," Kira hisses.

Our soft giggling fills the forest, replacing my wails from moments prior.

"I love you all so damn much," I breathe.

But the second we find Rainn and Lilian waiting at our den's entrance with excited smiles, sadness caves my chest in.

I wish Mom and Dad were standing there too. And I wish Noah had his dad to guide him through his first day as a father holding his child.

A tremendous sorrow crashes through our bond. Noah sucks in a tight breath, his arm stiff against my back.

Oh, Aliya… Are you—

Before Noah can finish his thoughts, Rainn snuggles up to his arm. "My big brother!"

Breaking into a smile, Noah nuzzles her head. "Hey, Rainn."

Rainn gives my hand a soft squeeze. "I've been so excited to see you both. I've heard how far you're progressing, Luna! You're doing so well!"

Lilian steadies me as she guides us around a boulder. "You are. I'm *so* proud of you both."

My shoulders soften. I don't have my parents, and Ritchie isn't with us, but Yasmine and Amy provide us with laughter, Rainn fills any space she enters with joy, and Lilian's soothing, nurturing scent fills just enough of the gap in my heart to carry me through.

But at the den's threshold, I freeze; Noah's newly-cooled exterior breaks into wracking tears.

Lilian's eyebrows arch. "Oh, my sweet—" Lilian reaches for Noah, pulling him into a hug. She kisses his head, over and over. "You're doing so well too, sweetheart."

Noah sobs against her shoulder, flipping my heart; I've never seen him trust her like this. But now that I am, tears slip down my cheeks.

"I don't know how to help her well enough, Mom. I just love her so much." Noah's voice comes out shattered, tearing at my core.

I grip Amy's hand tighter, unable to stabilize my breath. Noah might think I'm struggling through this alone, but with how deeply our souls have intertwined, I can feel my mate working through his own birthing process.

And Lilian holds her son through it. Releasing a wave of nurturing, soothing love in her scent, Lilian draws a helpless whimper from Noah's lips.

But I can feel the relief she provides his sore heart, stunning me speechless.

For the first time, I see it: I've been so worried about all the ways I could accidentally hurt dear Ari once they're born that I almost forgot how deeply I can help Ari feel loved.

Lilian's softened voice lowers Noah's shoulders. "You're going to keep being there for her, just like you're already doing, right? That's what she needs from you most, so you're doing just fine. It's all going to be okay. You'll both be okay."

"Okay. Okay, thank you." Noah nods, blowing out a slow breath. When he turns to me, his eyebrows arch once more. "I just love her with my whole heart. I can't believe I'm lucky enough to hold her pup."

"Oh, *honey*…" Lilian strokes his back. But as I waddle closer, Noah's tearful expression warms into a weary smile. We reach for each other, pulling each other into a tight embrace.

"I adore you," I whisper.

"I love you too—" Noah tenses as my forehead warps in pain, my next contraction hitting me hard and fast. "Oh, shit. Breathe, Aliya."

Sputtering out a short, fast breath, I clutch Noah's shoulders as hard as I can. But it's not enough; grabbing fistfuls of his shirt, I let out a heaving, low groan as my whole body tenses. A force beyond my control sends an undulating motion down my body, impelling me to stoop over and produce low humming sounds I've never heard from myself.

As Noah holds my hips steady, his refreshed mindset shines through his soft-spoken words against my ear. "Good girl. Good, you're doing so well."

But as my body bears down, forcing me to tense my stomach as if it's preparing to push, fear strikes my heart. My eyes jolt open, my active labor groans morphing into a cry.

Rainn gasps, and Lilian rubs my shoulder. "Oh sweetheart, take it easy, if you can."

I shake my head, coming up for air with heaving, groaning breaths.

Noah grasps my cheeks. "Hey, hey— You're okay. You've got this."

I shake my head again, gripping his hands. "What if I can't do this? I don't think I can, I—"

"Oh, A…" Amy's careful touch as she tucks my hair behind my ear sends me into panting moans—one contraction only leading to the next.

But Rainn rubs my back. "Wait, this is such a good sign! That means you're almost through it—this is just the toughest part before they're here."

I suck in a tight breath.

She's right; I feel it in my soul.

Gripping Noah's taut arms, I gaze up at him. "Oh, my God, Noah."

"Holy shit." Noah's eyes are as wide as mine, a hint of golden peeking through his teal irises telling me this reality is hitting his soul just as deeply as mine. He lets out a breathy sigh, kissing me with careful, quick pecks. "Goddess, *Aliya*—" He kisses me harder before leading me to our nest. "You're so beautiful—" His voice quivers through awe, pulling a touched whimper from my lips. "I'm so fucking proud of you, I can't believe it."

Despite my fear, the most vivid excitement I've ever felt in my body restarts my labor shakes, vibrating my body in Noah's arms.

Noah's chest tightens against my cheek. "Shit, let's get you laying down in your nest."

"I was about to say—" Rainn trails off as I speed-waddle from her side.

No one has to convince me to move: some sort of knowing guides me, urging me to pull my mate to my nest.

"Good girl. Follow your instincts." Noah's purring voice sends a pleased shiver down my spine.

With our hands clasped tight, we step into our nest, our dearest loved ones easing my body into a cushy blanket pile. No one has disturbed my nest—not even Natalia, our Pack Doctor waiting here with a bright smile despite her busy schedule.

This task feels like an insurmountable mountain trail, stretching miles above my head. Yet it's here. My body is ready to bring Ari into the world.

I'm tempted to slip into fear, an icy chill striking my core at all that could go wrong.

But my wolf takes full control. Noah attempts to get behind me to hold me through active labor, but my wolf is adamant I remain on my side, clutching Noah tight.

"I can't let go of you. Lay with me." Nuzzling into Noah's chest, I purr through my tightening abdomen.

"Okay. I've got you." Noah holds my waist steady.

I blow out steady currents of air against his chest, my belly tensing as another wave drags my belly down, down, down. I have no qualms about yelling my heart out, the sharpest pressure I've felt yet weighing down on my pelvis.

"Holy shit, this is happening. I can feel it too," Noah whispers.

My heart spikes in both excitement and fear as Natalia lifts my thigh.

"Pardon me, Luna. Let me make sure you're not straining—Oh!"

My heart flips as I glance between my legs to find Natalia beaming.

But it's Amy's delighted cry of joy that sends a thrill through my chest. "*Aliya*— I can see their head!"

Rainn's laugh is wet with giddy tears. "They have a ton of hair!"

Meeting Noah's startled eyes, I shake my head in disbelief. Noah pants alongside me, readjusting his clammy grip on my waist. Tears prick the corners of his eyes as he strokes my sweaty hair off my forehead. "Goddess, Aliya. You're the most incredible wolf—"

I cut off his words with a sharp cry, my features contorting as my body tenses.

Noah presses his forehead against mine. "You're so fucking powerful. Good job, sweet girl—"

But my eyes zip open. I force my claws to unlatch from poor Noah's arm, panting through each breath. "Noah, please—"

"Please, what?"

"I want you to be the first to hold Ari. I want you to catch them."

Noah's breath hitches. His eyes race between mine, torn between fear and absolute gratitude. "Oh, *Aliya*— A-are you sure—"

I break into a strangled groan. "Right now, Noah—"

"Oh my—" Noah cradles my sweaty head to his chest, his breath just as rapid as mine. "Someone hold her for me, please."

I reach for my best friend, only to find Amy teary-eyed with the brightest smile. As Noah trades places with her, Natalia leaving room for him between my knees, Amy dashes for me, hugging me to her chest.

Her voice buzzes against my ear, steady despite her pounding heart. "I've got you, A."

Instinct draws me to all fours. Amy joins me, allowing me to stand on my knees and hang my arms over her shoulders.

Noah's hot, wide palms sweep down my rippling back, following my rocking motions as I moan through searing pain. "Good, good girl— Oh, Goddess, Aliya, I see them too—"

The loving whimper in his voice radiates through me as my body bears down once more, everyone's hands on me just as encouraging as they are soothing; we're so loved. And by proxy, so is Ari.

Amy kisses the top of my head. "They're almost here, babe! You've got this—"

I press against her, unable to keep myself from screaming. The sound echoes throughout the den as Noah gasps behind me, his happiness in our bond bolstering my power. Natalia gives quick, rushed instructions in his ear as I check behind myself, fury striking my chest as a sudden pinch blasts up my spine.

"Sorry, gorgeous, sorry— I know it hurts, sweet Omega, we just have to turn Ari—" Noah doesn't meet my eyes until I groan, relieved they've finally stopped easing Ari into position to birth their shoulders. "I see their sweet face, Aliya. They have your beautiful lips."

The amazement in Noah's tearful smile stirs a renewed determination within me. I want to witness the love on his face when he holds them. I *need* to.

"You can do this," Amy whispers into my ear.

For the first time today, I nod in agreement—just before I bear down once more. I've never felt tearing pain like this, my body screaming alongside me like it's ripping in half. But Noah's thumbs massage me tenderly through my cries—until a small pop of Ari's shoulder slips from me.

I release a heaving sigh, a wave of relief washing down me as Ari slips from my body, caught by big, adoring hands.

Noah's emotions hit me before I can turn around to look at him, a chorus of our loved ones crying alongside his singing heart. When I flip over my shoulder, watching my weeping mate clear our baby's airway with his pinky finger, I witness the purest joy ease his frightened features, leaving the tenderest of love in its place. As Ari's first cry echoes throughout the den, spurring on a cheer, I burst into smiling, euphoric tears, gripping my heart as I breathe through the deepest love I've ever felt. Every inch of Ari is beautiful. Their flailing, tiny limbs are met by massive, loving hands, cocooning their startled body safely in Noah's arms. He stoops over, kissing their wet head with trembling lips.

Noah's aching voice comes out delicate. "Oh, I *love* them, Aliya."

Reaching for Ari, I'm overcome by hitching, giddy sobs as Noah eases our crying baby against my chest. When we learned about Lycan births, I was so afraid this portion would feel unnatural to me, ruining our joy. But as instinct urges me to lick Ari clean, serenity fills me; Noah and I bathe Ari's body together, preparing their skin for our loving touch throughout the rest of our lives. To my purest delight, Ari's tensed limbs soften beneath our tongues. I nuzzle them all over, wanting nothing but for them to feel at peace.

Noah shakes just as heavily as I do as he returns me to his lap, adrenaline thumping his heart against my back. As I clutch his sweet pup to my chest, I don't know where to look; everywhere I turn, there's someone I adore. Pulling Noah in for a deep kiss, I smile against his lips, snuggling Ari in our warmth as our friends drape us in cozy blankets. Noah's bare chest is hot against my back as Rainn and Amy help us undress, allowing us to cuddle Ari skin-to-skin.

"They're a whole eleven pounds, two ounces, King Luna," Natalia whispers.

Noah's jaw drops, and everyone's smiling, crying faces break into hushed laughter alongside us.

But as I look down, my heart skyrockets into my throat.

I didn't think our huge wolf baby would open their eyes so soon, but as Ari's cries ease into disgruntled coos, their grumpy little frown softens, revealing furious, dark brown eyes. Ari's vivid expression of disappointment in the cold, bright world spurs the freshest laughter from my chest.

"Oh, *Goddess*—" Noah whisper-laughs with me. We coo in adoration as Ari smacks their lips, their eyes lazing shut once more.

Noah's fingertips sweep over Ari's dark, thick hair as he sighs. "Well, shit. You don't ever need to worry about protecting this gorgeous pup alone. I'd die for either of you without a second thought."

I scowl, glaring at him over my shoulder. "Please, do not, Noah Greenfield."

Breaking into soft giggles, Noah kisses my temple. "Trust me, I wouldn't want to let you go, Luna. Especially now that I've seen just as angry of a little frown on your pup's face. I have a new sweet Omega to love now—well, as long as they still feel like they're an Omega, that is. They certainly smell like one, and it's—"

I hadn't processed it yet, but he's right; Ari's scent has Noah's most beautiful flowery hum to it, but with a spicy hint of jasmine. As Noah breaks into overjoyed, touched tears, I draw him in for a kiss, my eyes watering alongside his.

They're gorgeous, Noah. They remind me so much of the beauty I see in you.

As if he can't help himself, Noah releases the most delicious cinnamon-sweet Omega scent, filling the air with soothing comfort. As Ari's little body softens in my arms, easing their

furrowed expression into relaxed bliss, my soul reels in awe. I have two sweet Omegas now too; after all the abuse Noah's wolf has faced, he's holding our Omega pup so tenderly. I can't help but think that by holding our Ari, Noah's also cradling the Omega side of his wolf. The one that saved him, then saved us all.

As Ari snuggles into us, limp in relief to be warm once more, I can't stop kissing their soft little head, breathing in their sweet scent. Closing my eyes, I dive into our inner world. There, I'm stunned by what I find.

There aren't two of us here; there's three. The teeniest lump of fluff against Noah's fur is all I can see at first, excitement racing down my spine. My wolf nibbles at Noah's neck, her tail swinging wildly despite her exhaustion—rejoicing in Ari's newly solid presence. But when I finally see them up close, I can hardly breathe through how cute our pup is.

Hiding within Noah's fluffy, black belly fur, tufts of gray and black downy fuzz poke out in every direction. The littlest ears I've ever seen stick up, paws flopping like they don't know how to orient themselves just yet. As Ari lets out a squeaky whine, Noah's and my wolf break into a pant, overflowing with adoration. No matter how hard Noah tries to calm his vibrating wolf, Ari's tiny body excites their father into uncontainable tail wags.

Opening my eyes, I'm delighted to find Noah's slow, pleased blinks staring back.

After giving us our moment, Lilian, Rainn, Amy, Kira, Yasmine, and Dave take their turns stroking Ari's little tuft of black hair, sharing birthday wishes and telling them how much they're loved.

I pictured our little family as Noah, Ari, and me, but now that I see everyone together to celebrate this new pup in our arms, I realize they have the biggest, warmest family I've ever met, extending to the stranger wolves taking turns guarding our peace outside our den as the year's very first snowfall mutes the forest into a soothing silence.

I'm awestruck. I never thought this could happen to me. Not only to finally have a chance to give birth and raise the baby I've always wanted, but to also have such a loving community surrounding them from the second they're born.

There's not a moment Ari isn't cuddled—not even as Noah gently massages my belly through the afterbirth process, breathing through the last remnants of pain with me as we gaze into each other's eyes. My soul has placed full trust in him, my body loose and limber in his loving touch. Between tracking our newborn, golden, alert eyes stare back at me, Noah breaking into a touched, weepy smile whenever he sees my face.

Sweeping my forehead free of stray hairs, Noah drinks me in with his roaming stare. "You look so peaceful. I didn't think you could be, after all that."

"I'm madly in love," I whisper. "And I'm in love with how much you've fallen in love today too. I've never felt us so happy, Noah."

Shaking his head through a gushing smile, Noah sighs against my lips. "Me neither. You've given me the best day of my life, over and over again. Even just holding you in my arms makes me feel like every struggle in my life has been worth it, but now you've given me a whole other person to hold? You've really outdone yourself this time, Luna."

I giggle through fresh tears. "So have you, my King. And I'd do it all over again for you… But maybe in a few years."

Noah's bright laugh floats my heart to the ceiling, his vivid smile nourishing my soul.

And now I have his pup to hold too.

I can't wait to spend every day of the rest of my life loving Ari's sweet soul alongside Noah's. As Amy returns Ari to our arms, I'm beautifully overwhelmed—Ari's entire existence containing every droplet of cuteness I could ever imagine within one tiny body, and Noah's pupils expanding in adoration as he bundles our pup against his heart.

But as Ari's emotions melt into a steady, thrumming comfort, some part of them recognizing our familiar safety, I'm in awe of us; we create the deepest peace in this little being, even though we've only just officially met. All we're doing is holding them, nurturing them with milk and kisses, but that's enough for Ari to feel safe.

The power behind this thought startles me. For most of my life, I thought I had to be perfect. Really, I just had to be here.

It hits me then; my love has grown for someone else here too.

My wolf nestles deep in my heart in pure glee, immeasurable love surrounding her from every angle.

I adore her. I worship her guiding presence, and the beauty she brings out in me. Her strength is mine, and mine hers. I love being Ari's mother, Noah's mate, and our pack's King Luna alongside my King Alpha, and it's all thanks to her. I'm so proud of her for drawing out the courage within me to be myself, and I'm proud of me for trusting her, taking the leap to exist as myself—no matter how imperfect I still may feel.

Despite never having the courage to believe it before, it's true: I love myself.

I can't wait to teach Ari how lovable they are too.

$$\text{44}$$

Easing my hands beneath Ari in Noah's arms, I nestle our bundled pup in their crib. Within six months, Ari has grown into the squishiest, cutest little being I've ever witnessed in my life, their mittened hands rubbing over their cheeks every time they wake up and their gummy smile sending my wolf into zoomies in our bond. Tonight, sleepiness overcomes their whole body, one cheek still red from snuggling against Noah's warm chest. Their tranquil scent soothes my heart. As Noah and I gaze in absolute awe over them, just like the day we brought them home for the first time, Noah's warm palm on my lower back helps me feel just as cocooned and safe as Ari seems.

I bite my lip, gazing up at Noah's doting eyes over our pup. Adoration pours through me at the emotion in my mate's eyes—a love for our pup that only grows every day.

It makes me want him.

Noah straightens at the hint of desire in our bond, his eyes zipping to mine. With my palms settling against his chest, I stretch on my toes to kiss Noah as quietly as possible. Noah leans into my kiss, pushing a yearning ache through my core. I cup his cheeks, kissing him even harder between desperate breaths.

We haven't had penetrative sex since I gave birth, but I've told Noah I'm tempted to try tonight. Even as Ari has been sleeping on Noah, I've been planting sneaky kisses all over Noah's arms, shoulders, and cheeks, unable to stop loving on him.

So the second we're certain Ari is asleep in their crib, Noah draws closer, immersing me in an eager musk. I breathe him in, my wolf puffing her chest in pride at how riled up she's made her mate.

Lacing his palms beneath my ass, Noah hoists my thighs around his waist, moving smoothly to stay as quiet as possible.

After carrying me down the hall in silence, Noah shuts our bedroom door behind us with a soft *click*, careful not to wake Ari. But as we stare into each other's eyes, listening in for any sign of our little Omega stirring, my heartbeat picks up the pace.

Teal irises swirl into a light green before my eyes, taking my breath away; Noah looks ready to pounce.

But I don't feel a drop of pressure. I feel desired, washing away every concern I've had about my ever-changing postpartum body.

Easing his lips against mine, Noah gives me a whole-body kiss, pressing tighter against me as our mouths glide over each other. We keep ourselves hushed, but our bond fills the silence in my mind, erupting with a melodic, sugary lust.

Our emotions course through my blood, but their intensity doesn't fully hit me until Noah drops me onto the bed on my back, his hands splayed beside my shoulders. Dragging his stare down my body, Noah drinks me in.

"Beautiful." Noah's quiet, rumbling voice makes me shudder.

We take a moment to stare at each other—holding each other's cheeks, tracing each other's collarbones, and absorbing every minor emotion flickering through our bond.

"Noah, you make me feel at peace," I whisper.

His eyebrows warp as our bond swirls. Dropping to his elbows, Noah laces our body heat together. I hum as he settles into my lips.

You make me want to be seen, Noah mindlinks.

We roll into each other at the same time, my hands roaming Noah's back as he hikes my thigh higher on his hip. The mattress creaks as Noah grinds me into the edge of the bed, our lips colliding faster by the second.

But after a few tongue-heavy kisses, Noah stops.

Pulling back, Noah drags his cold nose down my bare sternum. His hot breath skates down my center, blowing soft currents of warmth down my chest until he pauses at my abdomen. Holding my hips in place, Noah lifts the edge of my shirt to kiss my loose stomach, every inch of my skin coated in stretch marks.

Noah's eyes flit up to mine at my flood of shyness in our bond, but Noah's purr sends another wave of heat to my groin.

He whispers against my skin. "Please, don't be hard on yourself. This gorgeous body gave life to our child, and there's nothing I can do that will ever thank it enough."

My heart flips. "N-Noah…"

His kisses dip lower, stopping just above my clit. Warm hands skate further up my shirt, rolling it over my breasts.

With Noah's gentle kisses over my breasts, my breath hitches. I immerse my fingers in Noah's hair just as his hands skate back down, easing my pajama shorts off my hips with my panties inside. The tip of his cold nose barely brushes my inner thigh, and I widen my knees, my heartbeat throbbing throughout every limb.

Noah's soft purr rumbles over my clit, and I suck in a sharp breath.

His eyes zip to mine, staring straight into my soul as he kisses my wet core. I clench with desire. His tenderness makes his every touch hotter, a heartbeat forming between my legs.

"I meant it, gorgeous Luna. You're my true King," Noah whispers.

My body flushes, fuzzy warmth cascading across my skin. "You're *my* true King, forever, Noah, no matter what anyone says. And for the record, your Omega side coming out to dote over Ari is the most beautiful thing I've ever seen."

Noah hums, giving me a slow kiss on my sensitive core. My knees squeeze his shoulders on their own, wetness pooling beneath my cheeks with the rush of pleasure he gives me. He's hardly even touched me yet, but I'm coming unraveled for him.

But I know Noah is enjoying himself just as much, drinking up my yearning breaths with low purrs. "You need this attention tonight, don't you?"

My soft whimper says enough, but my hips squirm at the thought of his hands, lips, and body on mine.

"Please," I whisper. "I've missed you while we've been so busy and exhausted."

"You don't have to beg me, my love. I've missed you too. And I want to take my time mating you until you're so relaxed that you can finally get some deep sleep. Would you like me to please you with my tongue first to hold you over?"

My heart flips. "Yes. But even if it helps me last longer after, I don't think I'll last long now."

Noah draws a deep, heated breath, allowing his exhale to skate over my bare skin through his nose. Desire coats our bond, making me shiver twice as hard as his breath continues to stimulate me.

Just when goosebumps reach my nipples, Noah's lips caress my soaked labia, making me jolt with pleasure.

His eyes flit up to mine, green with half-shifted lust. "Too much?"

"It's good today. So good that I can't hold still."

The second I say this, Noah kisses my pussy again. But this time, it's slow and tender, the crawl of his lips easing over my sensitive skin.

Goosebumps wrack my body, devouring my skin until I'm red-hot.

Oh, my God. My hormones are in full force, almost heat-like. It's the first time Noah has brought me to heat since I had Ari.

And Noah can certainly smell it, letting out a low, pleased purr. I sputter out a gasp at the vibration against my clit, but Noah doesn't give me a second to process how good it feels—he cups my ass in one palm, holding my wriggling hips in the other with a firm but loving grasp as he kisses me again and again, dragging more fluid from my core.

I can't stop the heat from talking. "M-more— Please, please—"

Noah growls, unsatisfied that he's making me beg. But the frustrated glint in his eyes only excites my wolf, lifting my hips to his mouth. His kisses morph into tonguing makeouts with my pussy, his breath colliding against my clit in pumping bursts between each lick. My legs shake beside his cheeks, my body rocking over his face.

I can hardly breathe through pleading moans. "Oh— Oh!"

Noah's tongue slathers every inch of my pussy, dragging back and forth until I'm soaked. My thighs widen as far as they can stretch. No matter how hard I want to rub my pussy all over his lips, my back keeps arching up off the bed in delight—until

I squirt hard, my orgasm surprising me with a vibrant burst of pleasure.

Noah holds my bucking hips in both hands, worshiping me with his tongue as it speeds across my flexing core. He drinks up the entirety of my orgasm, his low, needy growls buzzing my clit so deliciously that I grip his hair harder than I mean to, crying out in delight.

I collapse back onto the mattress, struggling to catch my breath. But when Noah stands, towering over me at the bedside, he's faring worse than me: the front of sweatpants stretches to its limits, forcing him to wince as he adjusts his eager shaft.

And I want to blow him more than ever.

I grip his hips with my thighs, locking my ankles behind them to draw him closer. Noah swipes his hand over his wet lips, stumbling forward as his chest heaves to catch his breath.

"Can I lick you into lasting longer too?" I ask.

Noah steadies his breath, still licking the taste of me off his lips. "Fuck, I-I'd like that."

I bite back my smile. Noah freezes, sensing I'm about to pounce.

Hoisting myself up on shaky arms, I flounder on my way to him. We both laugh at my wiggly limbs, still weak with how heavily Noah pleasured me. He helps me reposition myself onto my knees, and I bend to kiss his shaft. Noah's warm hand skates down my spine, my shirt still hiked over my breasts and leaving my lower back exposed.

I can't contain my yearning for Noah. I want him to feel how much I cherish him. How connected I feel to him.

But Noah doesn't expect the fervor in me; his lungs hitch as I drag my tongue over his cock, loving his soft warmth against my lips. I coat all of him in my affection, massaging the sensitive underside of his shaft with my thumbs to hold it in place for what I really want to do—kiss the fluid from his leaking tip.

As I stroke him, I kiss his reddening glans, again and again, until his hips jerk from the sensitivity he must feel, gripping my hips to stabilize himself. I purr, satisfied by how desperate he sounds. But that only makes Noah grip my pelvis tighter.

My pussy clenches, craving more of his reaction. I suckle my lips over his swelling shaft, applying soft pressure over it until his entire tip slips past them. I greet it with soft teases from my tongue. My eyelids flutter shut at the pleasure humming through our bond, Noah's shaky breath warning of how good he feels even though I've just started. Noah stoops over the bedside, his knees shaking. It only encourages my tongue to work faster. Harder.

I purr around his warm tip, drawing him deeper, and he huffs, jerking further into me. His tip brushes my soft palate on its own accord, forcing me to swallow hard.

Heat pools in my groin, building into a marvelous ache. It only makes me moan around his bulging tip again, spurring Noah into heavy, unrestrained groans.

Noah's stomach shudders against my head as I pull him as deep as I can. "O-oh, my fucking—"

Let yourself enjoy it, Alpha. I won't let it hurt me.

He softens his tense abdomen, flexing into my lips as they skate back over the end of his tip to catch my breath, giving him quick kisses.

But when I bob back down this time, I take him as far as I can stretch my jaws, holding him there. I swallow back spit, my eyes watering at how massive he is. But this makes Noah whimper out a moan, his torso squirming on the edge of release.

"Fuck, fuck, fuck—"

I hurriedly pull back, suckling over his tip. Using my leftover saliva dripping down his shaft, I stroke every inch of it, deepening my massage.

Noah groans, hardly able to keep himself from fucking my mouth as I suck faster and faster—until he can't take it anymore. Hot fluid spurts into my mouth, cutting off my breath as it spills from my lips before I can swallow it all.

By the time Noah stops moving, his gasps are raspy and heaving. And my groin aches with an intense need for my mate.

"O-oh, fuck, Luna, I—" Noah's voice shakes as he lifts my chin to gaze into my eyes.

When I meet his darkened cheeks and heavy-lidded stare above me, I shiver with excitement, knowing I made him feel just as good as intended.

A sly smile creeps over his face. "My feisty, feisty Luna. Let's clean those gorgeous lips."

I flop back onto the mattress, partly in submission as my wolf begs me to roll over for Noah. He pauses, taking in the sight. His smile is replaced by a serious, focused growl, leaving no inch of my body untouched by his stare.

As his big thumbpad swipes his cum from my lips, I skate my fingertips up his chest. He relaxes over me, his wet cock pulsing with arousal against my belly all over again.

Except this time, his muscles are fluid, his shoulders drooping over mine in a low prowl as he stoops to kiss me. Noah's lips are relaxed and pliable, filling our bond with absolute adoration for me.

But their tingly pressure against my swollen lips also fills me with a need I can't ignore.

"I want you inside of me."

My whisper escapes on its own, but I'm not embarrassed in the least. My limbs are loose and eager for Noah, my fingertips massaging his scalp until he lets out a hungry growl.

Then he suddenly tugs my hips off the edge of the bed.

"Oh! Noah!?" I burst into giggles, but Noah captures my lips with a mischievous smile.

I melt into him with a happy hum. His kisses spread soothing tingles down my neck and breasts, tickling down to my toes.

Kneeling at the edge of our bed, Noah settles me onto his lap, compressing me against the side of our mattress. We've kissed millions of times, but the cushy pressure of his lips feels so good tonight that when Noah pauses, too distracted by reaching for a condom, I steal his searching hand to cup it around my ass.

He chuckles, nuzzling my nose. "Feisty, feisty Luna. I'm not forgetting about you. Come here."

Smashing his lips into mine, Noah gives my ass a hard squeeze. I cup his cheek through a moan, kissing him even harder. Keeping Noah locked into our kiss, I dig through his bedside drawer with one hand, the other tracing teasing strokes up and down the length of his flexing shaft. It bobs harder and harder, nudging the condom as I slip it on. But when I lift my hips, walking my knees around Noah's thighs to straddle his covered shaft, Noah slides his fingertips up my inner thigh to toy with my wet core.

"Mmm!" I lean into our kiss, my shoulders raising as Noah swirls thick fingers between my legs.

He's so gentle that his touch feels even stronger, sparking warmth up my belly until I quiver through each breath. My pelvis presses down into him for heavier pressure. And Noah really gives it to me—all four fingers rubbing fast circles until my pussy gapes, begging him to enter me. With a harsh breath against my lips, Noah dips his fingers deep inside me, curling against my inner walls. I smash myself against his torso, desperate to plaster myself to him. My knees close in on his hips in an attempt to squeeze his wrist between my thighs, my pussy aching with want.

Noah slows, releasing a burst of soothing Omega scent. "Relax for me, gorgeous. It's been a while."

Nodding, I let out a pleased sigh. I focus on sinking into Noah's touch, allowing my open mouth to rub against his lips as my eyes laze shut.

"Fuck, there you go, Luna. You're doing such a good job."

Noah switches from slow teases to tender presses into my pussy. Thick fingers slink further with every massaging touch, giving me the stuffed sensation I crave. I can't help myself, panting against his lips as a flood of heat burns my cheeks. Noah growls, his free hand sliding up my rib cage until he can massage my breast just as tenderly. His thumb brushes my nipple back and forth between gentle squeezes, spurring a soft whimper from my throat.

"That's it," Noah purrs. "You're literally dripping onto my thighs for me, Luna, and I can't get enough. Keep going."

I moan into his mouth, nuzzling into him harder as his fingers ease out of me. They focus on a wider area, smoothing across every inch between my legs. But then his fingers slip deep into me in one swift motion, my pussy suckling over them like it's pulling him in.

My moan heightens in delight, puffing Noah's chest. Each time he slips his fingers out of me, he plunges them in faster, raising my shoulders with a burst of tingles as he palpates my G-spot.

"Fuck, you're such a good girl. Your body's opening up for me on its own. It's so fucking beautiful."

I can't process Noah's raw, dirty whispers, so I surrender to my wolf's desires in primal bliss. I rub my head all over his neck and chest, leaning into the lulls in Noah's musk until I encourage his scent to burst—coating every inch of me.

"Oh, Noah— *Noah*—"

Noah hugs me tight to his chest, kissing me with his full body. I purr, my tongue slipping across his in a tender makeout until my hips dip with need.

We can hardly breathe through our kiss, heaving into each other's gaping mouths as we grapple each other's backs, unable to press closely enough. With rapid flexes of my core, I yank his hand from me with a gasp, seconds away from coming again. I seek out his cock, grinding over it to coat it with fluid.

Noah leans into each of my rubbing thrusts, his golden eyes hazy with bliss. It sets a fire in me, and my grinding jerks over him in desperation.

"Fuck, I— I…" Noah groans against my throat, his hips pulsing upward to smash his cock against my pussy.

"I know. I need you inside me too."

I adjust his tip between my legs, locking eyes with Noah. Then I wait, allowing him to catch his heaving, yearning breath.

We guide him into me together, sinking him in, millimeter by millimeter.

Noah lets out a soft, shuddering groan. "Ah— *Luna*…"

I crave that sound, cupping his head and kissing him with slow, teasing licks of my tongue. I'm more than ready for him.

Dropping my hips, I sink Noah deeper each time, pressure hitting my cervix long before I can sink to the base of his shaft. Within just a few bounces, my body lifts my cervix out of the way, allowing me to shove him deeper. I moan helplessly against his lips, mating myself over his cock with slick, steady repetition.

The pressure his thick shaft applies feels so good that my inner walls grip him each time I rise in his lap, coaxing out more of his affection.

I can't help it; my body applies a steady massage over his shaft, my pussy clenching with every bounce. It draws a heaving groan from Noah's parted lips, intensifying his thrusts. Noah has to grip the bed behind me, pressing my back flush to it. His body rolls me into the side of the bed, each muscle grinding into my core with deep, satiating thrusts.

∽ Epilogue ∾

Four years later…

As our newborn drinks from my chest with satisfied purrs, I smile at Ari cradling a small, stuffed pup toy, cooing and nuzzling over it just like I am with his little sibling—our sweet baby, Brook.

Ari peeks up at me with ginormous, midnight-brown eyes, his little feet tucked under his butt. "Mommy?"

I break into the biggest smile I can manage at Ari's shy voice, wishing I had three hands to also stroke his dark hair; it's just as wild and luscious as Noah's, thick strands waving in every direction.

"Yes, my love?"

"Can I hold a pup in my tummy too?"

My eyes widen, and Noah drops his fork mid-stab, the sudden clatter of metal against ceramic making all four of us jump in the living room, no matter how sleep-deprived we all are, thanks to poor Brook's colic.

What the hell do we say? Noah mindlinks.

I don't know… The truth?

But doesn't that require a lot of sex ed? I don't know if I'm mentally prepared for that, Luna…

But I regain my soft smile. "Ari, not all wolves can carry pups in their tummies. But you can."

Ari gazes at the stuffed toy wolf cradled in his arms. Something about his sudden curiosity strikes me as deep and powerful.

He needs to hear this, Noah. I don't know why, but I just know we have to support him. It reminds me of when Amy told me I'd be a great mom for a whole town, inspiring me for the rest of my life. She spoke right to my core desires, and look where I ended up.

Noah nods, setting his plate down.

His hand eases over Ari's little head, his wide thumb on Ari's forehead making our pup blink his heart-killer, puppy-dog eyes up at his favorite person. I bite back my smile as Noah's heart aches in pain in our bond, which I've now come to recognize as Noah suffering through an Ari-cuteness overload.

Softening his voice, Noah smiles down at our precious boy. "Did you hear what Mommy said? You'll be able to carry a pup if you want to someday, buddy."

Ari shifts his gaze to me, and now my heart actually hurts for him; his relieved expression just furrowed into concern.

"Why not now?" Ari mutters.

Oh, Goddess. Noah takes a deep breath, avoiding my eyes as I bite back a laugh. "You're not old enough for that yet, sweetheart. Please, just be our pup first."

I try not to bust out laughing at Noah's distressed grumble, but Ari frowns, his brows knitting.

"But Daddy, what if I can't do it?"

My heart drops with Ari's. The bond we share grows stronger with each passing day, tearing a hole through me whenever he's this upset. But even though I can usually piece together how Ari feels, I hesitate, uncertain about the genuine fear in his side of our bond.

Noah's brows furrow. His bright eyes meet mine, his wolf on high alert as Ari's distressed pheromones erupt with his trembling bottom lip. *I just told him he has the body for it, so why does he seem so heartbroken?*

Ari verges on tears, cuddling his toy closer to his chin, but he's trying to stay composed with a tight scowl—as stubborn as ever to remain stoic, just like his father.

I scoot closer on my knees, unable to keep myself from holding him close. Cradling Brook closer to my chest, I stoop over Ari. "Oh, baby… It's okay if you need to cry. Can you tell me what you're feeling?"

About the Author

As a bisexual and transgender creator, River Kai specializes in LGBTQ+ Romance, Thriller, Sci-Fi, and Fantasy with mental health and disability representation, creating stories for readers like him to see they're not alone. While he writes in multiple Romance sub-genres, his stories share three recurring themes: empowering character arcs about healing from trauma; authentic representation of transgender or bisexual main characters with depression, anxiety, PTSD, and OCD; and a sweet-but-spicy emphasis on consent.